SUMMER OF
Glorious Madness

CHRISTY YORKE

ℬ

BERKLEY BOOKS, NEW YORK

$\mathcal{B}$

A Berkley Book
Published by The Berkley Publishing Group
A division of Penguin Group (USA) Inc.
375 Hudson Street
New York, New York 10014

Contact the author at www.christyyorke.com

PRINTING HISTORY
Berkley Signature trade paperback edition/July 2004

Library of Congress Cataloging-in-Publication Data

Yorke, Christy.
    Summer of glorious madness / Christy Yorke.—1st Berkley signature trade ed.
        p. cm.
    ISBN 0-425-19613-5
    1. Women physicians—Fiction. 2. Physician and patient—Fiction. 3. Separated peo-
ple—Fiction. I. Title.

PS3575.O634S86 2004
813'.54—dc22

2003063909

PRINTED IN THE UNITED STATES OF AMERICA

10   9   8   7   6   5   4   3   2   1

*For my mother and her sisters, who survived,
and in memory of my grandmother, Genevieve, who didn't.*

ACKNOWLEDGMENTS

Art is often beyond reason, as are the needs of the artist. I am so lucky to have a husband who soothes and grounds me, who nobly works a job he doesn't always like so I can continue with this crazy profession, and two children who think all mommies act this way and proudly show me off at school. Thank you Robert, Claire, and Dean. I love you.

I would not have lasted this long without the support, advice, and comic relief of friends. Andrea Symmonds, Sharon Hanson, Michelle Dega, and Jane Zink—you've been my best friends, my anchors, a wealth of parenting and literary knowledge, and a Book Club extraordinaire. Without Jane, I would run out of stories.

I would also like to thank Lauren Symmonds for keeping my children so happy, Vera Rasmussen for her one-woman publicity campaign, and Mrs. Symmonds for bringing her AP English class to Barnes and Noble. Oh, to be seventeen again.

My brothers, as always, provided valuable support and research. James: You are my mad gardener, and I mean that in a good way. David: Thanks for all the pep talks, and for the trips to Corinthian Island. I wrote the house for you.

Natasha Kern, you are my champion. We both know I'd have quit long before now without your strength and enthusiasm and common sense. To my editor, Leona Nevler: After I agonized for months over how a novel about artistry and madness would be received, you made me feel as if you'd merely been waiting for me to write it. In a business that is often cruel, you have always been kind.

There is a fine line between creativity and madness; I hope these pages honor those who walk it, or love someone who does. I want to thank my mother for trusting me with the story of her tumultuous childhood, and the manic-depressive disorder that led to her mother's suicide. You are, and always have been, a survivor.

SUMMER OF
Glorious Madness

Christy Yorke

My idea is this: The artist is extremely lucky who is presented with the worst possible ordeal which will not actually kill him. At that point, he's in business.

—JOHN BERRYMAN, POET

ONE

THE end of the marriage began with a secret, as most endings do. At some point during their fifteen-year marriage, Elizabeth's husband became dissatisfied and didn't bother to tell her. Instead he nitpicked about her weight, her hair, her silly fear of heights and flying. He dressed her, but somehow she did not see this for what it was—Will wanted to rebuild her. She looked back now with twenty-twenty hindsight and could not believe her naïveté; she was comforted only by the fact that the divorcing couples she counseled at her office in Sausalito had all suffered from the same blindness. A woman thinks the complaints about her hair are about her hair, instead of evidence of a deeper discontentment, a man believes his wife is merely having a bad day when she shirks off his arm in public. Partners hear the good news, not the bad, the news that won't change anything, the information that won't harm them. They ignore anything that might lead to the conclusion that love can, and does, wear out.

When Will's disgruntlement continued, accelerated, when he began to stay later at the hospital and took up golf, and other things, on the weekends, Elizabeth begged him to go to counseling with her. But she gratefully took him at his word when he said things were not as far gone as that. When they stopped having sex, she soothed them both with statistics, told him it was all right, many men lose interest over time. She went on a diet, suggested medications he could take, individual counseling, massage, more exercise. She bought books, analyzed away his quarrels and increased devotion to work as a midlife crisis, as his problem, not theirs. She gave him a hundred ways out, gave him feelings that weren't there until the night he avoided her even in his dreams. He moved to the very edge of the bed and didn't fidget, didn't turn over once, as if the slightest movement might be misinterpreted as an invitation. As if the clues had been there all along.

That night, Elizabeth put on one of Will's shirts and moved to the guest room. The weeks that followed were ones she wished to forget. First her daughter Chloe's disbelief and horror, then her own tears and entreaties, the pleas she'd never thought a grown woman, a psychiatrist even, could make. It was one thing to sit in her office and talk a desperate woman out of driving past an old boyfriend's house, to counsel the lovelorn out of making fools of themselves. It was another entirely to be the fool. She had made a career out of helping people control what they felt only to realize this was impossible.

Not only that, her husband's dissatisfaction was ruthless; Will recoiled from hysteria and compromise alike. He seemed soulless, filled with nothing but the determination to be unhappy.

He wasn't going to leave; he kept telling her that. He would stay, no matter what it cost him.

And finally, on a Thursday, she woke just like him, flat and wringed dry of emotion, nearly incapable of movement, let alone joy. Like an old down blanket, all its fluff and comfort gone. She lay there past the time when Chloe left for school, past her first appointment. Lay there until she heard Will come into the kitchen, whistling because he thought himself alone. And something pulsed. The big toe she'd broken a year earlier during a fall down the stairs began to ache. She moved a little, decided she was not comfortable in the guest bed at all. She got up, threw open the door, and found her husband making an omelet with bacon and extra cheese, two more things he denied himself when she was around.

"I want you to leave," she said, and when he couldn't suppress a sigh of relief, she realized he'd been waiting for this all along.

She would have thought being despised by her own husband was the worst of it, until she faced her fourteen-year-old daughter's tears, Chloe's fury and finally an ominous silence. Then came the shock of friends who thought she and Will had been the perfect couple, who weren't sure whose side they were on, and the call from Will's mother, suggesting Elizabeth had had an affair. The toilet backing up on cue, a week after he'd left, the breakdown of the Volvo in the middle of the Rainbow Tunnel, stopping traffic, the hesitant sympathy of the women she'd once considered her best friends, women who had always invited Will and Elizabeth over as a couple, and now did not have an even number for Pictionary teams. Women who did not want that kind of unhappiness rubbing off.

All this in the two weeks after Will left, when Elizabeth still had patients who needed her, a daughter who refused to be comforted, a full slate every day. She cried on the way to work each morning, cried at what used to make her happy, the view from her office of Marin, a breathtaking triad of hilly cities, wilderness, and sea. She cried every day but Thursday, when she felt that pulsing in her toe again, when she woke, for some reason, surprisingly dry-eyed. On Thursdays, she stretched diagonally in bed, made use of all the extra space, and remembered she used to make her coffee stronger, before *he'd* complained of headaches. Two weeks after Will moved to a townhouse in Tiburon, she drank it in an oversized cup, in *his* chair, the one that got the morning light, and tried to convince herself that the high-pitched hum of absolute silence could sound as melodic as music.

She began to believe, however superstitiously, that nothing bad could happen on Thor's day. She looked at Thursday as if it were a woman—the forgettable middle sister wedged between misery and mayhem, the neglected wife who finally made her stand, the wallflower quietly getting things done. Thursday, with its late afternoon productivity, most-watched television and NFL specials. The day ascribed to the god of thunder, rain and farming, all of which Elizabeth was for.

Two weeks to the day after she asked Will to leave, Elizabeth watched Jay Leno's gentle Thursday monologue, turned off the set before she had to suffer Britney Spears's belly button and spunk. She lay down, watched the clock edge toward midnight, toward Friday, free day, Freya's day, the goddess of love, beauty and fecundity. She had two schizophrenic patients to visit in the hospital in the morning, and the standard stomachache that always accompanied those visits. She pulled up the blanket, wished halfheartedly that she didn't know as much about medication as she did, because of course she knew what pharmacies lacked. A pill to transform them all into someone different. A red one to turn her into someone Will could have loved forever. A green one to make her brave.

She ought to replace the alarm clock; Thursday or not, the green digital numbers made her cry. They'd been married only a year when Will stopped at a garage sale and bought the contraption shaped like a gargoyle, with numbers where its eyes ought to have been. At midnight, when the double O's were monster eyes, Will had howled like a ghost, held the covers over their heads while making love to her. But even then, even in the very beginning, he'd looked sheepish afterwards, as if he trusted neither whimsy nor spontaneity, not even in himself. He was a general surgeon, like his father before him, a man whose hands never shook, who deplored risk taking and disorganization and scenes, who got angry only when a patient died before surgery, or when he opened someone up and found something he hadn't expected—a tumor missed in the ultrasound, a second kidney going bad. When *she* turned out to be something he hadn't expected. Uglier and less substantial, apparently, than she'd appeared at first glance.

She swiped her tears, watched the gargoyle eyes. 11:42. 11:42. 11:42. 11:43. The last she saw was 11:52, when she fell asleep clutching the sheet. She dreamed the sky was suddenly blotted out by birds, a coven of raucous ravens who circled Sausalito, then homed in on her townhouse. The ravens dive-bombed her chimney, darted through the scrolls on the wrought iron gate, rammed themselves against potted geraniums until dirt and crimson petals littered the terra-cotta courtyard like drops of old and new blood.

After the damage was done, they perched menacingly on the slim window sills and peered in, their silence worse than screeching. Then they began to peck. They pitted the glass mercilessly, glee-fully forcing cracks then thrusting their black beaks into the room and screaming.

The phone rang as a raven crashed through the living room window, and twelve more flew in with shards of glass in their beaks. Elizabeth sat up, abruptly awake, and grabbed the phone. The green eyes read 2:46. Friday morning.

"Hello," she said.

"Doctor Shreve? This is Officer Blakely. I'm over here at Bayview."

She gripped the phone. At times like these, she found it ab-surd that she'd gotten through medical school and an internship in psychiatry without anyone stopping her. Without someone looking into her eyes and calling her bluff. Only Will, in the first years of their marriage, had noticed how pale she got during rounds, how badly her hands shook before meeting a new client, but he'd chalked it up to low blood sugar, to the damp Marin air. He'd encouraged her to undergo tests for diabetes, anemia, hypothyroidism, and when those had come out negative, he'd bought her Power Bars to eat when she felt weak. Later, he lost interest in her signs of discomfort.

No one mentioned her mother.

"Yes," she said.

"Found a patient of yours in Golden Gate, incoherent, mostly, until he started asking for you. You want to come give him the seventy-two-hour job?"

Elizabeth loosened her grip on the phone, listened for Chloe down the hall. She heard nothing, just her own heart beating, the ticking of the gargoyle clock. She catalogued her potentially psychotic clients—three addicts, a dozen or more schizophren-ics she'd treated or committed, double that in mood disorders, both unipolar and bipolar.

"You have a name?" she asked.

"Jack Bolton," the officer said. "Thirty-six, shaggy blond hair, work boots and chinos from what I could see beneath the blood."

"Is he all right? Was there an arrest?"

"No arrest. He's a little beat up, but otherwise fine. Probably a fight, but we can't get any details out of him. We've run samples. We brought him in for a while, but he gave everybody the heebie-jeebies, the way he kept pacing, the look in his eyes. It was like having a caged animal in here. You just come and lock him up, all right? He's asking for you."

Elizabeth didn't have to search her memory. She prided her-self on remembering her patients when she saw them out of context, in the frozen-food aisle of the market, for example, or two rows down at the movies. She always touched their arms, like a friend, made some comment about the weather to cover up the moment when they feared she might expose them to their friends, might ask meaningfully how they were feeling.

She remembered Jack Bolton even more clearly than most. Eight months ago, in the midst of the rainiest winter on record, he had come in for depression. He and his wife had been in the process of separating, he'd been losing energy and the desire to work, despite the fact that he was a renowned landscape archi-tect and was beginning to get the high-exposure jobs he'd al-ways coveted. He hadn't been sleeping, he told her, for fear of the nightmares—ferocious dreams of trees shriveling, flowers withering, vines blackening in the sun and turning to dust. There had been some incident in a closed garage, car running, though he had insisted this was more exhaustion than a suicide attempt. Elizabeth had prescribed sleeping pills and then, when he began to sleep too much, antidepressants. He'd recovered fairly quickly, by spring if she recalled, and she had considered the episode an isolated one, an understandable reaction to the demise of his marriage, rather than a harbinger of clinical depression. The last session they had, he brought her a potted tree, told her Hercules had worn a strand of poplar leaves on his head when he'd descended into the underworld. She remembered now that the poplar had quickly outgrown its pot, that she'd planted it in her tiny courtyard and watched it grow six feet in half a year.

She told the officer she'd come in, then called the psychiatric hospital across the bay. After she'd begun the long process of Jack Bolton's admittance, she hung up the phone, was halfway to reaching for Will when she remembered she was alone. Her eyes welled up again. Now what? What did single mothers do in the middle of the night when they had to go out? Pluck a teenage baby-sitter out of bed at three in the morning? Call a friend who, with every imposition, better appreciated her snoring husband and her undemanding, self-sufficient married friends? Elizabeth put her head in her hands, wanted nothing more than to crawl back into bed and stay there until something changed. Until Will reversed himself, retreated to loving her, and returned her life to what it should be.

But a man was waiting across the bridge. Bloody, the policeman said. Incoherent and probably afraid. She picked up the phone, dialed the number she had memorized instantly, though the psychiatrist in her knew this to be a sign of desperation and little else. The hopeless hope of the unloved.

The phone rang twice, and when the woman answered Elizabeth clung to the second or two when she believed she'd dialed incorrectly, when she was certain it couldn't be true.

"Hello?" the woman said. "Is anyone there?"

Elizabeth leaned forward, had to touch her head to her knees before she found enough breath to speak. "Is Will there?" she asked.

"Hang on."

He came on quickly, the way a surgeon always does in the middle of the night, ready for any emergency.

"Will Verplank," he said.

It was too much, she decided. Too much to hear the woman in the background, saying something breathy, the sound of sheets sliding. Two weeks since she'd asked him to leave, but of course, in his mind, he'd been gone for years. He'd been gone nearly from the start.

How could she ask him for anything? The smallest request would sound exaggerated, every favor he bestowed would seem like some gracious gift on his part, and she couldn't stomach that. She found herself wanting to deny him even the slightest satisfaction with himself.

"I can't believe this," she managed to say.

"Beth." She imagined his sharp, hawklike features falling slack with disappointment, or perhaps even pinching with revulsion, at the sound of her voice.

"You've already got someone there? Does Chloe know about her?"

"Beth, it's three in the morning. You shouldn't be calling. Don't stoop to this."

She sat up abruptly, imagined what he'd look like with his eyes gouged out. Or with all that glorious black hair chopped off. "I'm not stooping to anything. I've been called into the city to commit a patient. I need someone to watch Chloe."

He must have put his hand over the phone. She heard his muffled voice, followed by what sounded like a little girl whine. Elizabeth concentrated on her breathing. Began to count each one, both the inhalations and exhalations. Was up to twenty-four before he came back.

"I'm not the baby-sitter," Will said. "You'll have to figure out something. This is the way it's going to be now. I'm sorry."

She closed her eyes, drew her legs up beneath her. She still wore his shirts to bed; she'd confiscated every white Oxford before he left. In the beginning, he said it was the sexiest thing she did, putting on his shirt after he'd worn it, but by the end, it was one more thing that bothered him, her tendency to be in her pajamas so much when she was home. Her habit of reading and eating and, according to him, hiding in bed.

"I'm not asking you to come back, Will," she said. "I was going to ask you to come over here so I can keep the job that puts clothes on your daughter's back. I was going to consider you a human being, but now I won't." Her words were petulant, but that was because it was taking all she had to keep her voice steady. She had to curl her toes, grip the receiver until her knuckles glowed white.

"Oh, for God's sake, Beth," he said. "You're not exactly hurting. You can hire one of those round-the-clock baby-sitters. A nanny. Whatever. Eve's just moved in. I'm not going to leave her tonight."

"Eve?" she said. "Eve Tyson?"

Will said nothing, which said everything. Eve Tyson, one of his surgical nurses. The woman he'd sworn for a year he wasn't having an affair with. He'd gone so far as to call Elizabeth hysterical when she found one of Eve's miniscule sweaters in his car, pointing out how often he drove various members of his staff home after a late surgery. He'd called Elizabeth's fears groundless, even though she had eyes. Eve Tyson was thin and tiny—five-two, less than a hundred pounds, not even out of her twenties—and always a hit at hospital parties, where she liked to drink and show off the island dancing she'd learned on her many trips to the South Pacific.

Elizabeth tensed against the silence, imagined blond hair on the pillow beside him, his fingers pulling down the sheet, stroking luminous, springy skin.

"Chloe can stay on her own," Will said, softer. "She's old enough to be the baby-sitter. She's fourteen."

Eve, she thought, her shoulders sinking. Who shopped at the Gap, in the juniors department. Who knew the first names of the members of 'N Sync.

"I don't want her waking up alone," she said, her voice shrinking. "I could bring her there." And perhaps, when Will saw her, he'd realize exactly what he was doing, all the mistakes he was making. He'd want a woman, not a girl, and realize Elizabeth had only let him go so he could come back.

"No!" he said, and she jerked at the vehemence in his voice, stood as if he'd pushed her. She'd ordered him out hoping he'd see how strong she could be. She'd suffered every minute without him to prove she was braver than he'd thought. She'd cried every day but Thursday, hoping he would fight for her, and now she realized she should have cried on Thursdays, too. It wasn't going to happen. He'd made her order him out so he could leave without guilt, take up with Eve. So that, when someone asked, he could point out that technically she'd ruined her own life.

She yanked the alarm clock out of the wall. The gargoyle eyes went dark, and she kicked it toward the closet. She woke long before dawn anyway.

She began to cry, and instead of soothing her, he sighed. He said something to Eve and Elizabeth heard her stomping off, slamming a door.

"That's enough, Beth," Will said tiredly. "I'll come. Just for tonight. After this, you'll have to make other arrangements."

"Will . . ." She wanted to say more but what kind of words broke through to a man who was no longer listening? She couldn't even be kind; he wouldn't let her, wouldn't hear anything that smacked of what they'd had before. She'd lost not only him, but also the tender things she'd once said to him, all the words that lovers say.

"I'll have to take Chloe to school early if you're not back. I've got surgery at eight."

After he hung up, she walked shakily to her closet, longing to put on comfort clothes—sweatpants and flannel—but forced to wear one of her suits. Skirt, blouse, jacket, belt, hose, shoes, all cinched and tied. She went into the bathroom, splashed water on her red-rimmed eyes. Even her shoulder-length hair hung limp and unhappy, a more hopeless shade of brown than usual. She twisted it into a bun.

She kept imagining Will and Eve, wrapped together, legs intertwined. Dark and light, tall and petite, a cautious man and a risk taker, perfect complements to each other. She shook her head, walked down the hall and quietly opened Chloe's door.

Three things were obvious immediately—the scent of clove cigarettes, a sliver of light beneath the closet door, and the realization that once Chloe stopped talking to her, she started up with somebody else. Elizabeth hurried across the room, flung open the bifold doors. Chloe sat on the floor between her dresses, the phone not quite hidden beneath a tangle of black hair, the private phone line Will and Elizabeth had given her for Christmas obviously a horrible mistake. A clove cigarette dangled between Chloe's forefinger and thumb; ashes had made it everywhere except into the crystal bowl she'd brought in for an ashtray. Elizabeth allowed herself one moment's disbelief, one unrealistic wish that someone in this family would be more, not less, than she'd hoped for. Then she grabbed the phone out of Chloe's hand and put it to her ear. "Who is this?"

A boy laughed before hanging up. Chloe stumbled to her feet, tucking the cigarette behind her back as if this blinded them both to the smoke and stench.

"What are you thinking?" Elizabeth asked. "It's the middle of the night."

Chloe leaned sideways into the rack of dresses she no longer wore. Her year-round school had started a month ago, in early summer, and since then her acceptable wardrobe had shrunk to a single pair of skintight jeans and a choice of three cropped blouses. Since Will had left, she'd defiantly put on the mascara Elizabeth had prohibited; by dinner there were black clumps beneath her lashes. Yet this insomnia seemed most ominous of all. Elizabeth knew far too much about the effects of divorce on a child, particularly a teenager who was becoming unpleasant enough on her own. A year ago, Chloe was a solid B student, on the verge of real beauty as she grew into the sharp chin and cheekbones she'd inherited from her father, popular with a small but loyal group of friends, an all-star soccer player. Now she'd quit all sports, refused to talk at the dinner table, and apparently was aiming to die young. Elizabeth had told her again and again that the divorce had nothing to do with her, that she was loved as much as ever, and one night Chloe had broken her silence with one scathing retort. "Right," she'd said. "Like your love is worth anything."

"Put out that cigarette," Elizabeth said now. "You'll light your clothes on fire. For God's sake."

Chloe crushed her cigarette in the bowl, carelessly spilling more ashes on the hardwood floor. Elizabeth crossed the room, flung open a window. It would take Will a good fifteen minutes to get here now that he'd moved further out on the peninsula, to an exclusive, gated development in Tiburon. According to Chloe, who gave only the barest of descriptions, he'd decorated the townhouse surprisingly with gold-plated mirrors and fancy fleur-de-lis upholstery. Or had Eve been there from the start?

"Who were you talking to?" Elizabeth asked without turning around.

"No one. Just Jill."

The voice was not Jill's, Chloe's best friend since kindergarten. Sweet Jill, who Elizabeth knew for a fact never went to bed past ten o'clock unless she was baby-sitting—a task she did often and for good money after word spread that she brought treats for the children and played Candy Land for hours on end.

Chloe got into bed, pulled the sheets to her chin. Elizabeth had counseled dozens of children of divorce, understood the phases, almost like the stages of mourning, that a son or daughter went through when their parents split up. She knew all this, but knowledge was worthless when trying to come up with topics of conversation at the dinner table, statistics were useless when her daughter loathed her. Elizabeth believed in talking things out, was an especially adept clinician, an authority on the latest medications, but she also knew that sometimes drugs and talking were superfluous. The only thing that helped was time.

"I know you're angry at me," she said.

Chloe rolled her eyes.

"I wish you would . . ." Elizabeth had to be careful here. Not ask for anything, not demand too much. Not show emotion which, in both Will's and Chloe's cases, was likely to be scorned. If Elizabeth reminisced about the times she had dropped Chloe off at preschool and returned to find her in the exact same spot, limp and still weeping, Chloe would say she'd been glad to have a mother who worked. She'd survived, she'd learned to take care of herself, and Elizabeth should, like, get over herself. Then she would stiffen when Elizabeth hugged her; she'd turn on *American Idol* to squelch all further comments. The things Chloe said were superfluous, too. Elizabeth had already taught her something terrible: To expect to be disappointed in love. To keep devotion to herself.

"I wish you wouldn't smoke," Elizabeth said at last.

"They're only cloves."

"They're cigarettes. I won't have them in this house."

"Whatever."

"Not whatever. I don't want you damaging yourself just so you'll look cool."

"Cool. Right," Chloe said, obviously mocking her though Elizabeth was beginning to have trouble pinpointing the source of her screwups. Language or look or actions or attitude. Perhaps all four.

"Chloe, please. Let's not do this now. I've got to go into the city. That's your dad's car pulling up. Say hello, then I want you to go to sleep. It's three o'clock in the morning."

Chloe leapt up, shedding two unbecoming years in the process. "Dad's here?"

It was a terrible thing, hope. Deep and stubborn as weeds. Before Elizabeth could talk her out of it, Chloe ran down the hall, so sweet and light Elizabeth's heart ached. She prayed that Will would notice how buoyant his own daughter had become in the last two weeks, how fragile desire had made her, how much she needed to be lifted and held. Elizabeth stood by the window, listened to the slamming of Will's car door, the little girl plea Chloe could not suppress. Elizabeth held her breath, then Will said something quick and firm. There was a silence, then Chloe asked a question, apparently didn't wait for the answer. She came storming down the hall, swiping at her eyes. She got into bed without looking at her.

Elizabeth walked across the bedroom, still decorated in shades of lilac—mauve lace curtains, lavender walls, a purple comforter with embroidered magenta daisies. A little girl's room Elizabeth cherished all the more because Chloe could start to hate it at any moment. She leaned over her daughter. Chloe had caught a strand of the luxurious black hair she'd inherited from Will between her lips, and Elizabeth slid it out, tucked it behind her ear.

"I'm so sorry, honey," she said. "If I could change things—"

"You never fought. That's what I don't understand. You were, like, the perfect couple."

Elizabeth sat on the edge of the bed. "Maybe never fighting was exactly the problem."

She arranged Chloe's hair prettily on the pillow, noticed how long it had gotten. "No more growing up, okay? You just stay put from now on."

Once, this kind of request had brought a smile, but now Chloe turned over on her side. "I wouldn't go out there if I were you," she said.

Elizabeth stiffened, but of course she had no choice. She had her next words planned—a cool recitation of the patient she was going to see. Will would have no choice but to acknowledge how polite and sane she was trying to be. She had her shoulders back and stomach sucked in as she walked down the hall, so the slumping was that much more apparent when she came across both Will and Eve standing at the bar, helping themselves to her Scotch.

She was almost glad. Once they decided to be despicable, the tears she might have shed hardened into pellets of ice. There was only so much a woman could take before she gave up weakness for spite. Elizabeth glared at the two of them, standing shoulder to shoulder, brazenly grazing skin. She stomped across the room and yanked the glasses from their hands.

"How could you do this in front of Chloe?" she asked.

"Beth," Will said, "calm down."

She turned to Eve, who was white-faced but smug. Standing in Elizabeth's living room in ripped teenager jeans and yet another skintight sweater, hands clasped demurely behind her back. "I know this is tough on you," Eve said.

"You don't know anything," Elizabeth said.

She slammed down the glasses, walked across the room so she wouldn't be tempted to kick or pull hair.

"Chloe's old enough to understand," Will said. "People fall out of love. They find someone new. I think it will help her to see that life goes on."

Elizabeth whirled around. He was taking a seat at the couch, maneuvering his long legs beneath the coffee table. He wore boyish white sneakers, jeans, a Stanford sweatshirt he'd had for as long as she'd known him, sand-colored now though she recalled it had once been sky blue. His dark hair, as usual, was uncombed, dumped over his blue eyes.

"You think it will help her to see that fifteen years of marriage can be forgotten in two weeks? You think this is a good lesson for her to learn?"

He looked up and, for a moment, she thought she caught a glimpse of uncertainty, at the very least a retreat from cold, unassailable calm. A glimmer of someone familiar, a man who could blush, someone like the young medical student who proposed on the bus ride home, because try as he might he couldn't wring himself from the hospital for a proper date. A man who got down on one knee on that dirty steel floor and took a simple gold band from his pocket, along with a wadded-up piece of paper, obviously a page ripped from a book. Will had cleared his throat, swiped at his irrepressible hair, flashed a smile that, for longer than was healthy, was more than enough to hold her.

> *"She was a phantom of delight*
> *When first she gleamed upon my sight;*
> *A lovely apparition, sent*

To be a moment's ornament;
Her eyes as stars of twilight fair;
Like twilight's, too, her dusky hair;
But all things else about her drawn
From May-time and the cheerful dawn;
A dancing shape, an image gay,
To haunt, to startle, and waylay."

The women on the bus sighed, but Elizabeth looked out the window. She didn't like to dance, had learned from psychiatry to approach people slowly, to never startle. She'd met Will in a diagnostics class in medical school, and ironically the only person he'd failed to diagnose was her—her relentless work habits, her aversion to mountaintops, not only Mount Tamalpais, but others as tame and prehistoric as Ring Mountain, her need to put messes and houses and jumbled minds in order. He took her hand, whispered her name, and she made, for her, an incautious leap of faith. She decided he'd seen her faults and chosen to look past them; he'd invested himself not in who she was, but in what she aspired to be. She looked at the ring in his hand and gambled that she would grow into the woman he wanted. A gamble that would not pay off for either of them.

"Wordsworth," he said. "I haven't got words of my own."

He put the ring on her finger without asking the question, and in truth he never actually proposed. He took her acquiescence for granted, kissed her in celebration, accepted the congratulations of the bus people—a homeless man named Neptune, three rangy college students, two elderly sisters who smelled of oatmeal and missed their stop. They were married five weeks later in the chapel at the hospital.

Chloe loved that story; when she was five, she would settle for nothing else at bedtime. Elizabeth left out the part when Will noticed the gum on the knee of his pants and threw out the pair without even an attempt at a wash. She skipped over the epilogue, when Will bought a sports car and refused to ride the bus after that day. She told the story and remembered other poems left on her pillow, other pages ripped out of books. She cherished other people's words, treasured Will's endearing ineptness with language when everything else he did was so sure. It was only later that she became suspicious of his plagiarism, as if none of his own words could be trusted.

Eve stepped between them now, cut off their lines of sight. "I brought a present for Chloe," she said. "Lipstick."

Elizabeth's eyes had dried up but her hands began to tremble. She realized that Chloe had been wearing a shade of pink that hadn't come from Elizabeth's makeup drawer, that she might have known about Eve all along. "How long have you been screwing my husband?"

Eve gasped, but Elizabeth could tell it was all show. She was a pretty, little thing but she was muscular, rock hard. She'd graduated head of her nursing class, became the youngest surgical nurse at the hospital at the age of twenty-three. "Please," Eve said, "let's try to act like adults."

Elizabeth shook her head, turned her back on them once more. She heard Eve head down the hallway, open Chloe's door. Elizabeth didn't want Chloe to fight her battles for her, couldn't bear it if she taught her own daughter to be mean. But wasn't it just as bad when a split second of outrage was followed by a long exclamation of delight? When Chloe was won over so easily, by a tube of hot pink lip gloss?

Will pulled a medical journal out of his briefcase, opened it on his lap. "I'm telling you, Beth, you've got to think about letting Chloe live a little. Letting her go."

Elizabeth took a deep breath, gathered her briefcase and purse. It seemed foolhardy to ask her to care for someone else tonight, but she knew once she got to Bayview, she'd willingly relinquish her own problems for someone else's. Grief had made her a better psychiatrist; she listened well into the night if a patient needed her, listened long after the timer had rung. Another mind had always been her narcotic, an escape to a different world.

"I'll tell you what," she said, "when I get to a point where I can stand the sight of you, I'll listen to what you have to say."

She walked out before she saw his reaction, walked out while she was still shaking. The night was cool and dewy, her plans for late summer camping trips and Sunday barbecues crumbling fast. Within a month, when autumn hit, moss would be growing in the cracks of the sidewalk and it would take all the expertise and tenderness she had to keep some of her patients from taking to their beds until spring.

She got in her Volvo, was nearly to the Golden Gate Bridge before she'd calmed down enough to think of something other than Will's growing list of betrayals. She pushed aside the image of Eve tainting everything she touched, the amount of ammonia that would be required to erase the scent of her, and forced herself to remember what she could about Jack Bolton. The man had always smelled of grass, had usually sullied her carpet with a few precisely clipped blades, and had eyes the color of healthy Bermuda. He'd had a force her other patients lacked that made her spill her own secrets. Instead of soothing his nightmares, he altered her dreams. Back when Will had been complaining about her haircuts and pajamas, she'd woken with the scent of jasmine and mint on her fingertips, with a fierce yearning for fresh air.

She'd been relieved, she recalled, when Jack Bolton left.

TWO

With its sedate stone exterior and high-end, waterfront location, Bayview Hospital looked more like a prestigious law firm than a seventy-bed psychiatric facility, inpatient and out. Elizabeth had completed the last year of her residency there, was assigned, like any intern, the most dismal and hopeless cases. The catatonic schizophrenics who would probably never recover, the depressives who, every six months when they were committed, found a new body cavity to smuggle in sleeping pills. She'd slept fitfully on a cot in the interns' lounge, ate a thousand iceberg salads in the cafeteria. She'd even gone into labor while sedating a foul-mouthed, demon-plagued girl, but the scent of panic in the lobby—part cigarette smoke, part saline, part ripening, sweet sweat—still left her queasy. She pressed her palm to her stomach and, as always, fought the urge to run.

The television in the corner was tuned to a Suzanne Somers

infomercial, a pale-faced man perched on the edge of the sofa, clipboard in hand, as if something contagious might be oozing from the cushions. He flinched when a woman deep within the walls began to cry. Someone would go to her, comfort her, and if that did not work they would give her something to help her sleep. Elizabeth could explain that Bayview was one of the finest private mental health facilities in the country, yet she knew that would be like telling him someone he loved had a little cancer. Maybe it wasn't the worst it could be, but it was terrible enough.

The man wrapped his arms around his waist and began to mumble. After twelve-hour shifts, the exhausted nurses were often confused for amnesiac patients, the doctors sat slumped and depressed while convincing a man to go on living. She squeezed the man's shoulder, her rage at Will and Eve, along with her hospital jitters, subsiding as she neared the front desk. It was easier to believe that, while she was here, the world ended at the front door. Easier for the patients as well. She slowed her breathing to accommodate the limp, confined air, found the commitment officer and read the formal complaint.

Jack Bolton. Male Caucasian. 36 years old.

Incident report: 2:06 A.M. Arresting officer: Jim Blakely. Complaint called in at 1:32 A.M.—Man wandering through Golden Gate Park, hands and torso bloody, behaving wildly, aggressively. Feral, the woman said. The man kept to the bushes and looked feral. Taken into custody at 1:46. Initial resistance subdued. Abrasions on subject's chin, cheek, and left arm, indicative of a fistfight. Dilated pupils, possible drug user. Subject extremely agitated, emotional, suffering delusions of the trees coming to life. Blood and

urine samples taken. Suicide/homicide threat. Voluntary commit-
ment reluctantly accepted for 72-hour evaluation.
   Room 302.
   Meds refused.

She took the chart, headed toward the elevator. The carpeted
halls were hushed; the crying woman had been soothed. She
stepped inside the elevator, grazed the second-floor button,
pushed the third. Will had focused on her fear of flying, never
giving her credit for the phobia she confronted week after week.
She'd treated a number of patients in Room 217, the room her
mother had frequented. When the bed was empty, she sometimes went alone into the room just to prove there were no such
things as ghosts. It was the living who struggled for peace. She'd
gone into psychiatry for answers, had known what she wanted
to be from the moment of her mother's first suicide attempt—
thirty pills that would be pumped out, leading to more drastic
measures, a knife blade and, finally, a car. Even now, Elizabeth
couldn't look at a station wagon without expecting it to turn on
two wheels, to see a woman's hair whooshing and flapping
through the window like a last, frenetic wave. To see a baby, six
months old, sleeping unconcernedly in the backseat.

She emerged on the third floor, found Jack Bolton's room two
doors down on the left. She knocked softly, heard a masculine
voice telling her to enter.

She'd seen ransacked rooms and patients covered in excrement,
prevented girls from mutilating themselves and convinced men to
stop shooting phantom FBI agents in the closet. For a while, before Will left, she'd been able to go home and soothe herself with
the sanity of ritual—the same seat at the dinner table, the same

news channel even when the anchors got on her nerves, the same family sitting across from her, insulting her chicken cacciatore and slowly turning glum, but still, at heart, the same.

Now she just put on her face—neutral eyes, a sliver between her lips to keep her jaw from clenching, a guarded yet unthreatening stance, legs slightly apart. She was already considering the dosage of antipsychotic drugs when she opened the door to total darkness and a man said, "This is all a giant mistake."

There was fear in his voice, a glimmer of moonlight through the curtains, the outline of a chair next to the window. Elizabeth squinted into the darkness, her heart skipping a beat when she caught a silhouette of tangled sheets, blankets twisted into knots, but no sign of a man.

"I just want you to relax," she said. "I'm Dr. Shreve. I'm here to help you."

"Believe me, this was blown way out of proportion." His voice came from one corner, then a moment later rose out of the other. She took a deep breath to settle her heartbeat, to listen more closely for footsteps. "I didn't hurt anybody," he went on. "I swear it. All that blood . . . I must have cut myself in the bushes. Blacked out for a while. I was upset, I admit that. Having a bad day, no doubt. But you can't lock me up for that. I'm no lunatic. Give me a ticket, all right? Fine me, whatever. Just let me go. This is no place for a man."

His voice was crackly, as if he'd spent a good portion of the last hour trying to convince the residents and orderlies of the same thing.

"I'm glad you agreed to the voluntary commitment. We'll be able to help you that much sooner."

"Look, I don't know what they told you, but I've got three projects that need my immediate attention. I'm not some nut-case who put on a show to get a nice warm bed. There's been a terrible misunderstanding. They started thrusting pills at me the second I got here."

"We only want to stabilize you."

"I'm stable. I'm as sober as a man can be. I'll tell you flat out, I was an idiot tonight. She had all my plants outside, even the tropical palms, who can't stand five minutes of a harsh bay breeze, let alone an hour. I saw her picking apart those leaves and I lost it."

"Who had your plants out?"

"Those palms didn't deserve that kind of treatment. What did they ever do to her?"

"Was there a fight?"

The room swelled with silence. "I would never hurt her," he said finally, softly. "It doesn't matter what I can't remember. I'd rather be crazy than a brute."

Elizabeth stepped forward, still couldn't find him in the darkness. "Have you been suffering from blackouts? The last time we met, you were separating from your wife, dealing with depression. You seemed stabilized when we stopped therapy, but perhaps—"

"Perhaps nothing. Don't go diagnosing. You'll be wrong. I got confused tonight is all. A little worked up. I'm cleaned up now and ready to go. Release me and you'll never hear another word from me again. Guaranteed."

She was glad for the darkness. It was never pleasant when a patient saw how little he was believed.

"I'm afraid that's not possible," she said. "The papers have already been signed. You're stuck with us for the next seventy-two hours. Why don't you let me give you something to help you relax?"

This time his footsteps were obvious, slaps of flesh against the chilly tile floor. They would have taken his shoes. "I don't even use aspirin. I'm sure as hell not going to take some elephant pill that'll turn my brain inside out. I've got *gardens* to put in. I've got to be clearheaded."

His voice didn't rise when he got angry, but lowered to a grumble. An imaginative woman could mistake it for a growl in the throat. She slid her hand along the wall, bit her lip when she couldn't find the light switch on the first pass. "Mr. Bolton, I know it's terrifying to find yourself in a place like this, unable to leave. Trust me, all we want to do is help."

His footsteps ended abruptly in the far corner, then a second later his voice emerged right in front of her. "Do you remember my face?" he asked.

She saw an outline of blacker black, smelled his breath, which was surprisingly tangy and pleasant. She reached back again, this time found the switch and flipped it on. He stood in front of her blinking, dressed in a green hospital gown, thoroughly human. His blond hair was long and uncombed, hanging into his eyes, his hands scrubbed clean of blood. Beneath the scratches and abrasions on his face, his nose was elegant, almost delicately curved, with a lower lip substantially thicker than the upper one, as if he'd been punched, or was pouting. He seemed disproportionately muscled from the waist up, all arms and shoulders, then slender through the legs. He was not gaunt like so many of her patients, particularly the schizophrenic ones. He stood defiant for a moment, then his shoulders slowly dropped.

"No," he said. "You don't remember."

"Mr. Bolton," she said. "No one's calling you crazy, but tonight you were acting so strangely that someone called the police."

There was a cut across his left cheek, swelling around his chin. Wounds that might have been self-inflicted. She needed to write down her observations, but somehow he'd gotten hold of her hand. His fingers were so callused, he would leave a scratch mark in the soft flesh between her thumb and forefinger. She searched her brain for the name of his wife. She'd have to go through her files once she got back to the office.

"Annie," he said. "Annie Crandall."

Elizabeth slowly raised her head. Jack Bolton wore her face—neutral eyes, lips slightly apart, jaw slack. She withdrew her hand, took a step back.

"Mr. Bolton, I think—"

"I remembered your face."

"That's nice."

"I remember you prided yourself on knowing the Latin names of twenty-seven trees," he said, "from Salix babylonica to Ailanthus altissimo, even though the common name of the latter—tree of heaven—is a thousand times more meaningful."

She stared at him, felt suddenly, uneasily vulnerable, as if he'd just reached a finger down her throat and plucked what lay closest to her heart.

"Tell me what you remember about tonight," she said.

He walked across the room, slumped in the chair by the window. He had a tattoo across his left arm, the black lines of a raven. He doodled an intricate flower on the dewy glass, and Elizabeth began to notice the papers atop his ransacked bed and scattered across the floor. Dozens of torn scraps with pink, hurried writing. There were pink pens, too, piercing the tangled folds of the blanket, skewering pillows. He must have hidden them; no patient was allowed to keep potential weapons. She snatched a paper from the floor.

Twenty cowslips.
Keys of heaven, but keys to happiness?
Frog ponds, burrow. Stained glass ceiling?

The flower on the window was now an elaborate woodland garden flanked by maple trees with faces emerging from the bark. Elizabeth crossed the room. She noticed another wound on his arm, a puffy bruise surrounding a fresh, jagged cut.

"Mr. Bolton—"

"Look, you'll have to call me Jack if you want to get anywhere. Don't you remember that, Elizabeth? Don't you remember you called me Jack?"

She did not remember anything of the kind, but she also couldn't remember the drive over here, how she'd managed to keep it together, the last time she'd really laughed.

"I'll look over my records," she said, scribbling a note. "About tonight—"

"Annie shoved my hand away. Told me to run. But I can't ground the vision in reality. For all I know, it's an image from a dream." He pressed his palms to the glass as if he could muscle out the panes. But they were specially made, three inches thick, with bars on the outside just to be sure. "If it happened, it was after she sat on the stoop, torturing those plants despite what she knew about them. Just because you're no longer somebody's wife doesn't mean you have to be cruel. Isn't that right, Elizabeth?"

She wrote another note, though it was little more than a doodle. She was as exhausted as she'd been after Chloe was born, when she'd had a colicky baby in one arm and notes from the department's Grand Rounds in the other.

"What did Annie know about your plants?" she asked.

He waved his hand as if this was common knowledge. "The same things gardeners have always known. That plants can feel things; they're as alive and sentient as we are. They react to threat. There's studies on this stuff. I'm not making it up. Annie's read them. She's been to my gardens. She killed that palm anyway, leaf by helpless leaf, so everything between us would be clear."

Elizabeth had seen the data on Findhorn, an astonishing, thriving garden in northern Scotland built on unfertilized, unamended sand and gravel, where the cultivators claimed to have used nothing more than love and good intentions. She'd read the reports and wondered why, if plants were so eager to grow, her well-fertilized, deeply desired roses were sulky rebels, dreary and stunted at two feet.

"Did you and Annie divorce?"

"Separated. I haven't had the time to file and she . . . God knows what she's doing."

"I'd like to talk to her," she said.

He shrugged, though she noticed he also stopped drawing. "I was happier than she was. You can't make a marriage out of that."

"I'd like to call her."

"It's your quarter, but I'm telling you, she's tired of talking about me."

He stood abruptly, came at Elizabeth so fast she wouldn't have had time to react to an attack, if violence had been his intent. She had scarcely lifted her hand to shield herself when he snatched the hospital pen from her fingers and tossed it over his shoulder. He wriggled a pink pen loose from its impalement on the pillow and handed it to her. "You need this one. Pink does wonders for your frame of mind. I mean, look at that." He took his chart from her hands, quickly covered up her observations with a sketch of violets. "I went online, bought out every manufacturer from here to Seattle. Doesn't that make you feel better?"

A smile might have escaped in her relief. "It's not me we're worried about."

"Why the hell not? You've got problems, too. You can't ask me to talk about myself, then keep interrupting the conversation with thoughts of what's troubling you."

She took back the pen, would write down delusions as soon as he turned. "Since we met last time, have you suffered—"

"And iguanas. You can't cry when an iguana's around. It's physically impossible. I was a fool to leave them with Annie. What if she dumps them on the side of the road or, worse, takes them back to the pet store? They can't live under those conditions. They can't stand the scrutiny."

"Mr. Bolton, can you tell me—"

He tried to yank out the drawers of the nightstand, but they were specially made for the hospital, fixed to open only halfway.

"What are you looking for?" she asked.

"You'd think they'd let me have something to write on. What kind of damage can I do to myself with a stack of paper, for crying out loud?"

"Quite a lot actually," Elizabeth said. "You could cut yourself. Or eat it."

"Please," he said, as if these notions were far crazier than a bloody jaunt through Golden Gate Park.

She ripped off a blank sheet from his chart and handed it to him. He pressed the paper to the wall, used another pink pen to draw an elaborate landscape of fountains, gardens and trees, his hand working quickly, eyes intensely focused on the intricate flowers like fuchsias and lilies of the valley, brow furrowed while he sketched the reflection of ferns on the water. He finished the entire drawing in less than five minutes, handed it to her. "A landscape design for your garden, now that it's all your own. I need another page."

She stared at the picture—fountain here, shade garden over there, a path of what appeared to be crushed glass or pebbles between rows of pretty perennials.

"How did you know—"

"It's a terrible thing to inherit a garden, then never make it your own," he said. "It ought to be a crime to leave junipers and Bermuda grass scorched and sulking in their plots. They might survive but they're not living. They go into a kind of despondent sleep, leave their despair in the soil, and nothing there will ever grow."

Elizabeth rubbed her head; at five in the morning, it was difficult to keep up with a patient like this, one who, she was beginning to believe, was displaying rapid flights of ideas, the first telltale sign of mania. "I like my junipers," she said.

"Junipers are fine. Lovely, if tended right. But planted en masse so they can be forgotten, never fussed over or gawked at or gussied up? That's worse than lazy. It's cruel. You're hiding behind your neat rows of potentillas. I'm telling you, Elizabeth, art is easier than you think. You find a pretty shard of glass in the street, mix a little mortar, and press it into your driveway. Presto, you've shown us your favorite color. That's an intimate thing. That's a gift."

"Let's forget my garden for now. About . . ."

"Did you see the article in *Architectural Digest?* The one about the botanical gardens I designed in Palo Alto?"

"Sorry. I don't have time to read much more than medical journals."

"It wasn't perfect, but it was close. Woodlands, the ruin wall, the rose gardens and fern grotto. When I'd get tired of one bed, I'd move on to something totally different. Artists were begging to get their work displayed in the sculpture allée; it was hard not to take everything. That project led to the one I'm working on now, the children's garden at the Londonbright Museum. I've started a dinosaur extravaganza, made them out of steel and moss. It's not perfect yet either, but I'm closing in."

"Perfection is a pretty challenging goal."

"For an artist, it's the only goal that matters."

He rose to the balls of his feet, then relaxed. Clenched his fists, bit his lip, began a fevered recitation of the plants he'd used in the botanical gardens, and she wished she'd convinced him to continue therapy last winter, had seen him through the spring and summer when she could have analyzed whether or not his depression dissipated only to leap into something else, the quick cycling assaults of mania.

"Has anyone in your family suffered from bipolar disorder?" she asked.

It was like watching the lights go out before a bombing, a last ditch effort to escape detection and harm. He stuffed his hands in his pockets, locked his stance, snuffed what he could of the light in his eyes by narrowing them at her. She hated to startle him, but from the fear in his eyes, she knew he had considered this possibility himself. One night, when his heart was racing and his thoughts skipping from gardening to mythology to world history to art, he must have thought, *What is happening to me?*

"I beg your pardon?"

"Bipolar disorder," she said. "Manic-depression. It's more common than many people think. One person out of a hundred will suffer from the severe form."

He stopped moving, but the muscles around his mouth still strained, his bones vibrated with suppressed energy. He walked to the bed, sat on the very edge. "I'm fine."

She moved beside him, sat close enough to hear the racing of his heart. "You were depressed the last time I saw you. I thought it was just a normal reaction to the separation from your wife, but now I wonder if it might have been a harbinger of something more. You might be at the beginning or even in the midst of a manic phase."

He shook his head, scoffed. "I've never felt better."

"Exactly. At the beginning, mania—"

"I can't believe this. You're taking what's been the most creative period in my life and turning it into something perverse. I've gotten more done in the last few months than I've accomplished in years."

"You lost your wife," she said.

He shook his head, fast. "That had been coming on for a long time. Everyone who divorces is not some lunatic."

She watched his fingers tap his knees, zigzag up his thighs. He noticed her gaze and tried to still himself, but then his foot started up.

"Of course not," she said. "And perhaps tonight was merely an aberration. A reaction to the loss of your plants and a blackout that will never happen again. We'll let you go on Sunday and everything will be fine."

He glared at her. "You're mocking me."

"I would never do that. I want you to be well, but it's my job to point out what's rational."

"I thought your job was to make people feel better. Seems to me that's often the most irrational act of all."

"Maybe, but all we can do is try." She smiled. "Manics are ecstatic, at first. You fall into mania the way you fall in love. Your entire vocabulary translates itself into secret, tender code; every thought is a grand, romantic scheme. Manics have phenomenal energy. They hardly sleep, are intensely aware of their surroundings, extremely sensual. No problem seems too difficult to solve. They're full of ideas, exuberant and charming."

He laughed, tapped both feet now. "And this is a bad thing?"

"It is when they lose control, exhaust themselves. Like a love affair, mania either ruptures or cools. Ideas come too fast, all that clear thinking is replaced by confusion. Memory goes, joy is replaced by fear and irritability, even rage. Exorbitant bills come for those exuberant purchases, and spouses leave in tears, friends tell them they did things they cannot believe. They seek out psychiatrists, medications, overdoses."

He looked toward the window. "I think you've gotten me confused with a poet."

"Maybe. Poets have the highest incidence of mental illness, at nearly fifty percent. Rhyming actually increases during mania."

"Poets behave exactly how people hope they will. They fulfill our ludicrous expectations."

"There is also often a seasonal element," she went on. "Manic by summer, depressed in winter. Like your plants, Jack, centered around light and inspiration."

He leaned in close, and she smelled the grass she remembered, felt a blast of heat, as if she'd been brushed by a hot summer breeze. "You called me Jack." He stayed there for a moment, then walked toward the door which was double bolted from the outside. "How's the poplar?" he asked.

She relaxed, relieved to get past the worst part of her job, the terrible, unwanted news she often had to deliver. "Giant. It grew six feet in six months, took over the entire courtyard. I've never seen anything like it."

He walked to the window, where the garden on the glass had dissolved. He started drawing in a new one, a hair's breadth more perfect than the one before. "It's the tree of courage," he said. "I'm glad it helped you throw out your husband."

Her heart picked up its pace again. She'd never mentioned what happened with Will.

WHEN the door opened Sunday morning and his psychiatrist stepped in, Jack Bolton took a deep breath. He was still shaking off the effects of the lithium and valproate he'd taken so they'd see he was cooperating. So they'd let him out. He felt slow and irritated by the unnatural gray of the sweet gum trees outside his window, disheartened by the blanched color of the room, a muted orange, the color of a dying tiger lily.

He sat motionless by the window, dressed in jeans and a white sweatshirt, canvas sneakers with no socks. He heard his sister's clunky boots step from the corner. "Hello. You must be Dr. Shreve. I'm Mary Bolton. Jack's sister."

She traitorously shook the doctor's hand, tossed her long gray hair over one shoulder.

"It's nice to meet you," Elizabeth said. "I'm sorry I'm late. There was a tussle in the lobby. It happens sometimes, though in this case, it wasn't a patient trying to get out, but someone hoping to get in."

"Sounds like someone who ought to be here."

"Maybe. The man looked pretty enraged, to tell the truth. A little worse for wear."

Jack stiffened, but didn't look up.

"How's he doing?" Elizabeth asked.

"He's drugged up and pissed," Mary said, and Jack smiled at his reflection in the glass. "He just wants to get back to his plants."

"I've started the process of releasing him," the doctor said, "but I still have concerns. My professional opinion is that he's suffering from bi—"

"He's high energy," Mary said shortly. "Always has been. There's nothing wrong with that."

"No there isn't, if it doesn't ruin your marriage and lead you into Golden Gate Park with blood on your hands."

In the silence that followed, Jack searched for but couldn't find any soft spots in Elizabeth's thoughts. She'd come in the full professional—rigid posture, dull brown suit, hair coiled into that ridiculous bun. Stern, but sad. Like a hesitant seedling, he thought, that comes up at the wrong time of year and has to be coaxed to grow.

"The gods were all voyeurs," he said. "And it's a good thing. When the god of light secretly gazed upon the flower princess Nanna as she bathed in a stream, the marriage of light and flowers was born."

Elizabeth's face flushed; it was the first color he'd seen all day. Mary stepped forward, flooding them all with the scent of the marijuana she still smoked. "I'm on his side," she said.

"If that's truly the case," Elizabeth said, "you might want to start listening to what I'm telling you."

Mary shrugged. She walked over to him, kissed the top of his head. She was ten years older than him, with deep creases fanning out from the corners of her eyes, a small, fading grin about her mouth. She was the only one he'd told about his clairvoyance, the company in his head, until she announced no one would take him seriously unless he wanted the unbelievable to be true. Tell everyone, she said vehemently, during her lesbian, Wicca phase. Dare them to doubt you, to look you in the eye and not believe.

"I'll see you when you get home," she said. "I'll be in the store."

Mary started out, then changed her mind and reached into her purse. A tin of Altoids, tortoiseshell comb, and bottle of flaxseed oil later, she handed Elizabeth a card.

"I run a book shop; Jack and I live above the store. My main occupation is astrology. Come sometime and I'll work up a chart for you. Cancer?"

"Taurus. I have to tell you, I'm not much of a believer in ast—"

"Funny," Mary went on. "I see Cancer in you. Protectiveness. Never venturing too far from home."

Elizabeth stepped back. "Well, it's Taurus. I was never happy about that. Being compared to a bull."

"Hmmm. There's a lot more to it than that. We convert the birth time to Greenwich mean time, then convert that to sidereal time, then find the ascendant. Really, it's quite a process. Nevertheless . . ." She walked around her, pinched Elizabeth's skin above the wrist. "I suppose Taurus works, too. Steady and conservative. Very concerned with dignity."

Jack laughed, turned back toward the window. After Mary had gone, Elizabeth walked over to him, pulled up a chair beside him.

"Mr. Bolton," she said. "How are you feeling?"

He turned to her slowly. She must have taught herself not to shrink from that look, the one that blamed her for flatness of emotion or too much of it, for diarrhea, blurred vision or nausea, dry mouth or the dry heaves. It was obvious she did not believe Socrates at all. Madness was not a nobler thing than sober sense. She admired bursts of genius less than geniuses who married and enjoyed their children. She valued masterminds who survived.

She touched his hand. He looked down, noticed hers was smaller than Annie's, softer, free of the calluses Annie had built up in the gym. A pale hand which had not done much gardening, a fact which distressed him more than his whitewashed eyesight.

He swatted her away. "I can't see color," he said. "Look out the window. Even the petunias are gray."

"We can adjust for that. It's a common side effect of heavy dosages of lithium."

"Can you imagine? A gardener who'd mistake the shyest rockrose for poppies? Who'd be just as happy with baby's breath as Mexican hat." He glared at her.

"If I needed people to like me," she said softly, "I'd choose another profession. The color will come back, I promise. Believe me, Technicolor is not everything. There's joy in earth tones, in middle ground."

He kicked back his chair and stood. "Am I free to go?"

"It shouldn't be long now."

He wanted to hate her, but her thoughts kept getting in the way. It had taken her an hour to get out of bed this morning. One hour just to convince herself to put her feet to the floor, to get dressed and do the things that needed to be done. She felt blinded by the dim dawn light, like anyone who has spent too many hours with the shades closed, too many days indoors. She wasn't hungry and didn't eat. She picked the dullest clothes, but her eyes defied her; they were amber, the exact color of the gems it had taken him three painstaking weeks to embed in the concrete at the Londonbright garden.

"I'm sorry about your husband," he said.

Her face gave away nothing, but he felt her mind spinning, searching for rational explanations. "Did you hire a private investigator to check me out?" she asked.

He didn't blink. "No."

"Then how do you know about Will?"

He shrugged. "Hard to say. You ever think you remember something, but can't place the memory? You ever get a chill down your spine in the middle of a hot summer day? Maybe it's wishful thinking, or maybe it's somebody's wishes."

"You believe you can read minds?"

"Not if you'll call it a delusion and lock me up for another three days," he said. "Let's just say, if you were in this brain with me, you'd feel anything but alone. There's so much stuff coming in, I can't tell what's mine and what's yours. You know any psychiatrists with a fear of crazy people?"

She hesitated before she stood, tried to subdue her trembling. If they were in any other situation, he knew she'd walk away. But in here she was as straightjacketed as he was, reined in by ethics and professionalism. She could fight back only with facts.

"Clairvoyance is almost certainly a manic hallucination," she said. "Emanuel Swedenborg, a great Swedish scientist, believed he conversed with inhabitants of other planets. Henry James saw a shape, night after night, squatting fiercely in the corner of his room. These weren't men suffering from paranoid schizophrenia but from the kind of bipolar disorder I think might be plaguing you."

He concentrated on the sun hanging low outside the window, perched like a canary on one of the branches of the sweet gum. If he was what she thought he was, he wouldn't be able to control his thoughts enough to make a good argument, would he? He'd be powerless to defend himself.

"You're wrong about me," he said. "I care about plants, and I didn't want to see them hurt. I went a little crazy, no doubt about it, but the real lunacy would have been to not feel a thing. There's your psychopath. The man who doesn't give a damn what happens, who gets hurt. Believe it or not, Elizabeth, you don't have to be normal to be sane."

She pretended to be busy with her Palm Pilot, but he knew she was just buying time, trying to come up with statistics, more anecdotes to convince him. "I believe you need not only lithium," she said, "but therapy to deal with the fallout of mental illness, your own disbelief and fear and anger, and the reaction of your family and friends. I've got an opening Thursdays at three. It's a group meeting, which I think will help."

He bristled. "Maybe you didn't understand me. Maybe you thought a lunatic's words don't count for much."

"I never said—"

"I've got the museum garden plus two residences to complete. I work seven days a week, dawn to dusk, sometimes longer. Look at me. I'm not a threat to anybody. I can't even see color. Notch me up as another success story."

"Mr. Bolton ... Jack. Bipolar disorder starts out so innocuously, so *pleasantly,* I understand it's hard to see the train coming."

"Or," he said, "perhaps there's no train at all."

She kept her calendar open. "If you stop taking lithium, there's a good chance you'll suffer a repeat of the other night."

He pinned her with his stare, and for a moment her mind was so obvious, it *couldn't* be a hallucination. She was a child, floating in a thick salt lake, the one her parents took her to each year before her mother got bad. Unable to swim, they'd still set her free, knowing the heavy water itself would support her. She'd floated weightlessly, drowsily, cupped in liquid as warm and soft as arms. It was the last time she felt safe.

"What happened to your mother?" he asked.

She jumped back, looked so frightened and still childlike he instantly regretted his words. He wanted to take her in his arms, hush the suddenly panicked thoughts in her head, and plant snow in summer all around her, which in the heat of the day sings gospel, along with the winter-loving camellia, who lets out one glorious note when she blooms then goes still.

"Please," she said. "Stop."

He turned away, cut the line to her mind. Ever since he was a child of five, enamored with the power he had in the garden, the mammoth vegetables his little hands could grow, he'd heard the warlike voices of the marigolds planted to keep away bugs, the lonely pleas of the lawn no one ever walked on, the whimpers of his mother's thorny, drought-tolerant shrubs, as gray and defeated as she was. When he was ten, the neighbors' thoughts started creeping in between the ivy—the elderly woman across the street fretted over the roses she was too frail to tend, the widower up the road couldn't bring himself to weed the garden his wife had cherished. Jack went door-to-door with his pruners if only to give them all some peace. At eighteen, he spent a year in Berkeley's landscape architecture program, but despite all the talking, found the lectures surprisingly silent. He wanted to be out turning that vacant lot into the jungle maze the neighborhood kids wished for. He dropped out and bought a lawn mower, began taking maintenance jobs. He deadheaded roses and hid his wariness of couples who vacationed in Tahiti for the lushness, yet refused to put serious time and money into their own gardens.

Once in a while he got lucky, stumbling across a client who wanted something striking and unusual—a ten-foot-high, earth-and-canvas sculpture near the driveway, no matter what the neighbors said, a full wall devoted to exotic succulents, or an artistic allée, parallel lines of trees interspersed, in one case, by gold spheres, a design which netted him his first real critical acclaim and the opportunity to move up to estate-sized landscapes, botanical gardens, and edgier commercial design.

When his marriage failed, he accused Annie of marrying him for the money, though they both knew it was years before his bank account increased that she fell for him. She saw his ad in the newspaper and asked him to install a low-maintenance herb garden in her backyard—basil and oregano for cooking and the rest of the plants as well-behaved and gray as wormwood. But when the garden was done, and she went to get him a glass of water, he noticed she opened the wrong cabinet, she didn't know her way around her own kitchen. She couldn't tell basil from oregano, and besides that she had red hair and skin as pale as northern light; she'd been taught to mistrust the sun. So he dug up the herbs, exchanged them for pink bergenias and blue delphiniums. Orange poppies and the dazzling mahogany painted tongue. He planted her a rainbow garden she could see from inside, and when he met her on the back porch, expecting a tirade, he found her crying. He reached for a lock of the hair that had fallen in her face and slid it between his fingers. It was an astounding color, as bold as red geraniums, as rich and vibrant as the life he imagined they would have.

At the beginning, she cried at his impulses, found his presumption charming.

He looked at Elizabeth. "I'm sorry," he said.

Elizabeth shook her head, cleared the tears from her eyes. "I left a message on Annie's machine. She hasn't called back."

"He might have erased it."

"He? Is someone else living with your wife?"

"Maybe. She's been seeing someone."

"You didn't mention that before."

"I didn't think it was important. As I said, Annie and I have been separated since December." He clasped his fingers around her elbow. It was warm today and she must have been miserable in her brown suit. What on earth was she thinking, wearing wool when they still had a few weeks left of summer?

"Could you have fought with him?" she asked.

He shook his head. "I'm not jealous of Annie's lovers. I'm happy for her, if you want to know the truth. She put up with a lot." He ran his hand down to her wrist. "Why don't you spring me and we'll go see my dinosaurs? We can pretend we're two perfectly normal people out on a pleasant Sunday outing. You can give me the benefit of the doubt."

He felt her go rigid beneath his fingers, but by then it didn't matter that she would refuse. By then, he knew she was wrong about him. He *could* stick to one thought. Sometimes, in fact, he couldn't be swayed from it. He was convinced she was one of those women who looked better outside, in full sunlight, than she did under artificial light. There was no doubt her freckles erupted in fair weather, her hair transformed from a uniform swath of brown into a hundred individual colors, strands of burgundy and wheat and copper. Sadness, and an idiot of a man, had lured her inside, when he was certain her body craved just the opposite.

"I'm sorry," she said. "That wouldn't be right."

He wasn't sick. How could he be, when he fell in love just like that? His entire vocabulary translated itself into secret, tender code; every thought became a grand, romantic scheme—a way to get a guarded woman to plunge her nose into flowers like Nanna herself. Love was indeed a lot like mania. And there wasn't a doctor on the planet who could convince him this was bad.

THREE

CHLOE Verplank could not believe anyone paid two hundred bucks an hour to get advice from her mother, when it was obvious Elizabeth made things up as she went along. For instance, the Great Doctor said a child's core personality was intact by the age of five, when in fact Chloe became an entirely new person the first day of freshman year. She stepped onto the asphalt parking lot of Eastside High and, instead of taking advantage of a clean slate and her one chance to look irresistibly breezy and nonchalant, she turned even more pathetic: She fell in love with the first boy she saw.

She plunged from demanding her best efforts in class and soccer to wanting nothing more ambitious than a date for homecoming and the chance to let Skitch Priestly copy her homework word for word. Her clothes had more aspirations than she did, arranging themselves on her body according to Skitch's favorite color; her passion for soccer fizzled like an all-girl party after she discovered Skitch did not like sports. She'd even lost control of her daydreams; Academy Awards and the Nobel Prize in medicine were muscled aside by the perfectly imagined moment of her first kiss.

Someone should have mentioned that ninth grade was a black hole. She'd gone in all smiles and eagerness, had no idea the colors and moods would all be black. Three days in, she found herself snapping at friends, waking up stiff and disgruntled and amnesiac about anything that had mattered before. One low grade on an essay and she refused to write another complete sentence, one scoff at her plans for medical school and she decided community college was just as good. One September morning so blue and warm and still, when Skitch Priestly did not appear in homeroom, and she took up ditching with a vengeance. She caught the bus to the beach and lay motionless with the cassette player on repeat, Josh Groban's operatic voice crooning to her again and again and again.

On weekends, when she used to rise at six-thirty for soccer camp, she now slept until noon. She discovered a fondness for hunger pains and diet sodas, was suddenly a supermodel of self-restraint. When she dipped to that magical below-average weight for her height, she celebrated with an even more stringent diet, one that blurred the line between weakness and bliss.

On school days, she ate nothing but rice cakes, spent the majority of her time trying not to play the fool. She didn't *always* show up in Skitch Priestly's path. Today, for instance, she managed to keep her back to him for close to fifty minutes during biology, which meant paying attention to Mr. Redman, better known as Mr. Retchman, who had been talking the entire hour without coming up for air.

"Kingdoms," Retchman said, "encompassing the three great divisions of natural objects, the animal, vegetable, and mineral. Then we move on to phyla, the major primary subdivisions of the animal kingdom, and within that the classes and orders, the usual major subdivision of a class or subclass in the classification of plants and animals, consisting of several families." When Retchman talked to his wife, Chloe imagined the woman putting her hands over her ears and screaming.

Chloe flicked at the pink eraser shavings on her desk, noticed the message scratched into the wood near her hand. For a good thirty seconds, she stared at her desktop, disbelief turning to suspicion then finally to a tentative flush of pleasure, a tingle that crept like a hesitant spider from the tips of her fingers to the palm of her hand.

Chloe Verplank is HOT.

She glanced up, but Retchman was only down to genera, the usual major subdivision of a family or subfamily in the classification of plants and animals, usually consisting of more than one species. Her best friend, Jill Dixon, sat in front of her, her frizzy blond hair bobbing as she furiously took notes.

Chloe glanced beside her, her cheeks warm. There was Zach Meyers, boy genius, who had practically run people over trying to snare Jill as his lab partner. Across from him sat Billy Tidman, who was going with Lucy French, better known as Lucy Will French-Kiss Anyone. Joe Divers, so thin and nice to girls he had to be gay, Ian Schmoltz, who couldn't string a coherent sentence together unless it had to do with football. That left only Skitch, who she might have turned her back to, but whose every breath still caused a shudder throughout her body, a blissful, consenting sigh.

She'd never had a boyfriend, but she knew this much about getting one: She'd have to fight every honest instinct she had. The girls who went steady were normally vivacious but had learned to be grim, the ones who got kissed had all dropped out of gymnastics and refused to go on family vacations, regardless of how much fun they'd had last summer. Her best move would be to avoid Skitch Priestly entirely, but her body refused to co-operate. She turned just enough to find Skitch stretched out languidly at his desk, staring right back at her.

She jerked forward, and he laughed. He'd called the other night at two in the morning, ostensibly to borrow her biology notes. But when she'd tried to give him the answers, he'd suddenly launched into the opening lines from *Peyton Place,* the first school play of the year in which he intended to play the lead.

"Indian summer is like a woman," he'd said in his contrived but still heart-stopping actor's voice. "Ripe, hotly passionate, but fickle, she comes and goes as she pleases so that one is never sure whether she will come at all, nor for how long she will stay."

Her skin tingled, practically danced. Skitch Priestly was a dead ringer for James Dean in looks, attitude, and no doubt doomed future, and last year at middle school, Chloe had been invisible to him. She'd been cloaked by her own contentment, hidden by her childish pleasure in playing goalie and garnering the attention of her parents, and now it was as if he admired her weak spot, a stress fracture that only emerged under the weight of black holes and disillusionment. She wasn't hot until people began to disappoint her. Until she realized love could simply stop, that happiness could be faked, that the kind of passion she desired must never have existed in her parents' hushed, cream-colored bedroom, because after it was over, both of them had been able to go on.

Chloe pretended to take notes. It would have been helpful to have Retchman's ability to stave off breathing, because noisy little gulps kept emerging from her mouth. When the bell rang, she rushed into the hall, too keyed up to wait for Jill the way she usually did. Thank God her father was picking her up today. Since he'd left, he'd stopped asking questions, didn't worry about the status of her friendships, never wanted to know if something was wrong because she was so quiet. He just took her to dinner as if that made up for everything, bought her whatever she asked for, and kept glancing at his watch. It was almost like being alone.

She opened the main doors, was the first outside. It was a picture perfect September afternoon, the sky and bay blended into one magnificent color, a single breath of blue. She searched the street for her dad's Mustang, but instead saw the silver Saab. Her father's new and ridiculous girlfriend, Eve, in her embarrassing miniskirt, leaned against the hood and waved energetically, like a game show contestant. Chloe rolled her eyes and turned away. She imagined Eve stomping her tiny foot, perhaps reaching for her cell phone and tapping in Chloe's dad's number with the tip of a perfectly painted pink fingernail. She imagined the things Eve said about her when she wasn't in the room—how morose she was, how naïve and selfish to want her parents together, even when this no longer made them happy. She imagined Eve smirking, cigarette and whiskey in hand, (though she didn't smoke and drank only wine) at Chloe's belief that there had simply been a misunderstanding between her mother and father, not some long-growing, now impassable divide. Yet Chloe clung to the few things she knew for certain: Her father was not the kind of man who left. He'd forgotten he wasn't that kind of man.

"No Daddy?"

Skitch stood beside her, not at all the kind of boy she'd thought would make her weak in the knees. Not a true bad boy, like the ones who shot up in the parking lot or hid guns in their lockers, or even a geek destined for future millions. He was nothing but an actor, good enough to play the lead in a high school play but never more than the chorus in college, a teenager who already seemed to sense the disappointment that lay in wait and, therefore, drank a lot and went through the prettiest girls in school like candy.

Before she met Skitch, Chloe's vision of true love was surprisingly specific: A brooding artist who had once lived on the coast of Hawaii but had to move inland, a man so haunted by a freakish boating accident and a dead sister that he hardly spoke and never smiled, until he met her. The fantasy still charmed her, sometimes even wormed its way into a Skitch dream, scenting it with tropical hibiscus and saltwater, until she tenderly shooed it away. Skitch talked to everyone and had spent his first fourteen years in suburban San Jose, tragedy-free. He was friendly but not popular, cute but not gorgeous, rude but certainly not mean. Nothing criminal or heartbreaking or crazy, nothing compelling enough to lose her mind over, and she didn't delve into what wanting him said about her—the need to choose someone more important than the person she chose.

"What kind of name is Skitch?" she asked.

He laughed, leaned toward her ear. "You're gorgeous and you don't even know it," he said.

Her face warmed as he walked away, going from tepid to flushed in a matter of seconds. He probably said the same thing to every girl, but she still had trouble resisting it. She rose on tiptoes, felt her stomach flip and flatten, as if the last of her baby fat was dissolving with the onset of adult desire.

Jill emerged tentatively from the science hall, more frizzy hair than head, lost in last year's baggy jeans and a Backstreet Boys T-shirt. Chloe cringed for her, wanted to tuck her away in some dark corner until she could introduce her to the Real World, where it wasn't enough to be just smart. Look at Chloe's mom— graduated head of her class, a savior to her patients, yet still cooking for three and unsure what to do with all the leftovers, afraid of every day but Thursday. Genius, in fact, might actually be bad for you. A lonely detour around an otherwise happy life.

Jill spotted her and, for a second or two, long enough to make an impression on both of them, Chloe did not wave her over. She hadn't counted on desire being so exhausting and jealous. She hadn't figured on it costing her her friends. It took relentless vigilance to keep on loving Skitch when he wasn't yet worth it, but the alternative stared her in the face every night at dinner, the alternative piled their plates with more unwanted food and smiled when her heart was breaking. The alternative was the potpourris and ruffles that were already taking over the living room, as if her mother had conceded defeat.

Slowly, almost reluctantly, Chloe crossed the courtyard. Yesterday she would have told Jill about Skitch, but today she knew Jill would only warn her about his succession of girlfriends and penchant for drinking, his mediocre grades in everything but drama. Today she realized best friendship could rupture as abruptly and absolutely as love, in the time it took for one, but not the other, to grow up.

"Sorry," she said. "I had to get out. Retchman was killing me."

Jill shrugged, but Chloe knew she wasn't about to forget the slight. Jill's memory was superhuman, absorbing thousands of trivial details that would appear only on tests.

"Yeah," Jill said. "Whatever."

Jill had been her best friend since kindergarten. They'd slept at each other's houses nearly every Saturday for eight years, but this Saturday Chloe knew she was going to cancel. This Saturday, she'd be with Skitch Priestly, and by Sunday more than just her weight and ambitions would be different. She'd have changed the person to whom she was most devoted.

"Were you talking to Skitch?" Jill asked.

"Yeah."

There were a million things Chloe could have inserted into the pause that followed. A confidence, a giggle, a squeeze of the arm. A million things she might have said yesterday but which today seemed sacred. Hers alone.

Jill shuffled her books from one arm to the other. "Are you okay?"

She could see Jill was about to cry, and it occurred to her that this was the reason neither one of them had been kissed. No boy wanted to make out with a girl who might weep at first contact. Skitch would certainly reject a girl who turned a little fooling around into a promise, into more than it was.

"Eve's here," Chloe said. "I've got to go."

She walked down the steps, met her father's slim, fair-haired girlfriend by her Saab. It hadn't taken Chloe more than a day to figure Eve out. She always smelled of Obsession perfume, which seemed a little obvious. She jogged five miles every morning, bought her size-6 clothes at the Gap, and stared at Chloe's father with a hunger that ought to have brought him to his knees, but which, from what Chloe could tell, registered at the level of a patient's hypochondria; he smiled at her sympathetically, but in

SUMMER OF GLORIOUS MADNESS 55

actuality considered her a bit hysterical. He had no idea he was being stalked.

Eve was unfailingly polite, especially to people she didn't care for. She said please when asking Chloe to pick up her socks, never made a meal without including one of Chloe's favorites. There was no reason on earth to believe that Eve hated her, but Chloe knew it was true. Eve's pink lips were always smiling, but her gray eyes were cold.

"Sorry, honey," Eve said, putting an arm around her. "Your dad got called in to surgery. I'll drop you at your mom's office. Okey-dokey?"

Chloe "slipped out of her embrace. Eve was always saying things like "Okey-dokey" and "Later, alligator." She requested catalogs from Baby Gap and Fisher-Price, and put an antique bassinet in the corner of the bedroom when she moved in with Chloe's dad. Even Chloe cringed when her father threw his dirty socks in it, mistaking it for a hamper. Even if Eve was the enemy, Chloe couldn't help feeling sorry for a person whose heart was bound to get broken.

She got in Eve's car, flung her backpack over the seat. Eve gave the varsity basketball players another perky, game-show wave, as if she'd just won the grand prize sports car, and started the engine. She smiled at Chloe. "How was your day?"

Chloe rolled her eyes and turned toward the window. She had yet to tell Eve that all that jogging wasn't reaching the cellulite on her upper thighs. She hadn't confided that sometimes, when Eve leaned in to kiss Chloe's dad, he kept his eyes open, and now she wondered if these omissions were signs of childishness, of the person she no longer was. The last vestiges of the girl who was nice but not much else.

She turned. "Are you going to marry my dad?"

Eve's foot slipped off the clutch; the engine sputtered and died. She gave the boys a phony dumb-blonde grin (Eve had graduated top of her nursing class; Chloe had seen the diploma) and started the car again. "Oh, honey, I can't tell you that. But believe me, before we make any decisions, we'll come to you."

"Please," Chloe said. "Don't."

She rolled down the window, couldn't wait for Eve to get moving. The scent of Obsession was suffocating. She didn't know how her father stood it.

"Did your dad say anything to you about marriage?" Eve asked, finally pulling into the street. "Is that what this is about?"

"It's not about anything. I was just wondering."

"You're sure?"

Chloe shrugged. Eve and her dad were another disappointing case of lackluster devotion. If Eve had really been his soul mate, the one person worth ruining his marriage for, the two of them should have immediately stopped guessing what the other was going to do. They should have filled the holes in the each other, doubled the people they were alone, not become less. Their condo wasn't that big, yet the second Eve moved in, she lost her confidence inside it. Chloe's dad misplaced his laugh.

Eve tapped her nails on the steering wheel. "It's too soon to think about any of that," Eve said at last. "Just moving in together was . . . Well, you know your dad. He isn't exactly known for his shock value, right? He's already stretched himself pretty far."

A hint of acid crept into her voice. Chloe sat up, intrigued. "All I know about Dad is he's a good doctor. When all else fails, he's always that."

"He'll be the youngest chief of surgery," Eve said. "Mark my words. He knows the game. He never does anything unseemly. God forbid."

Chloe found herself warming to this unusually petulant woman, which made her next remark all the more surprising and cruel. "Like, for instance, screwing one of his nurses while he's still married?"

Eve swerved into the oncoming lane, then overcorrected. She glanced at Chloe, bullets in her eyes.

"Oh, honey, you know that's not true."

Chloe shrugged, keeping silent while they headed to her mother's office—more a bunker than a medical center. Three stories of foot-thick concrete, and for some reason all the windows on the dark, north side. The sign on the building read: Martin Branch Psychiatric Center and Day Spa, the day spa being a recent endeavor, instigated by her mother's partner, Stuart Cohen, who believed hot stone massages and herbal wraps were essential for sanity.

The second they pulled into the parking lot, Chloe grabbed her backpack and jumped out. Eve leaned over and spoke through the opened window.

"Later, alligator," she said.

The truth was, it didn't matter how short Eve's miniskirts were or how nice she forced herself to be. She was still banking everything on a man who opened his eyes when he kissed her.

"After awhile, crocodile," Chloe said.

THE office building gave Chloe the creeps. She hurried across the chilly lobby floor, past the sounds of the rain forest emanating from the day spa. She bypassed the creepy elevator, where she might get confined with one of the crazies, a term her mother had banned her from using, and headed for the stairs.

The stairwell was poorly lit, with an unnerving echo; each step on the metal treads reverberated five or six times, until it sounded like an army coming after her. The building was full of shrinks and patients, yet always felt deserted; the crazies were probably peeking out of offices and air ducts, waiting until the coast was clear, and Chloe could hardly blame them. Hot stone massages or not, every time they came back constituted a failure.

Doctors Elizabeth Shreve and Stuart Cohen shared an office on the north side of the third floor, with views of the bay. They had a perky receptionist, exotic fish and a Bose stereo system, though no amount of new age music covered up the sounds of a grown man crying.

Chloe emerged on the third floor, where the hall was so plushly carpeted and soundproofed, she heard her own heart beating. She hurried to her mother's door, prayed for an empty room. In typical ninth-grade black hole fashion, she was broadsided by a waiting room of nutcases. An old woman in girlish clothes wriggling sensually on her chair, a long-haired man beating a rolled-up magazine on the coffee table, a frail girl attempting to disappear into the corner. Worst of all, a broad-shouldered, middle-aged man had already spotted her. He rushed forward, hand outstretched.

"Hello," he said. "I'm Corporal Louis Fields. You must be Colonel Xavier's daughter. You look so much like him. My goodness, those are his eyes exactly."

He had a military haircut and an exuberant, flip-flopping shake, like a fish on a hook. She pulled her hand away fast, turned a panic-stricken gaze on Carrie Willis, the receptionist and protector of the sane.

Carrie was already out of her chair. "Thanks for the introductions, Corporal," the receptionist said. "I'll just take the colonel's daughter over here and get her enlisted."

Carrie had red, curly hair and a nose ring her mother made her take out during office hours. "Your mom's starting a new group," she whispered. "We didn't know you were coming today."

"I wasn't supposed to. My dad bailed."

Chloe slid a chair snugly against Carrie's desk and plopped down. She took Retchman's homework out of her backpack, but was really trying to figure out a way to call Skitch without it looking like she was interested; maybe she could ask for his notes, even though she never saw him taking any. She could feign interest in the school play, and was considering which part to pretend to want when the door flew open. A man in work boots, dirty jeans and a green T-shirt strode in, infusing the room with the aroma of grass. Everywhere he stepped, he left clumps of mud and petals on the gray carpet, as if he were laying a path to find his way out. He had hair the color of golden yarrow, a sprig of which came off in his hands when he brushed a lock out of his eyes. He looked around the room at each of them. "Well," he said, "I see I'm in the right place."

"I'm Corporal Louis Fields." The middle-aged man stretched out his hand again. "You must be Colonel Xavier's brother."

The man's eyes sparkled as he shook hands. "Why not?" He glanced at the girl in the corner, who flinched and dropped her head. The old woman tucked her legs up beneath her and grinned flirtatiously. The drummer, oblivious, intensified his beat. He mumbled something that sounded more like curses than lyrics.

Finally, the man's eyes fell on Chloe and she fiddled with her homework. Who would he think she was? Clearly, the only problem worth having was an eating disorder—high achievement *and* thinness—but she was not down to anorexic levels yet. Depression, perhaps. Suicidal tendencies had a certain cachet, implied an admirable amount of raw nerve, but frankly she found the whole I-don't-want-to-live thing a little shortsighted. What if your dreams would have come true tomorrow? What if you'd been destined to fall in love the next day?

The man kept staring at her, and her skin began to sting. She pretended to study, but he had already crossed the room. He took the seat beside her.

"I hated the sciences," he said. "What could be worse than the reduction of true love to chemicals?"

She realized her paper was turned upside down, where he couldn't possibly read it. When she looked up, she was pinned by the greenest eyes she'd ever seen.

"Let me guess," he said. "You're Colonel Xavier's child bride."

She laughed while the military man approached the girl in the corner and held out his hand.

"The shrink's daughter," Chloe said.

He glanced at the closed door. "You think she'll go easy on me?"

"I don't know. My mom takes sanity pretty seriously."

He laughed. "I'm Jack."

"Chloe."

The drum solo revved up, and the drummer suddenly screeched, "Fuck!" He hit the wall, began to pummel the sides of the fish tank. "Goddamn motherfucker!" The girl in the corner turned her face toward the wall, scrunched up like tissue paper. The old lady closed her eyes and smiled.

Chloe snorted. Jack suddenly turned to her. "Hawaii," he said.

"Excuse me?"

"A beach shaped like a crescent moon. Enclosed by cliffs so completely, it's a wonder it's ever been found. That mean anything to you?"

She clutched her notebook to her chest. "Oh my God. I've got a poster on my wall of a place just like that. I've always dreamed . . . Hawaii's, like, my fantasy, but my mom won't fly." She grabbed his hand. "Do it again."

He laughed, turned over her hand. When he let go, she found the fragments of a leaf beside her lifeline, flecks of gold dirt on her palm. "It doesn't work like that," he said. "Thoughts just come and go. Fly in and fly out."

"That's awesome."

He looked down, seemed to notice, for the first time, the clumps of dirt on the knees of his jeans, hardening to rocks. His eyes widened at the sight of the debris his boots had left behind, genuinely surprised, it seemed, at the mess he'd made.

"Bet my mom will have a rational explanation for that," she said.

"Sure. Delusions. She might be right."

"Oh no. She's not right."

She said this firmly. Her mother could rationalize anything, including the reasons for despair, the benefits of loneliness. She was so good at it, she no longer clenched her teeth while lying; she might have even believed what she said. Chloe used to take her mother's word over anyone's, until those nights after her

mom moved to the guest room. Until she heard the bullet-like indifference of her father's voice, and how her mother still pleaded
her case. Until she realized that no one can control what they
feel. No one.

"I want to try it," she said.

She expected him to laugh, but he merely closed his eyes. "Let
me set an image in my head." He paused. "All right. Shoot."

She felt a thrill, studying a man's face without worrying she'd
get caught. She noticed a scar along his left cheek, a scab on his
chin, dirt in the pores of his cheeks. He had stubble, a few longer
hairs in the hard-to-shave crinkle beneath his lower lip. She let her
gaze wander, spied a tattoo of a raven on his left arm, assorted
scars on his hands, black smudges across his knuckles. His skin,
she thought, was tinged slightly green, like tree bark at the end of
a long, wet summer.

"Getting anything?" he said without opening his eyes.

She leaned forward, tried to pick up some sensation, but she
was distracted by the smell of grass and a sudden craving for
sunshine, by the drummer shouting "Motherfucking shitface"
and a suspicion that her mother was having trouble concentrat-
ing on paperwork in the next room while the afternoon light
danced across the leaves of the purple ash outside her window.

She tapped his hand. "Sorry."

He opened his eyes, smiled gently. The military man reintroduced himself to the petrified girl, this time with a bend in his
knees, a more tentative smile.

"I don't know if mind reading is a talent you'd want anyway," Jack said.

"Why not? I'd know what people are really thinking."

"Some people are better left to your imagination," he said.

The door to the sanctum opened and her mother walked out in her usual attire—slim black skirt, silk blouse, trim blazer, hose and pumps. Chloe did not know how she lived in those torturous garments all day. At least her partner, Stuart, got away with wool slacks and sweaters, now in a slimmer size than before. Stuart must have been on the Atkins diet; in the last few weeks, he'd reveled in the weight oozing off him, regardless of the fact that the results looked unhealthy. He'd become a rag doll instead of a teddy bear, all limp and floppy, the color and oily texture of the cheese he could eat to his heart's discontent.

Her mother saw her and smiled in surprise, then tempered the grin for her patients. Chloe hated her mother's stinginess with smiles, along with her rock-solid professionalism, as if her patients cared, one way or another, how happy she was. As if they weren't, like most people, completely and utterly wrapped up in themselves.

She touched Chloe's shoulder. "Your dad couldn't make it?"

"I'm not staying here."

"The session's only an hour. No one will bother you."

Chloe glanced at Jack, who was now humming a Hawaiian tune. He turned his gaze to her mother, smiled at her innocently.

"Why don't you all go inside?" her mother said to the group. "I'll be right in."

The old woman wriggled off her seat, the girl in the corner practically flew past the man still hunting down the relatives of Colonel Xavier. The rock star thumped the back of the chair, the door to the office, the soft spots on the side of Jack's head.

"Hey!"

Chloe's mom put her hand on Jack's arm. "He can't help it. I'll explain inside."

Chloe counted how long Elizabeth left her hand on Jack's arm. One one thousand, two one thousand, three. Elizabeth removed her hand, slid it guiltily, Chloe thought, behind her back. Chloe got to the door before either of them realized she was trying to escape.

Jack appeared at her side, slipped two flattened nasturtiums from his pocket into her hand. "There was a group of men called the Sun Brotherhood," he said. "They lived in a meadow of nasturtiums, lived for art and the simple loveliness of life."

Chloe saw her mother leaning in, a smile tugging at the corners of her lips. She dropped her hand from the door, had nowhere to go anyway.

"The flowers grow wild on Angel Island," Jack went on. "Right over the old gun batteries. There's a meadow there that, I swear to you, will answer any question you have."

Her mother came up beside them. "You'll stay here for an hour?" she asked Chloe. "Please? I can't concentrate in session if I'm worrying about you."

Chloe had begun to hate her. Hated the fact that her mother cried with the water running, trying to drown herself out, and had yet to call Eve names. Hated her for not holding on to her father tighter, hated her for proving there was no guarantee of anything, hated her for being alone. Hated hating her, hated wanting to make her happy and being unable to do so. Except in little spurts, in a rare and unexpected acquiescence.

She bowed her head and sat.

FOUR

BLANCHE Armstrong killed her marriage with a thong. Her husband of forty-four years took one look at her parading around in nothing but a string of yellow silk and packed his bags. At sixty-eight-years-old, Rudy Armstrong told his wife he was horrified by the things Viagra could do. He wanted to play a little golf, go out for steak on Friday nights, and fall asleep untouched. He sure as hell didn't want a wife coming on to him night after night. Seeing Blanche naked and wild-eyed was worse than embarrassing; it drained what little desire and respect for her he had.

Blanche stood in her underwear, dumbfounded. Couldn't he see that just having the guts to buy that thong had shed thirty years from her face, that the silk itself had magical properties, dividing lumpy old-lady flab into two enticing half moons? She shook her head, didn't bother to put on a shirt even when he walked out the door. She stood by the window, where any passing

Joe could see her, and felt more horny than sad at the sight of his tail lights. Now she wouldn't get even her monthly fix. Six months ago, Blanche had started asking for sex for the first time in her married life, and dreaming about it endlessly. Even Rudy's dry kisses and cantaloupe squeezes had gotten her going. Sometimes, when he left the room, she touched herself until she came again. For six months, Blanche's libido had been rising; the once-dry hollow between her legs had swollen to a sweet-smelling pool, her breasts ached almost continually, leaking ambrosia, she imagined, instead of the milk she'd once nurtured her children with. She'd begun ogling the box boys in the supermarket, taking water aerobics from Sergio instead of Judy, and marveling at the jolts through her body every time a wild-haired skateboarder whizzed past her in the park. For six months, she'd been going back in time, so when Rudy drove away, she had the legs for it, but didn't run after him. She needed someone who could keep up with her.

She announced this to the group of misfits she'd been paired with in Dr. Shreve's office and was met by stunned silence. The doctor wrote an umpteenth note, the sorrowful girl in the corner slumped as if desire itself was a twenty-pound weight, two men she would like to sleep with right this minute looked at her aghast. Only the handsome gardener seemed unoffended; he nodded and paced to the window, leaving a trail of lawn clippings behind. Blanche could no longer control her imaginings, nor did she want to; she wondered if her sweat would turn green when he touched her with those leaf-stained fingers. She imagined petals tumbling across her swollen nipples, their bodies slurping loudly with sap, the ugly marbling in her legs transformed to vigorous green veins. She was certain he tasted like grass.

"Blanche contracted syphilis forty years ago," Dr. Shreve said.

"She was treated and the primary infection was suppressed, but apparently not eradicated. Very rarely, a patient will have an extended latent period after the initial infection, then sprout a case of neurosyphilis. I asked Blanche to join this group because, like the rest of you, her problems and potentials go beyond the physical. In Blanche's case, we've treated the spirochetes with penicillin, but the changes to Blanche's cerebral cortex remain, her own mixed feelings remain. She never really wanted to get well."

"The lusty wiggles," Blanche said and eyed the gardener.

"Fuck!" The drummer suddenly lurched from his chair, flung his arm around wildly. His eyes rolled back in his head, his face contorted, and Blanche was halfway out of her chair to help him before the man simply fell back to his seat. He took up the relentless beating right where he'd left off.

"Gary Griffith," Dr. Shreve said, "is another who sees opportunities within his illness. Gary, why don't you explain your condition to the group."

The drummer flung back his hair. He had a large, chiseled face, with a nose that appeared to have been broken a time or two and a swollen mouth, as if he'd spent the morning locked in a luscious kiss. Blanche wiggled to the edge of her chair, felt the moisture saturating the slim thong she now wore everywhere. Even strange tics could not put her off; she wanted him, too, and the man who'd mistaken her for Colonel Xavier's first wife. At one point in her life, before Rudy and the kids, before thirty extra pounds and the sagging properties of disillusionment, she'd been picky. The boys she'd dated had to be rich or handsome, and when they took her home, she gave them the length of one kiss to impress her. If sparks didn't fly, she never saw them again. At one point in her life, she'd thought she could have anyone and liked no one, but now the opposite was true. At sixty-five, with a barrel for a body and a smell like humus rising out of her crevices, she couldn't entice anyone, yet wanted them all.

"Tourette's," the drummer said. "I've had it since I was a kid."

"Tourette's syndrome is an attack of the primal brain," the doctor said. "The hypothalamus and limbic system. The disease causes involuntary tics, movements, impulsivity. Oversimplified, sufferers of Parkinson's have a deficit of dopamine, and Tourette's patients have too much. The answer is usually Haldol, but Gary resists medication."

The grass man, as Blanche called him, tapped his foot to the drummer's rhythm. Gary looked up and smiled. "I do my best music when I'm off Haldol," he said. "I rock."

His hands moved so fast, Blanche imagined he could touch her everywhere at once. Would he stop trembling, she wondered, if she took him in her arms and held on tight? If she kissed him deeply enough, could she suck the wildness out of him?

"Everything that's happened to me," Gary went on, "every joke and straight-A boy you'd never know carried a knife are my *scars,* you know? They fed the music. It's my mom who can't take it. She wants a son she can admit to having."

"Gary—"

"I'm not blaming her. She wants me to have an easy life, like everybody else."

"There are no easy lives," the doctor said. "That's what this group is about. We all need support personnel."

Blanche turned toward the other one, the military man, who was studying the mousy girl in the corner as if she were a shiny treasure he could not believe was still there for the taking. They had linked up, she saw—the drummer and the grass man, the mouse and the confused greeter, and she'd been overlooked. She closed her eyes, felt the heat between her legs and such a tingling across her skin she swore she gave off a glow.

She opened her eyes to find the greeter introducing himself to the girl once more, and the drummer finally finishing his song and dropping his arms, exhausted. But the grass man stared at her with a smile that suggested she was not invisible and might, perhaps, be growing brighter. Like a passion flower that, instead of fading in the blistering summer heat, grows more vivid every day.

The doctor turned to the couple in the corner. "How about you, Louis?" she asked.

Louis Fields extended his hand to the most beautiful girl in the world. He was only halfway to touching her, but mentally his arms were already holding her tight. He'd taken one look at her trembling, birdlike hands, sun-starved face and concave posture, and felt a call to action. Sometimes all the unfamiliar faces overwhelmed him, but not today. Today he recognized someone: The person he'd been destined to tend to and love.

When she shirked from his hand, he only felt more sure. He turned toward the group, placed his hand on his heart. "Louis Fields, Twenty-Seventh Infantry Brigade, Fort Bandon, Iowa."

He must have stumbled upon a gathering of Colonel Xavier's relatives—Colonel Xavier's spinster sister behind the desk, the old woman his despicable first wife, the dirt-covered man his brother. The boy who'd exhausted his hands but now smashed his feet into the floor was surely the son who would never amount to anything. Only the girl did not belong. She was a creature all to herself, thin and pale, with blond hair so fine and sleek it looked like the gold he'd panned in the Colorado before joining the Army, before Amy, before he began to drink.

"Do you remember why we're here, Louis?" the spinster asked.

He scratched his chin, didn't care much. Didn't care about anything except tugging a smile from the beautiful girl. "Can't say as I do."

"We decided to form a group on Thursdays, to help each other with the things that medication can't cover. Our reactions to being thought of as different, for instance. The retreat of family and friends. Do you remember me? You've been coming to me weekly for five years now."

He looked at her, incredulous. He knew this for a fact: Though he recognized Colonel Xavier's features in her face, he'd never seen her before in his life. Not her or the old woman or the dirt man or the drummer boy. None of them except the girl, who had lived all along in his dreams.

"There's some mistake, surely," he said.

The spinster picked a file off her desk, walked around to show it to him. The others, except the girl, gathered round.

The folder was full of photographs of a middle-aged man who could have been a relative of his father's. The man had the same clueless grin in each picture, was seated in the same chair in this office week after week, according to the dates in the corners of the snapshots. A physically fit, decent-looking man—though he could use a change of wardrobe, slacks and V-neck sweaters instead of the jeans and sneakers of a teenager. A man growing steadily older, the fissures fanning out from his eyes growing deeper and splitting into new channels, his short military haircut going white.

"Do you recognize these?" she asked.

He shrugged. "Nope."

All a big misunderstanding. He turned to the girl, smiled. She seemed to be trying to fuse with the chair, meld her bones to wood. He experienced such a sudden glut of tenderness, he imagined himself a hollow man, filling up with the first thing he felt.

The spinster—some kind of social worker, he decided now, with that monotone voice, those slow, nonthreatening movements—put a hand on his arm. "How old are you, Louis?"

He laughed. "Nineteen."

The others looked at him, then at each other. Probably they'd been fooled by his baby face. The recruiting officer, Colonel Xavier, had been dubious as well, until Louis showed him his birth certificate.

"Where do you live?" she asked.

"In the barracks, of course. Until they ship us out."

She closed the file, squeezed his arm gently. He had a quick impression of her doing the same thing before, but he couldn't place the memory, thought perhaps he'd seen something similar on TV.

"What year is it?" she asked softly.

He narrowed his eyes. They were all watching him, even the girl, and he wondered if this was some sort of trick. His stomach tightened; an army of goose bumps marched down his arms.

"1977," he said. "Jeez. What do you take me for?"

The girl gasped, and he turned her way. She met his gaze for a split second before turning away, and in that time the knot in his stomach dissolved, the goose bumps receded. He looked around the strange room, didn't know how he'd gotten there. He didn't recognize a single thing except the high curves of the girl's cheekbones, the naturally pink hue of her lips, all the more dramatic because of her sun-starved skin. Her hair reminded him of the streams of gold he'd panned in the Colorado. He stepped forward to introduce himself.

"Hello," he said, "I'm Louis Fields."

The girl, Kayla Donovan, could not go any deeper into her chair. If her mother hadn't insisted she attend Dr. Shreve's group, if she hadn't driven her to the office herself, Kayla would be in bed right now, sinking into the comma-shaped hollow her body had painstakingly impressed into the mattress, watching Oprah or, more likely, eyeing that sneaky sliver of sunshine that always managed to outwit the drapes.

She glanced behind her, but the chair was already flush against the wall. She'd like to melt into the porous plaster, reappear on the other side alone, but any move seemed impossible with that befuddled man still staring at her. Staring at her like she had something he needed, something that might keep him alive.

Her heart pounded erratically, hard enough, she thought, to leave marks on the inside. She gathered her courage, stood with surprising haste for someone who had, for all intents and purposes, given up forward motion.

She was no longer fast, not even of average speed. Dr. Shreve overtook her before she reached the door, slipped an arm around her waist. The doctor was so kind and soft spoken, such a highly sought-after psychiatrist according to Kayla's mother, who was paying the bills, that Kayla didn't expect such an iron grip. She had already progressed a year into therapy before she realized she was being prodded and twisted into a more acceptable form.

"Try to relax," the doctor said. "We're all friends here. This is Louis Fields. He's suffering from a rare case of Korsakov's syndrome. He's got no short-term memory, remembers nothing after the age of nineteen. He can retain three, perhaps four minutes at a time. In a couple minutes, he'll introduce himself to you again."

Kayla turned to the man who had now confiscated her seat. He laid his arms where hers had been, closed his eyes, sniffed the odors she'd left behind. Her stomach turned, not in an altogether unpleasant way. She felt a stirring of curiosity at his interest, was glad she'd showered that morning, something she might not do for another week.

"There's little we can do for him physically," the doctor went on. "The memories are gone. We can't reverse brain damage. But I think a consistent environment, the same caring people week after week might eventually give him a kind of peace, at least a vague sense of familiarity and safekeeping. We all need continuity and purpose, don't we? Somewhere to go, something to look forward to. Now how about you, Kayla? Will you tell the group a little about yourself?"

Kayla shook her head vigorously. Talking was out of the question. Dr. Shreve had no idea how much it took for her to simply show up. First she had to give in to her mother's pleas to get out of bed—a feat which could take hours—then find the energy to dress in jeans that hung loosely on her knobby hips and floral blouses she must have admired at one point but which now hurt her eyes. She had to suffer her mother's pensive glances in the car, take the last few steps alone. She'd dart across the chilly lobby of the medical building, ride the elevator with strangers who, once in a while, shattered the strictly maintained silence with nervous laughter and chitchat. She had to look in Dr. Shreve's eyes every week and admit that, despite all the fancy drugs and psychotherapy, she did not seem to be getting any better.

"Do you mind if I share a little information about you?" the doctor asked.

Louis Fields had opened his eyes and was looking right at her. Her first instinct was to turn away, but she was pinned by the hunger in his eyes, by the astounding and invigorating notion that, while she was at a loss to help herself, she might have something someone else needed.

"Okay," she whispered.

Dr. Shreve squeezed her arm. "Kayla suffers from long-term clinical depression. For some people, depression springs from environment and circumstance. In Kayla's case, it's nearly entirely biological. We've tried a number of different classes of antidepressants; Prozac has been the most successful. Kayla might not have noticed, but I think it's starting to help."

Kayla had certainly not noticed, not until Louis Fields stood once more and held out his hand. Not until she realized the pounding in her chest was in her head, too, and it had a surprisingly upbeat, Jamaican kind of rhythm. That she was already smiling, anticipating his introduction.

"Hello," he said. "I'm Louis Fields."

The doctor turned to the last man in the room, the gardener who stood at the window studying the leaves of the purple ash. "This is Jack Bolton," Dr. Shreve said. "He started with me last week."

Jack heard them turning to look at him, heard disgust at his disheveled appearance and ludicrous guesses at what could be wrong with him. Even a bit of lust. He heard everything except what really interested him—the breeze picking up outside the double-paned glass. It took all he had to remain motionless, to stay in that airless room when he had so much work to do.

He'd come for only one reason, and she was waiting for him to speak.

The latch on the window was stiff from disuse, but he managed to pry it loose, slide open the heavy panes. He breathed deeply, sucked in the aromas of jasmine and cut grass and salvia and roses. Mint and rosemary and thyme and the last of the lilies. He took in so many heady fragrances, he began imagining things—Superman, for one, on the roof of the building across the street. Parading around in full costume—red boots, blue padded shoulders, an emblazoned S on his chest—and waving at cars going by.

"Jack?" Elizabeth said.

Superman raced across the roof, red cape flying, hands outstretched while he practiced takeoffs. Jack feared he was suffering one of the hallucinations Elizabeth had warned him about until the caped crusader did something all too human—he stopped just short of jumping, came to an abrupt halt at the edge of the roof. Someone on the highway honked their horn.

Elizabeth was still waiting, but Jack had nothing to say. He hadn't spoken to Annie since last Thursday. His scabs were healing, the police had not contacted him, no one had emerged to accuse him of a brawl; the whole night was an aberration. He still couldn't remember more than Annie sitting on the stoop, ripping apart his plants, then waking up a few hours later in the bushes of Golden Gate Park, but he had found himself thinking about Annie more than he had in months. About the last things she'd said before they made the decision to split, mainly that he'd catapulted from obsession to absurdity, engrossed himself in plants to such a degree he'd made them more animate than he was.

"I didn't sign up for this," she'd said, pacing across the kitchen she still hadn't organized, past cupboards whose contents would still surprise her. "For you. For a man I can't predict, whose interest I can't even hold. All summer I couldn't get your attention. You were so happy without me, it was like a slap in the face. Now this depression . . . it's not right. It's not natural. You can't imagine what it's like. Apparently I'm not even reason enough for you to live."

He'd never been depressed in his life, and tried to manhandle it. Ignore it. But it was like trying to garden in winter—not only pointless but a lesson in humility. It was so dark. The winter sun had not broken through the fog and clouds for twenty-eight days when he stopped going out, when he and Annie broke up, when he finally made that first appointment with Dr. Shreve.

Remembering wasn't all it was cracked up to be. He wanted to look forward, not back, relish the opportunity to create a spectacular garden at the Londonbright, enjoy his newfound energy and enthusiasm, no matter what the doctor said. He was fine, enjoying his sister's company so much he had not yet moved to his own place. Happy again, not obsessed and absurd as Annie had suggested, but reinvigorated by his landscapes, by the seemingly limitless possibilities floating around in his mind. Never better, in fact, though this room was stifling. If he ran full speed, he could leap through the window to the boughs of the ash—Yggdrasil in northern myths, the tree that supported the entire universe. He heard its powerful humming, the stretching of its massive roots beneath the building, where an opportunistic vinca followed along.

"Jack?" Elizabeth said. "Can you tell us why you're here?"

He marveled at the care she took with words, how lightly she tread, how much she gave to other people when she was falling apart herself. He felt ticklish around her, barely grazed and wanting more. "To see you," he said at last.

He felt the surge of the old woman's desire, the retreat of Elizabeth's mind into patient-doctor transference while her body withdrew behind that awful faux pine desk. Sometimes he felt overloaded by other people's thoughts and wished someone would listen to him. He could take a cue from the loquacious pumpkin, which sprawls over fences, grows straight into the neighbor's garden in order to be heard.

But he wasn't going to talk *here*. In front of these people. Elizabeth turned to her ubiquitous notebook, and that was the last impetus he needed to leave. He walked out of the office, closed the door on the lovely sound of her voice. The receptionist was talking soothingly on the phone while Chloe sulked. The girl was doodling rather than working on homework.

"You want to go listen to some plants?" he asked.

Chloe glanced at the receptionist, who had turned toward the wall and was saying, "Now, honey, just breathe. Don't think beyond that. All we want is for you to take a nice deep breath."

Chloe shoved her papers in her backpack. She bent over Carrie's desk, scribbled a note the receptionist did not glance at.

"Don't say that," Carrie went on. "Oh, honey. Don't. Just hold on. The doctor will be out of session soon and I'll have her call you."

Carrie Willis listened to the pleas of the mother whose son had run away, fought the concerns she had about her own son, who hadn't been particularly happy either. By the time she'd

convinced them both that everything would turn out well, the
waiting room was empty.

ELIZABETH took the tram to the top of the hill, her stomach in
knots that began to unwind when she saw the amazing structures of the Londonbright Museum. On a steep, slide-prone,
fire-ravaged hill in Oakland, they'd carved out what looked like
a dinosaur graveyard—a multilevel, interconnecting skeleton of
bone-colored structures, the center buildings a pile of skulls and
ribs, the adjacent ones wings, tails and forelegs stretched out in
their death throes. She nearly didn't get off the tram, it was so
breathtaking, then she remembered why she'd come and hurried
toward the children's garden that was still cordoned off beyond
an ivy-covered wall.

The museum's head landscaper, Daniel Puckerbaum, met her
at a gate that resembled a giant worm—an arched steel frame
stuffed with potting soil and strange, corkscrew-shaped plantings, giving the invertebrate a crazed appearance. A worm with
a mind of its own.

"It was fine," Daniel Puckerbaum said to her without a greet-
ing. "Done. We were set to open the first day of fall. We'd told
him that. Then two nights ago I get a call from security that
something's going on in the garden. Two A.M., I show up to find
him out here working the bobcat. Tearing the place to shreds."

"Jack," she said.

"Mr. Jack-in-the-Green himself, shouting over the equipment
that he couldn't sleep for thinking about it. Some crazy burrow he
wanted to put in. Some underground cave kids'll be having sex
and breaking their necks in."

He opened the gate, led her through. She took a few steps down the amber path and caught her breath. It was spectacular and sad. A garden of dinosaurs spared by the asteroid only to be humbled by the greater force of nature. A pterodactyl grounded by ivy-covered wings, a herd of triceratops sunk into scrub oak. Even the mighty tyrannosaurus rex had been overtaken from the inside out, her stomach eaten away by moss until it was a cavity fit for seven children, an ancient cave where secrets could be told.

Every square inch of the five-acre plot not used for walkways or dinosaurs was covered in greenery and flowers. Ferns and star jasmine, phlox and reed grass, rhododendrons and African daisies. Every square inch was gorgeous except for an unsightly chasm directly in front of her. Beside a giant abyss, a bobcat sat with mud and debris still in its teeth.

"He's here somewhere," Puckerbaum said. "Showing the girl around, even though we've got a couple weeks to go and he's nowhere near done. I'm telling you, if we don't open on time, he'll never get another job in this town. I was against hiring him in the first place, but Mr. Jones loved that design of his. *That* design. The one he just ruined."

"I'll just go look for them," she said, starting down the winding amber path.

"You're wasting your time," Mr. Puckerbaum called after her. "He's a waste of your time."

Elizabeth did not look back. She ran her hand over the smooth, concrete back of a giant snail, its tail molded into a perfect, slow-curve slide. Dangling from the pterodactyl's wing was a large rope swing, its seat shaped like a mammoth's tusk. She called out for Chloe, heard nothing in reply but birds.

Her headache was getting worse, spreading clear to her neck

and shoulders. She'd stepped out of her office at the end of the hour to find Chloe gone and Carrie nervously holding out a note. Elizabeth had to get her partner to cover her last appointment for her, fight traffic across two bridges, and battle her own imagination every step of the way—visions of Jack taking Chloe along on some manic compulsion to skydive, or leaving her at the Londonbright in a common bipolar fit of forgetfulness. The fact that none of this terror would have occurred to or mattered to Chloe seemed like some kind of bell toll. An ominous portent of things to come.

She heard laughter near the T-Rex, hurried toward the rope ladder Jack had hung from the dinosaur's belly. Dangling on the top rung was the unmistakable sight of her daughter's bare foot, ring on the middle toe. If she could have reached her, Elizabeth would have yanked her down, hard. They were both on the cusp of cruelty; they'd only just begun to disappoint each other. No matter how much Elizabeth talked, she would never make up for the voice that was missing. No matter how many crises they averted, Chloe would never be happy enough to suit her.

"Chloe, get down," she said.

The foot jerked back into its hiding spot, then Chloe stuck out her head. "Hey," she said.

Elizabeth stepped back, searched the gardens for Jack. If he'd abandoned her daughter to this place she would do worse than terminate their professional relationship; she would wish him ill. She'd do it even though, in the last few nights, her dreams had begun to sprout with green.

Chloe eschewed the ladder and leapt down. There were grass stains on the knees of her sixty-dollar jeans, willow leaves in her hair, and so much bluster in her eyes Elizabeth decided she needed to sit down. She folded herself into a comfortable, rib-shaped boulder, turned her face to the sun.

Chloe kept to the dinosaur for protection; Jack stepped right into her light. He was whistling, carting six flats of spongy moss.

"If you ever take my daughter without my permission again, our relationship is over," Elizabeth said.

He stopped the tune, looked so stricken she turned away. He set the flats on the ground, sat beside her. "Yes," he said. "Okay."

"You have no idea. To come out of my office and find her gone. To not know . . . Even with good intentions, you can't take someone's child. Not today. Not anymore."

He was pale now. "I had to get out and she looked like she needed to see something pretty. It was wrong of me. I'm sorry."

Elizabeth turned to Chloe. "I'll talk to you on the ride home. Why don't you go up to the museum. Look around a bit. I'll meet you there."

Chloe shuffled from foot to foot, finally put her hand on her hip. "He didn't force me," she said. "I wanted to come. I shouldn't have to stay in your office like some three-year-old. If you and Dad can't—"

"I'll talk to you on the ride home," Elizabeth interrupted icily.

She watched the furious set of her daughter's shoulders, a new and unsettling sway to her hips as she stomped away. She found herself visualizing a defiant, exotic weed rising up in the soil, a soon-to-be rampant creature willing herself to be.

"She's good with the flowers," Jack said. "Gentle, easily impressed. They like her."

"Mr. Bolton—"

"Here we go again."

"You're my patient. Chloe is not part of the deal."

He leaned back. "I see."

"There are rules here."

"Obviously." He turned until she couldn't see his eyes.

She softened her tone. "You didn't stay very long today. I really think the group can offer understanding you won't find anywhere else. We can all help each other."

"Gardens help me more."

She looked back toward the bobcat, the mess he'd made, though she noticed he had carefully avoided damaging any plants. "How can you expect to finish on time?"

He shrugged. "I don't."

"Mr. Puckerbaum says you'll lose this job if you don't finish."

"Mr. Puckerbaum is a mutilator of plants. You should see his pruning technique, if you can call it a technique. More like mass murder. Leaves quiver when they see him coming. I kid you not."

She struggled to hold on to the anger, but it was tough once the first smile leaked out. "Jack, be reasonable."

He cast off his sulk, turned to her, eyes glittering. Eyes like the best day of summer—shimmering green and growing fast.

"I had an inspiration Tuesday night. Underground tunnels the kids will have to find their way through. If we put in a glass ceiling, we'll have enough light to plant."

"Jack—"

"Mr. Puckerbaum would like this place done by autumn, but he'd also like every bed filled with boxwood so he can prune it with a chain saw and be done. I don't create anything for Mr. Puckerbaum."

"I don't know if you can let kids play underground without supervision. There might be insurance issues."

"We'll have a few troublemakers," Jack said. "You can't help that. Some people don't understand the life force of a plant, the *intent*. Plant clematis beside a trellis and it will grow straight for the pole. Plants *know*. I don't worry so much about the trouble-makers. Later on, nothing they plant will grow. Let me show you around."

She was going to refuse, until she noticed the clematis and cape plumbagos had indeed grown unerringly toward their sup-ports. Until she realized she had never missed the scent of flowers until this moment, when she was surrounded by them.

"I hid the velicoraptors in there," he said, leading her toward a densely planted jungle. "Trust me, they were even terrifying to make."

They headed down a series of steep terraces, past jungles and grasslands and shimmering pools. Below the museum garden, an old man crouched in his meticulously tended backyard, studying every angle of every cantaloupe before he plucked a single fruit.

"That's Carl Ludwig," Jack said. "When the fires came through, he lost everything. A fifty-year-old garden gone like that. He was out here the next day, planting seeds."

"Such a community. Gardeners."

"Oh no. I go crazy watching him. It takes him an hour to prune a single shrub, a week to decide where to place a filbert when it's obvious there's no place for it except out of the shadow of the elm. I told him I'd work in his yard in exchange for not having to witness so much wasted time, but I'm beginning to think he enjoys my frustration."

He led her to the base of the hill, where a beautiful silk tree spilled over from Carl Ludwig's yard. The old man had picked one perfect cantaloupe, and cut it open with his knife. He offered two luscious slices over the top of the fence.

"Nice garden he's making, huh?" he asked Elizabeth. "A little grand, but nice."

She took a bite of the fruit, her eyes widening at the sweetness. "That's delicious," she said.

Carl smiled, revealing a mouthful of charming, crooked teeth. Jack was looking up at the garden he'd made, his eyes narrowed as if, from this angle, he was seeing bare spots and more work than he'd thought he had left.

"We'd better go," he said.

"You know my favorite part of gardening?" Carl called after them. "The mornings when I don't do any work at all. When I convince my Judy to leave the home for an hour or two. You should try it sometime. Put down your tools, forget about planting for a while. Hold a woman in the garden and just be."

Elizabeth swallowed the last of the cantaloupe, but the taste would linger in her mouth for hours.

They headed back up the path, Jack assigning personalities to each plant. "Trumpet vines are show-offs," he said. "Athletic and they know it. They'll cartwheel all over the place. And the creeping fig is sly, starting out small and charming, then a month later devouring everything in its path. Did you know the scent of flowers intensifies when the blossoms are ready for mating?"

They stopped in front of an extraordinary series of ponds, each dyed a different color and bubbling like tar pits. Jack had carved slate into stepping stones of bullfrogs and lily pads.

"Tell me what you hear," she said.

He shook his finger at her. "Don't turn psychiatrist on me. We were having such a nice time."

Her gaze skipped along the frilly tassels of the eucalyptus tree. It wasn't hard to imagine it thinking itself the showgirl of the tree world. "It would be something," she said softly, "to know what plants had to say."

They were silent, then Jack took her hand. He pulled her onto the first bullfrog, a gurgling pool of red water at their feet. "Close your eyes."

He'd pulled her close enough that she could feel the beating of his heart; she smelled grass again, and hibiscus and thyme.

"Relax," he said, closing his eyes. "Listen."

She closed her eyes, heard the obvious chatter of leaves, a whiny branch moaning beneath the weight of a thrush, the ballerina sighs of the water hyacinths performing figure eights in the blue pond.

"What do you hear?" he asked.

"Leaves?" she said. "The trees swaying."

He slid his hand up to her elbow, an innocent but still alarming move. She wondered where Chloe was, and why she'd never noticed before that it took such a little stretch of the imagination to believe in so much.

"It's not so much words as emotion," Jack said. "It's summer, the honeysuckle is still in full bloom, and for a few more weeks there's nothing to worry about. Nothing but full sun and long, drowsy days."

She began to breathe easier, relax into his hand.

"They wilt if they need love or sunshine," he went on. "They pout if you go away too long."

She laughed and opened her eyes. She leapt from frog to lily pad, laughing again when she made it past the final, sizzling pond and landed on solid ground.

She watched the X-Games descent of an oak leaf, the 360 layout halfway down. When Jack stepped off the lily pad and took her hand, she forgot her daughter was waiting, she didn't struggle to get away. The dirt was ground so deeply into the lines of his palms, they'd taken on the appearance of leaf veins, and she was visited by the strangest thought, a fantasy not at all suited to her: He was part plant himself.

"You haven't been taking the lithium," she said.

"No." He snatched the oak leaf out of the air, pressed it into her palm.

She might have remembered to argue if the leaves hadn't begun to rustle, if the late afternoon sun hadn't stalled in the boughs of the oak tree and dozed. If he hadn't gone on to say, "Your thoughts come with a cloud of perfume. It's like tasting you."

She closed her eyes, felt a loosening in her stomach, a warmth spreading up through her shoes, as if the heat was coming right out of the earth. She thought she ought to say something psychiatric, but she couldn't think of what.

FIVE

I N the short time he'd been living with Eve, Will Verplank had spent a small fortune in recompense. She never complained about his late nights at the hospital, but by the next afternoon it had cost him the price of a cashmere sweater. His monthly on-call weekend had resulted in three romantic dinners during the week. Even his daughter, who had stopped shopping at the Gap after spotting Eve there, had appropriated Eve's technique. Every time surgery cut into one of their visits, he coughed up a meal at the restaurant of Chloe's choosing, usually some place with onion blossoms and a dubious sanitation history. Tonight Chloe directed him to Shasta Pizza, a seventies relic with wall-to-wall pine paneling, diamond-patterned stained-glass windows, and so much purple lighting he checked for marijuana plants in the salad bar. A Pac-Man video game blinked in the corner; the radio was tuned to disco, a medley from Donna Summer.

Chloe eyed the crowd, let out her breath in a rush. Will looked over the teenaged mob, was relieved to find only a few pierced eyebrows and, by today's standards, relatively tame fashions—clunky, thick-heeled shoes, a preponderance of the color black, faces brushed with white powder. Good kids, he imagined, who liked the look of daring but not the permanence of tattoos, who would scrub their faces when they got home and kiss their parents goodnight.

Chloe chose a heavily shellacked picnic table, promptly turned her shoulder to him so she could see her friends.

"I'll go order," he said. "Pepperoni all right?"

She shrugged. "Whatever."

Will walked to the counter. The kitchen was open to view, which seemed to him a terrible idea. Two long-haired men talked rock bands while sprinkling bluish slices of pepperoni onto prepackaged crusts. He opted to go vegetarian, ordered a medium plain and two Cokes. He brought the sodas back to the table, where a boy had already confiscated his seat.

Even beneath the fish tank lighting, Will could tell Chloe was flushed. She'd taken off her jacket, exposing a hot pink tank top with *Princess* printed in gold glitter, rhinestone-studded jeans that clung precariously to her hips. The boy's clothes were even more unnerving, rubber band tight and black from head to toe, like a bat. Will set down the drinks.

The boy stood, offering his hand with more confidence than some of Will's interns. "I'm Skitch Priestly. I'm in Chloe's biology class."

Will wanted to ask what kind of a name was Skitch, but he got distracted by the lipstick left behind on his daughter's straw, a smudge of russet.

He shook the boy's hand. "I'm Chloe's dad."

"Right. The surgeon."

Will took back his seat, stretched his neck. The kink in his spine had come on yesterday, while removing what he hoped would be a benign mole from the cheek of a long-time patient, then had erupted full force last night when he answered the phone—another girlfriend of Eve's—and realized he was a little disappointed that Elizabeth had stopped calling as soon as he asked.

From the beginning, he was unsure whether she was weak or strong. They met sixteen years earlier, when Elizabeth stumbled into an oncology class ten minutes late and coughing, her hair a collage of hastily strung barrettes, her nose red and runny. Seats that had been open a moment earlier filled up with coats, then Dr. Gruden, who had gone into academia because he couldn't stand working with sick people, threw a box of tissues at her feet. "Take your mucus and get out," he boomed.

She happened to be right in front of Will when she started to cry. He'd never forget his reaction, because for once in his life, it had nothing to do with medicine. He didn't mention fluids and bed rest; he only wanted to shield her from Dr. Gruden's wrath. Her tears beguiled him, fooled him into assuming this tender and beautiful, frail and tractable creature was the woman he would get. He touched her hand and she went still, and he imagined she would always be that easy to soothe. He chalked up her brave smile to strength of character, to great chemistry between them, to fate; only later would he find out she always froze under pressure.

Will had never missed a day of medical school, but he led Elizabeth out of Dr. Gruden's class without hesitation. In the hallway, she sniffled loudly and he placed his hand tentatively on her shoulder. With a jolt, she fell right into him. He placed his arms around her hesitantly, sure that at any moment she would recognize him as a total stranger and push him away, but instead she held on. She mistook him for someone familiar and devoted to her which, for that moment at least, he was.

He was not concerned, in the first years of their marriage, about her panic attacks. When he came out of the bathroom in the middle of the night to find her turning the house inside out, terrified he'd left her, he felt flattered, more than anything. He held her, stroked her hair, told her he would never leave. But once she started to believe him, he wondered if he'd spoken too soon. Once he told her he would love her no matter what she looked like, she made a habit of taking off her makeup the moment she got home. Sometimes she went to bed as soon as she got home from work and put Chloe down; it seemed she stopped being glad to see him, and that's when his exotic dreams began. He dreamed of being an astronaut instead of a surgeon, of tempestuous redheads, of the most alluring life he could think of—the opposite of the one he had. A life without her.

He couldn't help it; she got on his nerves. Her never-ending exhaustion, her talk of Chloe and work and little else, those same old tears whenever he brought up the idea of flying to Hawaii. What was he getting out of the marriage? That's what he wanted to know. She was rarely home to cook, was a timid lover, a surprisingly inefficient housekeeper. She tried to get him into therapy, but he suffered enough of her analysis at home. He began to work more, took up jogging, requested Eve Tyson in his operating room so he'd feel something youthful and lively for a change, a skin-tingling infatuation with the woman's pink fingernails and bawdy college stories, her tales of adventure in the Mexican interior, of scuba diving with sharks. He began going to dinner with doctors he didn't like just to keep from sitting at the table with Elizabeth, where he cringed at her careful recitation of her cautious day—the same restaurant for lunch, one patient getting well only to take on another with the same problem. He exhausted himself trying to feel more than regret. She wasn't the one for him; he felt it in his bones and his bones horrified him. He nearly crumbled under the realization that he lacked the integrity he valued most. In a last ditch attempt to save the marriage Elizabeth didn't even realize was failing, he found a baby-sitter for Chloe, bought two tickets to Cancun. But the morning they were due to leave, Elizabeth wouldn't come out of the bathroom. Her fear of flying was almost charming until she curled up next to the toilet, until she began to ruin his plans. He admitted it wasn't his best moment when he cashed in her ticket and flew to Cancun alone, but at least when he sat on a white sand beach three thousand miles from home, he felt more than regret. He sipped his margarita and longed for someone better.

He said some things he later regretted. When she finally asked him to leave, his euphoria made him a little cruel. There was no call to compare her to her mother, particularly since he'd never known Lila Shreve, but after the words were out Elizabeth surprised him by stopping all pleading. She got in the last word by not saying anything; she merely walked into the bathroom and waited for him to leave. She became the person he wanted after he was already gone.

But now he had Eve. Now he could go to Cancun whenever he wanted, though he and Eve had yet to fit a trip into his busy schedule. He was expected to be cruel to Beth, was surprised at how quickly he took to meanness. He was as bad as a bully. He'd had to call her this morning just to get it out of his system, and he behaved horribly, completely out of character. He told her he was going to file for divorce tomorrow, even though he'd been in no rush until that moment. Her shocked silence secretly thrilled him, as if it was possible to detonate old habits, dynamite away respectability and remorse. Hating her was the closest he'd come to loving her in a long, long time.

"Do what you need to do," Beth had said in a disappointingly even voice. "I've got more important things on my mind. Our daughter, for instance. She took off without a word. She didn't want to wait in my office, so she decided she could just leave with a patient of mine. Went all the way to Oakland to visit his garden."

"Hold on," he said. "You left her alone with one of your patients?"

"I asked her to wait while I finished a group session," Elizabeth said icily.

"But obviously there was another patient waiting. Man or woman? Stressed out or psychotic? You know, Beth, sometimes I wonder just how careful you are."

When she laughed, he had to move the receiver away from the ear, it was so unexpected. "You know exactly how cautious I am," she said. "Anyway, you were the one who canceled on her again."

"Surgery got moved. You know I can't help that."

"You never can."

"Beth, what do you want me to do?"

She sighed, and the pain in his spine erupted, radiated to his unsuspecting ribs and hips. Eve had wonderful, strong hands. She'd massage his back if he asked her to, but since she'd moved in, he'd stopped asking her for things. For massages and sex and a refill on his coffee. For reasons he didn't care to analyze, he'd started working late and jogging again. He'd taken up those dinners with the doctors he didn't like. Anything to keep from sitting at the table at home, listening to one more drinking and sex story from Eve's college days and wondering if either of them could figure out what the other needed without being told. Wondering if panic attacks were contagious, since he was now the one pacing around his house in the dead of night, terrified of losing something even though he had everything he supposedly wanted.

"I want you to talk to her," Elizabeth said. "I want you to find out what's going on."

Will sat on an uncomfortable bench in the Shasta Pizza Parlor and had a pretty good idea. He stared into the eyes of a boy who had probably made his own erroneous assumptions about Chloe, assumptions Will dared not imagine, if he wanted to let this boy live.

"I'm trying to get Chloe to try out for drama club," the boy said.

Will glanced at his daughter, who was furiously drinking her Coke. "Chloe? An actress?"

Last he'd heard, Chloe wanted to be a doctor, but he had to admit they hadn't talked about careers, hadn't discussed much of anything since he'd moved out. Since Eve moved in. Chloe opened her mouth, but the boy with the made-up name jumped in before she could speak. "She's a natural. I can always tell. Think about it, Chloe. All right?"

Chloe went from sulky to brilliant with such speed, Will realized he had no idea who this girl was. He wasn't sure he wanted to know. The baby he'd pushed in a stroller down to the lagoon, the child whose coos had been answered by birds, now blared Murderdolls to scare away the doves from her windowsill. Anyone who chose clothes like hers and such hideous swaths of blue eyeliner was working on a whole other level. He'd loved wrestling with her when she was ten, was more than willing to pay for college in another four years, but everything in between he'd happily cede to Beth. Everything else, frankly, just scared him.

He hunched forward, the pain in his spine reaching monumental proportions, truly excruciating agony with no basis in fact. X rays had shown no ruptured discs; his bones were healthy and square. It was phantom pain, the med school disease when students came down with whatever they were studying that week. He was forty-two years old and no better than an adolescent, surrounded by the people he said he wanted yet utterly alone. A middle-aged man suffering all the symptoms of teenage angst.

He grimaced against the throbbing while Skitch Priestly smiled, and a hum broke through Chloe's throat. Skitch laughed softly and sauntered back to the teenagers who, Will noticed now, were all girls except for him.

"Well," Will said. "That explains why we came here."

Chloe wouldn't meet his gaze. She made precise rips in her white paper napkin, feathering it along each edge. In addition to the lipstick and eyeliner, she'd painted her cheeks with two arcs of coral blush.

"Your mom said you left her office with one of her patients," he said.

She made twenty tears on each side of the napkin, her capacity and apparent fondness for destruction unnerving him as much as her ghoulish green nail polish. Everything unnerved him now. His patients' inability to stay off cigarettes and out of the sun. His own relentless, unrealistic expectations. Teenagers in black. Boys who laughed like that in the presence of fathers.

"Your mother was really worried. You can't just take off like that."

"I'm fourteen," she said without looking up. She was fidgety, showing off parts but never the whole of her face, as if she didn't want him to notice how much baby fat she'd lost, exactly how much had changed. The only things he did notice now, it seemed.

"I know that," he said.

He'd wanted all that wrestling to make her tough and unafraid, but he had no idea if it had worked. She no longer let him touch her first. All the hugs had to originate with her.

"Exactly. I can take care of myself."

"It isn't just a matter of age or strength," he said. "It wouldn't matter if you were twenty-four. This is about consideration. You tell people when you're going to leave."

She looked up, becoming strong the way her mother did. All at once, as if it were a trick up her sleeve. "Like you did," she said.

She had the bite Elizabeth lacked, the staying power he'd never mastered, and at fourteen this was terrifying, a recipe for criminal acts and mayhem. "We've been over this a thousand times," he said. "We ran out of love. I wish it hadn't happened, but it did."

"*You* ran out of love," she said. "And if that's true, I don't know how you stand it. If love can run out, then I don't even want to go on."

He waited for a hint of a smile, some comforting sarcasm. He got nothing but eyes exactly the shape and color of his own staring back at him, burning with twice the fire. "Chloe, what's going on?"

The napkin was beginning to disintegrate under the sweat and tyranny of her fingers. The faux wood table was dotted with white flakes, a blizzard.

"Nothing," she said.

"You're not yourself."

He was mesmerized by the relentlessness of her hands, going here, there, destroying another napkin, trying to gouge a green nail into the shellac on the table.

"Da-ad, that's impossible."

He wished those long-haired boys would hurry up with their pizza so he could take her home, get back to Eve. He glanced at his watch, wondered if Chloe feared these dinners as much as he did. If he was as strange and unbecoming to her as she was to him.

"Which patient did you leave with?" he asked.

She eyed Skitch, blushed when he returned the stare. Will would have given all he had to be someplace else, to erase the vision of his fourteen-year-old daughter looking through lowered lids at a boy who had one thing on his mind. The pain in his spine was suddenly welcome, compared to the things he could imagine happening next.

"This guy," Chloe said. "Jack. He's got this garden in Oakland? At this totally hip museum? That's where we went. It's so awesome. You gotta come see it."

"Museums were always your mom's thing."

She sat forward, actually focused on him for a moment. He nearly reached out, but by then her gaze was gone. "Who cares about the art? The gardens are the reason to go. It's, like, another world. You can go inside the belly of a dinosaur, Dad. Fly on the wings of a pterodactyl. And the plants! Jack got me thinking about growing something. You know? Something of my own? Maybe vegetables. Everything Mom buys from the supermarket totally sucks. But if I had, like, cherry tomatoes warm off the vine, I could become this total vegetarian. I'd plant zucchini, carrots, spinach, even bell peppers. I mean, I know I despise them *now* but it would be so, like, miraculous to grow my own. I couldn't not eat them. And Jack? He read my mind. I swear to God. It was so totally cool. Mom's out with him tonight. He wouldn't come to her office except for that weirdo group."

Will stared at his daughter. The pizza came at last, but while Chloe dug in, oblivious to the pepperonis he hadn't ordered, he just sat there, hands pressed flat on the table. He'd lost his appetite, had lost a lot more than that, he realized. "Your mother knows better than to make exceptions like that. It's not professional."

"Yeah, maybe. But she's doing it anyway. He's got this, like, force about him. I swear to God, he does something to the plants. I heard them *breathing*."

"You do realize why he's seeing your mother in the first place. You do realize what it is she does for a living." He hated the sound of himself, the bitter, petulant soon-to-be ex-husband, more the child than his child, but that didn't mean he could stop. He was suddenly grateful for the ache in his spine. He was terrified of what he would have left when the pain stopped.

"He was nice to me," Chloe said quietly.

"I'm glad. But a doctor has to draw the line between work and friendship. Psychiatrists especially. Otherwise, you can't be objective. You can't help."

Chloe glanced at Skitch, who appeared to be acting out some part in a play because he stood in front of the table, flailing his arms and projecting his voice above the beeping and munching of Pac-Man. "Maybe she likes him. As more than a patient."

He could see she was waiting for a reaction, but since he'd finally broken free, since he'd taken up with Eve, since he'd ruined everything and mended nothing, his feelings had tunneled inward instead of out, and started to spoil. His face might show nothing, but pain coated the underside of his skin like a layer of silt. He went about his business, but he was having trouble seeing the point of it all. Every movement felt heavy. He found it difficult to lift a fork, to breathe, to admit to the damage he'd done. "That's up to her."

"Yeah. I guess it is."

They ate in silence. He managed to get down half a slice of oily pizza, then pushed the plate away. He sipped his Coke. He realized he hadn't told Eve he was having dinner with Chloe and would be late. He should be thrilled she'd only buy a new coat online, rather than fly into a panic calling hospitals and the police. He should be grateful she was nothing like Elizabeth; she wouldn't worry about him at all.

". . . over there and see," Chloe was saying.

"Sorry?"

"I said I want to go over there and see what's going on."

"Chloe . . ." He had a sudden craving for ice cream, the good stuff. When Chloe was young, he'd taken her to Baskin-Robbins most every Sunday. She'd always ordered orange sherbet. She wouldn't try anything else.

Now she sat back, crossed her arms and sulked, and if he'd had any energy left, he might have walked out, expecting her to follow. If the pain in his spine hadn't been so intense, he'd have assumed he could still predict her favorites. But right now he wasn't taking any chances.

"Go," he said. "Just for a few minutes."

She was gone in a flash. She slipped in between two girls, looked reverently at Skitch. Will nursed his Coke, wished for something stronger. He pulled his cell phone out of his pocket, had his own number in mind but punched in different ones. He got the answering machine, did not hang up though later he would wish that he had.

"Beth," he said, "it's me. I'm at the pizza parlor with Chloe. She mentioned what you're doing tonight. Your . . . date. I'm surprised at you. This is completely unprofessional. I thought . . ." He had no idea what he'd thought or, even more worrisome, why he was calling the wrong woman. Why he was getting upset *now*. He hardly felt like himself anymore. He imagined, at any moment, he might start wearing black, convincing girls to do things they'd never dreamed of, performing soliloquies in public. He might become the self-absorbed, unpredictable teenager he'd never been in his teenage years, when he'd been totally focused on his future as a doctor. He might, he realized, even prefer himself this way.

"Anyway," he went on, "I just wanted to say . . . Dammit. Forget it."

He hung up, feeling ridiculous and lonely. He wanted Eve, whose face lit up whenever he walked into the room, who had been flirtatious for years before anything happened, brushing him on rounds then looking over her shoulder and smiling innocently. Eve, who did not backslide into flannel pajamas after she made him hers. Eve, who wept at funerals and terrorist attacks and those sappy cotton commercials, who cried for understandable reasons. Eve, who was clear. Who loved her job but wasn't married to it, who loved him more.

He tapped his fingers on the table, decided to offer Eve dinner at her favorite restaurant in San Francisco. He finished his Coke, was given a free refill, and still Skitch acted out some ridiculous part, complete with falling to his knees, hand over his heart. Finally, when he'd been ignored for half an hour, Will paid the bill and stood. He felt ancient walking over to that group. Achy and unnecessary. Skitch stopped talking in the middle of a line about a curse.

"Chloe," the boy said. "Your dad."

Chloe turned, her face flushed, hands clenched so tightly, he imagined a stolen hair or handkerchief hidden in her fists. She got up grudgingly and followed him, head down.

"Come on, Dad, it's early."

Skitch came up behind her. "If Chloe wants to stay, I can give her a ride."

"Yeah, Dad. I'll be home by curfew."

"Or Stacy could drive," Skitch offered. "I'm still on my learner's permit, but Stacy's had her license for a year. If you're more comfortable with that."

Will was not comfortable with anything, that was the trouble. Not with the ferocious determination of teenagers to get what they wanted, not with Elizabeth's caution or Eve's nerve or his own seemingly bottomless dissatisfaction. Certainly not with his daughter's blue eyeliner and pleading eyes, and the knowledge that it didn't matter what he said. If he didn't let her stay tonight, she'd come tomorrow. She was already gone.

"Stacy can drive you home," he said.

Chloe threw her arms around him, but let go before he could even bend his head to her hair. "Thanks, Dad," she said, sliding her hands in her pockets, inching one step closer to Skitch.

"I'll call your mom. One minute past curfew and you're grounded for a month."

Chloe rolled her eyes, stepped out of touching range completely. "Jeez."

"We'll have her home on time," Skitch said.

Will narrowed his eyes at the boy, didn't like him one bit. Didn't trust all that charm and politeness. Didn't like the glow in Chloe's eyes.

He went back for his jacket, dialed Beth's number again and this time left a quick, factual message, telling her Chloe would be coming home with a friend.

He drove home slowly, heading along the greenbelt on Paradise Drive, past the houses screwed onto pilings over the bay, then north toward Ring Mountain, which Eve felt should have been developed rather than saved by the presence of Indian petroglyphs and the Tiburon mariposa lily, which grows nowhere else. Just before the mountain, he turned onto a windy, private road toward Redwood Village—not a village at all, but an exclusive, gated community of plush townhouses and single-family homes nestled around a dozen spindly redwoods. The trees had been planted after the old growth grove was chopped down, giving the development its name.

He'd chosen a corner townhouse with an unexpected and, to

Eve, alarming view of San Quentin. He probably should have waited to invite Eve to move in, but in his mind he'd been waiting for years. He'd been as patient as time. Eve decorated the place spectacularly with gold linen draperies, chenille sofas, and gilded tables. She told him about the community swimming pool on the other side of the complex, which he hadn't realized was there.

He pulled into the garage, stayed in the car with the engine running. He used to dream of being an astronaut; in the last few days, he fantasized about ramming the car through the garage wall. Breaking studs in two, sending sheetrock flying. He'd pancake the gold-plated shoe rack, take out a gilded vase or two, muddy the impractical white carpet with tread marks. If he made a quick turn before the kitchen, he'd shatter the crystal hutch, pulverize a few of Eve's prized Lladros. If he was lucky, he'd crush every last martini glass, get all the way to the bedroom and that antique bassinet before he finally came to a halt.

If he and Beth were still on good terms, she'd diagnose him like crazy. Passive-aggressive tendencies. Borderline antisocial disorder. If they were still on good terms, he'd tell her the truth: He wasn't nearly as violent as he wanted to be. A man who couldn't figure out what he wanted, who couldn't love anybody right, ought to at least have the courage to raze everything, to rumble through his life like the 1906 earthquake, when the entire Point Reyes peninsula moved twenty feet in a few seconds, and absolutely everything changed.

Beth might consider him a natural disaster, but the truth was he still struggled to do no harm. He cut the engine, walked past the intact shoe rack, gave the gilded vases a wide berth. He headed into the sleek black and white kitchen, where he noticed two clean plates in the sink, the aroma of mint jelly and burnt lamb chops. He entered the dining room, saw the candles burned to stubs, a champagne bottle turned upside down in a melting bucket of ice. Eve sat at the far end of the table, dressed in the red silk dress he'd bought her after he'd canceled their weekend in Mendocino. She had swept up her blond hair with gold barrettes, but one side had come loose and now flopped over her eye. She sipped the last of the champagne.

"I thought we'd chel-celebrate," she said. She tried to stand, but missed the grip on the back of her prized Victorian chair and started to fall. The first tremor passed through him, an obvious hesitation before he moved to help her. "I got the promotion," she said. "Head of nurses."

He led her to the living room sofa. He'd forgotten she was up for the job. He'd forgotten a lot of things, it seemed, like the way lipstick smeared her teeth after she drank too much, how unlikely it was that he'd ever join her scuba diving in the Cayman Islands. How frightening it was to change his mind so often, as if he had no control over himself whatsoever. As if no one did.

Eve laughed, then got weepy, and he thought, *Oh hell.* She'd been so much prettier before he kissed her. She'd come into the operating room with a lightness to her step, bopped her head to the Lena Horne CD he always played during surgery. Later he would soothe himself with the knowledge that she'd been happier without him, whether she admitted this or not.

"I'm sorry," Eve said. "Sorry for crying so much."

"I should have called."

"I wanted to celebrate. Oh. I'm going to be sick."

She stumbled to the bathroom. A moment later, he heard her

retching. He looked around the room, nothing spared from his loathing. Not the elaborately curved and hard-to-clean legs of the coffee table, nor the too-cushy cushions, nor the overabundance of gilt. Not that ridiculous oil painting of cherries above the fireplace or the view of himself in the gold mirror.

Eve came back flushed, shame-faced, steadier. She leaned against the wall, pressed her palms against the terra-cotta glaze she'd hired a decorator to put on.

"Are you all right?" he asked.

"I think so."

He went to the bar, poured himself a drink. He glanced at the clock, wondered what Chloe was doing, thought about the first time he'd tried a father-daughter camping trip and Chloe cried for her mother until he took her home. He remembered wishing his daughter older. *Faster,* he kept thinking. *Faster,* so she wouldn't be so scared anymore. So they could talk and do things together.

"Congratulations," he said to Eve.

She nodded, kept her gaze pinned on his face.

"I took Chloe to dinner," he went on. "We ran into some boy." He thought of the giggles he'd heard as he'd walked out of the pizza parlor, how he could no longer isolate his daughter's voice in the mix. *Slower,* he thought. *Slower,* so we can talk and do things together.

He returned to the couch, rested the tumbler on his knee. Eve still stood by the wall. He noticed the whites of her fingertips.

He wasn't trying to draw things out, to be cruel again; he just wanted to think before he acted. He wanted to keep from making another mistake. He was getting the feeling he was reckless without even knowing it.

"The thing is—" he began, then noticed she'd gotten completely sober. She'd narrowed her eyes, as if she was calculating what he had to offer. As if he hadn't been the only one imagining driving through this house.

"Don't be a fool," she said.

He bumped his glass with his knee. "I beg your pardon?"

"You heard me. Don't be a fool again."

He looked right at her, admired her nerve but not much else. Beth had once said she hated her mother not for her instability, but for her inability to be happy. The way she could ruin a wedding with her bawling, shatter any perfectly fine day. And he realized, when he'd spoken so cruelly, that he hadn't been accusing Beth of becoming her mother. He'd been comparing Lila Shreve to himself.

"Eve—"

"First there were Chloe's feelings to consider," she said. "I understood that. You couldn't say anything, couldn't make any changes until Chloe was older. Then Elizabeth seemed, what, too fragile? You were waiting for her to really get her practice going, have some things of her own. Well, here we are. Living together with a great big black hole where our future ought to be. The word love is spoken like a curse in this house. I want to know if that's what you think it is."

She squeezed her hands together, but was otherwise calm. Perhaps he'd been trembling all along, was one of those fault lines that, instead of reaching the surface, implodes on itself. He felt sorry about everything, but regret was beginning to wear on his nerves. A man could stand only so much remorse before he decided he couldn't possibly be the source of every unhappiness, that he didn't, or shouldn't, have that much power.

"You can have this house," he said quietly.

Eve's bottom lip quivered, but otherwise she just smoothed down her dress. "I see."

"I don't want to hurt you anymore. I don't want to be the cause of any more hurt."

She nodded, stepped back. "That's a good one," she said. "That'll help you sleep at night."

When he said nothing, she tapped those pink fingernails on the wall. "I don't want this house," she said. "For God's sake. It looks out on a prison."

She walked into the bedroom, packed slowly, gave him all the time in the world to come after her. But he sat. He drained his Scotch. He listened to the faint hum of music through the shared walls and decided he hated more than this house; he hated the entire complex, every subdivision from here to Sausalito. Perhaps the entire, ostentatious peninsula.

She came back in fifteen minutes with a suitcase, which she dropped on the floor in front of him. "You know what's sad?" she said.

Me, he thought. Me.

"You're like a boy in a field of fireflies," she said. "You keep catching them and putting them in jars, and they keep going out."

She picked up the suitcase, walked into the garage. He listened to the hum of her Saab, the squeal of the garage door as it closed behind her, the engine fading as she drove down the street. Then the faint, unknown neighbor's music again, followed by the beating of his heart.

He stood up, poured himself another drink. He walked to the window, looked out at the lights of San Quentin winking on and off just like Eve said, like imprisoned fireflies. It shamed him to feel such relief at his freedom, but he must have been spending too much time with teenagers because he got over it fast.

SIX

*L*OUIS Fields stared at the note he carried. Unsure how it had lodged itself between his thumb and forefinger, he was nevertheless intrigued by what was obviously a message in his own hand. He held it up to the sunlight, realized the paper wasn't the only mystery. Why, for instance, was he hiking through a grove of oak and buckeye trees, trailing behind the oddest assortment of people he'd never met? Was he on the mainland, or were the flocks of herons and egrets a sign that his battalion had made an island landing? Why was he hurrying, when had he last eaten, was it something more than hunger that gnawed at his stomach when he stared at the note?

The heat was visible today, shimmering three feet above the parched ground. Even the hardy bottlebrush, growing in the pockets of shade beneath the buckeyes, looked limp and forlorn. He spotted water through the trees to the west, a sliver of sandy cove, and he felt sleepy, still halfway in a dream where he accepted even the most ludicrous developments, including a glimpse of abandoned missile launch pads.

A stranger bounded into the path and plucked the note from his hand. "Hey!" Louis cried, trying to snatch it back, but the man was animal quick, like a jackrabbit darting in and out of trees.

Louis worked to make sense of things, envisioned a training exercise and the man, camouflaged in green, posing as the enemy. His foe disappeared amid a grove of juvenile redwoods, their trunks already two feet wide. Louis looked for tracks, found nothing in the bone dry soil though the man had been wearing heavy hiking boots. Twenty feet from where he figured the thief to be, he caught a glimpse of a green bandana, a splash of unkempt blond hair. He headed that way, then heard a footfall behind him. He turned to find the man back where they'd started, holding up the note.

"They say redwoods have no memory," the stranger said. "It's how they can stand to go on so long."

The bandit read the note, looked ahead to the oddball group slumping against tree trunks. When the man walked, he placed his feet so carefully he didn't damage the only thing that was thriving, an ugly relative of parsley. He handed back the note. "You have no idea how lucky you are," the thief said, then silently rejoined the group.

They were all begging for water, melting beneath the miserable heat. Louis was surprised to find he was not even sweating. Not until he read the note:

Remember her.

He felt a child's weariness, leaned against the trunk of an oak so smooth it felt like baby skin. The heat was suddenly a palpable thing, like a sheet laid atop him, restricting both his breathing and mobility. He would like a dark beer, a lager. It seemed like forever since he'd taken a drink. He'd like to ditch the army entirely, apologize to Amy and lie beside her until their muscles grew soft enough to take on the shape of each other. He looked at the note. Was it Amy he was supposed to remember? But that was ludicrous. He always remembered Amy, the freckles across the bridge of her nose, the uninhibited way she danced when other men were watching, her intolerance of weakness of any kind, including the sad drunks in her bar, the kittens she'd found mewling in the alley, men who asked for too much. If he sometimes felt like the jumbled pieces of a puzzle, then Amy was the border, a place to start and stop.

She was a cocktail waitress by night; a writer of twenty half-finished manuscripts by morning. Stories and men disappointed her. Charming black-haired pirates ruined an otherwise fine novel with a streak of childishness; Louis spoiled her carefully planned romantic dinners by drinking too much, by one misspoken word. Amy had such a keen appreciation of the difference between what she could imagine and what actually was that Louis found it best to be more fantasy than man. He never drank beer around her, gave up the gold panning and river running for a desk job in her father's insurance office. He never asked why she wanted him to dress up for a night of TV, never argued, but one afternoon he got to her door and couldn't bring himself to knock. He stumbled backwards in a daze of his own sudden and fragile desires, unknotted his tie and strung it on her doorknob.

When he stepped into the recruitment office he hardly knew what he was doing, but within minutes all that changed. Within minutes, he was transformed by the power of Colonel Xavier's voice, the shocking revelation that bravery could be taught. That

night, when Amy threatened to leave him, he heard the unflattering workings of her stomach in the place where his pleas
might have been. He felt exhilarated walking out on her, but it
took a series of creamy, dark beers to keep up the elation. By the
twenty-eighth lager of the evening, he felt fine—sudsy, warm,
and deadened—and when he passed out and woke two days
later, boot camp was unnecessary. He awoke a perfect soldier,
unconcerned about the future, his private ambitions demolished. He awoke not knowing what day it was, and five minutes
later awoke again, each moment a universe, fully contained and
separate, like a series of boxcars unhinged.

Now, a man whose skin seemed to take offense at the heat,
turning red and puckery, stood in front of the others. "Dr.
Shreve asked me to come along," he said. "For those of you I
haven't met, I'm Dr. Cohen."

The old woman contorted herself, trying to find a comfortable
spot on a stump. She wore purple shorts and a threadbare white
T-shirt without a bra. Louis stared at her chili-pepper breasts
pricking the thin cotton, an unsettling mix of arousal and disgust
warring between his legs. "Can you believe this weather?" she
said. "Makes a girl want to peel off her clothes one by one."

Louis stepped back, fairly confident he didn't want to see
that, but the doctor only laughed. "Don't tempt me, Mrs. Armstrong," he said. "Angel Island's got all sorts of secluded spots."
She laughed like a sixteen-year-old. Pulled her feet up beneath
her as if she were away at camp and contemplating how much
she could get away with.

The doctor tried to take a step and stumbled over little more
than a twig. The woman with the tightly wound hair hurried to
his side, linked her arm through his.

"You're getting clumsy in your old age, Stuart," she said affectionately.

The doctor laughed. "Let's thank Mr. Bolton for insisting we take the ferry over."

Louis realized he was in the woods, possibly on an island with all the egrets and herons flying about. He held a note in his hands, recognized his own writing, as well as a relentless fluttering in his stomach, a surge of tenderness for the expatriate redwood growing in the middle of the path. He ran his hand down the lone, spindly youngster, which would probably not survive. In high school he'd learned that coastal redwoods grow shoulder to shoulder in dense stands, as if they all spring from one great tangle of roots. He'd once entered Rockefeller Forest near Highway 101 and been rendered mute. It wasn't a grove of ten thousand preposterously tall redwoods so much as a gothic cathedral, the twenty-foot-wide trunks split into grooves which ended in narrow arches, solemn needles of light filtering in from above.

Amy would rip this exiled redwood from the ground, but Louis knelt down, covered its roots with more dirt. He eyed the people he didn't know, a thin man who, when he thought no one was looking, lowered himself tiredly onto a fallen tree, a woman with her hair imprisoned on her head taking over the talking, a green man pacing, a young man fidgeting, an old woman flirting—a strange battalion, to say the least. He felt sleepy, anxious to dream, but before he could close his eyes he saw a flash of color, a young woman trying but failing to blend into the trees.

Her first mistake was wearing a bright floral blouse, the second trying to creep past a soldier. He stood straight, looked at his writing, then at the girl. He thought of Amy, but today he lost even that familiar thread. The girl was obviously not a threat; the slightest noise terrified her into immobility. She was so thin she disappeared behind the slender pillar of an adolescent buckeye, reemerged nervously on the other side.

Even from a distance of ten feet, he could tell she cried too much. She had river channels at the corners of her eyes, hooded lids that made her seem drowsy, an enchanted princess falling under the hot, somnolent spell of the woods. Her hair was milky, almost a liquid, a girl dissolving before his very eyes. When she finally thought it safe to move she made no sound. She was so light she didn't even break the brittle leaves beneath her feet; she left no trail behind, and this similarity shimmered across the surface of his skin like a refreshing breeze.

"Hello," he said softly, careful not to startle her. "I'm Louis Fields."

She surprised him by not bolting, by offering a tentative smile. "Yes, I know," she said. "I'm Kayla."

He felt around in his pocket, found a pen he must have put there. He pressed the note to the trunk of the oak, struggled with the cap. He felt out of sorts, impatient, as if he'd been dropped into some pivotal moment with no warning or preparation. As if all the time in the world had suddenly dried up.

He opened the pen and wrote another word.

Kayla.

He expected relief, but instead felt a surge of anger, a pining for things he might have lost.

Kayla was careful not to touch Louis's shadow, or any part of the tree he leaned against. But not so careful with her heart, which had begun racing the moment Louis Fields looked at her, *recognized* her from before. She stayed in the shade not to avoid the relentless sun, but to hide the flush on her cheeks. Apparently, incredibly, ten years of painstakingly accumulated bleakness was no more substantial than cardboard, knocked over by the flimsiest breeze of hope. Louis Fields stared at her and, bam, she went from needing nothing but sleep to wanting all kinds of unnecessary things—a man to look at her without pity, a movie that made her laugh out loud, the lovely view of a man's face in repose.

She stumbled over a root, and Louis caught her, encircled her wrist with his large hand, ran a finger over the white lines that bisected her veins, scars that had healed nicely. She closed her eyes, heard half a dozen bird calls, the snapping wings of grasshoppers, a chipmunk chattering gleefully. And above it all, her rapid breathing, as if she'd been running for months without realizing it, just to reach this point.

"Kayla," he said.

She opened her eyes, which was a mistake. As soon as their gazes met, he dropped his hand. He blinked and didn't know her. She gulped in hot, unwieldy bits of air, turned away as tears stung her eyes—not only at his sudden disregard, but at his luck. What an unfair advantage to not care what would happen next. To not care.

She stomped her foot, hating her grandmother, two aunts, and a distant cousin for not being more successful suicides, for not sterilizing themselves, at the very least, before they passed on this ridiculous weakness, this melodrama, this traumatism by mood. Mood, which by definition is subjective, unreliable, subject to manipulation and controllable by a stronger will than hers. A thing people tried to talk you out of, as if despair and a way with a razor blade were merely daredevil tricks that would bow to pleas and common sense.

Other girls had cursed their acne and buttery thighs—imperfections you could cover up, things that would pass. At sixteen, she despised a part of herself even her best friends doubted existed—her inability to control what she felt. Despite a dozen good friends and middle class accouterments, regardless of a talent for figure drawing and high SATs, she could wake on any given day and long for death, be completely unmoved by sunshine or the entreaties of the people who loved her.

The extended depressions started in high school, when the breezy, fashion-conscious girls she'd once emulated began to seem superficial and ridiculous, too giddy to be real. She slept more, smiled less, stopped going to football games and parties. She felt saddened by dusk and broken fences and the chaotic flights of moths on the lawn, as if everything was in some state of mayhem or decline. By college, she was in steady despair. She dropped out of nursing classes that should have been easy for her and cried over nothing, over everything, over crying in the first place.

By the time her roommate discovered her in the bathtub, the bloodstains on the tiles were permanent, and so, apparently, was her unhappiness. Five years later, she still lived with her mother, not trusted to be alone. Her friends got married and stopped calling, exhausted by her steadfast unhappiness, while she was locked up, force-fed, bound and shocked, talked to and yelled at, put on every drug in the book, none of which changed one essential fact: She didn't want to be happy either. All strong emotion hurt, rose from the same untreatable heart.

She slipped away from Louis, crept lethargically into the woods. She felt exhausted by this last-minute heat wave. It had been over 100 degrees for a week and she wasn't the only one suffering. Drive-by shootings were up, some lunatic was leaving watermelon-sized zucchini on every doorstep in Mill Valley, and even her mother, a Phoenix transplant, had ignored the warnings of rolling blackouts and turned the air conditioning down to sixty, saying she'd already suffered enough.

Kayla struggled up a small hill and was rewarded with a view that stretched from the Richmond Bridge to the East Bay to San Francisco. A view so stunning, it brought tears to her eyes, made her crave tranquilizers, a lobotomy, anything to let her stand there and enjoy it without wanting more or less.

She turned away from the water, spotted a more manageable sliver of beauty, a tiny meadow through the trees. Relieved, she headed toward it, began to smile despite herself when she caught a glimpse of sun-colored nasturtiums bobbing in the breeze. She had nearly reached the first flower when a beast leapt into her path, his hide as unkempt and green as the forest floor. She jumped back and screamed, held her arm over her eyes to shield the blow, which never came. When she finally dropped her hand, Jack Bolton's palms were turned up to placate her. His voice was as unthreatening as falling leaves.

"Sorry," he said. "I didn't mean to startle you."

"I thought I saw—"

"That's the nasturtium meadow," he said. "It's for the doctor's daughter. For Chloe."

She looked around her, saw no signs of an animal. "Oh."

"What you want are lilies of the valley. They're the flower of the Virgin. Legend says they sprang up wherever she cried, created beauty out of sorrow."

She shook off the last of the fear, looked longingly toward the field of gold. "I don't want a flower sprung from tears. I want to never cry. To dry up."

He touched her arm. Instead of claws, he had dirty, rough calluses. Fingers that smelled of the earth, deep down. "They grow wild on the island," he said. "Near the lighthouse."

She started walking. "I better get back."

"Have you heard the story?" he went on, keeping step beside her. "There was a lighthouse keeper, a woman, who rang the bell by hand when the mechanisms broke. She did it twenty hours straight one day to save men she didn't even know."

Kayla stopped walking and closed her eyes. She marveled at the efforts people made. "I'm tired," she said.

"Sadness is exhausting. People have no idea."

She thought he was mocking her until she opened her eyes and saw the expression she'd recognize anywhere, the relentless tug on his smile lines, the unmistakable droop of looming melancholy.

"Nasturtiums are an antibiotic for the mouth, did you know that?" he said. "Great for a disinfectant, and the blossoms improve the sight. The flower has even been used to treat emphysema. An amazing plant, really. Radiates a tremendous force of heat and light, represents the polarities of winter and summer. It replenishes itself. It might bloom forever if given the chance."

She imagined him talking all day, talking when no one was there to listen. He snatched a candy wrapper off the ground, stuffed it in his pocket. Ignored the bees she swatted at. Picked at the bark of the trees.

"Dr. Shreve keeps trying to get me to do something," she said suddenly. "Just one thing. Take a walk or go to the movies. I only feel worse, thinking about the simple things I can't do."

When he stopped moving, his eyes got brighter. She wondered if there was an energy source deep within him that crackled day and night.

"Gardens have amazing healing powers," he said. "Trees will let you cry as long as you want."

"Mr. Bolton—"

"The trouble is winter. It's hard to tell the difference between what's dead and what's merely dormant. Impossible to tell what will survive until spring."

A leaf had gotten pinned in the corner of his bandana. She wondered if, beneath the sheen of his eyes, he was just as afraid as she was. If his greatest wish was to be normal.

He jerked as if she'd shocked him, clutched her harder by the elbow. "You really believe we could survive in a world full of thinkers?" he asked. "Engineers building things, warriors tearing them down, and no poets around to cry out? You think we'd survive long without a conscience, without the people who dare to feel?"

"*I* won't survive long," she whispered, then darted away.

Jack reached out too late to draw her back. His brain felt like fireworks, every idea brighter and more elaborate than the one before. He thought he was keeping all the productions straight, but now and then an inspiration fired ahead of schedule. Now and then he scared somebody, and he worried that he was only getting worse.

He looked toward the group Dr. Cohen had gathered into a circle. Jack liked Elizabeth's partner, the warmth in the man's eyes despite the sudden decline of his body, his exuberant, comic-strip thoughts and the absolute absence of fear, as if the worst had already happened and he had nothing left to be afraid of.

Louis Fields made a place for Kayla beside him. Elizabeth sat near her partner, hands folded tightly in her lap, not dressed for the woods at all. She wore leather sandals that were now scuffed and dusty, a short denim skirt and white polyester blouse that did not breathe, that was giving her fits.

For once, Jack wished for a little quiet. He started to pace, pounded his feet into the ground when he realized there wasn't a place on this island, or anywhere, that he could be alone. A dying redwood moaned, the wildflowers made heartbreaking pleas for water. The dehydrated lilies of the valley had hardly been able to lift their heads as he led the group past the old detention center, where hundreds of Chinese immigrants had carved their poems into the walls while being detained for months, even years. There was a sadness to the island he'd never noticed before, perhaps the reason why the lilies of the valley had sprung up in the first place, rising from the tears of ghosts.

He longed for his tamed gardens, trees he could transplant, reconsiderations and reversals not only welcome, but often required. He wanted to sit with Carl Ludwig and decide which of the old man's apples should stay and which should go. Reduce death to an unemotional, necessary decision, then haul it out of sight to the dump.

He stepped backwards. In the span of a minute, he thought of Superman and drum solos, silk sheets and sunlight mistaken for an intruder, a knife blade through a slit in the curtains. Heat, drought, roots stretched as far as they would go, then curling up, defeated, still not sensing water. The dinosaurs at the London-bright, not ready for viewing despite demands and fury, and his sister staring at him while he spouted a dozen new garden plans and cleaned the kitchen in record time, an anxious look in her eyes.

He saw Elizabeth watching him, then rising from the circle, felt the weight of her worries—Chloe's unappealing metamorphosis, a confusing round of calls from her husband, and most alarmingly, a transformation in herself, her sudden enthrallment with her neglected courtyard garden. The bluebells and forget-me-nots she planted the last three nights by moonlight, the smell of dirt still clinging to her fingers when she slipped into bed, her tears sliding out onto her pillow, as if she weren't crying at all but merely watering the garden in her dreams.

The thoughts kept coming. An aged body smoothed and sexualized by lingerie, a cat killer named Amy, a boy with rhythm who was labeled a freak. And beneath it all, the soil hoarding its nutrients, the grasses killing each other for moisture, the redwoods coming to a standstill, forgetting even to grow.

He shook his head to clear it, turned from the group. He stopped treading lightly, stomped to drown out the gleefulness of the beetles, feasting on rotting pulp, a dozen more uninvited thoughts. He reached the first of the redwoods, leaned his forehead against its prickly trunk.

His thoughts stilled a little. At least, he recognized them for his own. His admiration for the tenacity of dandelions and the clever sweetness of honeysuckle, which masks how aggressively it grows. The ivy-covered sauropods he'd decided to add to the Londonbright, no matter how far behind schedule this pushed him, and the devastation to his plants if an unlikely snowfall should occur. If it froze in January and February, turned to icy rain in March.

Elizabeth found him, put her hand on his arm. "Ssssh," she said. "Hush now."

He hadn't realized he'd been making sounds, hadn't known

how much he wanted her until he attempted to normalize his face and his breathing, to be the kind of unremarkable man she'd choose. The night in Golden Gate Park was a blur except for the striking similarity of dried blood to mud, his own lack of horror until a woman saw him and began to scream. He didn't remember exactly when he'd started to become afraid of himself, but he did have the solution. He could not be a monster if he was falling in love. He could not be a wild man if he was gentle enough to hold her.

She surprised him by not pulling away or taking on her psychiatrist's voice, by doing three things he hadn't expected. She held him back. She rested her cheek on his shoulder. She acted as if he wasn't the only one with something to prove.

ELIZABETH started to play music again. Will had always insisted on classical during dinner, but now she chose tunes she could sing to. Singers a woman her age shouldn't even know, like those pretty 'N-Sync boys and peppy Sheryl Crow. She played the stereo in the absence of Chloe, played it louder than her daughter was allowed. She fell asleep to jazz, awoke to the blues, which the radio station played from five to nine. She wanted voices. Her sorrows turned to poetry. Company in bed. She moved a speaker outside and sang about heartbreak while kneeling in the garden.

"Tell me, tell me baby/How come you don't want to love me?/Don't you know that I can't breathe without you?"

She cried during ballads, but she'd also begun to find dirt dear. After a night in the garden, she liked to watch the water in the shower run brown. She got up half an hour earlier each morning to check if the star jasmine she'd planted had bloomed.

She pressed her nose to the roses that were, at last, beginning to swell and darken from her care, and picked weeds without gloves until her fingers were stained with green pulp. She forgot her cravings for coffee, started each day instead with dew on the hem of her robe.

With the heat wave as an excuse, she left the windows open in her office. She moved the Swedish chairs beneath the sill, imagined a steady stream of losses and unrealized dreams floating out through the branches of the purple ash. Despite her long hours—ten hours straight this Friday—when she got home the residue of the garden still clung to her. Sometimes, when she was especially tired, or surprisingly not sad at all, she imagined the garden was full of sentimental witches. One step into her courtyard and they relieved her of the ability to think straight. She forgot the lines and pleas she'd been planning to use on Will, no longer saw the harm in meeting Jack Bolton for dinner. The path to the mailbox was a minefield of tenderhearted spells, which was why, when she saw Jack's name on the package, she only considered sending it back for a split second. She only hesitated until she shook the box and heard something dainty and irresistible clinking in response.

She cut the tape, removed the tissue paper, pulled out a flamboyant, glass-tiled flamingo. She ran her fingers across the shimmering tiles in shades of chartreuse and iridescent blue, neon pink and sunflower yellow, all summer colors. She suffered one moment of clearheadedness, when she knew she ought to recoil from such intimacy, when she was certain accepting the gift crossed, even demolished, some line, then the spell took hold again. She laughed at the proud gaze of a bird with a copper stake for legs. She turned the tiles to the light, cast a rainbow on the wall, and realized her house was painted beige, filled with brown furniture, and that this said something about her she didn't particularly like. She had never changed her favorite color, but from then on she decided it would be red. A note had been taped to the flamingo's beak.

Dinner at The Blue Whale or gnomes will be next. Surrender.
Jack

Her heart skipped lightly, so that for a moment she had to rise on her toes to take in enough air. She was paid to imagine the worst—the surrendering of teenage girls to cruel, convincing boys, of wives to abusive men—but wasn't it just as plausible that the best couldn't happen unless it was envisioned first? She tucked the note against her chest and imagined the finest things that could be surrendered—a chunk of fear, an ugly self-image, sorrow. The belief that she'd been deeply, intrinsically flawed, that she was past the point in her life when she could launch a man's pursuit.

Tonight she showered and dried quickly, dressed in a cream cashmere sweater and the first pair of blue jeans she'd bought in ten years. She sang along to the haunting Sheryl Crow song she'd grown to love so much.

"Just a pill to make me happy/I know it may not fix the hinges, but at least the door has stopped its creaking."

She pulled up her hair, put on blush, newly purchased pink lipstick. She walked out, still singing, and found Will in the living room, sitting on the arm of the couch. He stared at her, eyebrow raised at the low-rise jeans she'd found in the juniors department of Macy's.

He said something she couldn't hear over the music, and she felt reborn simply by not asking him to repeat himself. She walked into the kitchen, poured herself a glass of water. The music stopped abruptly. He came in after her, leaned against the far wall.

"Chloe ready?" he asked.

She whirled around. "You were supposed to pick her up from school. It's your weekend."

They stared at each other. She'd never known a mother who worked up slowly to blind panic. Her heart began to pound; in seconds, her palms were slick.

"My surgery ran late," he said. "I called the school, asked them to tell her I'd pick her up here."

Elizabeth dropped the glass in the sink and lunged for the phone. She found the speed dial button for Jill Dixon. The girl's mother answered on the third ring.

"Fran, it's Elizabeth Shreve. Is Chloe there?"

"Chloe? No. Did the girls have a play date?"

Even in the midst of her panic, Elizabeth marveled at Fran Dixon's determination to resist time, to continue to call her fourteen-year-old daughter's get-togethers play dates.

"Can I talk to Jill?"

"Of course."

Elizabeth heard the woman talking to her daughter, urging her on when Jill resisted. "Mrs. Shreve?" Jill said finally, reluctantly.

"Listen," Elizabeth said. "I know you and Chloe protect each other, but right now I need to know where she is. It's important."

"We're not that close. Not anymore."

"You know that's not true. She's been spending all her time with you. She's—"

"Mrs. Shreve, I haven't seen Chloe for, like, five days. Not in school, not afterwards. She hasn't been around."

Elizabeth breathed deeply, beginning to realize the enormity of the disservice she'd done to her patients with teenagers, the unfair skepticism she'd displayed at their accounts of unrelenting rage. Until this moment, she hadn't understood the depth of betrayal the mother of a lying fourteen-year-old could feel. She'd had no clue that a father could mean it when he told her he despised his own son.

She heard sniffles on the other end, Jill beginning to cry. "Honey," she said.

"She's, like, ruining everything, if you want to know the truth. I don't care what everybody else is doing, and Chloe didn't used to care either. Now I'm, like, the only freak show around here. The only one who actually cares about her family, who tries to get good grades."

"Jill, Chloe hasn't left you."

"Oh yes she has. She's left you, too. You know she has."

Elizabeth ran her hand across the counter, could not believe the amount of dust that had accumulated in a week. She used to clean at night, but now she gardened. She tracked dirt in rather than sweeping it out, and though a month ago this would have alarmed her, today this slow triumph of nature was the only thing that gave her any peace.

"I'll talk to her," she said softly.

"Yeah, well, good luck. Skitch is the only one who gets through. She's, like, with him twenty-four seven. You can tell her it would have been nice if she'd said good-bye."

Will retreated to the living room while she hung up the phone, came back with a drink for her. She downed it before realizing it was the Scotch only he liked. She wasted valuable time coughing.

"She's not there," she said when she could. "Jill says she's with someone named Skitch."

"I met him at the pizza parlor. Let's go sit down."

"I don't need to sit down," Elizabeth said. "I need to know why you're not surprised by this. I need to know why I wasn't informed."

He crossed his arms, drew back. "No one's hiding anything from you. I told you a friend was bringing her home the other night. I left that message."

"That message basically accused me of malpractice."

"Technically, the message before that accused you of malpractice. I was concerned about your lack of professionalism. I still am."

She shook her head. "I thought she'd been with Jill all these nights. Chances are, that's not the only thing she's been lying about."

He had the nerve to yawn, right there in her kitchen. "I think you're overreacting."

She flung the glass without thinking, marveled at the accuracy of her instinctive aim. The glass hit the center of the tile backsplash, exploded into a shower of dangerous debris. Will stepped away from the glassy shrapnel but otherwise revealed only a slim, satisfied smile, as if a juvenile display merely substantiated his dissatisfaction with her. She wondered at her ability to go on hating him. Just how long it was going to last.

"I am not overreacting. She's been lying. She hasn't been going to school. Jill hasn't seen her."

He stiffened, alarmed at last. "I don't believe it. Chloe wouldn't jeopardize her schooling."

"Oh, for Pete's sake. If she's falling in love for the first time, school is a throwaway. It's the first thing to go."

"Beth—"

They heard scuffling on the porch steps, someone attempting to ease open the squeaky screen door. Will ignored the obvious sound of footsteps, bent to clean up the shattered glass. On her own as usual, Elizabeth marched into the living room, stopped Chloe in the process of tiptoeing down the hall. For a split second, Elizabeth thought her daughter would play the part right—look sheepish, stammer an apology, perhaps even cry. But in addition to dropping out of soccer and taking up smoking, Chloe had also been preparing for a fight.

"Sorry I'm late," Chloe said. "I'll get my things."

"Whoa," Elizabeth said. "Hold on."

Will came into the room, towering over both of them, scarecrow thin no matter how much he ate, that plume of black hair still in need of a cut. New patients always backed up when they met him. Their hands shook until he spoke, until he held their hands with both his own and they realized he was indeed warm-blooded. That he could, if the mood struck him, be kind.

"Here we go," Chloe said, rolling her eyes.

In a flash, Elizabeth had her daughter's arm between her fingers. "Don't you dare roll your eyes at me."

"I'm not rolling anything," Chloe said, twisting away.

"You will not just sashay in here and act like everything is all right."

Chloe's nostrils flared, but she remained silent.

"Where were you?" Will asked. "Do you have any idea how worried I was?"

"My guess would be not at all," Chloe said, glaring from

behind a curtain of bangs. "My guess is you forgot about me completely until your receptionist reminded you to pick me up."

They were all silent. Elizabeth glanced at Will's face, could not tell from the stony expression if he admitted to these truths or not.

"We were both worried," she said. "I called Jill."

Chloe glanced toward the phone, the back door, her room. Elizabeth could practically see her mind working, calculating each lie's chances of being believed. "Jill's got this, like, vendetta against me. She's totally jealous of Skitch."

"Who's Skitch?" Elizabeth asked. "What kind of name is that?"

"He's this guy in drama. He wants me to try out for the school play."

"Why haven't you told me any of this before?" Elizabeth asked.

Chloe flinched. "Why haven't you asked?"

Elizabeth took Chloe's chin in her hand. "Are you sleeping with him?"

"Mom!"

"I'm asking you a question, and believe me, this is not a good time to start lying. We can get you into Dr. Sykes for an exam and birth control. I won't say a thing."

"I don't believe this." Chloe jerked away. She began to tremble, then to cry. Will turned to Elizabeth, seemed to be waiting for her to remove this distraction so he could get back to Eve. Restore Chloe to a girl he could remotely stand so he could pay better attention to his girlfriend's charms.

Elizabeth rubbed her temple, wondered if either of them had any idea how much it took for her to not scream and cry like a fourteen-year-old herself. She imagined walking out of this room without another word. Just grabbing her keys and going, pretending *she* was the teenager and no one could stop her.

"Chloe," Will said at last. "This isn't like you. This sneaking around. These lies."

"What you mean is it's not like you," Chloe countered. "I'd die before I'd let love mean as little to me as it does to you two. Before I'd suffer a marriage like yours."

She ran into her room and slammed the door. Will stood staring after her, arms hanging awkwardly at his sides. A pitiful sight, a surgeon with nowhere to put his hands.

"She's growing into such a lovely young woman," Elizabeth said.

A little of the horror drained from Will's face; he managed a chuckle. It wasn't much, but Elizabeth decided to stay as long as he was smiling. To give herself that much.

"I should have told you about Skitch," he said.

"Really, what kind of name is that?"

He reached out, appearing to aim for her cheek then deciding, at the last second, to settle for her shoulder. He touched it once, barely skimmed the surface of her sweater, then let go. Still, that was enough to get her thinking all kinds of farfetched thoughts. To imagine the last few months had been one huge mistake, and that it was possible, after someone broke your heart, to let them stitch it back together.

"You're not going out," he said, more a statement than a question.

She bristled at his assumption, felt another spell slipping in beneath the window sill, reminding her of what lay right outside her door. "Oh yes I am."

He looked at her, then sat down on the couch. "Ah. The dinosaur guy."

"Eve can wait while you sort this out."

He shook his head. "Eve's gone."

Elizabeth felt a moment's thrill, followed by the disappointing realization that this changed nothing. Will had stopped loving her long before Eve.

She went to the couch, sat beside him. "Wow," she said. "You ruined that in record time."

"I wasn't very good to her."

"Well, that's a given."

He laughed again. "How come you weren't funny before?"

It was the perfect moment to lean against him, to claim what was still hers, but she was no longer sure how to touch him. Where to put her hands. What would be accepted and what rebuked. She couldn't speak either; she couldn't answer his question with Chloe in the next room and Jack Bolton expecting her at a cozy, nonprofessional restaurant. In fact, it might be one of those questions better left unanswered forever, so they could each have their own story, their own side.

"I'm not going to handle this for you," she said. "I've got plans. You can take care of Chloe."

He stared at her as if he'd been expecting another answer, as if she was becoming just as unfathomable to him as he was to her. And though she expected this to give her at least a little satisfaction, she felt irritated instead. As if he wasn't trying, had never tried, to understand her.

"As far as I'm concerned, there's nothing to take care of," he said. "She's growing up. She's got to start taking responsibility for her actions. If there are consequences, so much the better."

"What you mean is, you can't be bothered to talk to her."

"I mean you hold her too tight."

Elizabeth stood and grabbed her purse. She still felt the warmth where Will had touched her, or perhaps just a coldness everywhere else. What she'd missed most when she'd moved into the guest room was not conversation or sex, but something she hadn't even realized was a luxury: A body to touch. A warm back to curl up to, even when he was feigning sleep. Another person in the room, breathing.

But in the month he'd been gone she'd started to believe it was better to be abandoned than ignored.

She opened the front door, saw a thick mist rolling in, a setup for traffic accidents, for disaster. But what scared her more was staying here. Waking up in the morning and discovering even less had changed than she thought.

"Just so you know," she said, "Chloe would listen to you. She'd turn herself inside out just to hear what you have to say."

"Beth—"

She slammed the door behind her, was nearly to her car when she noticed he'd come out and was standing by Jack's flamingo. He touched one jagged edge, a sliver of chartreuse.

"What on earth is—"

She slammed the car door on the rest of it, turned on the radio, found the pop station she'd come to love.

"Just want to tell you don't worry," she sang. "I will be late/Don't stay up and wait for me."

SEVEN

*I*N any other location, Annie Crandall's well-kept bungalow would have garnered admiration or, at least, no complaints, but behind Jack's garden the house nearly winked out. Dwarfed by black granite monoliths, sea-glass walkways, and blue-stained retaining walls, the beige house was little better than a garden ornament, and a faded one at that. Elizabeth pulled up in front of a row of incongruous ten-foot-tall saguaros, pruned oddly, an arm hacked off here, a crown there, a mutilated army. Each was surrounded by bloodshot rings of wilted black daisies and trampled crimson poppies.

Elizabeth stepped from her car, wondering if Annie Crandall had done the damage. Perhaps there were spells at work in her garden, too. Elizabeth had been on her way to dinner with Jack when she'd suddenly taken a turn toward the Mission District. She wasn't doing her job unless she understood what happened to Jack that night, and when she glanced at herself in the rearview mirror one too many times, when she put on another coat of lip-stick, it suddenly became very important that she do her job. She heard songs about broken hearts and tried to think about Will, but the fog was particularly grassy and pungent, as if it had trapped all the garden scents of the day.

She headed up the glass-tile path, unsettled by a swath of or-ange zinnias, many lopped at their heads, then charmed by an undamaged grass checkerboard sown in behind. The miniature squares of blue and gray fescues were now leggy and competi-tive; in one corner the gray grass stood alone in total domination.

Every drape in the invisible house was closed. She knocked on the door, listened for sounds of movement. She saw the curtain flutter behind the large bay window, but no one came to the door.

She'd been trained to let people come to her in their own time, to never force the issue unless a life was at stake, so it was with both misgivings and a bit of exhilaration that she held her finger against the buzzer. She was not leaving until she had some answers, until she could offer Jack something more than educated guesses. She imagined the grating noise of the door-bell slithering under beds and into closets, beneath the skin of a woman who seemed to want only to be left alone.

Within seconds, the door jerked open, only to get snagged by the security chain. A woman glared at her through the slit, stun-ning without makeup, fitter than Elizabeth was even in her best dreams. She wore black sports pants and a pink Lycra sweatshirt, had pulled her red hair up into a ponytail. The kind of woman, Elizabeth thought, who ran marathons just for the fun of it.

"Do you mind?" Annie Crandall said. "We're trying to sleep here."

Elizabeth's watch read 6:38. "I'm sorry. It's very important. I'm Elizabeth Shreve. Jack's psychiatrist."

The woman didn't blink. For a good thirty seconds, Annie held herself so still Elizabeth couldn't make out her breathing, then she closed the door to unhook the safety chain and reopened it just enough to slide out sideways. Behind her, Elizabeth glimpsed a bed standing incongruously in the middle of the living room. A tangled mound of blankets, a tray table crowded with vials and pills, and the iguanas Jack had talked about lounging under heat lamps in their cages.

Annie closed the door behind her. "I got your messages."

"You didn't return them."

"Jack's no longer my problem."

Annie pumped her fist a few times as if she'd lost feeling in her fingers. She walked to the end of the porch, looked over those spiky birds of paradise, the sentry-like cacti, remaining arms raised to stop guests. She had exquisite fingernails. French manicured, glossy, perfectly arched. She looked glamorous in athletic clothes, like a tennis star who rarely wins but gains a passionate male following on the Internet.

"I'd like to ask you a few questions," Elizabeth said. "Can I come in?" She started toward the door, but Annie moved nimbly to block her.

"We can talk here."

Elizabeth glanced at the house, listened for sounds from within. She heard nothing but a lawn mower rumbling down the street, a siren off in the distance. There were too many scents for the tiny garden, causing her to wonder if there was a second, better-protected layer beneath the smashed poppies—low-lying

thyme and lavender and temperate glories of the sun ripening in
secret.

"I was hoping you could fill in some of the blanks in Jack's
memory. What happened the other night, when Jack came back
for his plants?"

Annie leaned against the door. "It was a mistake," she said,
"asking him to come by. I was hoping . . . You know the things
you think, after enough time has past. You start forgetting how
bad it actually was, you give him virtues he never had."

"You wanted him back," Elizabeth said softly.

"I don't know. I do know he wasn't interested. He couldn't
talk about anything but the garden and how I hadn't tended it
well enough. He was irate over the state of the zinnias and, I'm
sorry, but I think I've reached a point in my life where I should
count for more than a plant. So while he was working on the
garden, I brought out his palms. I wanted to show him the natural order of things. I wanted to prove I was done."

"Were you?"

Annie glared at her. "Yes. You have no idea what it's been
like. He was always energetic, always taking on more than
he could chew, but last summer it got out of hand. I'd come
home from work to find my entire yard ripped out. Bushes
and trees moved, a trail of dirt through the living room, a
brand new porch demolished. He'd spend a fortune on stone,
treat it like treasure, then abandon it the next day in the street.
I'm the one who took the calls from the city, who had to deal
with the threats of fines and lawsuits if we didn't clean up the
mess. Can you imagine what the neighbors said? The looks I
got? And that's not the half of it. He bought me three hundred pairs of silk pajamas, all in different shades of blue. Do

you have any idea how much that cost? I don't care how much he's making now, it's not enough to pay for his pink pens and flights of fancy."

Her freckles disappeared when she got angry, blending into a solid flush of pink. She had green eyes speckled with gold, girl-next-door looks and a kind of flustered way with her hands, as if she was being asked to do things she was not capable of. In Elizabeth's experience, it was almost always worse to be the normal one. The one who had to water and weed that madcap garden, get dinner on the table and hold down a stable job. The one who was expected to soothe every fear and compulsion with tenderness and patience, to balance the eccentricities by becoming inordinately, crushingly sane.

"Did you come to believe he was ill?" Elizabeth asked quietly. "Was that the cause of the separation?"

Annie stepped back, her flustered hands suddenly still. "That's for you to decide, isn't it?"

"I'm not here to make judgments, only to help. Did Jack change in the years you were married? Did he get, for instance, more moody and impulsive?"

Annie's face shut down. "Look, I hope you help Jack. I really do. But that's up to him. My marriage may be over, but that doesn't mean its secrets are open to strangers."

"I respect that. But something led Jack to the park with blood on his hands and I'm afraid if I don't find out what, it will happen again."

Annie stared at her, showed only the faintest evidence of a twitch. "Last summer he was happy," she said. "No, not happy. Euphoric. Full of energy and ideas and this incredible enthusiasm for everything but me. I'm not saying I didn't want him to have a good time, but I'd like to have been part of it. I would have liked to be taken along."

"Of course."

"Then he came to this screeching halt," Annie went on. "Winter came on and he stopped working. He couldn't get out of bed. Nothing I said or did made any difference. It didn't matter one whit that I was there."

"Depression is a fierce attack on the mind," Elizabeth said. "Unstoppable, sometimes, no matter what we do."

"He must have come alive again," Annie said, warming to the subject now, beginning to pace across the porch. "Apparently all he needed was to get rid of me. I used to think he was complicated, deep. It used to be almost charming, his fits of pique, his excesses, the extravagant presents he'd lavish on me, the dreams he had. I used to think he would actually accomplish some of them, that he'd do something so grand it would make him *happy*. But you know what? He doesn't want to be happy, not in winter or summer. Happiness is a normal, everyday kind of feeling. It's getting up and enjoying your eggs, cherishing a blue sky and not wishing for rain. That's not Jack. He's incapable of satisfaction. His whole reason for being is to change things, make them more beautiful. He'll even tinker with the people he supposedly loves."

Elizabeth tried to restrain the flinch, but it was there. "Could you tell me what happened next? After you brought his palms outside?"

Annie stopped her pacing at the door, clutched the knob. "He left."

Elizabeth stared at the glow of the woman's knuckles. "You were seeing someone. Was he here that night?"

"I was entitled to some tenderness. I'm not going to defend that."

"Jack was found with blood on him. Do you have any idea how it got there?"

In the pause that followed, they both heard the slamming of the back door. A man's grumbling, a car starting up in the alley. Annie went pale, flung open the door.

"Annie, please," Elizabeth said, stepping forward, putting her foot in the door before it closed. "It's important. I think—"

"It might have been all right if he'd gone crazy for *me*," Annie said. The statement took Elizabeth by such surprise, she stepped back. Annie shut the door quickly and bolted it, then Elizabeth heard her racing toward the back.

She stood there for a moment, stunned and suddenly uncertain. How could this garden be Jack's? All the buds on the asters had been sliced off and left to rot.

He had trouble sitting still. Last night, a dozen new designs occurred to him at once and Jack forewent sleep to fill two sketchbooks with lakes and caves for his dinosaurs, a third with visions for a mythical garden he'd been commissioned to landscape in Napa. At breakfast, he arranged the designs on the table, hopped from chair to chair to pick his favorites—a sago palm stegosaurus and the grotto of Calypso, so beautiful a man could get lost in it for seven years. His sister, Mary, eyed him from the counter while he ate five cups of yogurt, then three bowls of Cheerios. He ate while marching around the table, and Mary counted each revolution, her mouth moving silently, while she made him a ham sandwich he could take to the museum.

"You'll be all right today?" she asked nervously.

She was dressed in her usual ankle-length wool skirt and flannel shirt, her long gray hair already coming loose from its knot, her mood ring turning a dark gray when she touched him. She smelled of cinnamon incense and the marijuana she smoked to relax.

"I'll be great," he said. "I'm telling you, Mary, it's like something's clicked on. Designs are coming to me whole, down to the last pebble and ground cover. Sometimes they're coming two or three at a time."

"You're going to have to sleep sometime."

"Maybe not," he said, laughing. "Maybe not."

Jack finished another five cups of yogurt, which luckily he'd bought by the crate. In the last three days, he'd been eating nonstop, could not fill himself; everything he did was relentless, including his twelve-hour shifts at the museum. This morning, he arrived at the Londonbright by seven, posted his fifty new designs on the T-Rex's tail. He heard the groans from the crew, reminded them they were paid by the hour. It was obvious most everything in the garden would have to be changed.

He demolished, transplanted, repositioned paths until night. He paused only long enough to order new plants, a dozen peppermint eucalyptus trees and thirty cassabananas, huge trailing vines that bore slender, two-foot long orange fruits that were not only sweet, but a cure for tonsillitis. In the belly of the diplodocus, he removed the wooly thyme in favor of velvety lamb's ears. He yanked out the daisies Daniel Puckerbaum had, without Jack's consent, planted throughout the garden and replaced them with exotic red mangels, giant beets that grew two-feet long and weighed up to fifteen pounds. He ate Mary's sandwich and, still famished, had one of the workers pick him up four hamburgers and six crunchy tacos. By the time he was well on the way to changing everything, it was time to meet Elizabeth at Ruby's, an Italian restaurant in the city.

He wished he'd brought his sketchbook. While he waited for her at the table, he was beset by another brilliant idea: He'd plant the Garden of the Hesperides, tended by four topiary nymphs, the daughters of Night, and a contorted filbert posing as the sleepless, hundred-headed dragon. He glanced at the inviting white tablecloth, a perfect sketchpad, and tried to divert his attention by rearranging the silverware, getting up and pacing in front of the phone booth until an elderly woman hung up nervously. He cased the restaurant from front to back, peering around walls and dividing screens, smiling at startled busboys and talking to patrons who mistook him for a restless owner. He quickly forgot the nymphs' garden when he realized what this restaurant needed was light—French doors, skylights, a solarium-style roof. He'd bring in date and cabbage palms, ivies and citrus trees—oranges, lemons, limes, even the virburnum-like oriental euodia.

The vision was certainly worth the price of one tablecloth. He hurried back to the table, took out a pink pen. He smoothed out the linen, began by drawing brick floors in place of the hardwood, ferns and palms and misters to keep everything moist. A pond in the corner, a babbling brook between tables, a waterfall over the steps to the back room. He appropriated a good portion of that awful parking lot, remodeled it into an outdoor dining area with a series of three pergolas, each draped with crimson jewel bougainvillea.

Something tugged on his enthusiasm, prodded his lovely

imaginings like a bully with a stick. Something pungent and
nasty replaced the aroma of garlic; the room, which a moment
ago was bordering on steamy, now felt cold.

Jack looked around the room until he spotted a man limping
in the door, his nose and chin the yellow of an old bruise. Their
gazes met briefly, and Jack felt a surge of rage. He leapt out of
his chair, was steps from catching the man when Elizabeth
rushed in. She looked so enchanting in a teenager's jeans and a
cream cashmere sweater that he opened his fists, forgot where
he'd been headed. When she smiled and squeezed his hand
like a woman and not a doctor, he realized he'd been snagged
by the lure of someone who actually wanted to be with him.
Even when she was trying to cure him, he could see in her eyes
that she liked him like this.

"I'm sorry I'm late," she said. "There was a problem with
Chloe."

The man disappeared into the restroom; Jack laughed as the
sense of familiarity faded as quickly as it came. He led her to
the table, where she put her silverware back in order, hid behind the menu when he stared. She reminded him of a blue-
bell, which drops its head just after blooming as if it can't
stomach compliments, or believe how pretty it really is.

A sudden burst of Figaro came on. Jack squeezed his water
glass, felt the vibrations in his bones. He liked the Mexican
music his crews played, the lively tempo and easygoing acoustic
guitars. These bass notes slammed into his heart; lately, he'd
seemed a victim of anything with depth. Pained by poignant
music and poetry, overwhelmed by tentative beauty like hers.

"She's skipping class," she said, ordering sparkling water
when the waiter came, tapping her fingers on the table. "My

Chloe. My good girl." She looked up, blushed. "I'm sorry. Let me start the clock." She shook her head, erased emotion from her face. "We won't talk about anything but you. Starting now."

He laughed. "No way. Trust me, I'm dull as dishwater."

Figaro picked up a snappier tune, relieving him a bit. He rotated a shoulder, stretched his neck. His hand skidded across the table and he willed it to his lap. The man had not come out of the bathroom, but the pall over the room was gone.

"We're still doctor and patient," she said.

He narrowed his eyes. "All right, Doctor. I'm not taking the lithium. Let's get that on the table up front."

The waiter came with the water. Elizabeth ordered the antipasto, a cup of tomato soup. Jack went for the fettucine alfredo with extra cheese, soup, salad, a double order of garlic bread and a glass of Chianti.

"Jack." She did that all the time. Said his name then stopped, as if he stumped her.

"I can have a glass of wine," he said. "That's allowed, isn't it?"

"You can have a glass of wine. Let's talk about your medication."

"There's nothing to talk about. I don't need it. I'm feeling great, Elizabeth. Better than great. If I'm sick, I hope I'm contagious. Everyone should feel this way at least once."

"Mania can be extremely alluring. Sensual, expansive, intense, even brilliant. But at some point euphoria *will* turn to confusion. The ideas and emotions will come too fast."

"I'm disappointed in you. Why can't everything turn out well? Why can't I just enjoy myself? Let's call it a burst of creativity and leave it at that."

"I wouldn't be doing my job if I did that."

"I hate your job," he said. "Honestly, I don't know how you stand it. No one needs a shrink to tell them nothing lasts; that's all the more reason for me to seize the moment. I've gotten an incredible commission in Napa. A friend of Mr. Jones's, a real art connoisseur. I've even got ideas for this place. Look at this." He twisted the tablecloth, nearly sending glasses and silverware spilling to the floor. She struggled to keep everything settled, then peered over his shoulder.

"These ideas might not be cost effective," she said softly.

"That's the trouble with the sane. Always looking at the bottom line, what's feasible. If the world were populated by crazies, it'd be a magical place, guaranteed."

She smiled, then turned away to hide it. He'd sent that garden flamingo as a joke, but he'd spent twenty-five hours setting the glass tiles just right. He'd agonized over the colors, what to say on the note, over whether or not she'd put it up in her garden, and now he longed to ask her if she had.

"I don't doubt it," she said. "But then there'd be no one left to tend it, once you moved on to the next great design. Once the depressions came on."

"Tell me about Chloe."

"No."

He sat back, stung.

"This is your time," she said.

"Screw that. I've got too much time, that's my trouble. I'm sleeping so little and going so fast, I've got a year every day. Tell me about Chloe."

Elizabeth's face was professional and closed, but her body slumped. She looked longingly at his wine when it came.

"I don't know what I was expecting," she said. "Will never

helped much when he was home, and he isn't about to change now. I used to send Chloe to time-out for talking back and he'd rescue her, take her bike riding. He can't be bothered to do the work that'll help her grow up, so he just plays the good guy. He says she's spreading her wings. This is what fourteen-year-olds do."

Jack shook his head. He'd heard enough of Chloe's thoughts to know she didn't want to spread her wings at all, but close them around something she could keep. "She wants you and your husband back together."

Elizabeth's jaw twitched, but her face remained calm. "Most children want that. It can't always happen."

But he heard the uncertainty in her voice, either the beginning or the tail end of hope.

He devoured the fettucine, was still hungry after four slices of bread. He ordered cheesecake, two caramel lattes, and talked about his latest fascination with topiaries. The music changed quickly, jarringly, from classical to Smashmouth, as if a new, unruly shift had come on. The maitre d' marched toward the kitchen. One couple, oblivious, went on breaking up in the corner, the man rolling his eyes while he handed the woman a tissue.

Jack's feet danced beneath the table. The restaurant had twenty-foot ceilings, enough room for a dance floor perched over his stream, swaying from four sturdy ropes. Mentally, he flushed out his design, adding tiki torches, bamboo walls, reggae music to remind the couple in the corner they had rhythm, to induce a shy toddler onto the toes of her delighted father.

When he stood, Elizabeth eyed him warily. He wondered if she'd ever danced in public, or dared to sing out loud. She medicated away melodrama, talked people off cliffs, but such common sense might have disenchanted her marriage. It had certainly made her too slow to catch him. He jumped backwards, twisted his hips, and began to dance.

A man dining alone laughed uncomfortably. The young woman in the corner, egged on by a few Chiantis, cheered. Jack felt the music in his bloodstream, threw up a hand to follow its course. He began to sing along.

"Hey now, you're a rock star, get your game on, go play. Hey now—"

Elizabeth yanked him down with more force than he'd known she had. Her face was flushed and furious, even when the girl applauded. The music turned off abruptly, the maitre d' returned white-faced and apologetic. Elizabeth had already opened her purse, was trying to write a check with trembling hands. There were tears in her eyes.

"Elizabeth," he said. "Elizabeth? I can't be that bad."

She scribbled her signature and tore out the check.

"Elizabeth," he said softly, but she ignored him. She left the check on the table and walked out.

ELIZABETH stomped across the parking lot Jack wanted to replace with bistro tables and bougainvillea. She was in no shape to drive, had to focus entirely on keeping herself from crying. When the headlights from a glistening new Audi flooded her, she gave up the effort and lifted her hands to her face. She cried harder than she had when Will left, cried as she hadn't since childhood, when her mother was the one to mortify strangers with a dance, climbing atop tables and kicking over wineglasses with her bare feet.

Jack approached her warily, taking such care now she cried harder. She was not much of a psychiatrist if she couldn't even predict what he would do next.

"I'll bet your body dances while you dream," he said softly.

She turned away rather than admit he was wrong. Her dreams were as beige and scared as she was. She didn't even bother to remember them.

"What does it matter if a couple of strangers think I'm crazy?" he said. "Is it really the worst thing to make a little scene?"

Yes, Elizabeth thought. Yes. But she shook her head. "This is why you need to be on lithium. You've lost your sense of boundaries. What's acceptable and what's not."

"I don't think so," he said.

"You can't just walk around doing whatever you want. It not only dishonors you, it embarrasses those around you. It's not fair to put anyone in a position where they can't stand to look at you. Where they're ashamed of the human race."

She saw the pain on his face, but wouldn't take back the words. Will was right. In her office, Jack could sing all he wanted and it would affect only the dosage of lithium she prescribed. It would not affect *her;* it wouldn't make her remember.

"I talked to Annie," she said.

He cocked his head, as if he hadn't heard her correctly. "Annie?"

"I went there tonight. She didn't give me much information. I think there's an awful lot you two aren't telling me."

He looked down at his hands as if the blood was still there. "Was she all right?"

He turned her inside out, inserted jealousy where clinical

analysis ought to be, raised feelings she shouldn't have for at least another six months, after the divorce was final and her wounds scabbed over.

She started toward her car. "She's fine," she said over her shoulder. "She said she was never out to hurt you." She opened her briefcase, fumbled inside for her keys.

"I never want to hurt *you*." He stood right behind her, his mouth skimming her ear. "But that would mean never coming near you, skipping out the way your husband did before either of you had a chance to say something really breathtaking or mindless or cruel. I never want to hurt you, but I'm going to. I guarantee it."

Elizabeth heard her keys somewhere in her briefcase but she may as well have left them in the restaurant. She didn't want to go anywhere; she saw that now. She couldn't bear to go home to her usual fantasy, the one that both soothed and horrified her, when she imagined Will returned, their marriage restored without apparent damage or regret.

Jack reached around her and plucked the keys from their usual pouch, pressed his lips to her cheek. Just left them there, so that she filled up with the scent of grass and hibiscus and tentative desire.

He took her in his arms, held her, sang the same song he'd been singing inside, only softer, slower, like a ballad, a love song. "Hey now, you're an all-star, get the show on, get paid."

She wondered if, once she started crying, she'd never stop, but surprisingly the fit lasted only a minute. Then there was no excuse to stay there except that she hadn't been held in months.

He leaned back enough to see her eyes. "Come to Napa with me. I was planning to head up there tonight to look over Clyde

Cummings's estate. I've got to be back at the museum by Monday."

"To Napa?"

"You'll love Clyde. Sane as they come. It's Friday night. We could stay all weekend."

"Go to Napa with you for the weekend?"

She felt slow and obviously addled, because she didn't immediately scoff at the idea. She let a moment pass before she thought about professionalism, another two before she considered medical ethics, what Will would think, how she could possibly explain herself to her friends and Chloe. A good thirty seconds had gone by before she realized she was enjoying it, this brush with unexplainable behavior.

Yet she knew if she really wanted to cure Jack, she'd keep him close to home. She'd control the environment to isolate the heart of the disease. If she really wanted him cured, she'd stay.

She watched the tentacles of fog slide in from the bay, obscuring the restaurant which really was in need of more glass to let in the million-dollar views, more flowers to soothe wearied spirits while good food and wine did the rest. Just over the coastal range, she imagined, the sky was bone dry, as burgundy as the grapes in the vineyards.

"Say yes," he said, and she looked away, had to at least pretend to be the prudent one. She paused if only to fool herself into believing she hadn't lost all sense. Certainly, she was not moved by a silly pop song, by a young man telling her to get the show on, go play.

She paused, but not long enough to keep from shocking a mind reader. Not long enough to hide the fact that she'd merely been waiting for him to ask.

EIGHT

AFTER the temperamental, collared splendor of Marin, Sonoma County seemed a bit of an alley cat, rumpled and rangy and easy to please. In Sausalito, the scent of the sea always triumphed, but as they neared Napa, the fog vanished and Elizabeth smelled gardens. Vineyards. Bursting grapes and fields of lavender and cut grass, air so heavy and sweet the oak leaves stayed plump and purple all year. Hummingbirds, she imagined, ignored the feeders strung from trees and sucked the nectar right out of the air.

"Watching a Himalayan palm grow a foot a week is one of the joys of living," Jack said. He'd been talking about plants for an hour, driving his pickup with one hand while painting pictures in the air with the other. At some point, she began to see his sketches; he described a date palm and the pinnate leaves tickled her shoulder, the cab filled with the scent of figs.

"There's so much life in it, you can feel it rising through your fingers when you weed around its roots," he said. "And this is no tropical crybaby. It's hardy down to zero degrees."

Elizabeth took the cell phone out of her purse. She'd put off the call as long as possible, would happily hear about the growth habits of twenty more exotic palms than explain herself to Will.

"Tell him we've eloped," Jack said.

She laughed, pressed number nine on her speed dial, a satisfying demotion from the top spot Will's number had once held. She prayed for the answering machine, but Will picked up on the second ring.

"Will Verplank," he said, and though she inhaled the sugary air, she smelled Will. Stout aftershave, an evening cocktail, disinfectant still clinging to his hands.

"It's me," she said. "I wanted to let you know I won't be home this weekend. You can reach me on my cell."

She heard the television in the background, a horror movie from the sound of the screaming. She hoped Chloe would not have bad dreams, wanted to tell Will to leave his door open but knew any advice on her part would spark an argument—this time about the things she ought to trust him to do on his own.

"Where will you be?" he asked finally.

"Napa. I'm not sure where exactly."

"It's nearly eleven," he said. "You mean to tell me you don't know where you'll be sleeping?"

She closed her eyes, rested her head against the seat. Jack reached for her hand, and she felt the ridges of his calluses, the gentle but unyielding strength of his fingers, like a sturdy, wild palm himself. She expected to feel a guilty pang of treason, but was curiously, enjoyably, carefree.

"I'm with Jack Bolton," she said.

She heard more screaming on the television, and Will breathing, and Jack swallowing down the words he might have said if she was off the phone. Words she suddenly wanted to hear.

"All right then," Will said at last.

She didn't know if she preferred Will's righteousness or indifference, wished there was a third choice. "How's Chloe?" she asked.

"Watching a movie."

"Have you talked to her?"

"I was told I'm on my own here," he said. "I took that to mean I can handle things my way."

She squeezed Jack's hand, breathed deeply. "You don't have a way, Will."

She heard a terrible choking sound from the television in the background, then a more alarming silence, moody music starting up. Jack had pulled to the side of the road. He cut the engine, put his arm around her, and from that moment on she gave up trying to fight herself. She admitted it wasn't Will's next move she was waiting for.

"I'll call back when I know where I'm staying," she said, then hung up.

She marveled at the stillness of Jack's body. All evidence of manic energy was gone, or perhaps she'd absorbed it into herself. Her heart raced, her left foot tapped the floor, wherever they touched she felt prickly and warm.

"I can't believe I'm doing this," she said.

Jack laughed. "Let me introduce you to your wild side."

He smiled recklessly, the kind of smile she tamed in therapy but which now gave her a thrill. She had no idea where they were going, and the fact that it hardly seemed to matter made her feel Chloe's age, the most beautiful and adventurous thing on the planet. A far cry from how she'd actually felt as a child, when her father had posted an elaborate, minute-by-minute day planner on the refrigerator.

8:48: Drop Kylie at sitter's, Elizabeth at school. Take Lila to doctor's. Ask him, again, to lock the door.

9:00 - 9:59: Meetings, call insurance. Call doctor, make sure Lila is still there.

10:00: Use break to pick up Lila. Slip the tranquilizer in with her vitamins. Take phone off the hook.

12:56: Pick up Kylie. Wake up Lila. Make lunch. Coax Lila into giving the baby her bottle. Remind her to change her. Lock the door on the way out.

3:15: Remind Lila to pick up Elizabeth from school. Convince her to stay in the car.

On and on, until he could check off another day completed without disaster, until he finally fell asleep, exhausted, in the room across from his wife.

Jack released her, started the car again. "Did I tell you Clyde's an aerobics instructor on TV?" he asked, easing back into traffic. "Works out of a studio he had built overlooking his vineyard. He looks phenomenal, but he's a junk food junkie. Eats Almond Joys for breakfast."

"I was never much of an exerciser."

"Annie jogs. Up and down the hills in the city. She's a demon."

He stopped talking abruptly and gripped the steering wheel. They dove into a valley, the road paralleling a stream that had only a trickle of water this late in the season.

"When I told Annie I wanted to move to Bolinas," he went on, "she said she couldn't run in the country. She liked the feel of pavement slamming into the soles of her feet."

"How did you meet?"

"She wanted a garden."

"She was charmed by your work."

He laughed. "Maybe. Or else she'd never come across someone who could so easily ignore her demands. She wanted herbs and I gave her flowers. She was the youngest executive at her ad agency at the time."

Elizabeth imagined Jack luring Annie Crandall into the sunshine despite her fair skin and better judgment. A confident, independent woman helpless to stop a man from taking over her yard.

"I had no business to speak of when we met," Jack said. "It was something for her to look past that, to see . . . God knows what she saw."

"A man who breathed color," Elizabeth said quietly.

Jack took both hands off the wheel for a moment, then remembered to put one back on. They drove in silence, while Elizabeth tapped her foot on the floor and delighted in this impetuous creature who had apparently taken over her body, the one who made rash decisions, who said the first thing that popped into her head.

"I could never read her mind," he said. "I thought she'd be happy with a rainbow garden, and she spent the next year mowing down the tiger lilies. I thought she'd be thrilled when my career took off, but that's when she started looking at me funny. She complained about my hours, my intensity, my commitment to perfection. I was moody, I admit it, but that's the price you pay to get things right. I thought she'd give me more slack than she did."

"She wanted you to be happy," Elizabeth said. "It wasn't such an outlandish request."

"But it was!" he said, swerving into oncoming traffic, then correcting after the driver of a semi blared his horn. "You can't ask that of anyone. You can demand they treat you right or you can leave them, but you can't tell them what to feel. My happiness, or lack of it, was my own."

Elizabeth realized the air was not tinted purple, as she had imagined, but was merely the indigo of any night sky, the same color it was in the city when the lights went out. "Then why get married? Why was she there?"

He sped up, going sixty in a forty-five mile an hour zone, and Elizabeth forced herself to keep quiet. "Companionship, loyalty, faith," he said. "To accomplish something together, to do more. We had joyful moments, but that's not the same thing as happiness. Joy's a short-lived reaction to circumstance, while happiness is chronic. Frankly, I've never trusted it. Happiness is for old people. It's the reward after you're done."

She stared at him, feeling more sympathy for Annie Crandall than she had at the woman's invisible house. She turned toward the window, stared at million-dollar cottages and a small, stone winery illuminated with gas torches. They rolled into a black valley then wound their way up the other side, getting lost in the folds of a lush, velvet blanket.

They crossed into Napa County and reached downtown with its stunning array of pre-1906 architecture, an ornate mix of

Italianate, Victorian gothic, and Spanish colonial facades. Jack took a quick right, drove down a lamplit street of bistros and bed-and-breakfasts, and finally pulled into the dim parking lot of one of the plainest buildings in town, a faceless stucco hotel.

"I know it's not much to look at from here, but wait until you see their garden." He jumped out of the car, seemed to have forgotten their conversation while it reverberated in her. He was wrong. Joy was the untrustworthy one, the gorgeous but doomed high school dropout, while happiness was the boy you'd sat next to all your life. The one who knew all the answers and would quietly make millions. The one you were crazy not to love.

Jack had reached the door of the hotel and now came back. He opened her door, knelt down beside her. He put his hand on her knee.

"I'll get two rooms," he said. "Don't worry."

She raised her gaze, had started worrying an hour ago, when the valley had become so picturesque it no longer seemed real. When the real things in her life had begun to seem ugly.

CLYDE Cummings's twelve-million-dollar estate was breathtaking—a hundred-acre vineyard surrounding a Tudor-style, six-thousand-square-foot home. A private stocked lake, swimming pool and tennis court, an acre devoted to lawn, three more for gardens, all immaculately tended. First thing in the morning, Jack and Elizabeth drove through elaborately carved wrought-iron gates, inscribed with two C's in French script. The driveway curved in and out of sycamore trees, ending half a mile later by the mansion's portico and classical fountain— nine marble muses pouring water from their endless jugs.

A very fit, very handsome Clyde Cummings met them on the massive terrazzo steps, a giant Milky Way bar in hand. He had brilliant magenta hair, two stud earrings, and the kind of chiseled features rarely glimpsed beyond the pages of men's magazines. He pumped their hands vigorously.

"Thrilled that you've come," he said. "Thrilled. When Philip told me you were doing the Londonbright, I couldn't believe my luck. I've seen your work in *Architectural Digest*. Have I got a project for you. The more astounding the better."

He led them through a house full of antiques and stiff, priceless furniture, out the French doors to a lovely, formal garden. Enclosed by a semicircle of Italian cypresses, the gently sloping garden was divvied up into half-moon-shaped beds filled with clipped boxwoods, herbs, and heath. Brick pathways crisscrossed the plantings and led down to the lake and lawns and orchards, up to an elegant stone patio.

"It's beautiful," Elizabeth said.

Clyde raised an eyebrow. "Rip it out. All the plants. Every last brick. I'd just gotten back from England when I had it done. I don't know what I was thinking. You, Jack, are going to change everything. You're my wow factor."

He crammed the last of the chocolate in his mouth. His partner sat at a table on the patio, sipping a martini. A young man, barely eighteen and still towheaded, more gorgeous than even Clyde. Elizabeth tried not to look.

Last night, Elizabeth had heard Jack through the thin walls of the hotel, pacing, working feverishly. Now he opened his portfolio, handed over dozens of pages. "Modern but not necessarily abstract," he said, "the plantings mixed with art, a variety of materials. Metal, glass, concrete, stone. I want to focus on wild creatures. Gargoyles, dragons."

"Yes," Clyde said, wiping chocolate from the corner of his mouth. "Sirens and centaurs. Three-headed beasts." He studied each of Jack's designs, began to jog in place. "Beautiful but strange. A lot like me, hey Leonardo?"

The boy on the patio laughed.

"I'll need to take measurements," Jack said, "and I'll give you a set of rough plans if you need them, but the truth is I work better if I design as I go."

"I'm fine with that, as long as you make it look like I'm getting a say in the matter. That way I can brag that it was all my idea."

Jack smiled. "Agreed. There's a nursery in the valley that specializes in exotic plants. Corkscrew trees, unusual flowers, Alice in Wonderland–type foliage."

"Oh yes," Clyde said. "Alice in Wonderland. Everything turned on its ear. This place needs that. Believe me."

He looked up at his lover with such tenderness, Elizabeth felt as if she'd come between a kiss. The wind this morning was light and warm, scented of late-season raspberries, the last of the mint, and she realized she'd slept eight hours without waking for the first time in months. She'd listened to the trickling water from the hotel's fountain and dreamt of days with nothing to do, a stillness and serenity she hadn't even known she craved.

"Think of the Minotaur," Jack said. "The labyrinth. Ariadne's thread. We'll create a maze only Theseus himself could navigate. A tribute to love's way out."

He sat on the brick steps, turned over one of the sketches to use the blank back. Once his pencil hit paper, it didn't stop. As a child, Elizabeth had loved the story of Theseus and Ariadne, until she learned the end. Triumphant after slaying the Minotaur, Theseus deserted the woman who saved him, left her on an island without a word of farewell. She'd stopped reading myths after that, found them too hard on lovers.

Jack finished the sketch and Clyde quickly handed him another paper. Jack created one elaborate design after the other—living, green temples, a lagoon so breathtaking, Elizabeth imagined nymphs rising from the depths and dragging poor, beautiful Clyde and his lover into the water, never to be seen again.

Clyde touched Elizabeth's shoulder. "I feel lucky that he'll work for me. He's selective now who he takes on. He can't bear to be thwarted by someone else's banality and lack of vision. Isn't that marvelous? He can't *bear* it. Art matters that much."

Elizabeth looked over the estate that was already spellbinding and serene, and thought that while art might produce grandeur, in the process it often ruined things that mattered more.

Jack continued to sketch, while Clyde took the finished drawings up to his lover. The young man pushed aside his drink, took Clyde's hand while he looked over the designs. Their deep, blended voices rivaled the birdsong for sheer loveliness.

Elizabeth sat on the steps beside Jack. Each sketch was more fantastical than the one before. Gargantuan palms encircled by granite sculptures, fountains streaming out of mushroom heads, a statue of Nanna the flower princess falling under the enchantment of her own blossoms. Astounding but ridiculous.

Jack stopped drawing. "Clairvoyance is often little more than imagining the worst someone can think about you," he said.

"Jack—"

"I need to go to the nursery." He dropped the papers, headed back to the truck. She picked up the drawing of Nanna and was ensnared by her own eyes staring back at her, mesmerized by the petals bursting from every pore of her skin. She tried to rein in desire, then gladly gave it up as impossible. She gripped the drawing so tightly, Jack would later find smudge marks through the hair he'd freed from its bun, creases along the tendrils he'd drawn in like wisteria vines.

He was making her bloom.

She ran after him, put her hand on his arm. "Wait," she said. "I'm coming with you."

THE first time Skitch slipped his hand beneath the band of her pants, Chloe bolted. She fumbled for her shirt, put it on backwards, was out of his bedroom and down the stairs in a flash. If he hadn't caught her by the door, she'd have run home to confirm she still had speed, she'd have completed a mini-marathon just to prove she remained in control of her body. Even if she took off her blouse, she wasn't becoming one of those wan-looking girls who haunted the stage wings and cruised the hall outside the boys' locker room. Kissing Skitch where he asked didn't mean she'd stop eating. There was no solid proof that she used to be a whole person but now was only half.

Skitch snatched her hand from the front door. His shirt was off, his jeans unzipped, revealing surprisingly innocent-looking red-and-white-checked boxers. His parents were out to dinner, as they were every Friday night.

"Hey," he said. "Relax. We're not going to do anything you don't want to."

Which was not exactly true, considering what she'd swallowed, how many times she'd had to brush her teeth afterwards, how long and hard she shook. Still, she was less unnerved by what she was willing to do than the thoughts that accompanied the acts. When Skitch unclasped her bra, she imagined herself on the road to a fancy wedding, when she gave in to his pleas and crouched down, she was already twenty years down the road, designing their house with the bay windows and large lawn out back. When he was tender, rubbing his hand in perfect circles on the small of her back, she wasn't even there. She was shuffling down the street with him, gray-haired, stooped and satisfied, eliciting smiles from young lovers who could only hope to have such luck.

It had reached the point where she was actually glad for this weekend in her father's meat locker of a townhouse, especially now that Eve was gone. It would give her a chance to cool down from wanting so much. Saturday morning, she threw off the blankets, pulled the sheet up over her head. She'd stashed the phone beneath her pillow, and as she dialed Skitch's number, she vowed to never believe another thing her parents said. Contrary to their statements, love was not difficult to sustain at all. If anything it risked excessiveness, arising from the slightest invitation, multiplying on nothing but the sound of his voice.

"You ready?" he asked.

"I think so. I've got all the lines memorized."

"It's gonna take more than that. We're talking emotion, Chloe. Being real up there."

"I know."

"I'll pick you up at two-thirty. Wear something casual. Jeans and a sweatshirt."

She'd rehearsed the part of *Peyton Place*'s Allison MacKenzie so often, the twelve-year-old had become as unwelcome as a bratty sister who'd moved into her room. Chloe knew Allison's lines backwards and forward, but that didn't mean she could breathe life into them. No matter how many times she imagined herself standing on stage, taking Skitch's breath away, her rehearsals sounded wooden. She stared at herself in the mirror and felt queasy; she began, for some reason, to become afraid of the dark.

Chloe heard a footstep and peeked out of the sheet to find her father crossing to the chair by the window. When he sat, it was a testament to how much had changed that she didn't try to explain her conversation. She didn't say a single word.

"Your mother called last night," he said. "She's in Napa."

Chloe shrugged and sat up. She'd gone to bed after *Scream* and slept thirteen hours straight. She could force herself to sleep at any time, which was the one thing that gave her courage. If you wanted something badly enough, perhaps you could simply will it to be.

"With that patient," her father went on. "Jack."

Seeds had come in the mail yesterday. A padded envelope stuffed with thirty packets of oddities. Yard-long asparagus beans, sorghum sugar cane, which can be grown for syrup or chewed like candy, yellow heirloom tomatoes. At first she'd felt mildly offended, as if Jack considered her an oddity herself. Then she read his note.

Dare to grow into something different.
Jack

She arranged the seeds on her bureau as if they were jewels, then started to cry. She wept all the time now, for no reason except that her favorite cereals—Lucky Charms, Fruit Loops, Cap'n Crunch—were now too sweet, and the Thursday-night sitcoms that used to make her laugh seemed, suddenly, contrived and stupid, and the single clove cigarette she'd started with had turned into half a pack a day. She cried because she *was* growing into something different, someone she didn't even like.

"I've never known her to act so rashly," her father said. "It's unbecoming, frankly. I don't understand what's gotten into her."

Chloe snorted, stunned he could be so stupid. "For God's sake," she said, "she's found someone who's glad she's there."

Her father looked startled, but otherwise didn't move. God, she hated anyone over eighteen. She really did. They'd given up grand gestures, dashed their romantic hearts, strapped their souls to work and money instead of to the people who would really give them some peace. She might not be someone she liked, but at least she wasn't pretending to be happy while the person she adored got away. Even if it ended in disaster, at least she had the guts to go after what she really wanted. At least, at most, she believed in true love.

"Well," her father said.

She threw back the sheet, headed toward the bathroom down the hall.

"The day before our wedding, your mother said she wouldn't marry me."

She paused, curious despite herself. Lately, she valued the stories of her parents' dissatisfaction more than the ones of bliss. As if heartache, and what you did with it, was the thing that really proved your worth.

"When I tried to talk sense," he went on, "explain about the two-hundred guests arriving in the morning, she got so mad she smashed the terra-cotta planters I'd lined up on the windowsill. All ten of them, one by one. She threw every last creeping charlie out the window."

Chloe stared at him, incredulous. "Mom would never do that."

He'd gone so still the spider hovering on a web above his head began to crawl down. "She did," he said. "It took all night for me to soothe and reassure her. A whole night to convince her I was the right man to love."

Chloe shrugged. "I guess you were a good liar."

He jerked, sending the spider fleeing back up. She almost hoped for outrage. She would have liked to see him smash the porcelain tea set she'd had since she was a child, throw each saucer out the window then ask her to prove her love. She could have done it in a thousand ways, but he only sighed. "What shall we do today?"

She shook her head. Sometimes she thought if she poked him with a knife, he'd bleed but not show pain. If she called him names, he'd calmly accuse her of not meaning them, and she began to have some sympathy for her mother. She began, she realized with dismay, to root for Jack.

She went into the bathroom and slammed the door. She grabbed her toothbrush, furiously scrubbed her teeth and spit. She visualized herself in the woods, arms held wide.

"Hello!" she said, aiming for the unself-conscious, happy tone Allison MacKenzie used while conversing with trees. "Oh, hello, everything beautiful!"

She sounded like a robot, and she lay down her toothbrush, pressed her forehead to the mirror. Skitch respected only actors, and even then a small subset—those who played the stage, who toiled for the art and never made a living. She'd dreamed their whole life together, but that didn't mean Skitch had been dreaming the same thing.

"Chloe," her dad said from behind the door. "Come on out."

She opened the door, hand on her hip. He stood in the hall, as stern as ever, but also pitiful. Stoic without a reason to be, restrained without an audience. She didn't know how he stood it, being forty-two years old and all alone.

"Daddy," she said. She leaned against him, but only for a moment. She needed to shower, pick her most Allison-like jeans and sweatshirt, go over the lines again. She squeezed his shoulder as if he were the child and she had to disappoint him again. "I've got plans today. I'm trying out for the play."

Skitch picked her up at two-thirty, his learner's permit on the dash. One-way streets made him nervous, so they took the long way around and didn't talk at all, didn't even put on the radio. At the auditorium, he abandoned her for Mrs. Larrabie, the drama teacher who had seen Skitch's one-minute audition and instantly guaranteed him the lead. Chloe slid into the back row and tried not to be sick. Her palms were so slick they left a stain on the knees of her jeans.

Mrs. Larrabie cut off a girl's audition halfway through the monologue. "Don't try so hard, Angela. We'll find you a non-speaking part as one of the townspeople. Next."

Half a dozen girls were trying out for the role of Allison. Chloe bent forward, pressed her cheek to her knees. Skitch talked to Mrs. Larrabie over the auditions, and she imagined that voice in her ear day and night, telling her he'd never seen another actress like her, that the moment she stepped on stage, his heart was no longer his.

Two sophomores were instructed to take Mrs. Larrabie's drama class and return next year, then the teacher called her name. Later, Chloe would not remember which aisle she'd taken to the stage. She'd forget which lines she'd flubbed, how her voice had trembled, how loud the snickering had actually been, but forever after she would not read Grace Metalious. She'd disparage *Peyton Place* to all her friends.

She stood at center stage, pale and speechless, then Skitch fed her the first line. She knew from the moment she started speaking that it didn't matter how much you loved someone, you couldn't change for them. You couldn't suddenly become beautiful or brave or a natural on stage. You could dream only your own dreams, and hope they were met halfway.

She recited the entire monologue, not necessarily in its correct order, and Mrs. Larrabie was kind. The drama teacher told her the roles usually went to juniors and seniors. Told her to take beginning voice and try out for *Jesus Christ Superstar* in the spring. Another girl walked on stage and Chloe stumbled into the wings. She vomited into a trash can, but by then it was mostly water, a stream of yellow bile and little else.

Skitch didn't call that night. Chloe tried to force herself to sleep, but during the audition her body had begun to sweat and leak and vibrate; it slipped unceremoniously, disgustingly, from her control. She lay awake in her father's tomblike townhouse, knowing her dad lay awake and alone in the room next door. Knowing there was no guarantee of anything, of love lasting or life turning out as planned or even of a subsistence level of devotion. Knowing, suddenly, that most people coped with this horrible knowledge by ignoring it, by behaving like gardeners and savoring the anticipation of what might grow, rather than focusing on the few and sometimes unwanted things that actually did.

But Chloe wanted results. It wouldn't surprise her at all to learn that her body could not survive without Skitch, that it would refuse to eat and drink and spend itself in a flurry of desperate acts. She even smiled as she imagined all the damage she might do to herself, the regret Skitch would feel when he realized how far she'd been willing to go for love. For him.

She dressed quickly, tiptoed out the front door. The security guard at the entrance gate was distracted, watching one of the Star Wars movies, so she merely ducked beneath the electronic arm and began to run.

Speed momentarily returned, and she was at Skitch's house within half an hour. She climbed the trellis outside his window, stepped loudly onto the porch roof, not caring if she got caught. She rapped on the glass. It took Skitch a few minutes to wake, two more to come to his senses and spot her perched outside his window like an aimless, domesticated bird. He stared at her a full minute before moving, long enough for her to marvel at how much humiliation she could stand, to realize that, contrary to how it appeared, shame was making her strong.

He came to the window at last, opened it halfway. "What are you doing here?" His face was guarded, his voice like ice. Ironically, in that moment she learned how to act.

"I changed my mind," she said, pushing up the window and crawling through. Skitch backed up, but he was no longer a match for her. She had a hundred fantasies stacked up behind her, an army of doomed soldiers with nothing left to lose.

"Chloe—"

She kissed him before he could say anything else. Kissed him until she sparked his body if not his heart, until she was no longer that pitiful girl on stage but the willing one in his bedroom. She closed her eyes as she took off her blouse and didn't open them again until they'd fallen on the bed, until it was over. Until she felt the trickle of blood between her thighs and realized Skitch had never touched her with his hands. That he'd panted and groaned, but never said a word.

He rolled off. "You can't stay. My mom'll find you."

She searched for her blouse, couldn't find it in the tangle of sheets. She was beginning to shake now, and Skitch rolled his eyes, searched under the bedspread. He finally located the shirt pinned between the mattress and wall, and tossed it at her. He glanced at the blood on the sheets and winced. "Hurry up," he said.

She was surprisingly dry-eyed, trembling but underneath more calm than she'd been in days. It was a relief, in a way, to know she'd reached bottom, that it couldn't get worse than this.

"That was a mistake," Skitch said.

She even laughed at his statement of the obvious, at how oblivious he was to his own cruelty. At what it said of her, to love someone like this.

He stood by the window while she dressed, practically reeking of disgust. He didn't have control of himself either, kissing her one minute, covering himself in thorns the next. He strived for fury, but his gaze kept darting to the bed, to the bloodstains.

She walked to the window, felt her stomach rise when he reached out, then deflate when he merely pulled back the shade. She climbed onto the roof, had barely removed her hands from the sill when he slammed the window shut.

Once she hit solid ground, she felt twenty pounds heavier, so pudgy and marked no one else would want her either. She had left not only blood in Skitch's bedroom but her common sense and instincts for self-preservation. She ignored the light rain, walked home at a snail's pace. The sky was growing light by the time she let herself in the front door of her father's townhouse. He was pacing across the living room floor when he stopped short, stretched out his hand then dropped it.

"Chloe," he said, "I thought—"

He looked her over, didn't need to finish the sentence. They both knew the rest of it.

I thought you were better than this.

NINE

*I*n horticulture, anything is possible. Green roses can be cultivated, oaks taught to weep, dahlias grafted to the same stems as peonies. Nature blooms within boundaries, while human nature is limited only by morals and aesthetics, a hopefully well-established sense of right and wrong.

Until today, Elizabeth hadn't appreciated eccentricity. Everything she needed was on one shelf at Home Depot—a few marigolds, a dozen common boxwoods and two or three dwarf barberry shrubs. At her house, trees and plants were the unassuming frame and the building the picture, but in Napa, this time, the opposite was true. The charming bed-and-breakfast she'd once stayed at with Will had become a mere backdrop for a trio of twisted bay laurel trees, the restaurants they'd frequented afterthoughts to herb gardens. She sat forward, hands on the dash of Jack's truck, when the hilly vineyard she'd whizzed past unsuspectingly a dozen times before revealed its true shape. The grapevines were aligned in the shape of a bird.

It was like putting her hands in the soil and watching her fingers grow roots. The plants, and Jack, tied her body to the earth.

Jack drove toward the nursery, silent. Ten minutes from Clyde's estate, an ominous cauldron of storm clouds churned, the sky swelled with rare humidity. Elizabeth glanced in the rearview mirror, imagined a cyclone forming behind them, but when she turned she saw nothing but the black Audi that had been following them for miles.

"Do you know the man in that car?" she asked.

Jack glanced in the mirror and shrugged, still quiet and sulky. Every minute that passed in silence made her doubt her diagnosis. A commitment to a bad mood was as contrary to mania as sleep.

"Maybe," he said. "We're here."

They pulled into a gravel-lined parking lot, where a woman was attempting to muscle an odd, lime-green hydrangea into the back of her Subaru. They got out of the car as the man in the Audi parked beside a line of red wagons and left the motor running.

Jack hesitated before grabbing a wagon, then maneuvered it between bags of peat moss and compost. "It's just some guy," he said. "Prepare to be amazed."

He expertly guided the wagon into the toolshed that served as a sales office, through narrow aisles displaying fragile terracotta pots. The place looked like any other nursery until they entered the first greenhouse, then Elizabeth took Jack's arm.

The greenhouse was as large as an airport hangar, filled to the corners with plants that thrived in shade. An elaborate series of pipes and sprinklers hung from the rafters, and every two minutes a warm, gentle mist trickled over the giant hostas and begonias and feathery astilbes. The capricious maidenhair fern flashed its ruffly edges, then jumped back prissily when touched. Jack was already halfway across the greenhouse, shaking the leaves of the gregarious fiddleleaf philodendron, which had outgrown its aisle and the next one, amassed an orchestra of violin-shaped leaves.

Jack opened the back door, stood in the breezeway that led to a dozen more greenhouses. Though the air smelled of rain, it was a dust bowl compared to the humidity of the shade garden.

"This one," he said, pointing to the greenhouse on the far left, labeled "Oddities." He pulled the cart across the gravel path, smiled as he opened another door.

Elizabeth entered a garden circus, a big tent of million-to-one-shot plants. The first act was a polka-dot shrub with leaves large enough to sleep on, the second a birch tree growing upside down. In every aisle were sideshows of corkscrew-shaped flowers, thornless roses, grafted lily-irises with alternating petals of purple and orange. Trunks that peeled away their own bark to reveal skin the color of the sky, leaves as silvery and iridescent as fish. So much to look at, nearly too much going on. Jack left the cart near the door and took her hand, scratching her with cuts and calluses, the realest thing there.

The air inside the tent was heavy and damp and complicated, difficult to move through with any speed at all. Elizabeth took a languid step forward, felt like a tightrope walker becoming dizzy from the smells—drowsy humus, sour mint, a blast of sweet jasmine. She inhaled deeply and her bloodstream filled with orange blossoms. She thought of a hundred reasons not to kiss him, knew exactly how foolish it would be to risk her career, the small gains she'd made getting over Will, her precarious emotional balance, because of a momentary sugar high. But her senses were busy, her mouth watering for an exotic taste, her fingers sneaking toward him, an ear poised to hear what his reaction would be. If he could read her mind, he'd know what she wanted anyway. A kiss, and the birth of daring.

His eyes widened as she moved in. He hesitated at the first touch of her lips on his, then he slowly encircled her waist with one cupped hand, like a new tendril winding its way around the vine.

He kissed her lips, her cheek, the creases at the corners of each eye, each movement of his mouth as soft as rain, as soothing as a gentle climate after too many years up north.

"We've got to get the plants," he said. She pulled back, embarrassed, but he took her hand, held his open mouth to the palm. If she hadn't tilted back her head in pleasure, she might never have seen the man from the Audi watching them from behind a row of pink cabbage palms. He was blond-haired, wearing sunglasses and a leather jacket despite the greenhouse heat.

"There he is again," she whispered. "He *is* following us, Jack. Do you know him?"

He followed her gaze, seemed to tense but just as quickly relaxed. The man met their gazes, nodded an acknowledgment, then walked out of the greenhouse, letting the door slam behind him. "No."

"I think I saw him at the hospital," she said. "That day I released you, he was trying to get in. Why would he be following you?"

Jack led her between two wooden tables covered with pony

packs of delicate, unusual herbs. Ginger rosemary, a pungent cross of purple basil and oregano. "Who's to say he's not following you? Maybe Will sent him to find out why you're spending time with a psycho."

She stiffened when he laughed. She thought of his gardens and his wild grace, the way he made her feel both beautiful and electric. The way he made her *feel*.

"Don't ever call yourself that."

His laugh faded, but his smile stayed. "All right," he said, holding her with eyes like camouflage, for the moment the color of ginger rosemary. "I won't."

"Now show me these plants."

They started with the crossbred perennials, quickly filling up the wagon with the one gallon azalea that spread like phlox, the poppies that bloomed as true blue as delphiniums. They picked up another cart for the fuzzy-stemmed ivies, the black-bellied passion flower and twenty-eight varieties of bamboo, from rampant growers to a miniature with stalks the color of blood. Jack fell for each in turn, an easily won but fickle lover. This one enchanted him with her dainty white blossoms and love of full sun, that one replaced her with extravagant fall color.

Within the hour, most of the sales staff had arrived to help cart additional wagons. A salesman would lift out something new and Jack would agree to it on the spot. If Elizabeth so much as glanced at a plant, he'd order three. After a while, fearing for even Clyde Cummings's wallet, she strived to keep her gaze straight ahead.

Two hours later, with the twelve greenhouses noticeably skimpy, the sales staff loaded the plants for delivery. Jack took the tender vines into his own truck, then returned to the shed to write a check. He looked longingly around the rustic storeroom, the concrete floor and plywood potting table that served as a counter.

"You ever dream the same thing over and over?" he asked.

"I don't remember my dreams."

He narrowed his eyes at her, as if he didn't believe it for a second. "Well, I dream about this," he said. "A nursery of my own, a few acres I could design from start to finish, the way *I* wanted it. It would be a garden, too, a park, with a restaurant that served up the vegetables and herbs we grew. A place to read the paper or just unwind. I'd offer classes on gardening, how to listen to plants. Maybe it wouldn't sound so crazy in a place like this."

"I think that's a lovely idea, Jack."

He smiled widely, immediately launched into design ideas— the excavation of lakes, the planting of boxwood mazes and secret gardens, the installation of unfeasibly grand fountains and glass terraces. He reminded her of a boy with a rocket, more interested in velocity and style points than aim, charming but a little dangerous. She could certainly render a diagnosis, but with the orange blossoms still swimming in her bloodstream she'd rather contend that the ability to dream fantastically and unrealistically is the only way that art and innovation are ever achieved.

When they finally left the sweet air of the nursery, her head cleared, but not by much. The moment she'd kissed him, she'd also stopped treating him. It was difficult to fight an illness that, for a while at least, brought out a man's best.

She got into the truck, ran her fingers delicately over the vines in the back. Jack turned over the engine, set the heater on high. While they'd been inside, the temperature had plummeted. The black Audi had gone and the wind was now blustery and mean.

"I saw a property in Bolinas," Jack went on. "Amazing it's still available. Five acres, just past the lagoon. A grove of eucalyptus trees. I'd build the greenhouses first, live in a yurt if I had to, find the right chef for the restaurant. You ever been to Bolinas? Populated by crazies. They keep ripping down the signs to town so the tourists won't find it. I'd never advertise. The plants would tell people to come."

The psychiatrist in her reared up, but before she could challenge him, he pulled out of the nursery, abruptly changed the subject.

"What made you get into psychiatry?"

She breathed deeply. "I always wanted to be a doctor."

"Sure. Lots of kids do. Why a shrink?"

She pressed her hand to the window, wished the sun would come back. They passed the regal Rhine House at the Beringer Vineyards, and her mouth watered for a warm cabernet sauvignon, a cozy seat by the fireplace, the security of those stone walls around her.

"My mother," she said at last, then dropped her hand. "My mother suffered from bipolar disorder."

He stared at her so long, he nearly missed the street back to Clyde's estate. He made a sharp left, overcorrected, slowed down as he passed through the wrought-iron gates. But the jarring had dislodged one of the trumpet vines, sending a tendril down her shoulder. It lay there gently, like a hand.

"You wanted to cure her," he said.

Elizabeth shrugged, but the vine stayed put. "It was too late for that. I wanted to make sure no one else suffered like she did."

Jack pulled to the side of the road, beneath the sycamores, let the nursery truck rumble past. "Was she treated?" he asked.

"Yes, but not well. She was in and out of hospitals for years. Given shock treatments, opiates to calm her. There was no lithium then. She didn't have your opportunity to turn it down."

"I'm sorry, Elizabeth."

He touched the corner of her eye, where the tears had been piling up. He released a trickle as if he'd made an outlet through a parting of petals.

"Resembling, 'mid the torture of the scene," he said, "Love watching Madness with unalterable mien."

She swiped her cheeks. "You're rhyming."

"It's Byron. Other people's poetry doesn't count."

They were silent, which only magnified the hissing of the wind outside the truck, the cab rocking beneath them.

"If I am sick," he said finally, "then I believe love can cure me."

She pressed her head against his shoulder so he wouldn't see her eyes, so he wouldn't discover that she wished for this more than anything but had her doubts.

"Nothing," he said vehemently, "is too wonderful to be true."

Elizabeth had gardened as a child, before her mother got sick, then once more in the early years of her marriage. She and Will had paid their way through medical school partly by living on cherry tomatoes and zucchini each summer. Elizabeth had studied in the garden, eating fruit warm off the vine, but when Will finally opened his surgical practice, he ripped every last bush from the ground. He took her to dinner, ordered prime rib, and years later he was still calling tomatoes the poor man's steak, even though their crops had been abundant and sweet. He hired a maintenance man to cut the lawn and never let her put tomatoes back in their salads, even though, in many ways, those garden years had been the best ones they had.

Despite her recent visits to the courtyard, the lack of hard labor still showed. Elizabeth's arms ached after lugging a few five-gallon plants across Clyde Cummings's vast Napa estate. She turned her gaze warily toward the pewter sky, from which a light rain had begun to fall. She deposited the plants in the orange spray-painted circles Jack had marked on the ground, and occasionally a gust of wind knocked them over, spilling dirt and damaging the fragile stems of the trumpet vines, which snapped at the slightest touch.

She was still wearing her juniors blue jeans, which were now thoroughly stylish, torn and soiled at the knee. Jack had loaned her a button down work shirt, which smelled of him. Later, when she was told to stay away from him, she would not give it back.

Jack had disappeared into a tangle of shrubbery. She heard his voice, quicker and more high-pitched than it had been an hour ago, still picking up speed. She grabbed a shovel, began digging a hole in the moist earth for one of the Dicksonias, a palm-looking tree that was not a palm at all but a fern, imported from Australia. She was surprised at the things one never forgot—how to kiss and ride a bike, for instance, how to dig a hole as deep as the root ball and twice as wide. She turned the palm on its side and pummeled the plastic pot with the side of her fist. She was surprised when the tree cooperated, the crowded roots sliding out easily. She dropped the root ball in the hole, got on her hands and knees to refill the dirt, making sure, as her mother had taught her, to tap out all the air pockets.

She built a well and filled it with water, let it drain then filled the well again. She was glad of the rain, turned her face into the wind to cool down. She started on the next tree fern, her mother's simple-but-effective gardening wisdom coming back to her in a rush. Don't amend the soil around trees or the roots won't spread. Fertilize only lightly when planting, then heavier a month later. Never prune in summer, don't do anything but savor the garden in fall. She'd forgotten her mother had been something other than sick; a sprinter in high school, the girl a man chose to marry, an aficionado of bright yellow marigolds and purple Johnny-jump-ups. She'd picked trees for their pretty autumn foliage—oaks and liquidambars, smoke trees that turned an otherworldly shade of coral in October. She'd had fresh flowers in the house until the very end.

A saw ripped the air. Elizabeth headed toward the shrubbery where branches were splintering, leaves flying like shrapnel. Somehow Jack had wedged himself inside the scaly leaves of a dense arborvitae and was carving a hole with a chain saw. Ten minutes later, he poked his head through.

"Remember what I was saying about topiaries?" he said. "The possibilities are endless. Centaurs, dragons, mermaids watching over the lagoon." The bush seemed to balk at the suggestion, rustling, showing its thorns. She worried about scrapes and rashes, but had the feeling Jack would emerge unscathed.

A bolt of lightning severed the sky, followed by a quick crack of thunder. The rain came harder, but Jack had already started up the saw again.

She began to shiver. This rain was colder, more substantial, accompanied by an occasional fleck of ice. Clyde and his partner watched Jack's progress from the comfort of the covered patio.

The boy walked inside, returned a few minutes later with a sweater which he draped around Clyde's shoulders. Elizabeth looked at their fingers threaded together, and wondered what their parents thought, if the neighbors gave them trouble, if Clyde got hate mail. She wanted to ask them if it was worth it, but was ashamed to assume there was any answer but yes.

She shivered from head to toe, hurried to the terrace to join them. She searched for feeling in the tips of her fingers.

"Wow," Clyde said. "Look at that."

Elizabeth turned, saw the heart of the storm swooping in like a giant, mean crow. The hundred-year-old sycamores took on the wind, shielding the saplings like protective parents, but a forty-mile-an-hour gust snapped a gray-haired crown or two, sent boughs flying. The plants Elizabeth had just carted in scattered in all directions. The rain turned to sheets, and within seconds Clyde's reflecting pool was overflowing. Despite the tempest, Jack went on sawing. His arborvitae bent in the wind, but still revealed itself as a horse taking flight.

"He'll get electrocuted," Elizabeth said.

"He's mad." There was admiration in Clyde's voice, the kind of envy spawned whenever only one side was revealed—a man's bravery but not his battle wounds. Clyde and Leonardo braved the onslaught, ran into the rain like children who have no appreciation for the danger they're in.

Elizabeth remained on the terrace as the rain turned to dime-sized hail, a lightning bolt severed the sky no more than a hundred yards to the west. Clyde's lover held up his palms, then shrieked when the ice stung his skin. Even Jack had the sense to turn off the saw, but he merely slapped on a brimmed hat and picked up the hand clippers. He seemed oblivious to the damage in the garden, Clyde's decimated boxwoods, the tree ferns she'd just planted gurgling, drowning.

She closed her eyes, focused on her aches and shivering and tested Jack's clairvoyance. Gardening was not breathing; it could wait for fairer weather. She wanted a hot bath and warm wine and dinner. She wanted the same loving care Jack gave to his plants.

She opened her eyes, spotted Jack and Clyde and lovely Leonardo contemplating the remaining arborvitaes, oblivious to rain. "... nothing we can't do," Jack was saying. "Sirens and nymphs. A whole sea of them, if you want."

"Boys, too," Clyde said, eyeing his lover.

"Absolutely. I can use that row of hemlock, of course the box-wood, even the lantana if you really want to get crazy. We'll turn lilacs into fairies. Sumacs into piles of gold. And think about that underwater garden. We take that pond over there and ..."

She had no right to feel hurt, was ridiculous to allow tears. Last night, she never should have listened for sounds of him through the hotel wall that divided their rooms.

"Elizabeth."

Jack stood before her, dropped the clippers at her feet. She warmed up the instant he kissed her. He tasted like his plants, earthy and green, and she had the most fantastic vision while he held her, that she was being seduced and smothered by ivy.

She pulled back, blushing like Chloe might, hiding her gaze from Clyde and his lover, though they took no notice of her. Inside her soggy shoes, she wiggled her toes. She was imagining a green tinge to Jack's skin when he said, "Clyde's driver will take you back to the hotel. You can have a nice meal and a good night's sleep while I'm working."

She blinked and stepped back. She turned quickly, had to leave before she cried again, but he caught her by the arm.

"The storm will pass," he said. "I've got to move on these ideas now; they're one-way streets. You understand? They race through and don't come back."

"Yes, of course."

He refused to let go. "Annie used to say I didn't want to finish anything, but exactly the opposite is true. I'd give anything to complete one good design, start to finish, the way I planned it. I'd give anything to be *satisfied*. Can you imagine what kind of results I would get if I loved just one thing?"

Elizabeth sucked in her breath, but Jack had already let go.

AT ten, when the storm hadn't passed, and a golf ball–sized hailstone broke the skylight in the hotel lobby, Elizabeth retreated to her room, put on the warm, terry cloth robe she'd found in the bathroom, and turned up the heater. At eleven, when the weather service issued a high-wind warning, and the power went out in the hotel, she lit a candle and set it outside the door to her room. The owners of the hotel brought up hot chocolate, and she kept Jack's cup warm beneath a towel. She imagined him walking in stone cold and sullen that his day's work had been ruined. She practiced the words she would use to soothe him, words that, at first, sounded stiff and silly, but within the hour became routine and dear.

By midnight, when the winds had eased, she got into bed alone and thought of different things. How frustrating it was to wait for someone, even more excruciating to wait to find out what they would do. At some point during the night, she got up and drank Jack's hot chocolate. She wondered if she could truly ease any thirst but her own.

She fell asleep and dreamed two devil-like topiaries stepped out from her mother's garden to embrace her. They filled her mouth with holly, drew blood with their thorny leaves, might have suffocated her completely if her mother hadn't screamed. The plants turned menacingly, dragging their roots behind them as they chased Lila Shreve to her car.

Elizabeth tried to follow, but there were too many leaves, piles and piles she couldn't wade through. Her mother jumped into the station wagon, skidded out of the driveway. The demons pursued her up a monstrous hill.

"Mommy!" Elizabeth screamed, but the car was already out of control, careening toward the cliff. The station wagon seemed to fly for a moment, then went into a freefall, two hundred feet straight down. The topiaries walked to the edge and rooted themselves, stiff and silent as grave markers.

Even in her dream, her clueless father arrived too late. She pushed him away, but his muscles thickened, his skin took on the scent of pine. She opened her eyes to find Jack holding her tight. She buried her face in his shirt which now was the color of earth.

"You were calling for your mother," he said.

She closed her eyes. "My father must have had another woman," she whispered hoarsely. "He'd plan my mother's schedule, go away for the weekend, and come back sane enough to face the week. He never understood why I hated him more."

She picked a broken leaf off his shirt, studied the splintered veins. Her mother had been like that, fractured, headed in too many directions at once.

"It must have been awful for you," he said. "She must have known how awful it was."

"I don't know," she said. "She seemed so removed most of the time. I don't think we shared the same world."

"She never improved?"

"No. The U.S. approved lithium one month after she died, but she probably wouldn't have taken it. She begged my father to stop the shock treatments. To let her be. That's when she dropped into these terribly quick cycles. I can diagnose it now. Brief, severe mania with psychosis, then deep, long depressions. She terrified me when she was manic. I was never sure who I'd find when I came home from school. She might have cut off her hair or gathered all the terrified neighbors in the kitchen to watch her perform Hamlet. The depressions systematically got longer, and I was glad. At least when she was sobbing, I could predict what she would do."

Elizabeth sat up, the words coming quicker once she realized she'd never spoken them before. That Jack was the first one who'd asked. "I was seven when it happened," she went on. "That morning, she took my sister and me to the park. She was actually acting human, talking to the other mothers while I played on the swing and Kylie slept in her stroller. I'm telling you, Jack, when she was like that, when she was normal, there was no one else in the world I loved more. She was a tragic princess trapped in a terrible spell. Beautiful, maybe, underneath the curse."

Jack pressed his lips to her forehead, left them there.

"She wanted to go for a drive," she continued. "All she wanted was a breezy afternoon with her daughters, maybe a tour of the coast, a chance to sing along with the radio. One fine day, maybe, before it all got bad again. But I couldn't give her that. A friend had asked me over. We had this big argument; I said something awful. Told her I wished she wasn't my mother, that she wasn't such a freak."

"You were young. You didn't know what you were saying."

"Oh yes I did. I loved her more than anyone, but one normal day didn't count for much. I ran from her, thought she'd chase me down, do something manic and embarrassing in front of the mothers, but when I got to the corner and looked back, she was just standing there. Just watching me go. She put my sister in the car and started it up. The last thing I saw was that station wagon on two wheels as she turned the corner. They flew off the side of Mount Tam. The eyewitnesses said she looked like she was trying to fly that car."

He held her tightly. She wanted to cry, but no tears would come. Or maybe his skin absorbed them instantly. Either way, she decided she wasn't going to leave that spot. Not ever.

"How old was your sister?" he asked.

"Six months."

He pulled back, took her face between his hands. "Do you think I could hurt you?"

She wanted to lie, but had begun to believe he'd know it if she did. Had begun, perhaps, to believe too much. "I don't think you'd want to. But I know you could."

He dropped his hands, got out of bed and crossed to the door. She wanted him to come back, but knew the best thing would be if he didn't.

"Then I'm no different than any other man," he said.

She couldn't remember crying, but when she woke in the

morning, her eyes were swollen to slits. She walked into the bathroom where her jeans and work shirt hung over the rod, still wet. She splashed water on her face, widened her eyes enough to admit she looked ghastly. Her dark hair had slipped its bun and was as wild as Jack's, adorned with dirt clods and the fragments of leaves.

She turned on the shower, let the water heat up while she went to look for coffee. She opened the door to the living room, lifted her hand to her chest. The room was now a garden—the floors adorned with heaps of rose blossoms and oriental poppies, the chairs piled two feet high with sunflowers, coneflowers, delphiniums, and irises. Elizabeth leaned against the wall, was still there when Jack opened the door. He must have confiscated her key, and she tried to muster outrage.

"I don't think you—"

"You're fired," he said.

She took a deep breath which, with all the blossoms in the room, was her second luscious high in two days. She could think of a hundred things she ought to say, but all that came out was, "Oh, good."

He walked across the room. "I don't want to get worse," he said.

She kissed the hollow in his neck. "I won't let you." A lovely, unreasonable statement, the kind she hadn't made in years and suddenly vowed would be true.

"I don't want to get better either. Just stay like this. Full of energy and ideas and desire for you. Afraid of nothing except lovelessness and mediocrity."

"The nature of life is to change," she said.

He took her hand, led her to the bathroom. The room was now full of steam; she hardly saw it when he slid off the sash on her robe.

"You're wrong," he said, slipping the robe off her shoulders, stroking a finger across her breasts. "The nature of life is to move us toward that thing we're most afraid of. We're not done until we face it head-on."

He took off his clothes, revealing a teenager's body, lean, tan, and muscled, the kind that populated Chloe's favorite beaches. She touched his chest hesitantly, then more firmly, claiming his clavicle, the line of hair down his stomach, one hip then the other, thinking childishly, euphorically, the way Will never would have tolerated, *Mine. Mine*.

"What are you most afraid of?" he asked.

He opened the shower door, pulled her in. The nearly scalding water pummeled her back, and when he pressed his lips to her neck, she feared she was feverish, twenty-one again and expected to choose the right man without the aid of maturity or experience. When he cupped her breasts in his hands, she feared both the intensity and brevity of euphoria.

"Shut up," he said, pulling her closer. "Stop thinking."

When he slid inside her, she was afraid some things were too good to be true.

THE storm had swept away the trumpet vines. The rain gutter along the covered patio had snapped, and all the water from the roof had carved a six-inch deep channel from terrace to vineyard. The tree ferns Elizabeth had planted had been ripped out by a microburst, tossed unceremoniously into the reflecting pool.

Jack's topiary had been lopped off at the hips, leaving behind an unnerving hedge of four severed legs.

Show a manic a disaster and he'll find a million uses for the rubble, which was why, when Jack brought Elizabeth to the garden, her euphoria began to fade.

Last night, Jack had ordered on the generators, let the naturally occurring puddles define where Calypso's grotto would go. He exchanged the labyrinth for a rain forest jungle, turned the snails into the gardens, abandoned the ruined arborvitae in favor of a moldy thicket of holly, which he transformed into a circle of nine wood sprites, lithe green arms extended toward the sky.

By morning, the storm was in Idaho, closing Interstate 84 with four inches of freakish early season snow. In Napa, the rain and hail had washed away topsoil and the earth's underbelly steamed. Jack led Elizabeth into the circle of the holly sprites, already sprouting moss. She wore another of his shirts, an old pair of his sweatpants she'd cinched around her hips. She'd found clay-colored fingerprints on the inside of her thighs, an oval of grass blades on her stomach like the imprint of a kiss. He'd marked her; even under the surface she smelled him on her, in her. It was the opposite of lost sense—a mesmerizing swelling of perception. Her skin seemed buoyant; she noticed, for the first time, the variety of colors in tree bark and mold, the complicated scent of geranium blossoms, as if they were made up of every other flower on earth.

Jack leapt from sprite to sprite, pruning in smiles, high cheekbones, and winks. She'd been fired, she'd been soundly loved; she shouldn't analyze the jerkiness of his movements, or his humming that began as a show tune but quickly lost its way.

She turned her face to the sun and closed her eyes. She opened them again when the humming stopped. She found Jack on his knees, eyes squeezed shut. He pointed across the circle. "Stop it," he said. "Make it stop."

She looked at the hedges, saw nothing but the rings he'd carved onto every finger. She touched Jack's shoulder and he leapt to his feet, breaking off a sprite's hand at the wrist when he ran off, sending up a shower of holly leaves.

She caught up to him by the pile of glass pebbles he'd had delivered that morning; he was trembling over shades of amber and crimson and gold. The colors of autumn, the last gasp of leaves.

"Jack," she said. "What is it? What did you see?"

He turned to her, such panic and fear in his eyes, she looked behind her. She thought of the man who'd been following them, but the garden was empty. He shook his head, tried to smile, but at the same time rocked up and back. She remembered her mother doing the same thing, telling them one thing while her body screamed another.

"Nothing. Just a shadow." He laughed, ran his fingers through his hair. "I need sleep."

She held his arm the way no psychiatrist would. "You lie," she said.

He flinched. "The wind then. A trick of the light."

"Jack—"

"What do you want me to tell you? The thing that will make you right, or the one that'll make you stay? Tell me, Elizabeth. You decide."

But she couldn't. Her body was still cooling from his touch. She couldn't bear the truth if it sullied this morning, if it denied her what she wanted. She couldn't want anything but the truth.

"I have myself an inner weight of woe," he said, "that God himself can scarcely bear."

She shook her head. "No more poetry, Jack."

The grasshoppers stepped gingerly onto the saturated lawn, their snapping frost-bitten and slow. "You make me feel ashamed of what I've always thought of as a gift."

She blinked back tears, let go of him. "I'm sorry." She looked at the topiaries, imagined they *had* linked hands, stretched more gracefully toward the sky. She imagined they *did* have souls, that everything she so casually weeded, crushed or ignored was aware of her actions. "I'm not trying to do that. I just fear you're one of your morning glories. Twenty feet in a season, invincible in summer, but then the first frost kills it."

She was surprised when he smiled, as if the idea of spending all his energy and life in one fiery season was not such a horrible proposition. He returned to the sprites, picked up the clippers.

"We need to be getting back soon," she said, following him. "I've got to pick Chloe up at Will's by six. I've got a full slate of patients tomorrow."

He hesitated, then pruned in lips. "That's impossible. Look at all the debris. I can't leave it like this."

"I'm sure Clyde will hire someone to clean up."

"I've got to finish this, then figure out exactly how much we lost in the storm. I'll need to reorder, start on those glass walkways. I'll be trapped at the museum all week. I won't be able to get back until Saturday."

"Jack, I've got obligations."

In the distance, Elizabeth heard Clyde's voice, then a soft answer from his lover. A laugh, the cry of a bird.

"We'll compromise then. I'll work all day and we'll fly back tonight. They've got a small airport here. We can charter a flight. Clyde will pay for it."

She jumped back, literally shoved him getting away. "Oh no. That's out of the question."

He became the still one. "You're a psychiatrist," he said softly. "I figured you'd have something as treatable as a fear of flying worked out by now."

"It's not that. We've got a perfectly good car. We're not going to just abandon it here. Anyway, it's not that long a drive even if we leave—"

He took off across the patio, disappeared around the side of Clyde's house, and she had to admit her heart raced around him not only from desire, but from the same reason it had beat so madly around her mother, from the inability to predict what he would do.

She heard the banging, the wrenching of metal, as if it were inside her own head. She sat on the half-demolished patio, pulled her knees to her chest. Ten minutes later, Jack came back whistling. "The truck's having a little trouble," he said. "Looks like we'll have to fly."

She looked up, too outraged to speak

"Don't worry," he said. "Everything will be fine."

She shook her head, swiped at the tears that had started to fall. He was no different than Will, turning her terror into some ghost in the house only she could see. Making her deepest fears sound hysterical. "Of course. What could happen? No one dies before their time."

"Elizabeth—"

"I won't take Chloe to Hawaii; I lost my marriage because I wouldn't go away with Will, because I was always so afraid.

I get it. It's all my fault. How stupid and illogical I am to be fearful. How unreasonable to refuse to risk the people I have left."

"The world is a scary place," he said softly.

"Yes. It is."

She clenched her jaw along with her fists, which quickly led to a toothache. She waited for him to spout some gobbledygook about airline safety, the more likely chance that she'd die on the way to the airport than on the flight itself. She'd seen the data and none of it helped. Statistics only proved you had to leave a margin for error; one million flights without disaster set the stage for an accident on flight one million and one. She'd put herself through biofeedback, taken four different fear-of-flying courses, and every time she'd gotten to the airport for her graduation flight, she'd ended up sobbing in the terminal. She was not irrational at all, that was the trouble. Bad things happened every day. Terrorists struck the innocent, cars flew off cliffs, babies died. Geniuses had to do all their living in summer; she knew this better than anyone.

"Have you ever trusted someone to take care of you?" he asked.

She cried when Jack sat beside her, when she realized she didn't trust anyone. Not mothers. Not husbands. Not even God.

"The plane won't crash," he said.

She shook her head. "Don't mock me."

"I'm not. I'm telling you everything will turn out fine."

She turned to look at him. "You can't guarantee that."

"I can. I do."

"Jack—"

He took her hand, brought it to his chest. "You will get home to your daughter. It's so clear to me it's as if it's already happened."

"You're getting mystical now," she said, smiling despite herself, hope rising no matter how hard she willed it down, as if it was made of helium.

"You'll be fine, Elizabeth."

Her heart began to race, her palms turned clammy. She didn't trust anyone, and it would be insane, ridiculous, to start with a man who mistook holly for wood sprites, who had his deepest conversations with plants. A man who might be the very essence of unreliability, unable to control the very basics, what he thought and felt.

But he wouldn't look away, and even though her stomach dropped, the rest of her rose on tiptoes. The rest of her turned toward the sky which, in the wake of the storm, looked placid. As safe and buoyant as a warm salt lake.

TEN

*M*ARY Bolton was a firm believer that bad things came in threes. The blender sputtering to a standstill was normal wear and tear, the theft of her lucky bamboo the price of living in the city, her unease nothing but paranoia until Annie Crandall stepped into her shop.

Mary Bolton took one look at her sister-in-law and dropped into the chair behind the counter. Her hands hadn't trembled like this since Pluto had been in transit, a dreadful month that saw her cat run away and her long-time lover, Richard, announce he was gay. She opened her thermos of chamomile tea, took a few sips to calm her nerves. Annie strode through the store the way she'd attacked the aisle on her wedding day—shoulders back, red hair gelled to within an inch of its life, her shiny slacks swishing. The kind of woman who commanded spandex or silk, who made Mary feel every day of her forty-six years, every pucker, every line, every fold where even a man's shirt still pinched.

Annie had never come to the bookstore before. She'd returned the tarot cards Mary sent her as a wedding present, claiming she never played games. Her disapproving squint took in all of Mary's rings and macramé bracelets, finally came to rest on her waist-length, braided hair. Not only had Mary never cut it, she'd never colored it, and by her forties it had taken on the look of an Indian blanket, an intricate weave of browns, reds and grays.

"I need to see Jack," Annie announced.

And Mary realized it wasn't Annie's surprising appearance—the invasion of a determined Scorpio—that had set her on edge, but the look in Annie's eyes. The unusual glint of panic.

"He's not here."

"I've tried your apartment and the Londonbright. Is there some other job site I can check? I know you don't trust me, but believe it or not, I'm trying to help."

"It's a little late for apologies."

Annie tapped her fingernails on the counter, fingernails Mary couldn't help but admire. She'd never seen a hand so pretty, freckled along the knuckles, nails thick and glossy, tips painted white. She wondered when Annie found the time to get a manicure. She'd always marveled at her sister-in-law's immaculateness and scheduling prowess; Annie worked twelve-hour days at the advertising agency, trained for marathons, hosted baby showers and corporate luncheons, fooled around. Just thinking about it made Mary tired, despite the fact that she got up whenever she felt like it, closed the bookstore on slow days, had no one but Jack to care for, which lately was more than enough.

"Look," Annie said, "I'm not here to argue with you. I know how you feel about me. You can blame me all you want, but right now, I'm worried about Jack."

Mary turned away rather than admit she'd been worrying about Jack, too. Thursday night, she'd come home to a transformed apartment. Jack had lined the floors and walls with butcher paper, painted in every plant and flower in nature, along with a few winsome anomalies he'd clearly created on his own. He'd sketched ivy leaves on Post-It notes, wound them around chair legs and lamps, but when he reached the textured ceiling, the Post-Its must not have adhered. He'd used permanent markers right on the cottage cheese, shades of pink and purple in the shape of wisteria blossoms.

She'd found his working notes scattered throughout the house, notes that were surprisingly clear to her, as if siblings spoke in code. *Hanging gardens of Babylon. No proof. Blue glass pebble floor. Earth as sky.*

She was ten when he was born, the same year their father left and their mother took up palm reading to pay the bills. Her mother had a knack for saying what people wanted to hear, but was surprisingly reluctant to listen. She'd been astonished when her husband left her, though he'd been living with a girlfriend on weekends and threatening divorce for months. When the man she replaced him with couldn't find the right bedroom, she chalked it up to dim lighting and a long hallway, she slapped Mary for making up perverted, vicious lies. After a while, Mary stopped crying all the time, she learned that if she just lay still, it was over quicker. She hid out at the library, found her saving grace in a librarian who acknowledged terror and stretched closing time a little later every night, who hinted there was solace along the back shelf, in the astrology section. Mary devoured those sun-sign books, plotted her own chart, was soothed by the discovery that any pain she suffered now would be doubled in joy later on. As a Capricorn, she learned, she was resourceful and cool, which was why she was able to wash the blood and semen from her sheets without screaming. Capricorns, it said in all the books, never broke, no matter what was done to them.

They did, however, cry in relief when their periods came, and slide the bureau in front of their baby brother's door, in case the unthinkable should be attempted. Mary confronted the unthinkable early on, which had made a life of anything short of that seem less an existence than a relief.

She stared at Annie, who had an alarming ring of tears in her eyes. "I'm trying to help him," Annie said. "You have no idea. If I don't find him, if he finds him first, I . . ."

She dissolved into sobs. Mary drained her tea, wished she'd made it stronger. She'd never seen Annie cry, not at her own wedding, not when Annie's sister died of leukemia, not when Jack embarrassed her by singing a bawdy version of "Happy Trails to You" at a dinner party in front of all her snobby friends. She had pictured Annie telling Jack it was over in a cool, collected voice, that the demise of their marriage was all her fault, but now she admitted Jack could not have been easy to live with. While brothers could sometimes be considered charming when flawed, the best-loved husbands were the ones who improved.

Mary came around the counter, touched her sister-in-law on the arm. Annie turned into her, surprising them both.

"You still love him," Mary said.

Annie shrugged. "I never said I stopped."

"You don't try to change the people you love."

"You do if you're trying to save them."

Mary stepped back, fingered her braid. She didn't know

what to think and, frankly, preferred a universe where Annie Crandall didn't cry. The sun in Scorpio made Annie controlling and willful, occasionally vindictive, but the moon softened her edges, could even lead to sacrifice.

"I haven't seen him all weekend," Mary said at last.

Annie bit her bottom lip. "You don't know where he is? Really?"

Mary wished for a life with no one to take care of but herself, then quickly double-wished the wish away. "What's going on?"

Annie touched Mary's hand gently, something she'd never done before. "I'm sure Jack told you I've been seeing someone. You want to know what's scary?"

Mary shook her head vigorously, but Annie just went on. "I closed my eyes and imagined it was Jack kissing me. I went out looking for someone totally different, and unfortunately I got what I wanted."

Annie found one of Jack's pink pens on the counter, snatched a piece of store stationery. "Here's my cell number. Have him call me the moment he gets in."

"I'll ask him to, but Jack will do what he'll do."

Annie hardly seemed aware when she slipped the pen into her purse. Mary led her to the door, anxious for her to leave. She saw a waiflike girl heading toward the store, dressed in black leather on Sunday to horrify the neighbors, pierced at the nose to make her mother cry, and instead of ushering her in to offer tea and a reading, Mary waited for Annie to drive off, then put up the closed sign.

She went straight for a joint, inhaled the smoke deep into her lungs, but her body failed to respond. Lately marijuana had no effect on her; she hadn't gotten high in months. She'd grown middle-aged despite drugs, a city apartment, and as much pornography as she could stomach. She voted strictly Democratic out of habit instead of passion, was feeling in no way celebratory about menopause, despite what she said to her Monday night book club, and was, most alarmingly, beginning to forget what had happened in her bedroom all those years ago. She was beginning to think one man's barbarism had less hold on her than a lifetime of everyone else's good intentions, that she had no one but herself to blame for the things she lacked. For an empty bed and an untried womb, for loving but never being loved.

She put out the joint, wished for someone to rub the ache from her shoulders. Instead she picked up the Visa bill Jack had gawked at, unable to believe he'd run up so much, with so little to show for it. His South American ladybugs had been scattered throughout the city, the twenty thousand pink pens distributed to shops all over town. The glass tiles from Italy were used in a job in Mill Valley, the rare Australian tulips planted, without permission, in Golden Gate Park. The Korean grass and copper tubing brought dinosaurs to life at the Londonbright, which would not pay him again until the work was done, while the marble fountains and imported stone for Clyde Cummings's garden went well beyond the man's retainer. Mary opened her checkbook, paid the minimum. She put the bill in the mailbox and grabbed her keys.

She jiggled the handle on the door of her Jetta, pumped the clutch three times to get the engine to start. Where *was* Jack this weekend? She had assumed he was working a seventy-two-hour shift at the museum garden, or binging in a nursery, losing himself in plants. Lately, he'd taken such a leap in energy and confidence, displayed such a surge of *brilliance,* she'd chided herself for her discomfort, chalked it up to an unflattering pique of jealousy. He was happy. What kind of sister spoiled that?

Her kind, apparently, as she ditched her plans to head to the market and drove instead toward the Golden Gate. Would anyone believe her when she told them the color of Jack's eyes had changed? Gone from forest green to sparkling lime in a matter of weeks, as if he'd struck a match inside him, or was blanching. A man's happiness, she'd tell his psychiatrist, should not make people nervous. A smile shouldn't show such strain.

She passed through the Waldo Tunnel, and five minutes later pulled up in front of Dr. Shreve's office building, where she'd dropped Jack off once before. Only then did she remember it was Sunday and no one would be there. That these were the wasted minutes that filled her life, whole hours squandered trying to salvage people who didn't want or even need to be saved.

She shook her head, put the car in reverse. But before she backed up she saw a flash of blue and red on the roof. She sat forward, wondered if the pot had affected her after all. Superman stood, legs spread, hands on hips, on the edge of the bunkerlike three-story building. The wind caught his cape, rippled across his phony chest muscles. Someone honked their horn and he saluted.

She cut the engine, got out of the car. Clark Kent waved as soon as he saw her, and she waved back, smiling ridiculously. She prayed he wasn't some lunatic about to jump.

"Are you all right?" they both shouted at the same time.

Mary laughed, stepped forward. "I'm looking for Dr. Shreve. I forgot it was Sunday."

"Are you a patient?"

"Are you?"

He laughed, then coughed. His shoulders and chest were built up with foam, but his legs looked a little sickly for a super-hero. A teenager stuck his head out the window of a speeding Mercedes, shouted, "Hey Superman!"

"I believe her partner is here," Superman said. "Dr. Cohen."

"You're well-acquainted with psychiatrists, are you?"

"Go on in."

She walked into the deserted office building, found the psy-chiatrists' names on the placard. She took the elevator up, walked the long, hushed corridor. The door was unlocked, so she let herself in. The waiting room was dark except for the blue glow of the aquarium, silent except for the gurgling of the tank. An extremely slender, middle-aged man stepped through one of the office doors.

"I thought I heard someone come in," he said. "Can I help you?"

He brushed a tangle of graying hair from his dark, tired eyes, was dressed in oversized slacks and a V-necked sweater.

"I was looking for Dr. Shreve. I'm the sister of one of her patients."

"Why don't you come in?"

"No. It's all right. I'll call the doctor Monday. Sorry to bother you."

She glanced past him toward his office window, which was open despite the chill. A piece of red silk blew in the breeze, snagged by the sill.

She looked at him again, realized she'd taken in his thin frame, but overlooked the way he stood. He was flimsy, cer-tainly, a little concave, but he spread his legs, kept his hands on his hips. The stance of someone who could save you, if saving was what you needed.

She looked at the silk, then at his eyes, which were sunken but twinkling.

"Maybe I will come in after all," she said.

Elizabeth's partner, Stuart, had never tried to cure her fear of flying. Some phobias are there for a reason, he was fond of saying. Some people are best defined by the things they won't do.

He did, however, point out the inroads she'd made. Didn't she love airports, at least when she didn't have to fly? The tearful greetings and farewells, the unconcerned flight announcements, and the pilots, especially the pilots, who sipped coffee and strode casually to their planes, as if defying gravity was no more remarkable than falling asleep contented with the day. As if the most rational thing in the world was to believe things would turn out well.

Jack believed it; hours before they left for the airport, he got out his rooting hormone and insisted they plant every broken branch and stem that had not been washed away in the storm. Elizabeth imagined he did this more for her benefit than his, to distract her, exhaust her, and halfway through the planting of two hundred cuttings it began to work. She forgot the Latin names of the plants in favor of their scent and eccentricities. Melissa officinalis sparked visions of lemons, the stems of tanacetum vulgare leaked juice that soothed her hands. Lonicera japonica attracted bees, lobularia maritime looked and felt like snow, endymion hispanicus was the flower that reminded her of

Chloe, with leaves softer than a newborn's skin and flowers the blue of Chloe's eyes at birth.

By midday, her back ached so much she nearly forgot what lay ahead. A rash rose along her forearms and began to swell, and this also seemed Jack's doing because it lasted the entire time she was planting, then stopped the moment the taxi picked them up.

The fact that Jack got her all the way to the airport was something. Will hadn't enticed her out of the bathroom for the aborted trip to Cancun, world-class therapists had left her in the office, untreatable. The taxi deposited them on the tarmac and Elizabeth immediately spotted the single-engine four-seater. The peacefulness of the garden lingered because, instead of crying, she laughed. The Cessna was a child's toy, battery-operated, flimsy and comical. There was no way she was getting on that plane.

Jack rocked up and back on the balls of his feet, started talking about the smoothness of flight and quickly segued into a discussion of rugby. She lost the thread of his conversation, felt a flash flood of panic when she realized her fears might be nothing more than another idea he couldn't hold on to. Her pleas might not move him at all.

"Don't you think that's true?" he asked.

"What?" she said. "Is what true?"

"Women are stronger than men, if you adjust for muscle and body weight. They can take more punches, but they don't. They're not stupid. Men are just bored. We run out of conversation, so we hit each other. We can't come up with anything else. It's a terrible thing, boredom. Eats you up inside. Ask your patients; they'll tell you. Depression isn't anything more than disgust with yourself. You wake up and can't believe you have to spend another day with this person. You can't believe—"

She might have run away right then if she hadn't touched his arm, found his skin hot to the touch. "Are you feeling all right?"

"Of course. Couldn't be better."

His pupils were dilated, a bead of sweat had erupted above his upper lip. The pilot came out of the hangar office, a boy more than a man, hardly more substantial than air himself. She watched him tap the metal plate over the Fisher-Price engine, as if the echo imparted some significant data, and wondered exactly how many people she would have to disappoint with her cowardice. How long until the last one gave up.

The pilot waved, called them over. Elizabeth's legs actually gave way while she walked. Only Jack's grip on her arm kept her upright and moving. Her mouth was bone dry, and tasted slightly metallic. There was no question she would die on that plane. Those plastic propellers would drop during takeoff, or a wing would crack at the first sign of turbulence. Even if they made it all the way to San Francisco, the pilot of a jumbo jet returning from Honolulu would mistake them for a crow and crush them on the runway, but when she was sick on the tarmac and Jack merely rubbed her back, sang some silly song until she was through, she wondered if the way you died didn't matter nearly as much as whose hand you were holding at the time.

"Don't make me," she said.

He cleaned the sides of her mouth, took her face between his hands and held her with eyes the very color of the earth she clung to. "Trust me."

Somehow he got her all the way to the pilot, who introduced himself as Henry. On closer inspection, he was not a teenager but a solid twenty-one, dressed in shorts, an I ♥ Tahiti T-shirt and Teva sandals in the event of a water landing.

"Nice day for a flight," he said. "Glad you called. Now I have an excuse to meet my girlfriend at 3-Com."

He wheeled over a stepladder for a staircase. Elizabeth glanced back at the empty tarmac, wondered if Jack would chase her if she ran or, even worse, shake his head and let her go. She could sit down on the asphalt and refuse to budge, but instead, without actually understanding how she was moving, she heard the slap of her feet on the metal treads. Each step felt more absurd, willed from Jack's mind into her body. Jack helped her duck into the plane, where they crouched into pint-sized seats. The interior was clean but well-used, the seat cushions a little slumped, the whole thing smelling of Pine Sol and stale cigarettes. The sunlight hit the controls and nearly blinded her. She wished for whiskey, or something stronger. Something that would knock her out completely.

"You got anything to drink?" Jack asked the pilot.

The young man sealed the door, hopped into his seat. "Sorry. You can buy me a beer in Frisco, though."

He laughed, picked up the radio to go over the flight plan. He looked like a sweet boy, one who would let her off once she started screaming.

She was going to be sick again. She leaned forward, grabbed the sick bag, but nothing came out but saliva, tinted slightly gray. When they started to taxi, her throat swelled shut and she began to cry. Jack took off his seat belt, wedged himself onto the floor beside her.

"Elizabeth," he said, "I would never risk you. You wouldn't be here if I wasn't positive you'll be all right."

She could hardly breathe, gulped hard each time she sobbed. My God, how could her mother have done such a thing? Driven off a cliff, taken her baby with her? How could she not have wanted, been desperate, to live? What was more elemental than the need to protect yourself, preserve your loved ones, clutch your tiny but heartfelt life in the palm of your hand? She felt fury at any pilot who dared to take control of her destiny, at Jack who promised what he couldn't, and at herself for not being able to sit quietly, head on a pillow, calmly watching the cherished earth fly by.

Henry reached the runway and stopped. He glanced back, his easygoing smile gone, his hands firmly on the controls. "Are you going to be all right? I don't want any trouble."

Jack didn't budge. "I adore you," he said. "I'm right here."

She kept gulping, making tiny, baby noises that did nothing, got her nowhere. Her throat was raw, her nails had left gouges in her palms, and none of this was going to help her. Sometimes nothing did.

"Listen," Henry said, "you've got to make up your mind. We're clear."

Henry revved the engine, filling the cabin with thunder. Jack raised his eyebrow and got back into his seat. He fastened his seat belt, and at first she was so frantic she managed only a moan, a chirp. The squeal of a bird who can't fly.

"Go ahead," Jack said. "Let it out. Henry can take it."

Henry laughed, turned forward, and began to accelerate. Elizabeth couldn't believe they didn't realize she would go berserk, she'd make their last moments on earth hell. She fumbled with her seat belt, but at some point realized there was nothing to do but tighten it. She turned from the window, the view of the heavenly earth rushing by. She thought of Chloe and how she used to cry every morning before first grade. She had patted Elizabeth's face, clutched her long after the bell rang. Elizabeth couldn't convince her she'd return in six hours. "How can you be sure?" Chloe had always asked, and Elizabeth had answered as mothers do, promising what couldn't be promised, that love had guarantees, that she would always be there.

She took up Chloe's cry. They were gaining speed, the acceleration pressing them back in their chairs.

"Come on," Jack said. "You call that hysteria? I can do that in my sleep. This plane's going to be off the ground in a few seconds and then there'll be nothing you can do. Not one damn thing."

When the wheels left the ground, the scream took off, too. Despite his earlier laughter, Henry tensed, tilted the plane at what seemed an unnaturally steep pitch. Elizabeth screamed louder, and the air must have already been lighter, because the shriek changed tone, harmonized with the roar of the plane. It sounded like opera, dreadful and euphoric at once. Her ears clogged and she had to scream louder to hear herself. She saw Jack smiling, then the plane sliced through a cloud and leveled off beneath the sun.

Elizabeth stopped suddenly. Her ears popped, and she said, "Oh."

She felt the wobble of the plane against a mean-spirited wind gust, the razor sharp ripples of air a measly strip of metal beneath her. Her throat hurt, and her skin was now as pink as the fuchsias Jack had planted in Clyde's garden. Henry glanced back, a wary-but-gentle smile on his face, and she felt a flood of tenderness for him. A sudden desire to introduce him to Chloe.

Jack squeezed her hand, had been squeezing it all along. His face was gleeful, his eyes too bright though they suited her just now. The first disaster scenario had been averted; the propellers had continued to spin during liftoff. All that screaming had used up a good ten minutes. San Francisco was only another yell or two away.

"Ma'am?" Henry said. "You think I'd let anything happen? I got a girl waiting for me on the other end. That may not mean anything to you, but believe me, it means a hell of a lot to me."

She pressed her cheek against Jack's arm. She'd been crying all along and only noticed now that she was drying up. She counted the seconds she was alive. One, two, three, four, five. Each a perfect jewel. She wished she was this easy to please on the ground.

"I'm all right," she said. "I'll be good."

Jack laughed and kissed the top of her head. She heard his heart racing, the vibrations of his body caused not by the flight but by something deep inside himself, a motor neither one of them could reach. Henry turned forward, and she worried he would retaliate with a stall or a loop-de-loop, but he merely spoke into the radio, set a course for San Francisco Bay.

"Look at me," she whispered to Jack. "I'm flying."

WILL no longer watched the news. Not because of the endless recitations of human violence and tragedy, or the bumbling sportscaster who kept calling Barry Bonds "Bobby," or even the ridiculous banter of the anchors, talking movies between tallies of drive-by shootings. He stopped watching because of meteorology.

Citing no scientific data at all, the Channel 7 weathercaster had linked earthquakes to an aberrant climate. Snow in San Francisco and you'd better stock up on water, an unusually warm summer like the one the Bay area had just experienced and you'd be wise to look into land in Nevada, on the off chance the Big One split California from the continent.

Will stood at his living room window wondering why people, himself included, stood for it. All this talk of Armageddon, a perfectly lovely day perverted into a recipe for disaster. Why had it taken him this long to turn off the news or to decide, as he did now, that if the Big One came, he didn't want to be safe in Nevada but right on top of the San Andreas? Why had it taken him forty-two years to vow that the next time an earthquake hit, he'd be living somewhere he'd really feel it?

"Chloe!"

A long, teenager's minute later, his daughter trudged out of her bedroom in low-riding jeans and a halter top cropped above her navel. She'd been lying on her bed for the better part of the day, just lying there, not even listening to music. Will had tried to go through his patients' charts, but he kept getting distracted by the silence, by visions of where his daughter had gone last night and what he could have said when she'd come home. He'd been out of his mind when he'd gone in to kiss her goodnight and found her bed empty. Usually, this was when he soothed Elizabeth's panic attacks, when he preached logical thinking and composure. But apparently that kind of calm only emerged for an audience. Without Elizabeth, *he* was the one who called Chloe's friends at one in the morning, the one who wore down the carpet pacing. About the time he began to tremble, he admitted no one should have to love a child alone. It was too much emotion for one person to bear. It had been too much, all this time, for Elizabeth.

"What?" Chloe asked. He'd sent her straight to bed when she'd come back, hadn't trusted himself to say the right thing, to even be kind. Now she set her hands on her hips, looked so uneasy being in the same room with him that he laughed out loud at the caricatures they'd become. The sullen, angry teenager. The lonely, awkward dad.

"Your mom's not here yet."

She shrugged.

"Maybe we should go to Baskin-Robbins," he went on. "I've got a craving for orange sherbet."

She'd had nothing but half a bagel all day and this was obviously a warning sign, a definite cry for help. The daughters of doctors had a chillingly high rate of anorexia. There had even been a course on it in med school, six weeks of instruction on lowering standards, expecting less.

"I'm not hungry," she said.

Thinness wasn't his only concern. This whole weekend, she'd flip-flopped moods, sneaked out then crawled back, turned on the television only to walk out of the room seconds later. Her shoulders slumped but she clenched her jaw, she combed her hair perfectly but failed to wash the smudge of mascara from beneath her eyes.

"Is there anything you want to talk about?" he asked, forcing himself to keep his face impassive, to pretend he wanted nothing better than to hear who had hurt her, what kept her up at night.

She shrugged. "I don't know."

He stepped forward, even though Elizabeth was due home any minute. Even though he could have just waited. "Are you okay? Last night . . . I can't tell if you're desperate or defeated. It's starting to scare me, Chloe, that I can't tell."

She flinched. "You don't have to tell anything. Are you, like, Mom now?"

"I don't know what I am."

She stepped back, eyed him warily. "Well," she said, then went silent.

He'd set the thermostat too low. It was miserable in this house, frigid and uninhabitable since Eve left. The only inviting spot in the whole neighborhood was the community pool, but that had been confiscated by the young families who'd bought up the detached houses with the double-wide backyards. The Trumans, for instance, with their three kids under six, and that happy Labrador that loved to dive for rings. Will couldn't even reach the hot tub without tripping over inner tubes, goggles, fins, snorkels, sunscreen number thirty-six.

"Maybe I'll just go out," she said.

He caught her going past. "No."

Chloe stared at him, so stunned he realized he'd done her a terrible disservice by giving her gifts every time he couldn't make a soccer game, by replacing his presence with whatever else she wanted. It had made them both feel better, him wrapping and her unwrapping jewelry and CDs and blue jeans; it suggested they knew what to do to make each other happy. As long as the gifts weren't ridiculously expensive, he hadn't seen the harm. But now he did. His daughter had come to rely on him more as an ally than a dad, a distant, free-spending bystander, and now, if he was worthy of her at all, he'd have to betray her. Become an intimate and engaged enemy so she would grow up.

"Tomorrow I'm going to meet you at the principal's office," he said.

She widened her eyes. "I told you I wouldn't ditch anymore. Are you saying you don't, like, trust me?"

He smiled at her bid for pity, didn't feel the slightest bit tripped up. He imagined he was shedding strings—the thread that held him above the fray, another one that immobilized him in the face of Chloe's tears. He realized the pain in his spine had been gone since this morning, when he decided it wasn't the world or a woman that had to change, but him.

"I'm going to meet you at the principal's office," he said again. "I want to make sure I get a call every time you don't show up."

She looked trapped, in desperate need of a plot, but whatever she came up with wouldn't matter; the string of his ignorance was cut, too. She was no victim, and neither was he. She stomped back to her room, slammed the door. He glanced at his patient files once more, still couldn't muster the slightest bit of interest. He opened the front door, stepped out into what passed for his garden.

Every yard on the street was the same, a strip of grass and two broom bushes, the identical rows of townhouses like a string of abandoned caves. He flipped the switch for the fountain Eve had hung on the wall, a fountain he'd never seen running, since he always came in through the garage. It was a monolith of slate, nearly out of water. A small trickle twisted noisily down its rough flank. He'd admired the piece when Eve took it out of the box, but now he heard the motor more than the water, didn't find it soothing at all.

A car sped around the corner, skimming the side of a plastic garbage can and sending it flying. Will shook his head, thinking it one of the Ursery boys, who had had to do community service for whacking the rows of steel mailboxes with a couple of baseball bats. Then he saw the plates, the gleam of the Volvo. He stood there dumbstruck while Elizabeth parked in a skid and jumped out.

"You are not going to believe this," she said.

And whatever followed, he knew she was right. Her hair was down, tangled with blades of grass. She was dressed in another man's shirt and sweat pants.

"I flew," she said, hurrying up the path. "In a tiny, ridiculous plane. I did it, Will. Not that I ever will again."

She threw back her head and laughed. She twirled around and he reached out to steady her, then dropped his hand when he realized she was only dancing.

"You flew on a plane?" he asked, remembering that brief moment when he'd contemplated manhandling her out of the bathroom, forcing her onto that plane to Cancun. The fraction of a second when he'd imagined he had the power to make her change.

She laughed again, took his arm. Her fingers were marvelously cool, as if she'd dunked them in a snowmelt stream, as if she was immune to weather. "I did. I screamed."

His mouth twitched, she was so enchanting. "You did what?"

"I screamed. Made a scene like you would not believe. The pilot almost turned around the plane."

She smiled up at him proudly, and now he really wished that damn fountain was louder because his heartbeat was obvious. Ba-boom, ba-boom, boom, boom, boom. Like a child reduced to shouting when his parents would not listen. "You screamed," he said.

She noticed her hand then, still holding his arm. She drew back, ran her fingers through her hair which was not only wild, but smelled of exoticness, of blossoms found only in the tropics.

"Where's Chloe?" she asked.

He didn't, couldn't, answer. He'd once told a mute patient that the throat couldn't literally swell with emotion, and she had snatched the pen from his hand and angrily wrote on the examining table paper: YOU'RE WRONG. Maybe he was. Maybe there were moments when feeling superceded physics, when regret and newfound desire overpowered the simplest bodily functions, like falling asleep, like swallowing.

He picked up her hand, studied the half moons of dirt beneath her nails, the soil ground into her lifeline. She tried to pull back, but he held on. Too late.

"It was Jack," she said. "I think I might love him."

He let her go, and she slipped into the house hardly making a sound, still carrying the plane's weightlessness within her. She opened the door to Chloe's room, said something which brought stunned silence, then a reluctant laugh. Will leaned his head against the porch column, decided to call a realtor as soon as the two of them left. He'd pack a few things and move to a hotel until the place sold. He wasn't going to sleep in this house another night.

Elizabeth's arm was tight around Chloe's waist when they walked out. Which was a good thing because otherwise it appeared their daughter might bolt. Her face was frozen in a look of both disbelief and alarm, her gaze on her mother's neck, where Will noticed the bite mark as well.

"I told Chloe I'd meet her at the principal's office," he said. "I'm going to make sure they call me whenever she's not in class."

Elizabeth widened her eyes, and he laughed. "You don't have to look so shocked," he said.

"It's just . . . Really? You'll do that?"

"Yes."

When Elizabeth looked right at him, he decided he was going to do a lot more than that. He'd overhaul his entire schedule, make time for every other hassle that might turn out to be a gem.

"Thank you," Elizabeth said quietly. "Will you call me afterward? Let me know what the principal says?"

"I'm right here you know," Chloe said. "I can hear you."

Will turned aside guiltily, because the truth was, for a moment he'd forgotten his daughter. He'd been caught up in how long Elizabeth's hair had grown, the tips brown but the roots growing in red, as if something deep inside her was changing color. The way she tilted when she stood, one of their perspectives off. He adored his daughter, would do anything for her, but now he knew the truth. If we were lucky, we were given one person to love. If we were blessed, we loved more than one. He'd been blessed, and he'd managed to screw both up magnificently. He'd single-handedly ensured that no one was lucky enough to love him.

ELEVEN

THE night of the incident in Golden Gate Park, the police mistook Jack for an addict. They cited dilated pupils, erratic behavior, so much adrenaline his body hummed, taking on the frequency of static—all symptoms of drug use, but also of euphoria. Parents and law enforcement had no idea what they were up against. Forget the damage teenagers wreaked on their bodies to gain the acceptance of their friends; in private, they popped pills for bliss. For flushed skin and fits of the giggles. For a mind-boggling appreciation of the importance of chocolate and pop songs and love, for second thoughts replaced by unrelated third and fourth ones. For rewards without the work or the triumph, for what Elizabeth felt after her flight—charmed with humanity and devoted to all-out kissing, as if her life were still in peril and she might never get farther than this.

Jack and Elizabeth took a taxi from the airport to Ruby's,

where Elizabeth's car sat abandoned in the parking lot, then she drove him home. Jack let her talk or, more accurately, there was no stopping her. He recognized that symptom. A hundred breathtaking ideas flying at you, and you were expected to choose only one. Elizabeth had envisioned herself vacationing only in places she could drive to comfortably—the Grand Canyon, Reno, Victoria. Suddenly six more continents emerged on the map, and a trip to Europe was upgraded from impossible to improbable. Chloe's favorite beach might not be in Hawaii at all, but somewhere even more exotic—on a tiny island in Western Samoa accessible only by puddle jumper. There was no telling how adventuresome she might become.

Jack had begun his own adventure the moment he stepped off the Cessna and continued to fly. He stared at his rising hands, the dash, his feet hovering above the floor, anywhere but the places on Elizabeth he still wanted to kiss. No swollen lips or her astoundingly sensual collarbone or the bluish skin on the inside of her wrist. He wanted to relish her triumph, not ruin it with the news that euphoria was meant to last a moment, not a season. Too much of it and her body, like his, would start to tremble, too long and the humming would hurt her ears.

She left him on the sidewalk in front of his sister's house. Mary was probably waiting inside, worried where he'd been all weekend, but it was not his sister he sensed watching him. He scanned the street and sidewalks, might have seen a shadow in the alley but he had already skipped to other things, to the arch of Elizabeth's foot and vines that would thrive in pure darkness, to the way her hair fell into his mouth when she lay above him and which plants might take root on the moon. When his thoughts cleared the atmosphere, he felt a moment of alarm, then floated free. It was hard to fight anything that felt good.

He climbed the stairs to Mary's third-floor apartment, segueing from weightless gardening to a planet of tree kings he'd create if in charge of the universe. He opened the door to find his sister and Elizabeth's partner sitting at the dining table, sipping wine.

Mary jumped to her feet, rushed to embrace him. When Jack flinched, she drew back, looked him over carefully. She eyed the new cuts on his hands he'd gotten gardening.

"Jack?" she said. "This is Stuart. I think you've met."

Jack planted his feet to ground himself, struggled to give her his undivided attention. He glanced from her to Dr. Cohen, who had an orange lipstick mark on his cheek. A surprising color for his sister's rarely painted lips, though he saw now that it suited her, brought out the flecks of green in her eyes.

"Mary, I'm so happy for you," he said.

She told him not to be ridiculous, Stuart was just a friend, but when she touched him again, he noticed the heat of her skin.

"Hello, Jack," Stuart Cohen said. The psychiatrist got slowly to his feet, clutching the back of the chair for support. "It's good to see you. Mary was a little worried."

Jack glanced at his sister, saw the panic lines around her mouth, the salty residue of tears. Obviously, he was guilty until proven innocent, mistrusted on the basis of the things he might do. He stared confusedly at the wisteria blossoms on the ceiling. He recognized his work but couldn't remember what had possessed him to do it. He was done with flowers. On the plane, he'd been stunned by the magnitude of his misjudgment. His designs for Clyde's garden were prosaic; he'd caved in to the soft things people craved. When he returned, he would start anew, this time settling for nothing less than God's landscape, magnificent and stark, nothing fragrant or soothing, nothing too easy on the eye. Just earth and sky, rock and mud, a barrenness that brought epiphanies and tears.

He twitched with the compulsion to head back now, realized there was no reason he couldn't. The Londonbright could wait another week. Elizabeth would come to see him on the weekend. He'd tell Mary where he was going so she wouldn't worry again.

He headed toward his bedroom, saying nothing rather than risking a torrent of words. He was vaguely aware that he was going too fast; his feet were a blur, his hands still suffering a lack of gravity and reached for the ceiling. But his mind was clear. Once he started the real work in Clyde's garden, people would understand. *Architectural Digest* would come back. Offers would pour in. He'd make enough money to buy that five-acre lot in Bolinas and create a garden and nursery entirely his own.

He ignored a question from Dr. Cohen, the concerned look on his sister's face, and closed the door behind him. He grabbed a few work shirts from the closet. Mary came in as he pulled the duffel bag off the shelf.

"Mr. Jones called from the Londonbright," Mary said. "I'm sorry, Jack. They've turned the garden over to someone else."

He dropped the bag, turned. "You're not serious."

"He said it was mostly a matter of time constraints. They've got that big opening. They didn't think you'd get it done."

"Who'd they—"

"Daniel Puckerbaum's going to finish it."

Jack flinched, felt the terror of the plants as if he was heartwood himself, at the mercy of Puckerbaum's chain saw. He stared at his shirts, realized suddenly, briefly, that whenever he tried for something greater and more beautiful, he insulted what he already had.

"Your designs were wonderful. Mr. Jones told me—"

"I'm losing control," he said.

She nodded, as if this was the kind of thing brothers said all the time. *I'm losing control. I've painted wisteria on your ceiling and planted your balcony with vegetables.* She folded one of his shirts and set it neatly in the bag.

"Annie came to my store."

He glanced at the phone, imagined calling Elizabeth, asking her for something to help him calm down. He imagined the pause, then her recalibrated voice, the euphoria pinched back into guardedness. All her dreams of flight grounded.

"She seemed distraught," Mary went on. "And believe me, that's not a word I would ordinarily use to describe Annie. She wanted to warn you about something. Someone. Is everything all right?"

He almost laughed. The answer seemed as obvious as Puckerbaum's hatred of plants, but her eyes were hopeful; he could never bear to disappoint her. He'd leave before he'd let her see him crumble.

"I can't remember something," he said.

"That night."

His teeth began to chatter, and he willed them still. "I might have done something. Some man is following me."

"You need to call Annie."

He knew she was right, yet he walked into the bathroom and closed the door. He stood there for a moment, forced himself to look in the mirror. Before him was a stranger he'd shudder to meet on the street. Disheveled hair, bloodshot eyes, a twitch in the jaw. A wild man. He opened the medicine cabinet, took out the bottles of lithium he'd filled but never used.

He stuffed them in his various pockets, walked slowly back to the bedroom so he wouldn't jiggle, so Mary wouldn't hear. He zipped up the duffel bag. Mary sat on the edge of the bed.

"Where did you go this weekend?" she asked.

"Napa. The new garden."

"With your psychiatrist?" She watched him in that way of hers that was one part mother, three parts friend. Accepting but not completely oblivious to the mistakes he made.

"With Elizabeth," he said.

"She'll worry if you just take off. I'm guessing, but I imagine you don't want to do that to her."

His head hurt like crazy, like someone had gotten loose in there with a bat or a BB gun. No one deserved to be afraid of himself. No matter what he'd done, no matter what he couldn't remember, that sentence was too harsh.

"I love her," he said.

She had tears in her eyes. "You can go on medication, Jack," she said. "There's no shame in that. You can have a normal life."

He shook his head, humming yet almost out of words, losing gravity but also heavy. Exhausted. "I'd never be able to create what I do. I might be able to come up with a few pretty gardens, but I'm telling you, when you stood in the middle of them, you wouldn't hear a thing."

"Jack—"

"The man Elizabeth was with this weekend is not medicated."

"She'd want you well."

"If a normal man was all she wanted, she'd reconcile with

her husband. I know what I have to offer, Mary. A glorious summer. Three months when all the living gets done."

"I need you, Jack. Summer and winter. All the time."

He sat on the bed and wrapped his arms around her. His mind filled up with images of Superman and a Capricorn's fate to love those who were weaker. He stroked her hair, marveled at the restraint of the man in the other room who had not interrupted.

"When did you meet Dr. Cohen?" he asked.

"Just yesterday. He's miraculous."

He calmed a little, would like to go on believing in miracles. "He's sick," he said.

"Non-Hodgkin's lymphoma. He just found out. He wouldn't go to the doctor sooner. Isn't that ridiculous? A psychiatrist who doesn't know how to ask for help."

"You need to take care," he said.

She rested her chin on his shoulder. "I will. I'll take it wherever I can find it."

When Jack finally emerged from the bedroom, he found Stuart Cohen by the open window, gazing at the flat rooftops of the warehouses across the street.

"Not going to jump are you?" Jack asked.

Stuart turned around. "No," he said. "Are you?"

THE dinosaurs came to life at night, when shadows hid their wire construction. Under moonlight, their mossy hides were mistaken for fur.

Jack turned the key in the worm gate, almost hoping Puckerbaum had changed the lock. But the key turned, the door swung open, and for a moment Jack welcomed the inertia that overtook him. He imagined lying down right there and finally being still.

But the moment passed; the breeze stirred up the ivy, unveiled a spark of unrest in the garden. He opened the gate, was halfway to the T-Rex when he noticed the path beneath his feet was squishy. He squinted in the darkness, realized it was no longer a path at all. Puckerbaum had filled in Jack's burrows with tons of freshly poured concrete, fossilizing the twig thrones Jack had put inside. The man had laid a slab over gardens and amber paths alike. Jack looked behind him, made out his footprints across what looked like a giant parking lot. He stumbled out of the concrete, managed to get to the T-Rex he called Bessie, then wished the path had been blocked.

Zigzagging through Bessie's legs and around her tail was an incongruous plastic jungle gym—rings, tire swings, chain ladders and bars. A yellow curlicue slide protruded from the dinosaur's belly, landing in a pile of bark chips Puckerbaum had added, suffocating the showy pink-striped lewisia beneath. Beyond Bessie, a herd of metal picnic tables had cornered the stegosaurus; Puckerbaum had hacked the beast's bony armor to nubs. The pterodactyl had lost its exhilarating rope swing; a safer, Lego-colored model had taken over the fern grotto, was bolted to the ground.

Jack closed his eyes, tried to listen to the garden, but it was nearly silent. All the trees had gone into shock. There was only a hint of remonstrance left in the leaves, one last gasp of bewilderment. They'd been stripped of their sentience, relegated to scenery, and the fault was not Puckerbaum's. Jack was the one who'd abandoned them.

When the fury hit, he swore this time he would remember.

He memorized the flashflood of adrenaline, burned the surge of strength and mean intentions into his brain. It was pure revenge, he admitted, when he muscled free the chains on the climbing ladder. They made a delightful whooshing sound when he swung them, clunked satisfyingly against the metal picnic tables, dented plastic, severed swings with hardly any effort at all.

He swore, as he flung the chains into the freshly poured slab, that he'd remember how good the metal felt in his hands, how satisfying and easy it was to ruin things. When he ran out of ways to use the chains, he turned to his hands. He pried the plastic slide from Bessie's stomach as if it were a weed, and cried out not in triumph, but because he remembered something else. Another night, another ruined garden, another man with a cruel streak. He stumbled backwards, felt the garden staring at him blank-faced while he made out the grease on his hands and something darker, redder. While he squeezed his eyes shut and whispered, "Oh my God."

When the hand touched his shoulder, he jumped. Carl Ludwig stared at him with sad, gardener's eyes.

"Son," Carl said, "that's enough."

Jack put his face in his hands. The old man squeezed his shoulder, returned the chains to the ruined playland. Carl clucked over fallen swings and dented picnic tables as if they were babies, as if they were plants.

"No one but you would have known the difference," the old man said. "Most people don't demand so much."

"I'm sorry."

"This is no way to live," Carl said.

Jack stretched out his hands, as if he could distance himself from them, get away. "No," he said. "It isn't."

                          *   *   *

CHLOE waited beneath the covers, fully dressed in a floor-length skirt and red velvet blouse. Her mother always checked on her before she went to bed, but when she hadn't come by midnight, Chloe stuffed the bed with pillows and ignored an unexpected offense.

She opened her door soundlessly—caution that turned out to be unnecessary. Every light was on; Smashmouth blared from the living room stereo. Her mother had fallen asleep on the couch and was smiling disquietingly, hogging all the good dreams.

Chloe resisted the urge to poke her, to wake her with a sudden shriek. She was all for her mother's happiness, if Elizabeth celebrated the way other mothers her age did. With a new dress or a dishwasher. With a night out with friends instead of a weekend with an unpredictable man, with goofy Barry Manilow tunes instead of Smashmouth.

Chloe tiptoed, though it was obvious her mother was out cold, sailing along in some sappy Jack Bolton dream. She opened the door, stepped on the porch, wondered if she was dreaming, too. Their front yard, what little there was of it, had been transformed into a seascape. Between her mother's white roses were waves of blue hydrangeas and rhododendrons, foamy sprays of baby's breath and white salvia. The clematis that had never risen past the first rung of the iron trellis had been replaced with ten-foot crests of silver lace vine, gray islands of dusty miller and snow-in-summer. Two silver birch trees glittered, and another specimen sailed up the path. She was just beginning to feel afraid when Jack Bolton stuck his head out from behind the root ball.

"Don't tell," he said. "It's a surprise."

She nearly cried, until she saw he had already started. He took as little notice of the tears at the corners of his eyes as a maple tree takes of its sap.

"An elder," he said, setting in the root ball. "Not a domesticated tree by any means. It's strong, some say violent if attacked. It's said to be inhabited by witches."

She wanted to walk away, but was distracted by how far her mother's music carried, how little regard a grown woman had for the neighbors. She couldn't get over the sight of Jack Bolton's shoulders trembling while he adjusted the tree. She had thought her inability to control herself was something she would outgrow, but now she wondered if it was what she was growing into. If adults were even worse.

Jack filled the hole with soil, tamped it down. "Started your garden yet?" he asked.

She looked away, felt guiltier than she had in the principal's office, where she'd been scolded for a couple days of ditching as if she were undermining her entire future. "Not yet."

"You should. You're running out of time."

Steam flew from his mouth when he talked, the first hard evidence that, no matter what the day, summer was over. "What did you do to my mom?" she asked.

She wished she didn't sound so petulant, wished she could turn herself into whatever she wanted. A rock star. An athlete. A woman who wasn't afraid of anything. But not even her body was cooperating. Despite eating nothing, it had begun to swell up. It turned nauseous first thing in the morning.

"Is she all right?" Jack asked, looking past her.

She wrapped an arm around her stomach. "She's fine," she said. "She's great, actually."

He lifted his hand toward the window, and she noticed blood on his palms. He caught her staring, drew back his fist. "I wanted to leave the elder to guard you. The birches to remind you of summer."

He grabbed more plants, moving like a lost hummingbird, here then there, jumping at shadows, a heart pumping with fright. She realized he was little more than a stranger, and she edged toward the gate. He clutched her arm before she reached it.

"The snowdrops? Those I planted over there, the white ones with bowed heads? Those are for you."

"Mr. Bolton, I have to go."

He nodded, but didn't let go. His hand shook; every finger vibrated at its own frequency, as if he was made up of ten different songs. He looked around the garden. "I tried to do this one different. I didn't even think about making it perfect. I thought about making it right for you." He released her, ran a hand through his hair. Too many strands came out with his fingers.

"You don't sound good," she said.

"When the Angel of Sorrow breathed above the winter ground, he turned snowflakes to snowdrops. He brought the hope of spring to Eve after she was banished from Eden. He called the flowers fair maid of February."

She stared at the flowers, felt tears prick her eyes. She wanted him to read her mind and answer this question: Why couldn't she be loved? Or at least be like Jill who went on living while waiting for love to come later? Why was it better to be with a jerk than with no one at all?

"Fair maid of February," Jack said softly.

"What are you going to do?"

He picked up a fallen snowdrop and placed it in her hand. "Follow autumn. Don't worry about it."

She wasn't worried until then.

She stomped toward the gate, shoved at the latch. Who cared what he did, or who her mother loved? What did it matter whether any of them survived? But she made the mistake of turning around, hesitating one second too long. Even the most rational person in the world would have mistaken Jack for an aspen, a creature quaking from head to toe.

"You better not leave her," she said loudly. "She's, like, alive again. That's all I can say."

His body rocked forward and back, his head from side to side. He didn't know which way he was going, that was the trouble. "Don't tell her I've gone," he said. "Let her savor the garden. The last of summer. It's almost cruel how short a season it is. Shorter than all the rest no matter what the calendar says. It's hard to get everything in. Some plants don't even have a chance to establish themselves before the first chill comes."

She looked down the road, where she wanted to go but wasn't wanted, then walked back into the garden. She slipped her hand into Jack's. His palms were warm and soft with dirt. She wanted him to stop crying more than anything in this world.

She rose on tiptoes and kissed his cheek. "I don't think you're crazy at all."

She ran out of the garden. Ran as fast as she could, not pausing for second thoughts, not taking a single deep breath to clear her mind. Ran all the way to Skitch's house, where she climbed the trellis and knocked on his bedroom window.

He wasn't sleeping. He opened the window only a crack. "Go home, Chloe," he said, almost like a sigh.

The Angel of Sorrow had needed magic to turn winter into spring, but all she required was time. Patience. When she got home, she'd plant every seed Jack had given her; she'd build a greenhouse, if necessary, to give the plants what they needed to grow.

"I'm pregnant," she said.

THE group expanded to Tuesday, Tiu's day, the day devoted to heavens and war. Before Louis Fields opened the door of the doctor's office, he suffered an echo of what he'd seen before— Swedish furniture, shades of mauve and gray. It was a faint recollection, but he guessed there'd be a fish tank. Inside he found it well-stocked and bubbling. Inside he predicted six chairs would line the walls of the waiting room and he counted exactly that many.

He was sure it wasn't the first chill down his back.

The room was empty except for a slim, blond girl sitting in the corner, chewing on her fingernail, and he didn't bother to reach for his notepad. He already knew her name.

"Kayla," he said, and she looked up, smiled tentatively. The receptionist's desk was unstaffed, but Louis didn't report the incident to Colonel Xavier. He was more interested in the moisture at the corners of Kayla's eyes, the way she sat curled forward like a deflated C, hands stuffed between her knees, her hair oddly crooked.

He walked across the room, sat beside her, not too close. He glanced once more at the door, made sure they were alone, then began a song from his youth, one of the few he remembered fully. A silly song about a cowboy and his trusty dog. Halfway through he realized his voice was deeper than it ought to be, and he fell silent. By the time Kayla slid closer, he was stunned to realize he loved her without any notes at all.

"I cut my hair," she said. She ran her fingers through the uneven strands, the right side cropped to the ear, the left hanging at a forty-five-degree angle from chin to neck. It wouldn't matter what she did to herself, he would still love her, and this knowledge comforted him like a road in an unfamiliar jungle, a path he could, in a panic, follow out.

"It looks good," he said. "Edgy."

Her eyes widened, then began to leak tears. He was not shocked by this, as if she'd cried many times before, though he couldn't remember the reasons, and thought perhaps she couldn't remember them either. Sadness was a lot like amnesia, he imagined. It grew on you after a while, receded into background scenery rather than the details up front. It was easier to live with than to change.

The phone rang, but no one emerged to answer it. He reached for Kayla's hand, and she didn't pull away. She smelled of indoor things, of soap and scented sheets, dusty books and last night's spaghetti, spiderwebs and leather and lavender potpourri.

"I don't know what I do in the army," he said.

The ringing stopped, then a few seconds later began anew. He met her gaze, struggled to hold onto the moment, to not forget what had led him here. He took a chance and cupped her face with his hands.

"You're not a soldier," she said. "You're forty-five. You live at a home for people with mental disabilities."

He didn't blink, though his hands began to tremble, and if he'd wanted to he could have squeezed her cheeks until she cried out. He could have hurt her and forgotten the crime an instant later, not been held accountable for it, but he pressed his forehead to hers and closed his eyes.

"Shit," he said.

The door flew open and a young woman in a miniskirt burst in. Louis dropped his hands while the red-haired woman dashed to the phone, answered it brusquely, put whoever it was on hold. He glanced around the room, didn't recognize the walls but predicted six chairs would be there, and when he counted them he saw he was right. He remembered Kayla, didn't have to ask her who'd butchered her hair.

"Holy Toledos," the receptionist said. "You would not believe who I found glued together in the stairwell. Whoee."

She laughed, tossed back her flamboyant hair, went to the far door and knocked loudly. A few seconds later, the door opened and a woman in slacks and a cream-colored sweater stepped out.

"Aren't the others—"

The receptionist leaned forward, whispered something in her ear. Louis watched the woman's face closely, saw surprise quickly masked by a forced smile. "Well," she said. "Let's give them a few minutes."

She smiled at Louis and Kayla, opened her door wide. Kayla glanced at him, her eyebrows raised as if she'd just asked him a question and was expecting an answer. If he'd told her he loved her, he couldn't remember her response.

Kayla took a seat in the corner of the office. He wanted to sit by her, but didn't know if he was welcome. He opted to approach the desk, introduce himself to the woman with the cream-colored sweater. "Louis Fields," he said. "You must be General Xavier's sister."

The woman shook his hand and smiled. "I'm Dr. Shreve, actually," she said. "I want to talk to you about a job."

He glanced at Kayla, who was looking at him strangely. Head cocked, as if she'd just spotted a contradiction in him, a grimace when he professed to not be in pain.

"I have a friend who needs help in her preschool," the doctor said. "She runs a program for two- to five-year-olds. It's a well-respected school in Mill Valley, close to your . . . residence. A lot of the kids come from single-parent households. I think it would do wonders for them to have a consistent man in their lives."

"I have a job, ma'am," he said.

"Yes," she said, "but I'd like you to consider a change in profession. It would give you a chance to really do some good. It might suit you better than the Army, in fact. You know kids. They can't concentrate on anything longer than a few minutes. They're lovely that way. No time matters except right now."

Kayla moved behind him, as quiet and insubstantial as her shadow. He felt the weight of all those notes in his pocket, the ones he no longer needed. The ones that told him her name and age, but not what she thought of him. The ones that described her suicide attempt and the medications that followed, but not whether he eased her pain at all. She moved closer and he thought if she touched him, he might burst into tears. When she laid her hand on his shoulder, it was almost unbearable.

"Yes," he said, his voice hardly rising above a whisper. "All right."

"Wonderful," the doctor said. "Let me call Gail right now."

When Blanche Armstrong walked into the office on the arm of her lover, she noticed Kayla's hand on Louis's shoulder first thing. Had they all been seduced by this last gasp of summer, by some aphrodisiac houseplant Jack Bolton had stashed in the room? Her own blouse was still untucked and she struggled to fix it; she smoothed down her suddenly freewheeling gray hair. Gary's shirt was unbuttoned to the waist, and she wondered what would happen if she ran her fingers down his chest right in front of them. If they'd cringe or get caught up in the same notion she had, that at this point anything was possible.

The doctor's receptionist, Carrie, had found them on the stairwell, their pants around their ankles, the rock beats of their chests in sync. Carrie had been shocked into silence for a moment, then she laughed. Blanche tried to wriggle away, but Gary held her firmly, shielded her with his body and for once used his swearing for an appropriate purpose, to tell Carrie Willis to fuck off.

He'd pleaded with Blanche to stop crying, kissed her until she moaned through her tears. Whenever he twitched, he sent shivers down her body in anticipation of what he might use those marvelous gyrations for next. "Now," he said, after Carrie rushed off, "where were we?"

Blanche had not been planning to seduce him, didn't really think that she could. She'd heard him coming up the stairs behind her, banging out a rock song on the metal railing, so full of life and neurotransmitters she wanted to take him inside herself and see if she lit up. When he smiled at her, she felt sixteen years old and as pretty as a prom queen. Sliding her hand beneath his shirt was the whim of a girl who'd had three dates to the homecoming dance and divvied them up by the hour.

He didn't immediately pull away, for which Blanche would

always be grateful. He widened his eyes, which was to be expected, and looked at her as if she might be suffering an allergic reaction to one of Dr. Shreve's abundant medications. She laughed, brushed her fingers across his nipples.

"I didn't get good at making love until I hit forty," she said. "By then, my husband had moved on to golf."

He swallowed, which was lovely. He had one of those darling Adam's apples, which expanded to twice its size when he twitched. His left hand went flying and she grabbed it in midair, pulled it to her breasts, which were as ugly as pickles now but still capable of alarming amounts of pleasure. She hated every inch of her body, from the chicken skin above her ankles to the piggy folds beneath her chin, but loathing didn't stop moisture from pooling between her legs. Self-disgust didn't come close to stifling the moans that slid out when he squeezed her breast.

"Blanche," he said, and she kissed him on the cheek to silence him. She'd rather hear curses than her old-fashioned name.

"Close your eyes," she said, but he wouldn't. He tapped her back as if she were an exotic instrument he might have been born to play.

"I'm not very good," he said, and she was the one to close her eyes, so he wouldn't see her gratitude, or how desire looked on a woman her age. His hands strummed her back while he kissed her, and until Carrie Willis broke them up it was like getting back a year with every note. Like being reintroduced to the music of her youth.

She waited until the doctor hung up the phone, then marched to the desk. "Whatever's wrong with Gary has rhythm," she said. "You can't take that away."

"Hello, Blanche," Dr. Shreve said.

"Just because he doesn't tiptoe through life the way you do doesn't make him a freak."

Gary put a hand on her back and she realized she was shouting. She hadn't stopped crying since Carrie had found them and there were tears all down her cheeks. Dr. Shreve came around the desk with a tissue.

"No one ever said that," she said softly.

"Where's Jack?" Gary asked.

"He's not coming. He fired me."

She smiled when she said this, and Blanche's ears began to ring. The air conditioning that usually ran fullforce in the office had been turned off, replaced by something high-pitched, the hum of sudden and unexpected desire. She would always remember the thrumming of Gary's fingers on her back, she would hear his music in her sleep. And she knew this would have to be enough.

She sat on the couch. She'd had energy to burn ten minutes ago but now she felt her age and ten years more. She had no desire to talk about her problems, to let the group know she had seduced a twenty-two-year-old and he'd been sweet enough to let her. Gary would be kind, she was certain, when he told her this was never, ever, going to happen again.

She closed her eyes when Kayla spoke at nearly full volume about her compulsion to cut her hair, the walk she'd taken all the way to the corner. Louis ranted about the Army, didn't show much surprise when the doctor reminded him he'd agreed to change jobs. Blanche tensed while she waited for Gary to speak, then finally opened her eyes.

She found him sitting beside her, waiting for her to look at him. His smile gave her goose bumps. Sent her flying back another ten years.

"There's this woman," he said, and the hum in the room got so loud it was a wonder she could hear him. A marvel, really, that she took in every word he said.

TWELVE

ELIZABETH was fairly sure the group was meeting without her. Not only in stairwells but at coffee shops. Like teenagers who must gather in private to say anything of consequence.

She pretended not to see the hand-holding, feigned placidity when today's discussion kept regressing to sex. She saw them out, two by two, then closed the door to her office.

She called Mary's apartment but got only the answering machine. It had been two days since she'd seen Jack, and this morning she had started to feel edgy. As if everything might magically, horribly, revert to the way it was before.

She searched her Palm Pilot for the phone number of the Londonbright, had her hand on the phone when Stuart opened the door.

"Have you heard from Jack Bolton since Sunday?" he asked.

She might have reached for the chair to steady herself if

Stuart hadn't needed it more. He lowered himself carefully into the seat, swiped at a bead of sweat on his upper lip.

"Are you all right?" She touched his shoulder, felt a bone through the fabric of his sweater.

"I've got cancer, actually," he said, smiling. "I start chemo tomorrow."

Elizabeth stared at him, then knelt by the chair, took his hands in hers. "Oh, Stuart," she said.

"Not to worry. It'll all be all right. We'll talk about it later, but right now there's Jack. I was at his sister's on Sunday. He was peaking. Rambling and obviously suffering compulsions. He looked ready to crash."

She noticed now what she should have before—beneath Stuart's aftershave was a scent like Clyde's garden, the part too moldy and wet to plant in after the storm. "You and Mary Bolton?" she asked.

He laughed. "You and Jack."

She smiled back at him. "How did you—"

"She came by here looking for you. Jack's wife had been to see her. She was concerned Jack might be losing control."

She tensed the way she would at the top of a roller coaster, just before a monster drop.

"Jack's fine," she said. "Don't you think I'd know it if he was deteriorating?" Just like she should have known about Stuart's illness. "Don't you think I'd know it better than anybody else?"

"Elizabeth—"

"And if he has crossed some line, who's to say love can't cure him?"

"Honey," he said, his eyes sad. The eyes of a psychiatrist who has spent a lifetime with the delusional. "Mary's pretty worried. She hasn't seen him since Sunday night."

She stood, turning away like one of her patients who refused to suffer the truth. "He'd call me if anything happened."

"Let's go talk to Mary," Stuart said.

He had to grip her hand to stand. They walked slowly past his office, where the window was open and a cold breeze had scattered his session notes across the room. She shook her head, let go of him to close the window.

"I want you to think about something," he said. "Not whether or not love can cure him, but whether love, in his state, can be real."

She might have taken offense if she hadn't gotten sidetracked by the imprint of a sneaker tread on the sill. She ran her fingers over the scuff mark, closed the window, refused to think about a life without him. "I want *you* to think a little harder about taking care of yourself," she said. "You keep leaving the window open and you'll get weak enough to fly away."

She turned back in time to find him smiling. "Oh, Elizabeth," he said. "Wouldn't *that* be something?"

She shook her head, helped him down to her car. Half an hour later, they pulled up in front of Banned Books, a store wedged so tightly between a delicatessen and shoe repair shop its foundation had buckled. The front porch was losing bricks like baby teeth. Inside, the light was dim, the racks dusty, the air striated with layers of leather and incense and marijuana.

The books were ranked and shelved according to the number of banned lists they'd made, with *The Satanic Verses* and *Lady Chatterly's Lover* still holding the top spots. Stuart led her through a narrow aisle of heinous children's literature, subversive titles like *Watership Down, The Chronicles of Narnia*, and *Peter Rabbit*. At the counter, Mary Bolton sat creating an astrological chart that looked like a child's dot-to-dot. A joint burned in the ashtray beside her. Stuart raised his brow but didn't comment.

"Mary," Elizabeth said, "it's good to see you again. Stuart mentioned Jack seemed a bit keyed up on Sunday. How's he been since then?"

Mary stood heavily, her usually serene brown eyes full of worry. "I have no idea. I haven't seen him."

Elizabeth noticed more scents now—cinnamon-spiced coffee, the closed-up cabin smell of Mary's wool poncho, a girl's imitation Georgio perfume still nosing through the witchcraft section. She opened her purse, took out her Palm Pilot. Once more, she found the number for the Londonbright, used Mary's phone to call the curator, Philip Jones. She got his secretary, was put on hold while Mary picked up the joint and smoked it, looking Stuart right in the eye.

When Philip Jones came on the line, he didn't hesitate. "If Jack comes near here, I'll press charges."

Elizabeth closed her eyes. "What happened?"

"You're telling me you're unaware of what happened Sunday night, when Jack Bolton destroyed a good portion of the garden? Come on, Dr. Shreve. I find that hard to believe."

After their time in Napa, so did Elizabeth. After what she'd started to hope for, it was almost too much to bear. "Is he all right?" she asked softly.

"I wouldn't know. My immediate concern is ten thousand dollars worth of damage to my play equipment and two thousand square feet of ruined concrete. Jack Bolton may claim to be a gardener, but so far all I've seen is a man who destroys whatever he professes to love."

Elizabeth dropped her shoulders, opened her eyes. "I'm sorry," she said. Sorry for the garden and Philip Jones and herself, but mostly for Jack, who had needed her more than she needed him, and who had been ignored.

"I had to fire him," Jones said, softer now. "I admire his work, and I sympathized with his quest for perfection, but I had a board to report to. A garden to open. If he'd just finished what he started, none of this would have happened. Frankly, I thought version one was the best."

"He loses faith in himself," she said.

"So does every artist. The profession requires you to fake it. Do the best job you can, then pray it's better than you think."

"Let me know if he shows up," Elizabeth said. "Please."

She tried Clyde Cummings's number next, wasn't surprised when the housekeeper told her Jack had not been seen since Sunday. She gripped Mary's hand, told her what had happened.

"He's disappeared before," Mary said quietly. "A couple of times. He took off on a sudden road trip to Santa Barbara and forgot to call. He ended up once in Reno. Annie might know where to look."

Stuart put a hand on Elizabeth's arm, but jealousy was a luxury of peacetime. Mary gave her Annie's number, but the phone just rang and rang. Elizabeth replaced the receiver, leaned heavily against the counter.

Mary slid open the top drawer of her desk, took out a brown leather journal. "Maybe you should read this," she said.

Elizabeth caught the gentle gaze Stuart usually bestowed on women patients who swore their husbands wouldn't cheat, on mothers who refused to believe their teenagers took drugs. She snatched the book, opened it to find Mary's entries.

August 25

Jack laughs at my worries, tells me he's fine. It's impossible to reason with a man who gets so much done. His gardens are flourishing and the phone rings at least twice a day with pleas for his work. He swears he's never been happier, but it's a shore leave kind of happiness—frantic, undiscriminating, and drunken, full of things he'll want to forget. Last night he admitted he slipped back to Annie's. Tore out the water garden and replaced it with zinnias. Three hundred, all orange, so that on the next foggy day, she'd have sun. She'd have what he couldn't give her, the same thing day after day, a garden without moods. He expects the plants to do too much.

August 27

This morning, I woke to zinnias, too. Planted in my teacups, my Pyrex, covering the balcony which was lined during the night with my favorite magazines and four inches of potting soil. And I'm not the only one. Zinnias are now growing on my neighbors' porches, in city-maintained medians, spilling from store baskets which used to display vegetables. Stuffed into mailboxes, now mini-greenhouses.

Mrs. Forester nearly beat down my door with her cane. Said two dozen of her heirloom roses were viciously murdered, and she wanted my crazy brother locked up.

August 28

Jack removed all the zinnias, replaced them with succulents. Said the orange was making him sick.

August 28 - night

Woke to thumping. I came into the living room to find all the pots overturned, and Jack pacing. He was afraid there was already too much concrete in the city, that no matter how much greenery he brought in, it would not be enough. He thought he ought to go to Africa, where there was more land to work with. Within the hour, he was on the Internet searching for tickets; it was a full-fledged plan. I had to bring up his jobs, the gardens, his responsibilities, the bills he was mounting and needed to pay. I had no idea he'd respond so dramatically, that he could lose so much enthusiasm so fast. I didn't think caring about something could make him so sad. I felt like I spoiled his adventure. After he went to work, I cleaned the living room, was too tired to open the store. I went to bed and had the worst nightmare in full daylight. I was Annie, in love with someone I couldn't make happy.

The entries went on, but Elizabeth couldn't read anymore. She closed the journal, gave the book back to Mary.

"I don't know who this man is," Mary said, "but he's not my brother. I wanted to show him that."

Elizabeth shook her head, both for Jack and for herself. "Of course he's Jack. An exaggerated version, perhaps, but still the same at heart."

"He wouldn't read it," Mary said, "and I can understand why. No one wants to admit he's losing his mind."

Elizabeth couldn't speak, couldn't find even a single word to defend him, which seemed almost as bad a betrayal as failing to treat him in the first place.

"He courts madness," Stuart said. "Some people do."

Mary nodded. "He believes it inspires his gardening. And it's true, he didn't get the big jobs, the botanical garden and museums, until his designs turned more avant-garde, until he became more . . . flamboyant. Maybe madness *is* the fountain of creativity, but it's a fountain of wildfire. It creates a masterpiece, but in the process the source is destroyed. Is Jack supposed to sacrifice himself to give us something beautiful to look at, or is he the beautiful thing we should be trying to keep?"

Elizabeth looked toward the window, covered by shades with a beaded fringe. "He thinks I'm brave," she said.

Stuart put his arm around her. "You are, Beth."

She shook her head. "I'm irresponsible. I never should have let him off the medication."

Mary shook her head. "Don't kid yourself. You didn't have the power to stop him. Sometimes I think it's the sanest thing he does, refusing to take your drugs. He'd go as far as ruining himself to prove he's still got free will."

"But Mary," Elizabeth said, "he doesn't."

Mary sat down wearily, tucked her braid over her shoulder. Her eyes were brown, more almond shaped than her brother's, but somewhere in them Elizabeth saw a glimmer of Jack, of what Jack could be. Brilliant *and* serene.

"I've got to find him," Elizabeth said.

By the time she got home, Chloe was doing homework in front of the television, trying to write an essay while watching *Entertainment Tonight*. Elizabeth snapped off the set, expecting the usual grumble, but Chloe had turned an ominous shade of green. She ran into the bathroom and slammed the door.

Elizabeth stood perfectly still the way she had as a child, whenever her mother's voice began to rise. She had this irrational but comforting notion that if she didn't move, time could not go forward; disaster would pace in the wings. She was the playwright, as long as she didn't breathe.

She stood there until Chloe emerged from the bathroom, eyes on the carpet, palm against her stomach.

"That flu," Chloe mumbled. "It's going around school."

Elizabeth had raced home to make more calls, to comfort herself with action, but now all forward motion stopped. They both tried not to breathe.

"Baby," Elizabeth said.

"Dad called. He's staying in some hotel now, doesn't care what it costs him. He's, like, looking for a new house."

"Let's not talk about your dad. Are you all right?"

"Sure."

"How's Skitch?"

Chloe widened her eyes to keep from crying. "We broke up."

Elizabeth stepped forward, surprisingly unrelieved. She tried to want only what was best for her daughter, but sometimes got it confused with what Chloe wanted for herself. "I'm so sorry, honey," she said.

Chloe shrugged. "Whatever."

"What happened? Did he—"

"I don't want to talk about it, all right?"

Elizabeth tried to catch her eye. "Is there anything I can—"

"No."

Elizabeth rubbed the back of her neck. "Will you let me know if you want to talk?" Chloe shrugged, which Elizabeth took as a yes. "I'm going to be making some calls. A patient of mine is missing."

Chloe rubbed her sleeve against the corner of her eye, swiped one rebellious drop. "You mean Jack?"

Elizabeth wondered if there was some conspiracy to ensure she was the last person to know everything, or if she somehow sought out ignorance. If every mother and lover did. "You know about Jack?"

Chloe stared at her feet, and Elizabeth noticed a notch cut out of her hair, a quarter-sized circle shaved down to the scalp. She couldn't tear her gaze from it, found it as horrifying as a self-inflicted burn mark or razor cuts up the inside of Chloe's arm. A hundred questions bombarded her, but she focused on the one that hurt the most: What had she done so wrong that her daughter now loathed herself?

She took Chloe's arm, pulled her down on the sofa beside her. "Talk to me," she said. "Now."

When Chloe hesitated, the answer became clear. Elizabeth had done everything wrong. Smothered her, ignored her, worked during her formative years, spoiled her with toys and videos when she should have gotten down on the floor and taught her something worthwhile—the strategy of chess or how to crochet, skills she didn't have herself but ought to have mastered for her daughter's sake. She'd made a hundred million mistakes, just like any mother, and none but the truly hurtful ones mattered. Chloe was like any girl; she grew up and tried to ruin herself. If she survived, she'd become an adult.

"Chloe?"

"I'm fine, Mom. Just feeling a little sick."

"How did you know about Jack?"

Chloe breathed a sigh of relief at the change of subject. "I saw him," she said. "The other night. He was here when I . . . I went out for a walk, and he was in the garden."

"In the garden."

"He planted those snowdrops for me."

Elizabeth had pictured Jack working outside her window while she slept, planting a sea of flowers just for her. She had thought the pinnacle of love was to be a man's sole object of affection, but now appreciated how much better it was to find a man who loved what she loved, a man so full of emotion, he had love to spare.

"Did he say where he was going? How did he seem when you saw him?"

"He didn't tell me anything. And if you're asking if he was acting crazy, the answer is no. I mean, if he *is* crazy, then turning ivy into dinosaurs is the work of a madman. Looking for company in a deserted garden is a sign of lunacy. Loving anyone who isn't guaranteed to love you back would just be dumb."

Elizabeth spotted more wayward tears in her daughter's eyes, and she gathered her in her arms. She held her until Chloe could no longer stem them, and neither could she. She had no idea how other mothers stayed dry-eyed while their children cried. She couldn't separate Chloe's misery from her own; she didn't even want to. At this point, it might be the only thing they shared.

She helped Chloe to bed, tucked her in on one side while she got in on the other. She stared down at that exposed chunk of scalp, kissed the tender skin.

"Why'd you do this?" Elizabeth asked. "Your hair is so beautiful."

"I don't know."

Elizabeth stroked her daughter's hair until Chloe's breathing evened out, waited half an hour before saying, "You can tell me anything." It was the truth, but truth always had consequences. In any case, Chloe was already asleep.

*   *   *

IN Idaho, all the gardening was done. The same storm that decimated Clyde's garden stalled over Boise and blackened tomatoes on the vine. The maples that lined the streets around the
capitol building lost their leaves in a day, a full month early, after a series of ferocious winds. The brown inversion, which usually didn't block the sun and seal the cold into the valley until
December, had already sunk over rooftops, obscuring views of
the Boise foothills, which were frosted with two inches of rare
September snow.

Jack walked along the Boise River, which ran like a defiant
slither of wilderness through the vibrant capital city and was
now edged with ice. The walking path took him over bridges,
past the university, through a grove of bruised cottonwoods,
their late growth black and wilted. Everyone who passed him
smiled and said hello, seemed to take him for someone familiar.
He heard snippets of conversations about the BSU Broncos and
the rare and exciting prospect of opening the local ski resort in
October, but apparently the locals were used to bad luck and ugly
weather. No one said a word about the omission of autumn.

If he'd still been suffering from grandiose thinking, he might
have imagined he'd brought on the cold himself. He'd stood in
the United terminal at SFO, looking for a flight north, anywhere
that led to winter. All other compulsions were dead. He'd left
Elizabeth's garden before he could act on his second thoughts,
change the imperfect placement of the candytuft against the sim-
ilarly shaped white mums. He left wishing the plants wouldn't
shriek at him so much. He considered flying to Africa, driving to
Clyde's, then finally hit on the one destination that might give

him some peace. A place where the plants had gone quiet for the year.

He picked the flight to Boise because it was leaving in twenty minutes. Once on the plane, he drew the shade, refused to watch the sunlight hit the bay or the inveterate windsurfers wringing a few more hours from summer. He had not packed a jacket or sweater, was chilled by nothing more than the recirculated air streaming out of the tiny nozzle above his head. He read an article in the in-flight magazine touting the majesty and ferociousness of the River of No Return Wilderness, but when he got to the rental car agency, the clerk told him the roads into the area were already inaccessible, buried under a season's worth of snow in one massive storm.

He asked where he could find someplace quiet, and the man directed him, surprisingly, to the heart of town, Julia Davis Park. Jack parked beside the rose garden, where pink medallions and the lavish orange Montezuma had been frozen in perfect, full bloom. By the time he reached the low, tame river, he was shivering. He walked a mile, found a secluded spot amongst the cottonwoods, and sat on the ground. He took the five bottles of pills from his pockets, set them out in a row.

He could hear Elizabeth eight hundred miles away, or maybe anyone on the verge of hurting another can imagine what they would say. That the shame lay not in the illness, but in refusing to try to get better. That today's drugs were marvels, specific and well-aimed. Only the fears and phobias would be affected; his work, his creativity, his soul would remain untouched, as safe as black boxes found later among the wreckage. He had to trust her now, just as she had trusted him.

He looked at the golden leaves two-inches thick on the

ground, but saw Elizabeth's face—a copper glint to her brown eyes, lips shaded almost exactly the color of fuchsias and shaped like bows, the unusual vertical dimple on the right side of her mouth but not the left. He realized she'd grown brighter while he'd known her. Her season was not summer at all; they were separated by no more than a few months. He was struck by how his desire for her did not diminish even when his interest in everything else, including living, did.

He twisted off each safety cap. Suicide, they say, is not a solitary act. It's aggressive. Violent. There is no difference between someone who takes his own life and a suicide bomber who blows himself up on a crowded bus. There are always casualties—fatalities and the injured, innocent bystanders who can't get over it.

He understood this, and when it didn't move him much he poured out the pills and counted them. He felt heavy, nearly incapacitated, as if all his ideas, compulsions, and plans had been sitting in water inside him, slowly absorbing everything he had.

He didn't fear the repercussions of his actions. He was a gardener, so he could destroy what he had to, and withstand guilt. The only thing that bothered him was frailty; the things that, no matter how well you tended them, wouldn't flourish. He'd loved a woman at the height of summer and couldn't bear to disappoint her in the fall. He was a secret sympathizer of annuals, who disappeared in winter rather than hanging on, weak.

This first frost was mild, not even fatal to the thick grasses by the river, yet it chilled him to the bone. Last year, he'd been taken by surprise by the slow bleeding of his energy and enthusiasm; by the time he recognized his grimness and inertia, he was too drained to act. This year he was not so lucky. Imagining the dullness of winter was probably worse than living through it, but he'd been running on nothing but imagination for months.

He tallied twenty pills per bottle, one hundred sure to do the trick. He'd prefer magic and metaphor, a grand exit like the one engineered by Baucis and Philemon, who convinced Zeus to turn them into an oak and a linden tree, so they wouldn't have to live without each other. Baucis and Philemon, who eased their way into oblivion with their arms wrapped around each other, who were probably still intertwined to this day. Jack could imagine a hundred deaths as romantic and grand, but the real horror of slipping from mania to depression was the acknowledgment that most of what he thought about was just fantasy. Most of what he hoped for would never be.

A group of cyclists whizzed along the greenbelt path behind him, sending shock waves through the underbrush, tugging the last of the blackened leaves from the trees. The plants indeed did not shriek here. In fact, he had to struggle to hear anything at all. He spent half an hour just isolating the sounds of the clover snuggling beneath a blanket of leaves, the wild yarrow crackling from frostbite. He wondered if the hallucinations associated with mania had come early and now were spent, if the harsh truth was that he was nothing but a lonely and absurd plant ventriloquist, trying to keep himself company. He pressed his palms to his eyes, listened harder. Even the river seemed muted, thickened; the fallen leaves slowed the current like molten gold. He began to shake in earnest when he found himself alone in his mind.

He listened to the silence until he couldn't stand it, then as a hater of frailty, he listened more. Beyond the unbearable lay a true, immobilizing exhaustion. He dropped his hands, lay back and looked at the silhouette of branches, the sky not quite as somber as he'd thought, but made up of a dozen shades of brown. Beyond the unbearable, the solitude he'd feared was absolute and indifferent, in some ways a reprieve. There was nothing to listen to, no reason to move. He realized he'd never lived anywhere there was a true change of seasons, never raked the leaves and allowed himself a month of visual splendor, never cut the perennials to the ground and called it a day. He'd avoided snow and deciduous plants, assuming he couldn't bear to see creatures bowing their heads to darkness or struggling to stay alive. Now, beyond the unbearable lay what truly couldn't be endured—not, as he'd thought, the surrender and quiet that come before death, but the noise that rises up in its aftermath. The bereft breathing of the people left behind.

He looked toward the rumpled foothills, squinted through the brown haze to make out their pine-capped peaks. That article had been nothing but hyperbole. All rivers had no return; even the tamest led somewhere different. He had imagined a vast, cursed wilderness, would have been disappointed, no doubt, to drive up north and find condominiums, accountants in V-necked sweaters chipping on the golf course. A name provided a certain mystique, a sometimes frightening exoticness, but once it rolled off the tongue a few times it became common. River of No Return. Insanity. Bipolar.

Another cheerful Boisean hummed while she walked along the river path, then stopped abruptly behind him. "Do you need help?" she asked, stepping into the brush. "Are you hurt?"

He sat up, swiping the leaves off his shoulders. *Yes,* he thought. "I'm all right," he said. "I'm fine."

He waited for her to go. Beyond the unendurable, waiting was as good a day's work as any. It might even be the best. His senses were diminishing; he was gradually, surprisingly, adjusting to the cold. He waited more, let a moment pass without making a single decision, like a molten-gold river himself, slowing down but also gleaming. Then he reached for the pills, and took just one.

Elizabeth realized her mistake within seconds.

"I'm trying to find out if a friend of mine bought a ticket on your airline," she said.

"I'm sorry. We can't give out our manifests." The man on the other end of the line was polite but firm.

"I understand, but I'm this man's psychiatrist and I fear—"

"Hold on."

In less than a minute, another man, grimmer voiced, came on the line.

"This is Tom Glass, head of airport security. I'll need a name, ma'am, possible destination. Why don't you give me a summary of your patient's condition? Worst-case scenario."

Elizabeth closed her eyes. She was all for heightened security, background checks, whatever it took to keep people safe. She was as scared as anyone, but a life of worst-case scenarios hardly seemed like a life worth living.

"No, I don't think so," she said. "Never mind."

"Ma'am, this is a security issue now. If you think there's a man on board a plane who might be a danger to himself or to others, it's your duty to report it."

"I never said he was a danger," she said. "He's a patient of mine, and he left without telling me where he was going. I merely wanted to follow up, make sure he was all right."

"In this climate, I really think—"

"Thank you."

She hung up quickly, let out her breath. She'd called everyone she could think of, twenty of Jack's previous clients, the members of her Tuesday/Thursday group. She was prepared to hire a private detective; she'd fly to Africa if it would answer Mary's question definitively enough. Jack's gardens would go to seed without him. There was never a doubt the treasure was him.

She had a few email addresses Mary had given her, and she turned on the computer, stood there frustrated while her ancient PC attempted to connect to the Internet. The front door swung open suddenly and Will stepped in, key in hand. Fed up, she stomped across the room and snatched it from him. She tossed the key across the room, watched it slide into oblivion behind the desk.

"What are you doing here?" she asked.

"Chloe called me from school."

"Did she ditch again?"

"No. She was worried about you."

Elizabeth looked at him disbelievingly. "Well, I'm fine. You didn't have to come all the way over. Don't you have patients?"

"I canceled."

"You canceled?"

"I was worried, too."

"Worried?"

"Beth, this is a rather slow-moving conversation."

He wore chinos, which she hadn't seen him in for years. Brown loafers and a striped seersucker shirt, as if dressing for a leisurely day at the beach.

"Chloe told me you're concerned about that patient of yours," he said. "Jack Bolton."

Elizabeth saw the tic in his jaw, but she ignored it. She sat at the computer, cursed her slow modem, which had already tried to connect three times and now seemed to wail its frustration. Eeeeeeee-augh, eeeeeeeee-augh. Will stood behind her, so close she felt his breath on her neck.

Elizabeth shoved back her chair. She turned to face him, was infuriated by the tenderness in his eyes. "That's not fair," she said.

"What isn't? You falling in love with someone you shouldn't, or me falling in love with you now?"

She sank back to the chair. She was connected now, but she just stared at the screen.

"I'm sorry, Beth," he said.

She shrugged. It seemed exactly fitting that he was sorry for loving her now, but unapologetic for stopping short in their marriage. She was amazed he could know so much about her, yet not know that if he wanted to save anything, to spark passion, he would have to say more than that.

He remained silent, fidgeted with the pockets on his chinos, apparently surprised to find Velcro on the inside.

"It's too late," she said.

She heard him struggle for breath, and instead of enjoying the moment the way she did in her dreams, she squinted to make out the computer screen through her tears. She punched in Internet messaging, was once again stuck waiting for a connection.

"I thought . . . I thought I should have been happier," he said. "That something else would make me happier. I'd work all day and come home and feel like an outsider. You had Chloe. I didn't fit. I blamed that on you when I should have seen the fault in myself. But I *do* see that now. People change, Beth. You, of all people, should know that."

She clutched her hands in her lap. It simply wasn't in his character to pull her to her feet or kiss her when she hadn't yet consented. He didn't believe in taking liberties, coaxing love out of season the way you'd coax a tender calla lily to bloom indoors in January. He didn't know she'd been spoiled.

"I've got to find Jack," she said.

He knelt down beside her, covered her hands with his own. She opened her eyes and immediately wished she hadn't. He was the same man she'd been married to for fifteen years, the one she'd been desperate to keep. A black-thumbed, confused, subdued but ultimately good-hearted man, and it was an insult to want him to be different.

"I'm cutting back my practice," he said. "I'll have more time for you and Chloe. This time, I swear, I'm going to—"

"Will," she said. "Don't."

He studied her face. For a moment, she imagined he would run his fingers through her hair, see what could be coaxed, but then he stood up.

"I see," he said.

"Will." She stood up after him. The computer disconnected her. She put her hand on his arm.

"It's all right," he said, disengaging himself. "I just wanted to let you know how I felt. It was important that I tell you." He was already walking toward the door, giving up.

"You call that a plea?" she called after him. "You expect me to come back for that?" She shook her head. "You haven't changed one bit. You still expect me to do all the fighting. You still expect to come through love clean."

He stopped, and when she saw his face she knew she might alter his thinking a bit, but she'd never really change him. He'd always demand perfection in himself and others, he'd always need just a little more than what she had, yet he'd stumbled into a singular act of bravery, the most tantalizing thing he could do. He had dared to love her again when there was little chance she would love him back.

She crossed the room. When she leaned in, he widened his eyes like an awkward boy chosen first for softball. His surprise made her bolder, perhaps, than she ought to have been. She used her tongue to part his lips, her teeth to coax desire. She kissed him until he kissed her back, until she was no longer someone he could give up on so easily. Until she was his one regret.

She pulled back, flushed and full, like an aster just beginning to get its color. A flower not fully formed until the fall.

"There," she said. "That's how it's done."

"How what's done? A kiss or a reconciliation? Beth, I don't understand."

She was saved from explanations by a knock on the door. She gave Will a moment to stop her, to ask her to ignore the knocking so they could go on, but he remained silent. She crossed the room, yanked open the door, would always regret the moment it took to remember Jack had been missing. The hesitation before she fell into his arms.

"Oh my God," she said. "I thought you were lost."

Jack hesitated, too, before he returned her embrace, glanced at Will before he filled her with the scent of wood smoke and leaves. "Not quite," he said. "I was in Idaho."

THIRTEEN

*L*OVE worked backwards, Chloe had decided. Played its spectacular, grand finale at the outset, then reduced tension and momentum until the end. Love was anticlimactic when it lasted, delicate and tedious when taken to three acts, but apparently Chloe's father only found his rhythm after the audience went home. He'd always done his best work in emergency surgery, when everyone else had given up, so it was no surprise that when her mom left with Jack Bolton, he decided it was time to fight. He reset her mother's speed-dial buttons, putting himself first, and changed a light bulb that had gone out on the porch. He fixed dinner, took out the trash, and hung his sweater in his old closet. He stood staring at his stolen work shirts so long he seemed as clueless as Chloe was, unable to decipher the difference between what might have been and what could still be.

Chloe retreated to her bedroom, fell asleep for two hours

and woke up hot to the touch. She opened a window, breathed in the coolest night of the year so far, and noticed the man beneath the lamppost. He was smoking, minding his own business, but he gave her the heebie jeebies. He flicked a cigarette butt into the street so carelessly, she imagined he'd do the same to fireflies—pluck their wings and look on heartlessly as they winked out.

She turned from the window and sunk into bed, still exhausted. The hours of daylight were shrinking, but the days themselves had become endless. Her parents made sure she went to school, but she knew she was unteachable. She wrote the required position papers and turned them in not knowing if she'd been pro or con. She still inhabited her own body, but apparently the creature growing inside her was in charge. She couldn't even move where she wanted; she took paths that led nowhere, punched in six of her mother's cell-phone numbers and stalled at the seventh. Friends called her over during lunch and, though she wanted to gossip and attack dubious fashion choices more than anything in this world, she pretended not to hear them. She walked to the football track, where she was invisible to the jocks, and trudged around the two-hundred-meter track until the bell.

She listened for sounds in the other room, heard the shuffle of papers, the scratching of a chair. The days felt so long she had to nap in the afternoon, then had trouble falling sleeping later. She forced herself to her feet, padded down the hall, found her father on the sofa, medical journals spread around him. He wore one of the work shirts her mother had been wearing to bed.

"I thought you were sleeping," he said.

A half-lunatic had returned from the dead for her mother,

and Chloe felt filled with envy. That kind of poetry ought to be happening to *her*. Her Orpheus would not turn around in doubt, would not lose love twice and be torn apart, limb by limb, by a troop of maddened women. Her myth would end in quiet triumph, in a man and woman who loved so long and so well they were omitted from storytelling, too boring for words.

"Chloe?" her father asked. "You with me?"

"I'm pregnant."

She leaned forward, wanting to catch the full brunt of his fury. Wanting to hear she'd sabotaged the most important years of her life, perhaps ruined her future entirely. She needed more than a little nausea to make the creature growing inside her real; she needed outrage and her father's disgust.

He set down his pen, sat perfectly still except for a twinge beneath his cheekbone. She was envious of her mother, and she adored Jack, but she also knew the truth. *This* was the man her mother ought to love. *This* man, who had done enough things wrong to learn something. This man who loved best in silences. Who was finally becoming tender now that he chose not to speak at all.

"Daddy?" she said, sitting beside him. "Promise me you won't tell Mom."

"Chloe—"

"Please! I'll tell her. I swear."

He pulled her into his arms. She cried so hard her stomach hurt, sobbed until she thought she might lose the baby through anguish, a thought which made her cry more. Maybe this child was the only person who would ever love her. Maybe this was how it was supposed to be.

He rocked her until she quieted, carried her to bed as if she was still a little girl. He sat beside her, tucked the covers beneath her chin. If he mentioned an abortion, she would never forgive him.

"Your mother was so emotional when she was pregnant," he said. "Crying over crib sheets, too many pacifier choices." He shook his head. "I should have comforted her rather than coming home with a set of white sheets. But I wanted to fix things. You understand? She had a problem and I solved it."

Chloe thought of how many obstetricians he must know, which ones he trusted to fix the problem of a pregnant fourteen year old.

"She had to take a break from med school to have you," he went on, "and that was tough on her. That's the funny thing about your life before children. You have the mistaken impression you're the most important thing."

Chloe closed her eyes, thought of that night with Skitch, how much it had mattered and how little it was worth. He'd been rough, quick, and the sweat that had risen up through his pores had been surprisingly acrid. She hadn't even liked the smell of him.

"I thought you'd get in the way," he said.

She had. She'd ruined his concentration, upset his schedule and sleep, left a trail of bell bottoms and barrettes through what would have been his pristine living room. She'd challenged his commitment to his calling, and now that he was holding her, talking softly, she basked in the surprising conclusion. She'd made him more than a doctor. Coaxed him into loving her more than he thought he could.

"Then I saw you," her dad said. "This furious red face and a scream that curled the nurses' toes. I screwed it all up later, but that first time I held you, I got it right. Nothing in the world mattered as much as your happiness. *Nothing* matters as much."

She shook her head, didn't dare speak. Why didn't he just rage and tell her she was an idiot? Why couldn't he get it right at the right time? Be the loyal husband when her mother needed him, the irate father when it was called for?

"If you want someone to love you forever," he said, "why not let it be me?"

She started to cry again when she realized it wasn't only Jack Bolton who was clairvoyant, but all men. All good men. The ones who adore you despite themselves. Who love you no matter what you do.

THERE was a traffic jam on the Golden Gate while hundreds of people swam in the frigid bay, their arms marked up with numbers, braving hypothermia and sharks for a T-shirt declaring they'd participated in the Golden Gate Swim. Jack understood the quest to push the body beyond its endurance, but what he couldn't begin to imagine was the cold. Even the surface air was plummeting; he'd had to turn on the heater. Nevertheless, once he started talking, Elizabeth began to shake.

She looked out the window. "How bad did you hurt him?" she asked.

His memories, like his vision, were curiously flat. He couldn't believe the lithium worked this quickly, yet the orange Golden Gate was already the color of overcast. Elizabeth's shirt, which he knew to be purple, had faded to gray.

"I'm not sure," he said. "He showed up while Annie was

destroying my palms. He knew all about me from Annie and he thought it was funny. He had a pocketknife he could use to join in."

Elizabeth remembered Annie's garden, the lopped-off zinnias, the amputated saguaros. "He attacked your plants," she said.

"He really took to it. Stabbed and carved up the cactus, stomped every flower he could find. I tried to reason with him, but there's no talking to a bully. I had to go after the knife. I could hear the plants screaming. Each shout sizzled; it was like being struck by lightning."

"Oh, Jack."

"Even Annie saw he was going too far, taking too much pleasure in it. She was talking, pleading probably, but all I heard was the plants' wailing. I had to stop him. I don't regret that. I don't regret anything until halfway through, when I kept pummeling him even after he was on the ground. Every blow became more unacceptable, didn't it? Every punch made my mind more uninhabitable."

By the time his clothes were covered with Annie's lover's blood, the plants' keening had turned to sirens; sirens that turned out to be Annie's wails. She backed into a corner of the porch, called him crazy, incurable, but also told him to run. He took one step toward her and she held up a hand to shield herself. He ran out of the house, tried to run away from himself but couldn't. He ended up cold and delirious in Golden Gate Park.

He heard sirens again, quieter ones, Elizabeth's cries which she tried to muffle in her fist. The traffic inched forward maddeningly slowly; in an hour they'd hardly made any progress at all.

"I think she called him Bruce," he said. "He's been following us."

She dropped her fist, turned. "So he must be all right."

Jack shrugged, knew for a fact that all right was a relative term, ranging from bliss to a hair's breadth above devastation.

They crawled forward in silence. Once the swimmers passed beneath the bridge, the pace picked up. They reached the Presidio, headed toward the Mission District. He tried to pick out the smallest thought, any indication of what Elizabeth was feeling, but her thoughts were closed to him. Whether by choice or by medication, he was losing his talent for clairvoyance.

They pulled up in front of his old house, in front of Annie's, and Jack killed the engine. The few zinnias that had survived Bruce's rampage were still there, battered and ugly, another of Jack's impulses gone awry. He wondered if Elizabeth believed his love for her was a compulsion that would eventually end in the same disarray. If nothing he said counted once he went insane.

Annie walked out, the look on her face telling him everything—that he'd been getting sicker all along, that she'd put up with far more than he'd given her credit for, that she'd only wanted to be adored and defended, like a favorite, tender plant.

"She loves you," Elizabeth said.

She'd stopped shaking in favor of absolute stillness; he imagined she'd bolt if he dared to lean toward her. "But she doesn't like me much."

He opened the car door, walked around to his wife. Annie touched his arm, found a fragment of a cottonwood leaf, a stowaway from Idaho. She glanced toward the car, where Elizabeth was getting out.

"I've been looking everywhere for you," Annie said. "You don't know . . ."

"I'm sorry about everything."

She stepped back, unusually tentative, and swiped at her eye. "I don't know if I did the right thing. I was so confused, so furious at both of you. But I didn't want to get the police involved, so I kept Bruce here. He was bad, Jack. My sister took a few days off from the hospital to come help me. I was sure once we got him though, healed the worst of it, he'd calm down. Stop talking about revenge."

"I'm sorry," he said again.

"God, Jack, all I wanted was a grown-up. Someone who thought I was more important than plants."

"Annie—"

"He's a grown-up, all right, petty and jealous and mean."

Elizabeth had come up behind him. Annie dropped her hand, stepped back. She blinked twice, hard, both stronger and kinder than she'd led him to believe.

"He's been following Jack," Elizabeth said.

Annie shook her head. "He's crazy, Jack's crazy, apparently I'm a magnet for insanity. That knife . . . Bruce takes it with him everywhere, cuts his steak with it. He won't let me forget."

Jack stiffened. He'd gotten a hold of the pocketknife, he remembered. He'd thrown it into the bushes, he was sure. Elizabeth slipped her arm through his, and he wished it was easier for hearts to split in two, so he could offer something as meaningful in return.

"You never would have used a knife," Elizabeth said.

"She's right," Annie said. "You might have thought about it, but you tossed it aside."

This time.

Jack heard a car door slam, couldn't remember if he'd driven to Golden Gate Park or run the whole way, who he'd passed and what they'd said, if there'd been children in his path he'd frightened.

"Isn't this nice?"

Jack turned quickly, saw the man who had attacked his plants sauntering up the path, his face healing into contrasting colors, purple and yellow. "I've been waiting half the night at the good doctor's house, and it turns out you decided to come to me."

Jack smiled, because he was exactly right. He was done running. "Hey there," he said. "It's Bruce, isn't it?"

Jack covered Elizabeth's hand with his own, prayed that clairvoyance never dried up but merely changed directions. That she knew it was possible to be saved and still lose.

"You seem a little forgetful," Bruce said. "Want to see your work?"

He lifted his shirt, exposing a torso that was being held together by a patchwork of black threads, a rainbow of assault wounds, from purple welts to blue scabs to emerging pink skin. When Jack flinched, Elizabeth tightened her hand on his arm.

Bruce dropped his shirt. "Florence Nightingale here," he went on, glaring at Annie, "kept me so doped up I couldn't thank you properly. But you know what? She did me a favor. How do you scare a man who's not afraid to die? You make him live."

"What do you want?" Jack asked, shamed that he'd left Annie with such an ugly garden, with a need for such an ugly man. "A free punch?" He removed Elizabeth's hand, stood with his arms held wide.

Bruce laughed. "Too easy. I was thinking more along the lines of calling the police. Showing off your work to a wider audience. How does attempted murder sound to you?"

Jack turned to Elizabeth. Clairvoyance might be imagining the worst a man can do, or it might be expecting the best. Elizabeth looked in his eyes and handed him her cell phone.

"Sounds about right," Jack said, and he punched in 911.

CHLOE's dreams were relentlessly upbeat. Her belly grew and Skitch realized he loved her. He took her away to a remote, mountain hideaway, where all the girls wore smiles and T-shirts with BABY ↓ emblazoned across the front. He married her before the year was out, and the baby was born in June, the month of freedom, when the earth began to steam.

Her dreams were so good, when Chloe woke to Skitch sitting at the foot of her bed, she smiled as if she'd been expecting him.

He flipped on the light. "I haven't got much time."

She blinked at the sudden brightness, noticed the opened window, a clump of mud on the sill. Skitch wore a denim jacket over ripped jeans and a threadbare T-shirt. The eyes she dreamed blue with passion were bloodshot and brown. He smelled sour, of the aftereffects of beer.

She saw a light beneath the door, smelled coffee. She swore she was the only one who slept in this house anymore.

"Look," Skitch said, "I've been thinking."

She sat up, pulled the covers to her chest, wished the right words into his mouth. She didn't expect Orpheus's bravery, but she tried to will Skitch kind. It was horrifying to consider him the last battlement between her and years of total disillusionment.

He reached into the pocket of his jeans, took out a wad of crumpled bills. "This is all I've got," he said. "Cleaned out my savings. And this." He took a slip of paper from his jacket pocket, laid it on the lavender bedspread, the one her mother had helped her pick out ten years ago. The one she ought to replace with something more stylish and sophisticated.

Chloe said nothing. She saw the doctor's name, the address. She imagined a dark alley near the wharf, the smell of iodine and grief. Skitch's jittery gaze skipped across her face, but she couldn't meet it.

"This is the only answer," he said. "You know that. Jesus, Chloe, you're fourteen goddamn years old."

She'd run out of tears in her father's arms. She'd dried up when she'd realized he wasn't going to betray her secret to her mother, and he wouldn't demand answers. Somehow he would survive without knowing what she was going to do, without saving her, and there was nothing more she could ask of him.

"Get out," she said.

Skitch shook his head and stood. "Don't be an idiot. It's the baby or you."

She finally looked up. In front of her stood so much less than she'd hoped for, a mythless boy, perhaps less brave than she was. A fifteen-year-old who didn't have the guts to drive on one-way streets, who had yet to learn the basics of nobility. A kid not even close to being someone's father.

"It's all right," she said. "Go."

He backed to the window, bumped his head climbing through. She listened to him run down the street, then when all was silent she picked up the money.

She dressed soundlessly and jammed Skitch's note in her pocket, stunned to find herself longing for the days when her parents could stop her. She climbed out the window, already envisioning the deep breath she'd have to take before stepping into the doctor's airless office. There'd be little inside—a metal folding chair, concrete floor, a plastic trash can filled with tissues. A man would come out eventually, dressed not in scrubs but in dirty chinos, a T-shirt with stains that triggered the gag reflex at the back of her throat. She could nearly touch the bruised walls of the tiny room he'd lead her to; she heard the girl crying in the room next door, then the sputtering engine of the vacuum. It would all happen within seconds. Pressure between her legs then a sudden, hard tug, an unspeakable slurping sound. A quick glimpse of something slick and pea-shaped, streaked with blood.

Perhaps a good imagination was the foundation of conservative morals, because the moment she smelled her own insides, she changed direction. She headed toward the Banana Belt, the hillsides of Sausalito where the sun usually shined, and ended up in front of Jill's turreted house. She knocked on the heavy, antique door imported from Britain, though it was four-thirty in the morning and Jill's family had probably never been wrested from their sweet dreams at such an hour before. Jill's father answered, dressed in blue silk pajamas, a baseball bat in his hands.

"Chloe?" he said. "Is that you?"

"Can I talk to Jill?"

He looked past her, eyes watery and confused, as if this hour of the night had seemed more fiction than fact. As if an accountant in Marin, a man with an earthquake-safe foundation and a daughter who never got into trouble, lived only in the hours between dawn and dusk. He didn't move for a good two minutes, then finally stepped back to let her in.

"Does your mother know you're here?" he asked.

"My mother's in love."

He shook his head, as if trying to clear it. "Your dad then?"

"I need to see Jill."

"Chloe, you can't just come marching in here at—" He stopped in midsentence at the swelling of her tears, put a hand over his heart.

"Sit," he said. "I'll get her. I'm going to call your parents."

Chloe swatted her tears, sat on the pillow-happy couch. She coveted this room, all its gilded excesses and fluff. A surplus of cushions and bric-a-brac had always seemed to her the mark of a happy woman. She imagined Jill's mother at the end of each day adding another homemade lavender sachet, replenishing the crystal saucer with striped candies. There was nothing more soothing in the world than bunny knickknacks and a well-worn chair, except, perhaps, a mother who peeked into your room to make sure you were breathing, who stood ready with lullabies at any hour of the day or night.

Jill came downstairs dressed in surprisingly stylish pajamas—tie-dyed sweatpants and a Sheryl Crow tank top.

"What are you doing here?" she asked. "My dad is totally freaking out."

Chloe felt as heavy as lead, as if her body had revolted and seized up, reversed the growing process. As if she really was too young for love.

"I'm sorry," Chloe said.

Jill stood in the arched doorway that had been painted sky blue. "Sorry for being a jerk? Or sorry for being a jerk and getting dumped anyway?"

Chloe's eyes were leaking again. "I'm sorry for hurting you."

Jill flicked her hand. "Well, that makes it all right then."

"I'm not saying—"

"Just treat me like dirt, then when your love life doesn't work out, come on back. God knows I don't have any other friends."

"Jill, I'm having a baby."

Jill froze with her mouth open. She reached for the wall. "No."

"I think I'm supposed to keep it. It all makes sense, you know? The way everything happened. My dad moving out, then losing you and Skitch. It's like you're not allowed to keep anyone unless you can prove, from the start, that you won't fail them."

For a long time, there was no sound but Jill's father's unsettled voice coming from upstairs, and the ticking of the gilded grandfather clock in the corner. Then at last Jill crossed the room and sat beside her.

"That's baloney," Jill said. "You keep the people who forgive you no matter what a jerk you are."

Chloe lifted her shoulders. The three blocks to Jill's house had been the longest walk of her life, and she wondered if she would ever regain her strength. If there would be a tremble to her legs, and a quiver to her voice, from here on out. "What do you think I should do?"

Jill leaned against her, not as casually as she once had, but loose enough. Softening by the second. She gave her the only answer that could be trusted, the answer not of parents or lovers, but of friends.

"Oh, Chloe," she said. "I have no idea."

WILL found Elizabeth in the courtyard, ferociously planting bulbs. Tulips, crocus, daffodil, hyacinth. She dug unevenly, six-inches deep here, twelve inches there, then tossed in the bulbs and left them where they landed, upside-down or not. She left some holes bare and in others piled the bulbs ten deep so that in spring they'd have to fight for soil and air, for their very survival. Will knelt beside her, took the bulbs from her hands.

"Beth," he said, sorting and replanting in orderly rows. Uninspired gardening, certainly, but at least each flower would have a chance to bloom in its own time. "I called the hospital's lawyer, Bill Hailey. Attempted murder can get fifteen years to life in prison."

She kicked at the bulbs and glared at him, as if he'd pronounced the sentence himself. She knew Chloe was sneaking around, but had no idea their daughter was standing sideways in front of a mirror, taking folic acid supplements and throwing out her cigarettes. She had no idea things were only going to get worse.

He was up to three sleeping pills a night to deal with the knowledge he had. One to keep a promise, the second to refrain from ripping a boy to pieces, the last to stop himself from fixing the problem the way surgeons do, with a sharp knife and no turning back. With so many sedatives in his system, he dreamed an extra two hours, got in all the things he wished he'd done differently, like exposing Chloe to basketball and karate, activities that were reported to guard against girls' low self-esteem. He dreamed his daughter young forever, sailed her right through puberty without falling in love or ruining a thing.

The sleeping pills left him groggy, which was a good excuse to call in every favor he was owed. While his colleagues covered for him at the hospital, he sneaked to open houses. Yesterday, he found the home of his dreams, a house completely unsuited to the man he'd been before. More a tree house than a conventional home, on tiny Corinthian Island where there were only fifty-eight houses to begin with, most of them straight up. Perched on an alarmingly steep cliff, ninety-eight steps up from the road, it was a ridiculous house, three stories tall, painted lime green and purple, drafty and difficult to clean. An outrageously overpriced residence, half a million in view alone, with sweeping vistas of Belvedere Cove, Angel Island and, on a clear day, San Francisco. He fell in love with it the moment he imagined Elizabeth standing by the window and feeling like she was flying, without the slightest threat that she would fall.

He had a copy of the offer in his pocket, but his other vow was to not act the fool. Jack Bolton's arrest was pretty much the only topic of conversation he and Elizabeth had left. "He did try to kill him," he said quietly.

She glared at him. "The man was a barbarian. He was trying to get Jack to snap. A man has to defend what he loves."

"We're talking about plants, Beth. A few flowers people cut and trample a hundred times a day. There are no justifications for murder."

"It wasn't murder. Jack stopped."

He saw the opening, the tears in her eyes. He could put an arm around her, be there when she came back from the trial and Jack was sent to jail.

"What am I going to do?" she asked.

He stepped back, squashed a bulb beneath his shoe. "You'd better not do anything. One word and you'll jeopardize your career. You've been having an affair with one of your patients. You'll lose your license."

She shook her head. "I can't think about that now."

"You'd better think about it now. Excuse me for being unro-mantic, but is this man worth your entire career? The respect of your colleagues and friends?"

Self-preservation told him to look away, but he forced him-self to watch her. She looked toward the garden, where all the trees and shrubs Jack had planted were already on the scruffy side, the blossomless snowdrops now an eyesore. Everything, he hoped she saw, was in need of more work than she had antici-pated.

"If he's the man you think he is," he went on, "he'll get a good lawyer. If he *isn't* insane, he'll face up to what he's done. In the meantime, you've got a job to protect, a child to raise. A life of your own to lead."

"What kind of life will it be without Jack?"

Each word dangled like a separate spider in the garden. "Yes," he said. "Well."

"This is what you've never understood. Sometimes it's essen-tial to be irrational. If you think too clearly and make all the right decisions, you lose what matters most."

That decided it. He walked into the house, vowed to be down to two sleeping pills by this evening. He opened his daughter's door, knew from two decades in medicine that the changes his patients thought too insignificant to mention were often the ones that did the most harm. There was no longer a maelstrom of clothes in Chloe's bedroom. The wood floor had been swept and, if the shine was any indication, mopped. Chloe had put away her CDs, moved her textbooks to the shelves, dusted the aluminum blinds. She'd made the bed, fluffed the pillows, propped her old stuffed bear, the one that had been relegated to the deepest recesses of the closet, in the center of the ruffled, lavender comforter. Elizabeth walked in behind him and gasped.

"Oh my God," she said.

She touched his arm, rested her head against him for a split second, but long enough to get him hoping all over again.

"What's going on?" she asked. "Is it this thing with Jill?"

He closed his eyes rather than point out the ways she deluded herself. In the beginning, the worst she'd been able to imagine was that the colic would continue past two months, that Chloe's eczema might leave scars. She'd never considered SIDS or spinal meningitis, and Will realized this was what he should have cherished about her. She did what her mother couldn't; deep down, she thought all would be well.

"It's not Jill," he said.

"What do you know? What is it?"

Time ran out on promises when Chloe let herself in the front door. She walked down the hall, didn't seem at all surprised to find them in her bedroom, gawking at the cleanliness as if it only exposed the mess that had been there before.

"Where were you?" Elizabeth said. "Chloe, this is getting out of hand."

Chloe sat on the bed. "The meadow on Angel Island was just like Jack said it would be."

Elizabeth drew in her breath. "I don't believe this. How'd you get there? You can't just—"

"He's not crazy. If it goes to trial, you need to tell them that, Mom. I know it for sure now. He's not crazy at all."

When Chloe looked at him, Will decided that, if given another chance, he wouldn't even stress the karate and basketball.

He'd merely work out of a home office. He'd hold a scalpel between her and harm.

"It gave me the answer, just like he said." Chloe turned to her mother, looked her straight in the eye. "I need an abortion."

FOURTEEN

*E*LIZABETH emptied her pantry, disgusted with her shopping habits. She had never entered the cookie aisle at Safeway, never bought a single bag of candy except at Halloween. On the bottom shelf, she took out six different types of beans, but found no frosted cereals, no sodas. In the refrigerator, there were whole-grain tortillas but no whole milk. If cavities and a few extra pounds were all they'd been risking, why hadn't she given her daughter the chocolate she craved, why couldn't she have splurged on double fudge ice cream and smooth, expensive wine? Fat and alcohol might have killed her, but self-denial was making her cranky. Who wanted to drag out a hungry, puritanical life?

She settled for tea sweetened by an accusing bear with his feet full of hardened honey. She brought a tray to the living room, where Chloe sat curled up on the sofa. Will had deserted them, this time at Chloe's request. Elizabeth set the tray on the table, took her time pouring the tea into the dusty cups she'd been saving for a special occasion, knowing neither of them would drink it. She was only buying time.

Chloe pulled her knees to her chest. Somewhere, of course, there were perfect words for this moment, an imaginary mother speaking softly and setting things right, but Elizabeth stomped right over her. She was livid at the myriad ways a life could come undone, appalled that a thousand carefully tended days could, and would, be erased by one reckless moment. She'd forgotten the one good thing her mother had taught her, the most important thing: Savor the moment, because everyone was one misstep or bad break or poor choice away from calamity.

"Did you use birth control and it failed, or did you just assume one time wouldn't hurt?"

Chloe began to cry. Accusations, at this point, were ludicrous, yet Elizabeth struggled to come up with more. Without blame, the conversation could only get worse. They might freefall into a discussion of how those we trusted failed us, the variety of ways hopes could be dashed. One understanding word and the daughter she'd dreamed into Stanford, married to a gentle, fun-loving man, would be obliterated by this trembling, teary-eyed creature who needed mothering less than the name of a good doctor, a few years away at a strict school for girls.

"Or perhaps this has been going on for a while," Elizabeth went on. "Maybe even back when I brought up the subject of birth control pills."

Chloe cried harder, and Elizabeth stood. Maybe what Chloe had needed to see was not Elizabeth and Will's measured politeness, but role models of spite. She needed to see that a promise is made out of air and holds no weight at all, that real love is not as wholesome as you might think; anything of that power both creates and destroys. She needed to question whether any man was good enough, to hold back trust until the last second, when it alighted on a man who deserved it, not on the first one who asked.

"Maybe you planned this," Elizabeth said. "Imagined Skitch ennobled by the prospect of becoming a father at fifteen, transformed by the wife and baby he secured before graduating high school."

Chloe looked up, at least managed to glare. "I didn't plan it."

"Well, you certainly didn't plan not to do it. My God, Chloe. You're not stupid. You must have thought this was the way to his heart."

When she saw that she was right, all the wind went out of her. Chloe *had* thought sex was the way to Skitch's heart, and the idea of her baby unbuttoning her jeans and spreading her legs for a boy whose life's ambition was to play the lead in a high school play was suddenly too much to bear.

She sat down heavily beside her daughter, wanted to hold her but there was too much between them now. The sour breath of a boy, the blush of early pregnancy, a premature and awkward equality. "What does Skitch say?"

"He gave me a name, a little money."

It would have been easy to detest him, to blame that silly boy for a lifetime of smashed dreams. To go to his parents, ruin *his* life, but she was sure it was disintegrating just fine on its own. Three of her patients were men who'd been cruel, thoughtless boys—boys who believed they grew up by damaging someone else. Now they were men who spent their lives worrying the same would be done to them. Scared, frail men who couldn't sleep at night, dreading violence and villains meaner than they were.

"Did I teach you that you weren't whole without some boy loving you? Did I make you think you weren't good enough on your own?"

Chloe whistled in disgust. "Always you," she said.

Elizabeth shook her head. Chloe would never understand how inaccurate that statement was. Elizabeth had canceled all her appointments, couldn't even go to Jack when he needed her most. For years, the truly inconsequential things—from her fingernails to her sagging stomach to her talent for pottery—had gotten no attention at all. "Men love you or they don't," she said. "Not based on what you give them, but on who you are."

"Does Jack love you?"

Elizabeth drew back. "We're not talking about me."

"I think he does."

"Tell me how you got to Angel Island."

Chloe waved her hand. "The bus. The ferry. The nasturtium meadow was just like Jack said. I took one step and the flowers gave me my answer."

Elizabeth stiffened, and Chloe pointed a finger. "See that?" Chloe said. "That's what Jack has to live with. You *want* to think he's some kind of freak. That's the only thing that makes your magicless life tolerable." She scoffed and, ironically, that unpleasantness gave Elizabeth a moment's relief, a retreat into simple shame at her daughter's rudeness, a state any decent parent coped with a dozen times a week.

"I don't want to think anything of the kind," Elizabeth said.

"It wasn't some crazy thing. No talking leaves, if that's what you're thinking. It was just obvious. Jack thought the place had been meant for me, but everywhere I stepped I crushed something. I ruined it."

"Chloe—"

"I don't know how to tread lightly. I don't know what I'm doing yet."

Elizabeth touched her shoulder, careful not to squeeze too tight. "At fourteen, you're not supposed to know."

They were quiet while someone mowed the grass for the last time, slicing off scorched tips and the scent of summer, while a tiny creature became translucent.

"I have a good friend," Elizabeth said at last. "A doctor at the clinic."

"I can't think of it as a baby," Chloe said.

"No," Elizabeth whispered, thinking of the first time she'd seen Chloe, the flashflood of tears and panicky devotion, the sudden fierceness of her own breathing. "I wouldn't."

GARY told the guards he was Jack Bolton's little brother, and either they believed him or it didn't matter who he was, because they signed him up for the twelve-thirty visit. He didn't even gain attention for his tics. The other visitors were so self-absorbed, so concerned with *their* criminal, they didn't look twice at him as he twitched his way into a room lined on three sides with bulletproof stalls and black phones.

The guests picked a booth; Gary ticced his way to the one in the corner. Behind the partitions, the door opened and a line of orange-clad prisoners walked in, some sauntering, some pale as sheets, all with chains on their hands.

Jack blinked when he sat down. He'd probably been expecting

a lawyer or the shrink. Gary rapped his hands on the glass and didn't like the sound, an echoless thump.

Jack picked up the phone, the chain between his wrists clanking. Gary picked up the one on his side.

"Shit," Gary said. "Dr. Cohen told the group what happened. Man, I can't believe it. Had to see you with my own eyes."

Jack's face registered nothing. He looked washed out in orange; he'd lost a summer's worth of tan in two days. His cheeks had a new puffiness, as if they'd been pumping him with glucose instead of lithium. Sedating him with sweet things.

"Wow," Gary said. "Look at you."

Jack struggled to focus his eyes. "You're the first one who's come," he said slowly, thickly. Obviously, they'd tried to subdue him. "Other than the lawyer."

"Not even Dr. Shreve?"

Jack said nothing.

"You got a good lawyer?" Gary asked.

Jack shrugged. "Hard to say. His head's an oil slick. I don't approve of people who subdue their own hair."

Gary stared at him, his right arm twitching. "You do it?" he asked. "Try to kill that guy?"

Jack didn't blink. "I hurt him. There's no denying that."

Gary whistled. "Man. Bet he had it coming."

He waited for Jack's defense, had already imagined the whole incident and only needed Jack to verify the particulars. How the man shoved him first. How he would have killed him, if Jack hadn't fought back.

Jack remained silent, and Gary rapped hard on the glass. Jack didn't flinch; Gary had no idea if he even heard it on the other side. "What about your lawyer?" he asked. "What's his strategy?"

Jack smiled for the first time. "Insanity."

"Fuck." Gary had been chastised for cursing at inappropriate moments, and though he had no recollection of his vulgarity, he understood why he liked the worst words. Four otherwise harmless letters transformed him into a militant, suggested a deepseated anger that people forgave more readily than strangeness. Fuck, fuck, fuck. Crassness was one of the perks of the insane.

He sat forward, the tics going wildly to the right, then swinging left again. "You're as insane as I am," he said. "As anybody who refuses to be tamed."

Jack looked at the stalls across the room, the prisoners pressing their foreheads against the glass and saying things they knew they shouldn't, since every word was taped. "You don't understand."

"Sure I do. Don't listen to them, Jack. They'll ruin you. You gotta keep fighting. Jack? Jack, take a look at me. I can't time myself right on Haldol. I keep running into doors."

Jack's eyes were half-closed. He looked terrible. Bloated and drying up like that whale that had beached itself in San Francisco Bay and resisted aid, apparently preferring to die on its own terms.

"Shit," Gary said. "What the fuck have they done to you?"

"The lawyer ordered me a new psychiatrist. He likes lithium in large dosages."

"No! Fuck, Jack, don't give in."

Jack shrugged. "Houston Mike makes himself throw up to get a stay in the hospital wing. He says I'd be a fool to get better now. You've got the gay and straight tanks, thirty men apiece. Most guys know enough to request the gay tank. Ironic, huh? It's the heterosexuals who rape you."

"Jack—"

Jack jerked suddenly, the way Gary would, with the force of a tic. For a moment, he was his old self, caged and furious, then he slumped forward, went still. "There's no color in here," he said.

Gary glanced at Jack's marigold-colored jumpsuit, his own yellow shirt. "If you take away my tics," Gary said, and just then a huge one strangled him from head to toe. Contorted him to such a degree he couldn't breathe. Then it released him, leaving his skin tingling. "You take away my tics and what have you got? A mediocre musician you've heard a thousand times before. Your average self-absorbed *kid* who isn't going to give a shit about the desires of a sixty-five-year-old woman. I can tell you that."

Gary searched Jack's face. He'd wanted to satisfy himself that whatever Jack had done he'd done for a reason, that one mistake, one flaw, did not make you crazy or change who you were, deep down. He'd wanted reassurance that it was always better to be a freak than faceless, but Jack wasn't even looking at him. He had dropped the phone to his shoulder.

"The enemy is not manic-depression or Tourette's," Gary shouted. He pointed to the phone, which Jack finally put back to his ear. "The enemy is not mental illness. It's the response to it. It's our response."

"It's not the worst thing to lose color."

"Like hell it isn't," Gary said. "You're a fucking liar, Jack. A fucking lying jerk."

He threw down the phone, got to his feet. He paced the room, passed six weeping girlfriends, a stone-faced child, a father who kept screaming into the phone even after the pale, trembling prisoner on the other side took three steps back, pressed himself against the wall. He paced the way Jack had once paced across Dr. Shreve's office, but the guard merely stared at him. Time wasn't up. Finally, he walked back to the stall, where Jack still held the phone to his ear. Gary picked up his side, said, "To hell with you."

"They tell me I'm still suffering delusions," Jack said quietly, "but I don't think so. The lithium works like frostbite. It took my toes and heels first. Now it's creeping up the backs of my knees. It's so clever, I'm almost rooting for it."

Gary wanted to shake him but, even more, he wanted to protect himself. He wanted to get the hell out of there and breathe in the glorious scent of October, wanted to tic his way down the street and garner a hundred ugly stares by noon. He wanted to walk into the South Street Club, grab a pair of drumsticks, and stretch his solo into an hour, maybe two, accomplish a feat of human endurance never matched before. Then he wanted to find Blanche sitting in the audience and kiss her until she moaned like a college girl. He wanted to be the kind of freak who found a woman with her history told in liver spots beautiful.

Instead he reached into his pockets, came up with a handful of the dirt he'd scooped out of a particularly attractive garden in Pacific Heights, still blooming this late in the season. He'd hoped to get the loam to Jack, but the guards had informed him the only things prisoners could receive were one-dollar bills, slid through the slot near the door.

He crushed the dirt between his fingers, then smeared it across the glass. He was pleased by how well it stuck, how easy it was to make a mess of things, how fast the guard moved. "You made me feel like the worst thing in the world isn't being stared at," he said quickly, while the guard marched toward him, "but being overlooked."

The guard grabbed him by the collar, and Gary was led from the jail, tics in tow. He garnered a hundred ugly stares just walking to the State Street Club, played a one-hour solo that, instead of mesmerizing the crowd, cleared the room. When the lights came on, not even Blanche was there. His gyrations got worse until the manager handed him the card Blanche had left while he'd been playing, and then they stopped completely.

> *Thank you. I never expected more.*
> *Blanche*

And he thought perhaps the worst thing wasn't being overlooked, but being underestimated.

AT nine in the morning, while her friends started second period, Chloe dozed through Regis and Kelly. After lunch, she slept through Timmy's kidnapping on *Days of Our Lives*. At three, when the movers arrived at her father's townhouse, she ignored a spurt of energy and dug down into drowsiness. She slept through the screeching of packing tape, the rumpling of newspaper, the emptying of closets and cupboards. She would have slept while they loaded her bed onto the truck if her father hadn't come in.

He jiggled the blankets, tugged her hair. She woke long before she opened her eyes, clinging to the best dream she'd had so far, dual universes she could enter and exit at will—the first the life she'd chosen, the other the relinquished one. A baby to hold at dawn, when nothing but warm milk and whispers were demanded, and her arms free by evening, so she could be asked to dance.

But even in her dreams, her stomach hurt. Asleep or awake, the muscles in her lower abdomen remained taut and sore, coiled around emptiness as if refusing to accept defeat. She had not eaten anything solid in two days. She craved Mountain Dew, and drank so much her skin tingled.

"That's enough, Chloe," her dad said.

Chloe opened her eyes, found her father dressed in clothes she'd never seen before—sweatpants and a ratty gray sweater. He'd taken so many days off work he might have quit entirely. He and her mother divided the days and nights so that she was watched twenty-four seven; she couldn't even pee without one of them standing outside the door. Neither one had brought up her return to school. They had decided to be kind, and she marveled at her ability to feel nothing, as if emotions were not housed in the heart or brain, but in the deepest recesses of the stomach where a doctor could, if given the order, cut them out.

"I'm taking you to my new place," he said. "You're gonna love it."

She didn't have the energy to roll her eyes. She recalled another dream she'd had in the last eighteen hours of near constant sleep. She'd been standing on an endless icy plain looking for snowdrops, the kind Jack Bolton had planted for her, but she couldn't find a single sign of life.

"Later, okay?"

She realized she couldn't love him anymore. Not him or her mother, who had held her hand so tightly during the surgery that afterwards Chloe couldn't make a fist. She couldn't trust anyone who had allowed her to make such a horrible decision, who hadn't told her that sometimes, in the process of saving yourself, you cease to be worth the price.

"No, it's not okay," her dad said. "No one's expecting you to be cheerful, but you are required to stand. You can go ahead and hate me for saying it: Life goes on."

He took a pair of jeans and a sweatshirt from the dresser and tossed them on the bed. "Get dressed," he said. "I'll send the movers in in five minutes."

He left the room, and she debated about crawling back into bed, forcing him to tote her around like a baby. But picturing that hurt her stomach more. She dressed slowly, kept her gaze above her waist, on the window and the thickening fog. Her jeans were loose, the sweatshirt itchy against her sensitive skin. Her dad had left phone messages from her friends on the dresser, but she didn't look at them.

She found him by the front door, flipping his keys from hand to hand. "Don't you feel a little better already?" he asked.

Sometimes the only gift you could offer someone was a perfectly tendered lie. "Sure."

His face lit up, and she smiled at his gullibility, smiled despite herself. He took her hand. "I can't wait to see what you think."

She followed him to his car, had to grip the armrest when he gunned the engine and took off in a skid. Though she kept trying to care about nothing, she reached for her seat belt and snapped it on. Her dad tuned the radio to something jazzy. He hummed, tapped his fingers on the steering wheel.

"What's wrong with you?" she asked.

He smiled, nudged her with his elbow. "This is not a house for a normal man."

They passed the guarded gate and her father sat forward, hunched right behind the wheel as if he was making a quick getaway.

"So you're abnormal now," she said.

He laughed, mistook her condescension as admiration, which it might have been. "Yes," he said. "I guess I am."

They took Tiburon Boulevard to Main Street, passed Ark Row's swanky restaurants, where her father had twice taken her to dinner to make up for missed dates.

"Okay," he said, "here we go."

They turned at the stone pillars that guarded the single entrance to Corinthian Island, immediately met a line of traffic behind the mail truck. The street was barely wide enough for a single car, flanked by lush hillsides of trailing rosemary and ivy, windswept cypress trees and pines. The houses were multileveled, with substantial decks to take in the views. On the left, the steepest walkways appeared purposeless, disappearing five feet up in the fog.

"You can't be serious." She felt claustrophobic. Some lots were no more than twenty-five-feet wide, the houses nearly twice that in height. The fog was becoming especially intense, thickening to the consistency of cotton, which appeared to be consuming their car. Despite all the excess sleep, Chloe felt tired, weighted down by her clothes and mutilated hair. Even her breath was heavy. She could sleep twenty hours a day, she realized, and it wouldn't be enough.

"Just a little farther," he said. "Look."

The mail truck continued on Bellevue, while they took a left onto Alcatraz Avenue. The even-narrower street spiraled upward, neared the edge of the peninsula, where the hills matured into full-fledged cliffs, and the houses reached the two-million-dollar mark. She felt completely lost. Twice, it appeared the road ended only to turn at the last moment into an even-narrower opening. Finally, they pulled into one of the parking cut-outs. Her dad killed the engine.

Chloe looked at the multimillion-dollar homes, the majority in the typical north bay style—weathered gray cedar siding, evergreen foundation plantings, smoke spewing from well-used chimneys. Most surprisingly unostentatious, nothing too out-of-the-ordinary, which only proved that wealth did not beget daring. It affected much less than people thought. "Which one?" she asked.

He smiled widely, pointed to the top of the hill. "That one."

She followed his finger, saw nothing but an unimpressive shadow halfway to the sky. Compared to the Tuscan-style mansion going in across the street, its diminutive size ranked it little better than a shack, certainly not substantial enough to hold up to a good Marin wind. A spindly staircase spilled from the clouds and zigzagged down the hill like an old, cagey snake. "You've got to be kidding," she said.

He opened the car door, leapt out. "It's fabulous," he said. "Vintage. Built in the '60s, all wood floors, river rock. It hasn't even been remodeled. Wait till you see the view."

He started toward the wooden staircase, which she was certain would not hold his weight. The railings didn't begin until halfway up, and even then were spindly. For years she'd prided herself on her endurance, her six-minute mile, but she knew there was no way she could climb all those stairs. She wanted to sit in the car until her dad realized she wasn't coming. Until someone realized the things that were missing often took precedence over the ones that were there.

But her dad picked the same moment to make a spectacle of himself, racing up the stairs like Rocky. She wanted to give misery its due, waste away from sorrow, but when she laughed she realized this was more difficult and dull than she'd been led to believe.

She stepped out of the car. The fog clumped beneath the house, obscuring everything except what appeared to be a purple foundation. Her dad took the steps two at a time, lifting his arms and singing the Rocky theme song. She walked to the stairs and started up, but by the thirty-ninth step she was dizzy. She had thought she was done crying, but she was wrong.

She didn't hear her dad come down, but suddenly his arms were around her. He sat beside her on the stairs.

"Come on, honey," he said. "Please. I can't take it."

"I just don't get it," she said. "You'll have to climb these stairs every day. You'll have to bring up your groceries one bag at a time and there's no one here to help you."

He said nothing, just held her. Her stomach felt on fire, her teeth hurt. She felt the pain in every toe and finger, was aware of the separate pieces of her body as if they'd been set against each other. As if her body was at war.

"I want someone to read my mind," she said.

He leaned back to study her face. "Let me try."

"Don't make fun."

He put his hands on either side of her face, closed his eyes to concentrate. "Hmmm," he said. "Mmmm-mmmm."

She shook her head, hated him desperately.

"You're scared," he said quietly. "You're scared and sad and, at this moment, a hundred steps seems like far too much work for any view."

He opened his eyes, and she blinked back tears. He wasn't right, and it didn't matter. For a moment or two, he'd come inside her skin to look for clues.

"You want to know the only thing I've learned so far?" he said. "We've got two choices. Either we play it safe and don't care too much about anything, or we risk pouring our hearts and souls into something. It doesn't matter so much what it is—a house, a woman, a garden. What matters is that you pick something."

"I picked Skitch," she said, shocked now by the unworthiness of her choice. Relieved, a bit, at her ability to be shocked.

He shook his head. "I don't think so. I think you got picked. You got picked, you made some wrong choices, and thank God some things can be fixed. Not without heartache, and not without regret, but you are fourteen years old and entitled to your own future. The only thing you need to pour your heart and soul into now is you."

"Daddy, I'm sorry," she said.

He kissed her forehead. "Forget about it. Hey. Look at that."

The fog thinned, revealing what indeed was a purple foundation, and the oddest lime-green siding Chloe had ever seen. The trim was sunflower yellow, the front door red, like one of Jack's colorful gardens.

"Mom's not coming back," she said softly.

He glanced at her. "Maybe not."

They got to their feet, took the remaining sixty-one steps together. At the forty-eighth, the fog threw out a tentacle to unbalance them. By the eighty-ninth, they stepped above the clouds into a sky as blue as a robin's egg. The house was directly in front of them, purple and green, like old-fashioned hard candy.

"Wow," she said. "I'll bet the neighbors hate it."

Her dad laughed, put his key in the lock. She had only a second to take in the knotty-pine floors, the crimson walls and dazzling sea view through the windows, before six of her friends jumped out and yelled, "Surprise!"

Jill stood near the fireplace, along with Marcie and Patti Newhouse, and Patti's boyfriend, Max. Angela Yochum hugged her, Julie Defoe told her she'd missed the hardest test yet in geometry.

"All proofs," Julie said. "Totally freakin' impossible." She took Chloe's hand. "That must have been some flu. Jill said you were totally out of it. When are you coming back?"

Chloe watched Jill walk out onto the sunlit balcony. "Monday," she said, a decision she hadn't made until that moment.

She found her dad in the most outdated kitchen she'd ever seen, still in shades of pumpkin and avocado. The linoleum was cracked, the appliances practically antiques, and somehow she knew he wasn't going to change a thing.

He'd stocked their old camping cooler with sodas, left out a few bags of chips.

"I didn't think you knew who my friends were," she said.

"I do now."

"Dad—"

"They kept calling to see how you were, so I set this up. I thought it might help."

Chloe shook her head, looked out the window. The sky above the clouds was so blue and beautiful it hurt to look at it. She prayed that when she hit fifteen, she'd learn to tell the difference between sorrow and joy; she'd stop getting so confused. "You're, like, totally freaking me out," she said.

His trash bins had yet to arrive, so he lined up the empty pop cans on the counter, more like himself. Obsessed with order, with the way things should be. "Honey, that's just too bad."

"You can't wake up one morning and decide to be another person," she said. "You can't just start being nice. And even if you do, it doesn't change what's already happened, the mess you made before. It doesn't affect anyone but you."

He put his hands on her shoulders, smiled like he knew all this and none of it mattered, and she nearly blurted out that she'd never know the color of her baby's eyes. She nearly told him she could raise a dozen children, and none of them would be the right one.

"You think too much," he said. "You and your mother both."

"We can't help it."

He handed her a bag of chips. "Have some Doritos. Go say hi to Jill. Take a breather from the rest of your life and talk about boys."

He kissed her forehead, whistled as he escaped out the back door. Chloe swiped her eyes, headed into a family room dominated by glass and sky. She listened to a few more warnings about the makeup test she'd have to take on Monday, then walked onto the balcony.

Jill took notes from a world-history book, rewrote the text verbatim. She shook her fingers now and then, to ease a cramp.

"Thanks for not telling anyone," Chloe said.

Jill shrugged. She turned the page, started writing again. Chloe looked out on the sea of clouds below them, nearly thick enough to walk on. Springy too, as if she could bounce from one to another and end up in Belvedere, the San Francisco Yacht Club, clear across the bay.

"Skitch is going with Belinda O'Malley now," Jill said. "He's, like, totally in love with her."

Chloe waited for the pain, but it was a ping compared to the ache in her stomach. What stung more was her own stupidity, believing for so long that the devotion of friends and family was a lesser love.

"I'm such an idiot," Chloe said.

Jill stood, slipped an arm around Chloe's waist. They watched as one cloud, the weak seam, split and frayed, opening up a hole to the sparkling bay. Beneath them, closer than Chloe had thought, was the water, the whitecaps, a sailboat sliding through. She had nearly made out the face of the lone rider before the sky stitched itself together again.

"You could almost jump," Chloe said. "It's that close."

"You're not jumping, Chloe."

Chloe realized, with a ping of teenage regret, that she was probably right.

THE door sealed electronically behind her, then Elizabeth made her way down the hall. She'd used her credentials to arrange a private meeting with Jack, but the guard recognized a nervous lover when he saw one. He talked steadily, trying to relax her with a stream of inanities.

"They say it's gonna be a wet winter," he said. "That'll be good for the 49ers. They're always better in rain. And the mountains sure need the snow. Imagine the lawns in spring."

Elizabeth couldn't have spoken if she tried. Her mouth was dry and tender, bothered by bleeding gums that had sprouted up two nights ago, during her watch. She'd sat at Chloe's bedside, armed with chicken soup and aspirin, but not with the one thing they both needed—the ability to lift the decision to enter that clinic onto her own shoulders, bear it alone. All mothers, she would bet, maintained the same reservoir of heartlessness, stood ready and willing to sacrifice anyone who might cause their daughters harm.

The guard opened the far door, stepped back to let her in. The moment she saw Jack, seated in a metal chair behind a well-worn table, looking at her with a lithium haze in his eyes, she admitted that, ever since she'd fallen for him, her life had become an unmitigated disaster. She was in pain all the time; she couldn't breathe without hurting for the ones she loved. *This,* she thought, was why old people stooped and slowed down. Not because of the effects of aging, but because of the accumulated weight of the loves of their lives.

"You have ten minutes," the guard said.

The solid steel door clanked shut like an air lock, as if they were being left with only enough oxygen to say the most important things. Her life was a disaster, yet Jack's meadow had somehow led Chloe home, and Chloe had brought her father with her. Will had become part of their house without moving back in, he'd been devoted to Chloe, and Elizabeth couldn't ask for more.

Jack's gaze skipped from her lips to her cheeks, her nose to her eyes, from button to button. A prisoner of details.

She sat beside him and reached for his hand, ignoring the sight of the chain between his wrists. His fingers were cold, the undersides of his fingernails clean as bone.

"They've been treating you," she said.

"I'm frostbitten. The colors are gone."

"Do you know how much lithium you've been taking?"

"They don't tell me."

"There's a psychiatrist?"

"Mel something or other. The lawyer said there'd be a conflict of interest, you treating me and testifying."

Elizabeth stiffened, but she didn't want to talk about the trial yet. "Mel Herrara?"

"That sounds right."

"Well," she said. "Mel's very good, in his way. He prefers an intense assault of lithium at first. It can be a shock to your system."

Jack dropped his hands to his lap. Elizabeth had stayed with Chloe for three days, the length of time it took for everything to change, for spirits to rise and a girl to lose faith, for a woman's devotion to appear to sprout holes when, really, it was solidifying. Hardening around the things she'd learned to cherish.

"I couldn't come sooner," she said. "I'm sorry. Chloe—"

"The lawyer wants to try the insanity defense."

She sat back. "Oh, Jack."

"A regular trial and I'm almost certain to go to prison. We prove the insanity defense, and they'll send me to a psychiatric hospital. I could be released within sixty days if I respond well to medication. He'll need you to testify. Tell them I'm crazy."

It was almost comical. For every step she took, another leap was demanded. Every declaration of love required more proof. She began to cry. Jack *was* crazy, an unstable fool with plants and pens, a danger to a woman's fearful peace of mind. A green man, wild and brilliant and life-giving and fierce, capable of both creation and destruction until someone unqualified to judge, someone like herself, decided he should be stopped.

She put her head in her hands, stunned that it had taken her fifteen years to start hating her job, a decade and a half to recoil from the responsibility of deciding whether human behavior was right or wrong. Jack pulled her hands from her face, cradled her cheeks in his palms, and she cried harder. She hadn't expected him to touch her.

"I won't testify," she said. "I won't do that to you."

"The lawyer swears it's the only way."

"You're crazy, Jack. Just not in the way they think." She smiled, touched a still wild strand of his hair. She missed the flecks of grass and dirt that usually came off in her fingers. "I'll talk to your lawyer," she said.

"I have to warn you, he gels his hair."

Elizabeth laughed, grabbed his hands again. "Have faith, Jack," she said. "Be fearless."

He squared his shoulders, but his face still dissolved into anguish. He pressed his face into her shoulder and cried like Chloe had after the doctor was done, like she had after she finally got Chloe to sleep, like anyone would when, despite the presence of people who love them, they know they've been abandoned.

FIFTEEN

*T*HE waiting room of Scott Malkowitz's office was a replica of Elizabeth's own. Decorated in shades of gray, with the same, scuffproof leather chairs, an identical L-shaped arrangement along the walls. The lawyer had a south-facing view instead of a northern exposure, but it was just as chilly, stiff and formal at best. For the thirty minutes she was kept waiting, Elizabeth felt like she was staring at an unflattering self-portrait, or the ten extra pounds that clung to her on videotape. Even when faced with the evidence, she couldn't believe she looked as bad as that.

She skimmed *People,* marveled at how many supposed friends betrayed the intimacies of Jennifer Aniston's marriage, how many thoughts and opinions could be squeezed out of one person. Even therapy left patients with some secrets at the end.

The secretary finally led her in. The inner office was, thankfully, far different than her own. Modern and stark, the paintings

Pollock-like splatters, the floors an unforgiving granite. Two angular armchairs squared off in front of a stainless steel desk more suited to a butcher shop than a law firm.

Scott Malkowitz greeted her. His hair was indeed as slick as Jack had suggested, knotted at the nape of his neck. "Mrs. Shreve," he said. "Glad you could come."

She shook his hand, flinched from the iciness of his gold bracelet. "Mr. Malkowitz."

She sat in one of the chairs, tried to get comfortable. The lawyer whispered something to his secretary, who swished out, closing the door behind her. He sat behind his desk.

"The trial begins January 14," he said immediately.

"That far off?"

"That's early, believe it or not. That's because I have some pull."

He smiled and she thought he might have been handsome once, was probably still handsome to women who liked jewelry on men and the thrill of wondering whether a glint in the eye meant seduction or cruelty. She glared at the pinstripes in his gray suit, hated them without reason. He had no personal photos anywhere, and this struck her as suspicious. Mary Bolton had researched every lawyer in the city and only hired Mr. Malkowitz after determining he was the best. He could win freedom for Jack, but in the process might sacrifice a host of lesser, intangible things.

"Here's the plan," he said. "You're going to testify, but not as a professional psychiatrist. We'll leave that to Mel Herrara. Frankly, at this point your professional testimony doesn't count for much. You slept with the defendant. That's known by me, by you and Mr. Bolton, and apparently by the victim. Mr. Bolton also told his wife, Annie Crandall, and we need her testimony for other reasons. The point is, your relationship will be brought up. I recognize this may damage your career, but we're going to use it to Mr. Bolton's advantage."

Elizabeth's career was the least of the things she could lose. She strummed her fingers on the armrest, playing a quick-paced, Gary Griffith rhythm. "How?"

"You're going to say you began to feel in danger. As time went on, as the relationship progressed, Jack's moods spiraled out of control and you feared for yourself, for your estranged husband, particularly for your daughter. Jack's violent attack of the Londonbright garden, his rash decision to fly to Idaho and contemplate suicide, only confirmed your suspicions that he was unstable and dangerous. If he could hurt property and even himself, he might very well come after you. It was heartbreaking, but after he told you about his attack of Bruce Koswolski, you decided to end things. There was no other choice; you realized he was insane and, worse, he was capable of great harm."

Scott Malkowitz sat back, satisfied with his summation. He buzzed his secretary, asked her to bring in coffee. "You take cream and sugar?"

Elizabeth walked to the window, looked out on a row of magnificent Pacific Heights mansions she'd once fantasized living in, but which now struck her as excessive. Behind her, she heard the clanking of dishes and spoons, a feminine step, the door closing. A shadow passed her shoulder, then Scott Malkowitz stood beside her, holding out a steaming cup of coffee.

"Dr. Shreve," he said. "I'm not as heartless as I appear."

She ignored the coffee, blinked back tears. She'd be damned if she'd say those things about Jack. He'd loved her when she felt most unlovable; she'd defend him even if some found his actions inexcusable. Every man, and every woman for that matter, was capable of violence, had better be capable of it when defending what they loved. Jack's commitment to living things was the clearest evidence yet of what was right with him, not what was wrong. It was what she loved best about him. The more devoted you were, the less meanness you tolerated.

"We are trying for the insanity defense," he said. "It's terribly hard to prove, and impossible if I can't count on your help."

"I'm not going to betray Jack," she said, turning from the window.

"Isn't sending him to prison a betrayal? Isn't letting him deteriorate when he could be successfully treated a kind of unfaithfulness? If you don't do everything you can to save him, whatever the cost, isn't that treason?"

She closed her eyes, but not before she admitted he was clever. And right.

"Seems to me," he went on, "the person who really loves him won't get up on that witness stand and praise Jack Bolton's character. She'll rip him apart. She'll prove he's not a little crazy, but completely out of his mind. Nutso. Capable of anything, and in need of serious psychiatric treatment. Jack Bolton will break your nose as soon as shake your hand, and he'll do it without malice. He'll do it because he can't contain his own thoughts; he's got even less control over his feelings. He'll fail the irresistible impulse test every time. He can't curb his hands, his heart, or his mind. He thinks flowers talk to him and moss has feelings and, frankly, he holds plants in higher regard than people. The person who loves him will sacrifice her good name and Mr. Bolton's esteem to keep him out of harm's way."

Elizabeth opened her eyes. She had no doubt her license would be suspended or revoked, and she was fascinated by how little this bothered her. As if she was already someone else, wearing the brighter, more lively clothes of a stranger.

"Yes," she said. "I see."

"Good."

"I'll need to see Jack," she said. "Explain this to him."

"He knows our game plan," the lawyer said, placing her coffee on the tray, taking his seat behind the desk. "And that's another thing. Your testimony must be that you've ended the relationship, that you still fear him, so of course seeing him is out of the question. It's fortunate you requested a professional visit the other day. We'll say you were there to make arrangements with the new psychiatrist and were relieved when you got out in one piece. Mel Herrara will take it from here."

"You've got this all worked out."

"I believe that's my job."

She returned to her chair, folded her hands on her lap. "What's Mel's assessment of Jack?"

"He doesn't think we'll have much trouble proving delusions, even a psychotic break. Annie Crandall will help with that."

"Annie," Elizabeth said, leaning back.

"She was there during the attack, and last year when the illness began to show itself. She's got no problem calling him crazy."

The intercom buzzed, and the secretary announced Mel Herrara. Elizabeth stiffened, knew an ambush when she saw one. Mel Herrara strode in, a towering, bearded man, combative in his clinical style, even confrontational in his walk. She'd heard a few glowing reports of Mel's assault therapy, but she'd personally taken on three of his ex-patients. Spent a month just coaxing them to speak the truth.

"Beth," he said, holding out his hand. "Not a good time for you. I'm sorry."

She didn't rise, held his hand only briefly. He took the seat beside her, opened his briefcase. "Scott wanted us to get together. These are the preliminary reports on Jack Bolton. He's got an amazing capacity to withstand the effects of medication. I don't think I've seen another case as far gone that hasn't resulted in suicide."

Elizabeth closed her eyes. She knew the truth then, couldn't understand how she'd missed it for so long. Jack didn't respond well to lithium because manic-depressive was the least of what he was. The artist, the genius, the rest was immune.

"Most insanity defenses are won on the basis of psychoses," Mel went on. "Schizophrenia, paranoid delusions, a complete break from reality that robs the patient of the ability to understand the nature of his actions, to tell the difference between right and wrong. Our goal of proving not guilty by reason of insanity as a result of an affective disorder, an irresistible impulse, well, that's another ball game. It's been proven in only a few jurisdictions. We're going to have to validate the insanity of compulsion. The irresistible need to do something that makes no sense. The way Jack Bolton is with his ridiculous gardens, for example. Jumping from one wild idea to the next, compelled to destroy more often than create, with no regard for waste or cost or feasibility. He's at the mercy of his own ambitions. A walking bomb or phoenix, depending on his mood. They've had to completely revamp the garden at the Londonbright, by the way. Children were getting scared of the velicoraptors. Teenagers were found making love inside the T-Rex."

"Mel agrees with me," the lawyer chimed in, "about you not seeing Jack."

"Absolutely," Mel said. "Not only for the sake of the trial, but for the patient's well-being. If we get him to an institution, he'll need months if not years of treatment. A combination of lithium, anticonvulsants, perhaps electrotherapy, depending upon the level of his depression, which he seems to be sliding into with great haste. You know my success rate with bipolar patients. A nonstimulating environment is essential. The same institution, the same room, if possible. Bipolar patients often live like teenagers, on the verge of breakdowns and foolish stunts every second. An unethical love affair . . ." He waved his hand, narrowed his eyes at her. "Well, that plays right into the grandiosity and recklessness of mania, doesn't it? When we get Mr. Bolton calmed down, I predict he'll see things more clearly, understand better what he put his wife through."

It wasn't the stainless steel table that bothered Elizabeth now, but the lack of greenery in the office. No doubt, whenever Scott Malkowitz or Mel Herrara walked into a room, all the plants went into shock. They sensed a lack of tenderness and, like her, tried to remain still enough to escape without damage.

"I have a group session to get to," she said, standing.

"Beth," Mel said. "I just want to do what's best for the patient."

She stared at him. "His name is Jack."

"Ms. Shreve," the lawyer said. "Are you on board?"

He must have set the thermostat below seventy, because she

was chilled to the bone. He must have counted on her willingness to do anything.

"Just tell me when to show up," she said.

KAYLA Donovan had given up cigarettes and sleeping pills only
to become addicted to the way Louis Fields fell in love with her
twice a week.

Two days before their group, she was pumped up, not hoping
but expecting to be chosen. By Monday, she was flat-out predict-
ing she'd be loved. By the time the group met, and Louis turned
her way, she was prettier than nature had intended. Leggier
when standing on tiptoes, luminous when sure of so much. She
traded in timidity for impatience, tapped her foot instead of
blushing while waiting for him to introduce himself and be
won over, once more, by her charms. She didn't have to worry
about him bringing up her past, mentioning the things she'd
said about the surprising painlessness of a knife across the wrist,
the limitations of Prozac. She took a quick breath every Tuesday and Thursday, and started from scratch.

Such constant anticipation upset her sleep cycle. The first
time her mother found her rummaging through the kitchen before dawn, Sondra Donovan began to cry. When Kayla took to
bringing in the newspaper and making coffee, her mother
stared at her the way she stared at her friends' grandchildren.
With such hunger, it was a wonder it didn't eat her alive.

Kayla had begun to hear birds. Obviously, they'd been chirp-
ing outside her window all along, but for years she'd turned up
the television and slept too deliberately to notice. Now they
woke her early and, rather than putting a pillow over her head,

she opened the window. She tried humming along with the robins and found she liked the sound of her own voice. She preferred bluegrass tunes. It was the birds who left bread crumbs to lure her outside—a shiny rock dropped on the lawn chair, the last of the geranium petals they'd nested in strewn across the lawn. Sometimes her mother sat in the garden with her, offered her one of her novels. Kayla especially liked the western romances, with heroes named Blake who would lay down their lives for a woman.

There were days when she didn't cry at all, which might seem like a little thing to her once best friend Marian Foxworthy, who had graduated from law school, gotten married to an architect, and produced two perfect children by the age of twenty-eight, but which was as miraculous as life after death to Kayla. She began to pick up speed, to feel even occasionally silly, though she had yet to share her knock-knock jokes with the group. She was not Gary or Jack; she would have to be pried off her medication. She fingered the scars on her wrist religiously now, but even with such obvious reminders, she was still losing the sensation of hopelessness. Like childbirth and loneliness, once the moment passed, the memory didn't seem entirely real. She couldn't pinpoint precisely what had kept her in bed all those hours, why she hadn't grown exasperated with herself. She couldn't understand why she'd been so certain no one would ever love her, when obviously she was good enough to be loved over and over and over again.

Today she walked into Dr. Shreve's office and found Gary Griffith at the window, not bouncing or jiggling or thumping anything. He folded his arms across his chest and glared at Blanche, who sat on the edge of her chair, fussing with the creases of her polyester pants. The old woman looked ancient today, doubly wrinkled, hunched over and frail. She was dressed in one of those ruffly granny blouses, with a scallop right up to her chin.

"Hello," Kayla said.

Blanche looked up, widened her eyes in surprise. Kayla had put on jeans for the first time in two years, a pair of Calvin Kleins she hadn't worn since high school. They were loose on the hips, but apparently this was the style now. She wore the only turtleneck that still fit her, a size four, without a bra. Last week, she'd gone through drawers she hadn't touched in five years, discovering outdated baby-doll pajamas and an inordinate number of wool socks. She hadn't found a single scarf or bra, and she wondered if her mother had thrown them all out, fearful of the ways they could be knotted.

"Well," Blanche said, smiling. "Look at you."

Kayla warmed from head to toe. She felt a flood of goodwill, wanted to take Blanche in her arms and warm her up, too, but just then Dr. Shreve rushed in.

"Sorry I'm late," she said. "Louis's boss left a message on my cell. They need him to work at the preschool during our group. He won't be able to come anymore."

Kayla slumped, might have even sunk into her usual chair in the corner if it hadn't been Thursday, *her* day. If she hadn't felt so giddy, drinking coffee since dawn. She marched to the desk behind which Dr. Shreve was arranging her things, taking off her sweater, looking about as unprepared and addled as Kayla had ever seen her.

"We should go," Kayla said. "To the day care. We should give him our support."

The doctor looked up. Kayla had never spoken in that firm a voice, had always rushed her whispered words to give the others more time. Now they all looked at her aghast, as if she'd broken some cardinal rule. And perhaps she had. She'd gotten well first.

"I don't know," Dr. Shreve said. "He might not feel comfortable with us there."

"Of course he will," Blanche said suddenly. "He won't even know who we are." She turned to Kayla. "Well, some of us."

Kayla rose to the balls of her feet and hovered there. She looked out the window, saw a man dressed as Superman walking along the fire escape. When he put a finger to his lips, she smiled and was silent. Wonder had come for her at last.

"Still," Dr. Shreve went on, "I just came over from the city. To tell you the truth, I'm a little—"

"Let's go," Gary said. "We need another outing. Without Jack, we've got no oomph."

He began to twitch again, and when Blanche met his gaze, the gyrations got wilder. Ticced him two feet forward, twisted his arms around his waist. He must have been contagious, because Blanche was shaking, too. Trembling like a woman losing her strength, a woman who would soon stop driving at night and showing up for Sunday bridge parties. Who would spend her evenings alone, looking through photo albums.

"Apparently, you've all decided," Dr. Shreve said, and there was a note of peevishness in her voice. A lack of professionalism that made Kayla warm to her for the first time since they'd met.

Blanche walked around the table, put a hand on the doctor's arm. "I was thinking about Jack and this old folk song my mother taught me." She cleared her throat, glanced at Gary who

was watching her intently. Her voice wobbled at first, then grew
higher and stronger as she went along.

> *"There were three men came out of the West*
> *Their fortunes for to try.*
> *And these three men made a solemn vow,*
> *John Barleycorn should die.*
>
> *They ploughed him in the earth so deep,*
> *With clods upon his head,*
> *Then these three men they did conclude*
> *John Barleycorn was dead.*
>
> *There he lay sleeping in the ground*
> *Till rain from the sky did fall;*
> *Then Barleycorn sprang a green blade*
> *And proved liars of them all."*

Elizabeth Shreve had gone very still. Kayla came around the
desk, took her other arm.

"Don't you know the legend of the green man?" Blanche
asked. "Every time they kill him, he comes back stronger than
before."

"Anyone could tell that he loved you," Kayla told her.

It was remarkable to watch the shift from doctor to woman,
to be strong enough, for once, to do the holding. Gary stayed by
the window, his tics coming so smoothly they were almost like
music.

Finally, Dr. Shreve pulled away, swiped her eyes. "Sorry," she
said. "That was way out of line."

"Oh, poppycock," Blanche said. "We like you much better this way."

The doctor picked up her briefcase. "Let's go see Louis."

They took the doctor's car to the Wee School Preschool, nothing more than a remodeled home in Mill Valley, clad in dumpy aluminum siding. The play yard consisted of a few patches of crabgrass, a rusting metal picnic table, and two turtle sandboxes. Kayla could not imagine anyone bringing her child there in good conscience. They opened the front door, passed through a narrow hallway lined with cubbies labeled alphabetically—Ashley, Brianna, Brittany, Colby. Picachu rain jackets and Bob the Builder blankets hung from hooks or, more commonly, were crammed into the cubbies along with dirty Beanie babies and the Power Rangers that were not allowed during Show and Tell. They opened the far door, emerged in a large room where twenty-two children sat at tiny tables having a snack of goldfish crackers and apple juice. Louis dwarfed the small, plastic chair he sat in while filling Dixie cups with twenty goldfish apiece.

He counted each fish out loud, and the children chimed in at fives and tens. When he got to twenty, he looked around in confusion, then one of the children grabbed his sleeve and pointed to a boy standing at Louis's left. "James's turn. Give it to James."

The director came over, told Dr. Shreve how delighted they were with Louis's gentle manner, his extraordinary patience and willingness to spin the children like windmills again and again and again. How the boys, in particular, adored him, begged him to tell stories so they could fill in farting and peeing endings whenever he forgot what came next.

Blanche sat down at a table of girls who were creating stick figures with markers and glitter glue. Gary discovered the toy drums in the corner. Kayla remained near the door, might even have stepped backwards. It suddenly occurred to her that one morning Louis might not have the energy to fall in love with her. One wrong word, one second thought, and he might exchange the blissful torture of infatuation for an undemanding, slapstick movie, a long, uncomplicated nap. Even if she was the only woman he remembered, she had never been his only choice.

She reached for the wall, slid her hand across a finger painting that might have started off beautifully multicolored, but ended up brown. She'd trade a minute of feeling beautiful for an hour of knowing what he would do, one Thursday of being chosen for six days of already being picked. She'd bring her children here in a heartbeat, she realized, if she knew that Louis would be around to tend them.

She marched across the room, pulled up a tiny blue chair beside Louis's red one. She took his hand before he could reach for another goldfish.

"Hi, honey," she said.

He stiffened, and she felt the doctor watching them from across the room. Kayla waited for Louis to look at her, to remember. It was one thing, she thought, to be pretty enough to pique a man's desire, but it was something else to keep it. You had to be more than beautiful for that. You had to be interesting. Strong.

She squeezed his hand. God knows she didn't demand miracles. She didn't need ecstasy or giddiness—it wasn't necessary that her heart pound. All she wanted was a couple hours each day when she wasn't hoping for anything different. A moment or two when she wouldn't change a thing.

Louis looked first at her hand, then worked his way up her arm. The children had drawn a smiley face on his right cheek, and she smiled in response. She held the smile even when she saw no sign of recognition in his eyes. Happiness followed a completely different road than she'd imagined, a steeper trail even more demanding than the long, sad path around it. A hike, for sure, to the summit. A test of endurance and faith in the view to come.

He studied her nose, her lips. His eyes circled up, began to widen in both appreciation and familiarity. She squeezed his hand, brought it to her lips.

One of the children giggled. Two went over to the craft table, where they were making bugs out of egg cartons and pipe cleaners.

"Kayla," Louis said at last, without taking out his notes.

Her smile relaxed into a grin, then unwound even further into a sigh of contentment. "Sweetheart," she said. "How was your day?"

AFTER autumn, heavy metal hurt Chloe's ears. During winter, jazz seemed too snappy and love songs, like warm days in January, a tease. Chloe gave her stereo to Jill, went outside whenever her mother turned on the radio. The garden she began in October, in the greenhouse her father helped her build, was now flourishing, a fact which astonished her less every day. She'd had no faith that Jack's exotic seeds would sprout, and once they did, she realized she had nothing to do with it. She hadn't followed the directions on the packet, hadn't pressed the seeds a quarter-inch deep and kept them evenly moist for two weeks. She merely came home from school every afternoon to see what had grown in her absence, what miracles had been wrought when she turned her back.

She harvested sugar cane on Christmas, stocked the kitchen with fresh greens on New Year's Day. Her friends began to ask for tastes of her Spanish licorice, and though she enjoyed showing off what she'd grown, she might always be skeptical of sudden, unwarranted attention. Like Jack, she preferred the company of plants.

Today she repotted the peppermint eucalyptus, then filled her mother's car with the smell of mint. Her mom had continued to go to work, to clean, to garden, to hope for the best. She gripped the steering wheel tightly, and when Chloe sat beside her and made a fist she noticed their hands were the same size and shape, both freckled at the knuckles. When her mother pulled up in front of the San Francisco County Courthouse and didn't weep, Chloe decided it wasn't the worst thing in the world to turn out just like her. It wasn't the best thing, but it wasn't the worst.

They searched for a parking space, finally gave up and paid ten dollars to park across the street. Her mother killed the engine, and Chloe couldn't get out of the car.

"You don't have to go in," her mother said.

Chloe shrugged. She didn't have to get up in the morning either. She could stay in bed, pitiful and soap opera dependent, letting the things she'd lost steamroll what she had left. Or she could get over it, tend her plants and make something else bloom. She could choose the very thing most of her friends, except Jill, shunned: The path that would do her good.

"I want to," she said.

Her mother walked her across the street to the door of the courthouse. She looked up at the windows, stuffed her hands in the pockets of her jeans.

"I wish you could come in," Chloe said. "That lawyer is such an idiot."

Her mother smiled, blinked back tears. "I'm okay. Time doesn't change everything," she said. "Remember, they'll take you in as a group. You'll talk through the phone. Try not to worry about the others. Focus on Jack."

Chloe hardly flinched at the unnecessary advice. She squeezed her mom's hand, walked into the courthouse alone. She went through the metal detectors, was kept waiting with twenty other fidgety visitors. Finally, they were led into the meeting room; the guard took up his stance by the door. She waited for the others to sit, then chose a stall near the door.

Her mother had warned her about the shackles, but she wasn't prepared for the transparency of Jack's skin, the thinness even she didn't find fashionable. His trial was in two weeks and she wondered if he would make it that long. Every man she'd ever loved, from her father to Skitch to Jack, had turned out to be less than first imagined. Then she realized this hardly mattered, because she had turned out to be more.

She picked up the phone, and it seemed to take hours for him to pick up the receiver on his side, to say her name.

"I'm so sorry," she said.

Jack smiled sadly; it never reached his eyes. Someone had cut off all his gorgeous hair, shaved it to an ill-suited military buzz. "It's all right. It's not as bad as it looks."

He looked past her, probably hoping to see her mother. Chloe didn't pretend to understand Scott Malkowitz's tactics, but she

320 CHRISTY YORKE

recognized stupidity when she saw it. What good was saving a
man if you broke his heart in the process?

"How's your mother?" he asked quietly.

"She cries in the bathroom. Your lawyer spends an awful lot
of time telling her how she feels about you."

Jack blinked a few times, looked more closely at her. "You've
been gardening," he said.

She smiled, sat forward. "I built a greenhouse. Just one of
those kits. Dad had to help a little. I got your seeds going inside.
And vegetables. Some perennials I'll plant outside in the spring.
I wanted to bring you some of the sugar cane, but Mom told me
they wouldn't let me give it to you. You wouldn't believe the way
it grew, Jack. So fast and tall, it was like it wanted to reach
heaven in record time."

He smiled as she talked, got a spark in his eye that quickly
faded. She reached into her jacket pocket, took out the baggie of
seeds she'd brought to show him. It had taken her days to collect
all the kernels from the asparagus beans. She'd started a single
seed in a three-inch peat pot, and in a month the plant had
grown to ten feet. She'd had to repot it twice and stake the vines,
build a bamboo teepee when the beans and tendrils outgrew
their support. Nothing had given her as much pleasure as
watching it overtake everything, completely oblivious to the onslaught of winter right outside the door.

"These are for you," she said.

Jack looked at the seeds. "Chloe, I appreciate the gesture, but
they won't let me have them. Anyway, there's no garden in
here."

She hadn't even realized she was crying until he touched the
glass. "Don't," he said. "Please."

"Mom and I went to see the dinosaurs," she said through her tears. "They've ripped them all out."

He shrugged. "Things change."

"But you worked so hard. There was nothing like it. You had this incredible vision, this way with the plants."

"It doesn't matter."

"Of course it does. It was amazing and they ruined it. They didn't understand."

"I mean it doesn't matter what they do. If they tear it out or tame it. Once beauty is introduced it can't be denied. If you shut it out, it will come and get you."

She estimated he'd lost twenty pounds, all muscle. She studied his sunken, pale face, wanted him to hear the thoughts she didn't dare speak out loud. The strange visions she'd been having of becoming as rampant and fearless as asparagus beans, as miraculous and self-supporting as strawberry spinach. A plant that grew with no help at all.

But he merely stared at her, said nothing, and she figured if he'd stopped reading minds, it was time for the rest of them to start talking.

"You told me a garden grows just for the joy of it," she said. "If that's true, it doesn't matter what they do to you. How much medication you take. The plants will be waiting for you."

He leaned forward just enough for her to see she was mistaken. He wasn't entirely colorless. When he smiled, there was a green glint in his eyes.

SIXTEEN

THE defense called her to testify on a Monday, the moon's day, when her patient would have been Amy Wendt, who was afraid of air. Afraid of what she couldn't see, airborne viruses and bacteria and contaminated exhalations. Terrified of radiation and carbon monoxide and the thinning of the ozone. Elizabeth had been counseling Amy for a year, trying a host of anti-anxiety drugs that failed to dent her phobia. The trouble with Amy wasn't hysteria, but perfect logic. The biggest dangers in the world *were* invisible—poisoned air and unstable minds and the enemy within our midst. She was the sanest person around, Amy Wendt, but what did that get her? Logic was invisible, too, and full of fear. On their last visit, Elizabeth had done little more than hold Amy's hand and plead the case of the illogical—if we can't see it, perhaps it can't do us harm.

Elizabeth arrived at the courtroom to find Mary Bolton

waiting for her outside the door. "Don't go in," Jack's sister said. "Testifying is a terrible idea for you."

Elizabeth put her hand on the door. "Don't worry about me. We've got to do whatever it takes to help Jack."

"I've talked to him. He doesn't want you to sacrifice yourself. Listen to me. You've got a Mars transit in conjunction with Neptune. That's an explosive situation coupled with Neptune's disappointments. I don't see any way you can make this right."

"It doesn't matter. I have to testify."

"Please. I'm not making this up."

Elizabeth squeezed her arm. "I don't think you are. But I'm not letting Jack go to prison if I can help it."

She entered the anteroom, where she was to wait until they called her. Two women she didn't recognize were chatting; Elizabeth stared at her hands, tried not to bristle at the inane conversation. *Can you believe this rain? You've got to go to Maggie—best manicure in the city.* Elizabeth kept her head down, silently rehearsed the lines Scott Malkowitz had fed her.

When they called her, she smoothed her skirt, looked straight ahead as she walked into the courtroom. She didn't glance at Jack until she'd taken the oath, then wished she'd waited longer.

Someone had made a mockery of him, dressed him in an ill-fitting blue suit—tight through the shoulders, nearly popping its corny white buttons, the sleeves two inches short of his wrists. White sneakers, red shirt, blue tie, an American flag gone awry. His hair was all but gone, shaved to a dirt-colored prickle, revealing unusually delicate ears, a tiny bandage over the pulse in his neck. He never lifted his gaze from the floor.

Scott Malkowitz stood, looking slick and sane beside his clownish client. He wore a black suit, cream shirt, red tie. He

walked toward the witness stand, asked her full name and profession.

"Elizabeth Alice Shreve," she said. "Psychiatrist."

He asked her address, and she took the opportunity to steady
herself. During the recitation of her credentials, she uncrossed
her legs, flattened her feet on the floor.

"Have you treated the defendant, Jack Bolton?" the lawyer
asked.

"Yes."

"When?"

"This summer," she said. "And for a few weeks the winter
before."

"For what condition?"

"Bipolar disorder."

"Can you describe that condition please?"

She sat forward, easing into comfortable terrain. "Mr. Bolton
suffers from bipolar I, the most severe form of affective illness. Patients diagnosed with the disease meet the full criteria
for both mania and major depressive illness. They cycle from
short-lived periods of mania, grandiose thinking, high energy,
compulsions, sometimes delusional thinking, to longer-lived depressions, often resulting in suicide or suicidal attempts."

The lawyer stood beside her, leaned in as if they were colleagues. "During the summer, while you treated Mr. Bolton,
would you say he was manic or depressed?"

"Manic."

"Severely?"

She focused on the blue hair of an elderly woman in the jury
box, thinking it the color of glaciers. She realized she had no desire to go anywhere Jack couldn't garden. As quickly as she'd

found the courage to travel, she'd limited herself to the places another person wanted to go. "Yes."

"In your professional opinion, would you say Mr. Bolton was delusional?"

She spotted Mary Bolton sliding into the back row, wiping her eyes on the sleeve of her blouse.

"Yes."

"Of what nature were the delusions?"

She closed her eyes for the briefest moment, then turned to look at Jack. He had raised his gaze sometime during her testimony and now watched her steadily.

"He believed plants communicated with him," she said. "That he understood the desires of trees and flowers, and that plants responded to his presence and good intentions. He was grandiose. He believed he was here to create heaven on earth. To make the perfect garden."

She smiled when she said it, out of tenderness, respect. To her own ears, nothing she'd said sounded unreasonable, yet someone in the courtroom laughed. The judge asked for quiet.

"How did you come to treat Mr. Bolton this summer?" the lawyer asked.

"The police called me and asked me to commit him."

"On what basis?"

Elizabeth sighed. "He was found in Golden Gate Park."

"Found? Can you explain what you mean?"

"He was found wandering through the park, the bushes, acting strangely. Wildly. He was incoherent and . . . bloody. He had blood on him."

A man in the front row of the jury box sat forward, shrugging off sleepiness. Elizabeth glanced at the eleven people who would decide Jack's fate—five women, six men, ranging from a boy only a few years older than Chloe to the blue-haired woman in her sixties. Every fifth house on the street shelters a person with mental illness, which ought to mean two of the eleven would not be so quick to label Jack a criminal. Two of the eleven ought to harbor some secret compassion.

"He agreed to the commitment?" Scott Malkowitz asked.

"Yes."

"During the voluntary commitment, or at any time as your patient, did Mr. Bolton tell you what happened between him and Bruce Koswolski?"

Jack looked toward the door that lead back to his cell. He'd gotten through half a winter, and she hoped Mel Herrara had pointed this out. Sometimes the quality of living was inconsequential compared to the accomplishment of simply going on.

"Not until the day he called the police. Until then, he didn't remember."

"He didn't remember, or he didn't tell you?"

"I believe he truly didn't remember. One symptom of mania is blank spots in the memory. A patient wakes up in the morning and can't believe the things his friends tell him he did the night before."

"Things such as trying to kill a man?"

"Perhaps."

"Did he tell you his wife was having an affair with Bruce Koswolski?"

"They were separated. He told me she was seeing someone new."

Jack laughed out loud, and the courtroom stilled. The judge, a white-haired man who had been resting his heavy jowls on his palm, suddenly rapped his gavel.

"A warning, Mr. Bolton," he said. "Outbursts like that constitute contempt."

Scott Malkowitz did not seem the slightest bit perturbed; he might have even coached Jack to act up. "We apologize, your Honor," he said, then he turned back to Elizabeth. "You were treating Mr. Bolton last winter, weren't you? At the same time he and his wife decided to separate?"

"Yes."

"Do you recall what reason Mr. Bolton gave for the dissolution of his marriage?"

"I can speak to only one side of the story," Elizabeth said. "Annie Crandall was never my patient, nor did I counsel the two of them as a couple. I know only what Jack told me. She wanted someone steadier, more . . . average, more predictable. They had different ideas about what mattered most, where their lives should be going. They had different energy levels, wildly different personalities. I wasn't aware of the manic episodes he'd suffered the previous summer, but I'm sure they only added to Annie's dissatisfaction. My guess would be that she felt both exhausted and a little unnerved by Jack's mood swings, his garden binges. She'd come home from work to find last week's patio ripped out, the elaborate iris beds he'd spent months on replaced by a swath of daisies. She is a cautious person and he's reckless with funds. With design choices."

"You believe she felt frightened by her own husband," the lawyer said.

Jack's smile had faded.

"Yes," she said quietly.

"The defendant became obsessed with gardens, isn't that right?"

"He wanted them to be perfect."

"While you treated him, he took on two major gardening projects, became what we might call illogically passionate about both of them. In the end, he slaughtered one, abandoned the other. Is that a fair assessment?"

"He would get upset with what he perceived as imperfections in his designs. He came up with better, more elaborate ideas, and had trouble sticking to one plan."

"One of those major projects was the children's garden at the Londonbright Museum. The job of a lifetime, some would say, yet he continually delayed the project with change orders, midnight excavations, fanaticism about details." He walked quickly past Jack, causing him to flinch. "He was more concerned with the quality of life experienced by a trumpet vine than he was with completing the work on time or on budget, or with any resemblance to the design he was hired to install."

"As I said, he got frustrated with—"

"He destroyed much of the Londonbright garden after he was fired. Took what he professed to love and whacked it with a steel chain. Is that correct?"

She sighed. "Yes."

"He began an even more ambitious garden in Napa. A mythological design of nymph topiaries and the labyrinth of the Minotaur. Yet even those ideas weren't grand enough to satisfy him. He was set to demolish what he'd already started when he abruptly left for Idaho. Is that true?"

"It is, but you have to understand. A manic's mind is unfenced.

The trouble was not one unrealistic vision, but too many just possible ones. Jack saw labyrinths in hedges, lagoons in puddles, dinosaurs in steel and ivy, and each was entirely feasible for the moment he believed in it. From the outside, the mind of a manic looks like a mosaic, but go inside and you'll see it's one glittering, mesmerizing fragment at a time."

"Does a person in a manic state understand the havoc they wreak every time they change their mind? That, for every grand new scheme, every more fantastic design, there are two or three ruined gardens, an angry curator, a stack of bills, a wife who has been left behind?"

She glanced at Jack, who was now doodling on the desk. "No," she said. "Not always."

"Explain compulsions, if you will."

Elizabeth took a sip of water. "A compulsion is an irresistible impulse to perform an act, often one that is contrary to your own will. Bipolar patients, in their manic stages, might feel forced to act in ways even they perceive as senseless and interfering. They might become enamored with pink pens, for instance, not sleep or work for three days until they've bought out every stationery store in the city. They'll feel like they're suffocating until the compulsion is fulfilled."

The lawyer walked across the room, picked a point halfway between her and Jack. Then he turned, dropped his hands in his pockets.

"Would you say, Dr. Shreve, that you became one of Jack Bolton's compulsions?"

Elizabeth heard the titter in the courtroom. Jack set down his pencil. The last she saw of his eyes before he closed them was a hazy, unfocused green, like murky water. She wondered exactly how much medication Mel Herrara was prescribing. She searched the courtroom, found Mel in the second row, watching her closely. The moment she was off the stand, she knew a complaint would be raised with the APA and the Board of Medical Examiners for sexual misconduct with a patient.

"Perhaps," she said.

"Is it possible," the lawyer went on, "that Mr. Bolton felt like he was suffocating without you, and he pursued you with the same irrational desire that led him to pink pens and dinosaur gardens and the side of a river in Idaho?"

The members of the jury watched her closely, and Elizabeth understood Scott's true plan. It wasn't to prove Jack had suffered from the psychosis of an irresistible impulse, but to confirm something even more tantalizing: The inherent insanity of love.

She turned to the lawyer, folded her hands in her lap. "Nothing is too wonderful to be true," she said.

Jack opened his eyes suddenly, smiled. He sat back in his chair and crossed his arms.

"So," the lawyer said, lips pursed now, "you were aware that Mr. Bolton was still, technically, married. You yourself, I might add, had only been separated from your husband for two weeks when you started up a relationship with the defendant. You knew that Mr. Bolton was suffering from both compulsions and delusional thinking. You were called to treat him after he was found bloody and delirious in a public park, so you were aware that he was most likely a violent and unstable man. Yet during his time as your patient, you began a romantic relationship with him. Is that true?"

She didn't hesitate. "Yes."

The lawyer paused, as if her quickness had thrown him off

track. "How long did this romance with Mr. Bolton continue?"

She wanted to say it never ended, but had been coached to reply, "A few days."

"Was it sexual?"

He hadn't practiced that question with her, and she narrowed her eyes. "I don't see—"

"Did you have sexual intercourse with one of your psychotic patients?"

She blinked, questioning whether this was such a good idea after all, giving up everything—her career, her reputation, any chance of backtracking. When the moisture had cleared from her eyes, she noticed her husband sitting beside Mary Bolton. She hadn't seen him during her testimony, but of course, he must have been there all along. She saw the blue tie she'd picked out one Christmas, the same steady gaze that had, over the years, quietly made her stronger than she would have been alone.

She locked gazes with him. "Yes," she whispered.

Scott Malkowitz waited for the whispers and chuckles to die down, let the judge admonish the courtroom. Finally, the lawyer continued with the hint of a smile. "How many times did you have sexual intercourse?"

She turned from Will. "Mr. Malkowitz—"

"It's essential to know if this was an ongoing relationship, or simply a momentary collapse of good judgment on your part."

She glared at him, wondered if he really greased his hair or if it merely emerged from his scalp mucky and slick. "Once," she whispered, the memory of that morning in Napa flooding back. One morning worth a thousand.

"So after one sexual episode, you decided to end the relationship. Can you explain why?"

Elizabeth thought of that day in the car when Jack told her the truth. She'd looked out at the swimmers in the bay, but what she saw were broken things—torn stems and bloody men and her mother beating her then swearing later that she remembered none of it, that Elizabeth was making up stories. She thought of all that before she could stop herself, and Jack's smile faded. He dropped his hands to his lap.

"He'd . . . he'd been fired from the Londonbright," she said, trying to remember the script. "He was distraught over all the concrete they'd put in and . . . He believes we have to face our greatest fears, so he found winter. He'd saved the lithium I'd been prescribing. But he didn't take them. He came back."

She smiled where she shouldn't, and Scott Malkowitz stepped forward. "He came back, yet you ended it," he said stiffly. "Why?"

When Jack wouldn't look at her, she turned to Will, saw the tears in his eyes, an unexpected gift. She'd practiced the next words so often, she was surprised when they didn't come out stilted, when they sounded an awful lot like the truth. "Because I was becoming afraid of him. I was afraid for myself and for my daughter."

She felt, more than saw, Jack's head rise. Felt him pivot, turn toward her. She broke away from Will's gaze, found Jack's eyes wide and startled. And she realized how naïve she'd been, thinking an ally was always a friend. Believing a man like Scott Malkowitz when he'd told her he'd prepped Jack on what she would say. Of course the lawyer had wanted Jack to react with surprise, the way a betrayed man would. With shock and rage and sorrow. With madness.

"So you believed he might harm you."

She looked right at Jack. *No. Never.* "Yes," she said quietly.

"As Jack Bolton's lover, you believed he was capable of violence. As the defendant's psychiatrist, you believed him mentally imbalanced, incapable of distinguishing right from wrong."

She believed him capable of wonder, but she said, "Yes."

"May I ask, Dr. Shreve, why you got involved with him in the first place?"

Elizabeth kept expecting someone to object. At any moment, someone would jump up and say this had no bearing on anything, that it was just melodrama. But the courtroom was silent, waiting. Even the judge leaned forward on his hand.

The attorney had already given her the answer, an intolerable lie. She'd been lonely, abandoned by her husband, unsure how to go on alone, and had fallen for Jack's sensual, manic energy, his high-spirited charm. She'd needed companionship even though she'd known he was incapable of true feeling. Incapable of love, just as he was incapable of malice. He had all the intent of shrapnel, she was supposed to say. Dangerous but beside the point.

Elizabeth blinked, didn't bother to wipe her tears. It took everything she had not to get up and walk over to Jack, not to throw her arms around him and ruin everything.

"Dr. Shreve?" the attorney asked.

Elizabeth met Scott Malkowitz's gaze knowing he had a counterattack for any surprise moves she might make, knowing he was good at what he did and, with any luck, he'd save Jack from prison. Knowing he was the first person she'd truly hated.

She turned to Jack, tried to will him to look at her. "Because he was generous and kind," she said, watching Jack flinch. "Because he coaxed my daughter into the garden when she could have gone into her room and refused to come out. Because he taught me how to talk to plants and unwrapped six more continents on the globe. Because whatever line divides bizarre and original thoughts is porous and complicated. Because he loved me."

Even from the corner of her eye, she saw Scott Malkowitz's face redden, but she kept her gaze on Jack. When he finally looked at her, she smelled gardenias. Her nostrils flared, she felt woozy from so much perfume, then little by little the scent faded. Too quickly, there was only the barest hint of it, over-powered by the artificial smells of the courtroom, by furniture polish and floor wax and sweat.

"So what you're saying," the attorney said, his voice clipped and furious, "is that the defendant was contagious."

Elizabeth jerked. Even the prosecuting attorney looked stunned, as if he'd lost track of whose side they were on.

"I beg your pardon?"

"I said Jack Bolton was contagious. He got you believing in his delusions. In the necessity of pink pens and the tender-heartedness of plants. He infected you enough to ruin your judgment. You began to call creative what, a month earlier, you would have correctly labeled as psychotic. Isn't all this true, Dr. Shreve?"

Scott Malkowitz looked at her with murder in his eyes, and she stared right back. *You're just as capable of violence as he is,* she thought, and perhaps he heard her, because he stepped back, got a drink of water, ran his fingers through his glutinous hair.

"Just because a man can't control what he's doing," she said, "doesn't mean the things he's doing aren't good."

Scott Malkowitz squared his shoulders. "Did you try to medicate Mr. Bolton?"

"Yes. On lithium and anticonvulsants."

"Did he take the medication?"

"Only briefly."

"Why only briefly?"

"Many bipolar patients fear treatment because they don't want to lose the euphoric feelings that often accompany mania. They fear they'll lose their artistry and flair for poetry, that mental illness is so intertwined with who they are that it's inoperable. Like cancer of the heart."

"Did Mr. Bolton believe suffering from bipolar disorder made him special?"

"He didn't believe it made him anything other than what he was. A man who cherished life by cherishing plants."

"Yet he attacked a man, didn't stop until he'd nearly killed him."

"Yes."

"Was the defendant taking medication when he attacked Bruce Koswolski?"

"No."

"Would he have attacked Mr. Koswolski if he had been taking it?"

"Objection!"

Finally, the prosecuting attorney got his wits about him, but Elizabeth knew it was too late. Jack was back to doodling on the desk. At the next trial, someone up for murder would discover an elaborate pencil sketch of a cherry tree in full bloom. The judge asked Scott Malkowitz to move on.

"In your professional opinion," the attorney said, "did Jack

Bolton know what he was doing when he attacked Bruce Koswolski?"

"No."

"In your professional opinion, can Jack Bolton control himself?"

Elizabeth took a deep breath, finally able to state a truth that
would please them all.

"In my professional opinion," she said, "he doesn't even try."

Elizabeth didn't wait for the censure. After her testimony, she
called her patients to tell them she would no longer be practicing psychiatry. After an excruciating day in the courtroom, listening to Annie Crandall describe Jack as a man at the mercy of
his impulses, crazy for sure, blameless but also heartless, Elizabeth cleaned out her desk.

The next morning, she was back at the courthouse, taking in
every word. When the jury went into deliberations, she refused
to leave the courtroom.

Stuart, frail and bald after weeks of radiation and chemotherapy, met her there, armed with the last box of her personal
belongings—pictures of Chloe, three treasured volumes of poetry, two dozen pink pens she used religiously now.

"They may not suspend you," he said.

"They'll suspend me."

"You could try to look a little more upset."

She shrugged. "When I come back, I swear I'm painting the
walls purple."

Stuart laughed. He'd been on Mary's fat-rich diet since he
started treatment, and all the gourmet cheeses and deep-fried

onion rings were starting to do strange things. His chest had hogged the extra calories, buffing out two shirt sizes, while his legs remained wobbly and thin.

They waited. The jury deliberated all morning, then again after lunch. At three, a murmur ran through the courtroom. Spectators began filing back in. Mary Bolton pushed her way into their row, clutching a mangy orange rabbit's foot. "Never fails," she said, and tried to smile.

They waited while Jack was led in, white-faced, too calm. Everyone stood when the judge entered the room. The man looked over the verdict, glanced at Jack. He nodded and the foreman stood.

"On the count of attempted murder, we the jury find the defendant, Jack Bolton, not guilty by reason of insanity."

Elizabeth dropped her head against Stuart's shockingly spongy chest. She started to cry, every last tear she'd held back during the trial.

"You worry too much," Stuart said.

She cried harder, and laughed. "I'm sure I do."

"There's always a happy ending, given enough sacrifice and time."

She looked toward the front of the courtroom, but Jack was surrounded by the defense team, clapping each other on the back.

"Mel told me if they won, he'd request Fairhaven," Elizabeth said. "He told me to leave Jack alone."

"Screw Mel Herrara," Mary said, blowing her nose, smiling brilliantly. "He's got no soul."

Elizabeth waited for the crowd to clear out around Jack, then realized, too late, that he'd already been led out of the room.

Had he even known she was there? She didn't know the rules, had no idea if they'd take him away immediately or sit him down in some room and explain what was to come. She'd been so focused on the outcome of the trial, she hadn't stopped to consider what would happen next.

"Maybe Mel is just what Jack needs," Elizabeth said suddenly, clasping Mary's hand. "At least, there will be no room for argument. There's clear thinking and there's insanity, and Mel won't tolerate anything in between."

Stuart shook his head. "Stay away if you think it will help Jack, but I won't have you thinking like that. Do you really believe Mel Herrara can medicate out genius? Prescribe away love? You think that's possible?"

A year ago, a month ago, she might have said yes. But she'd been spending all her time with free thinkers, and wondrous things had begun to rub off.

Stuart led her and Mary out of the courtroom, turned a corner into an empty corridor. Instead of heading toward the stairs and the exit, Stuart ducked abruptly into an unused meeting room. He began unbuttoning his shirt, and at first Elizabeth laughed, thinking it some risqué joke, then her smile faded as she feared some new tumor. She was prepared for anything except what she saw—bright blue silk, an emblazoned red S over a set of foam chest muscles. Stuart stripped his pants, revealing tights and red boots, a bright yellow belt that held the costume to his emaciated frame.

He stood before them transformed, and while Mary applauded, Elizabeth wrapped her arms around him. He *was* Superman, the last defense against evil and madness. What would the world do without superheroes?

"I started putting on the suit a year after my wife died," he said. His arms, beneath the silk, felt soft and limp. "It made me feel good. I didn't have to do a thing to make people smile except show up."

"You've always been that way, Stuart," she said. "Superman or not."

Stuart walked gingerly to the window, but once he opened it, he rose to his full superhero height. Non-Hodgkin's lymphoma was unpredictable, more likely than Hodgkin's disease to spread beyond the lymph nodes.

Stuart checked the condition of the fire escape, the possibilities of flight from rooftop to rooftop. "You know the great thing about Superman?" he asked as he stepped, surprisingly sure-footedly, onto the narrow fire escape. "When he gets too sick and feeble, they find someone new to wear the suit."

STUART had to stop practicing, at least temporarily, as the cancer, and treatments, advanced. He moved into Mary's apartment in February, liked to lie on the couch beneath the window where he could see the sky. By the time the last rounds of chemotherapy were over, he'd lost twenty-eight pounds. The doctors couldn't guarantee that they'd gotten everything, but Stuart seemed oblivious to everything but Mary's cooking and tenderness, the unexpected gift of a woman who wanted to take care of him.

He took up astrology, was delighted to learn he had the same planetary angles as Jack Nicholson, an alignment which apparently made him irresistible to women. Elizabeth stopped by every day, usually on the heels of one of Stuart's patients who had brought casseroles instead of fears. Today, she stumbled into the brothers Stuart had guided through the minefield of transsexualism, putting on a drag show that made Stuart laugh so hard he fell asleep with tears in his eyes.

Afterward, Elizabeth drove to her old office, where someone from the Board of Medical Examiners had stripped her name from the placard. She'd been suspended for six months, would have to formally apply for reinstatement, and while some days she couldn't bear to drive past the psychiatric center, on others she took the highway deliberately, blared the radio passing by.

It felt odd to walk the silent hallway, almost criminal to ride the elevator three flights up. Carrie Willis had gotten a job in the Day Spa doing aromatherapy facials. Stuart had sublet their offices to Freudians. Elizabeth tried not to look toward her door. She opened the one to Stuart's office, was headed toward the closet when she realized someone had beaten her to it. The door stood ajar; the Superman costume was gone.

She opened the window, imagining sorrow as a ledge a heart-broken man retreated from with every "Hey Superman!" She sat in Stuart's chair and cried.

She'd gotten through each day the only way she knew how. By focusing on the garden Jack had started for her, on Chloe, on the things that flourished under her care. She did not give in to despair when her letters to Jack went unanswered. Winter shrouded everything, then withdrew to reveal what you'd for-gotten—the crocuses planted with haste but growing with cau-tion in the courtyard, green buds on a favorite old vine. Jack was wrong about one thing; winter was not dormant. Invisible things—roots and bulbs and heartwood—still grew.

That night, Elizabeth made her way to Chloe's bedroom, the

way she did every night even though Chloe's nightmares had abated. This time she sat in the chair by the window and stayed until dawn, until she'd absorbed every last, lonely minute. Until she had decided.

She woke Chloe gently, pressed her lips to her forehead. "I've got to go out for a while," she said. "You'll be all right by yourself."

It wasn't a question; it hadn't been for a long time. Elizabeth hurried to her car, took the directions out of the glove compartment, where she'd stored them for months. She headed through Belvedere, along the shores of the cove, past the stone pillars onto Corinthian Island. She followed Alcatraz Avenue nearly to the top, where ninety-eight stairs led straight up.

At her first glimpse of Will's house, she scolded herself for not realizing sooner that some people are more colorful than they appear at first glance, and some people are less.

She hiked the stairs, feeling the sting of muscles she'd have to build up, praying there was garden space at the top so vegetables, at least, would not have to be carted up weekly. She reached the red door a full ten minutes later. She knocked but got no answer. She tried the knob, found it unlocked.

He'd decorated boldly—an aquamarine wall, cherry-colored sofa, vibrant Mexican art. All the years they'd been married, he'd left the decorating decisions to her, and she wondered if his innate sense of style surprised him. If it saddened or encouraged him to discover that some talents would only unfurl while on your own.

She walked into the family room, opened the sliding door to the balcony. Will sat at a blue and gold mosaic table, sipping coffee, reading the paper. He stood when he saw her, gawky and newly sweet, a gift no less valued because it had been given twice.

She would have gone to him, so it was that much sweeter when he crossed the deck in two strides, took her in his arms. He pressed his face to her hair, ran his hands down her back, as if she'd changed form, grown muscle while he'd been gone.

He kissed her slowly, tentatively, and she lifted a hand to his cheek. He turned her in his arms so she could see the bay, her view, pressed her back firmly against his stomach, and she realized poets and pop singers had it all wrong. Falling in love does not prove anything. It's only an introduction, a position taken and still in need of validation. Next to come are the arguments she and Will would have to establish, the meat of the body they'd need to write, the long, convincing conclusion still to be made.

Falling in love is only the beginning.

THEY tried to tempt him with the garden as soon as he arrived, but he showed no interest, wouldn't tour the expansive grounds. He took to bed in the psychotic wing, refused mail and fruit and company, the things he loved best, the things they allowed him to refuse. At Fairhaven, they could do whatever they wanted to him, and Mel Herrara believed in doing a lot. Lithium, anticonvulsants, shock therapy, administered in high dosages in spite of Jack's protests, and later increased even further, to combat Jack's apathy. Because Jack was so committed to hating his psychiatrist, he didn't realize, for a good month, that loathing created its own ugly but forward motion. When you hated someone, you plotted their demise, prayed for their downfall. You couldn't lose all hope.

He slept a lot, or not at all. February passed in a monochrome haze—the corridors of the hospital a steel gray, the sky, when they forced him to look out the window, the color of storm clouds even when the sun was shining. One of the women on his floor got roses from her husband every Saturday, and she cried when Jack pointed out that all the petals were beige. Some days flowers and faces were less than beige, insipid and drab, and he refused to rise from bed, even when they injected him with something. Some days he wished he'd taken all the pills in Idaho, some nights he thought he had.

Four people on his floor had been in the hospital for more than a decade.

He knew Elizabeth would not come.

He hated his psychiatrist and cursed every pill, but one morning he woke to the first birds who'd come north, boasting of their accomplishment outside his window. He rose to an elbow before he remembered to fall back asleep, had a sudden, strong craving for pea soup. He threw his feet over the side of the bed, flinched from the ice cold floor. He grabbed a robe that had hung, unused, in his closet all winter, and put on sneakers. He decided to get the woman down the hall some beige daisies to go with her roses.

He asked one of the men who would never leave the way to the garden. He emerged outside on the day the first crocus bloomed.

Jack walked slowly along the concrete path, his legs trembling. He could not make a fist, took little breaths to keep from inhaling too much fresh air at once. Mel Herrara met him on a manicured but uninspiring swirl of lawn, past a grove of sycamores and oaks and a crumbling brick patio none of the patients used.

"You're an interesting case, Jack Bolton," the doctor said. "All winter I've been hammering you with medication, then, the first sign of spring, you get up on your own."

Jack stretched his arms. The sun was cool, still distant, but warm enough to raise the hairs on his wrists. He poked the grass with his foot, knew from its lackluster color that it had been planted in unamended soil, never given the nutrients it needed to survive for the long haul. He heard birds, wind, and, on a leap of faith, the yawns of awakening leaves. Maybe it ought to take a leap of faith to hear more. Maybe it was better to wonder about wonder than to ever know for sure.

"We need a gardener," Mel Herrara said.

Jack shook his head. "Oh, no."

Still, he had to close his eyes to keep from imagining it. Tree houses, catwalks between the branches, a jungle so gentle and beguiling, it might soothe the nightmares of the post-traumas, lure the agoraphobics outside.

"Just think about it," Mel said.

"I'm not staying." Jack opened his eyes, but the tree houses were still there. The catwalks defiant, practically built, planted with ivies that flourished in a maritime climate, less striking, perhaps, than his exotic summer gardens, but more likely to survive. A garden that was meant to be here.

"No," Mel said softly. "I don't think you are. I wonder if I should have merely waited for spring."

Jack turned to him. "No. You were right."

The two men looked at each other, then Mel touched his shoulder. "You can do whatever you want in the garden, with only one requirement. You must finish what you start. Pick one design and see it through. Convince me, Jack."

A blast of wind hit them, and Jack shivered. March in Marin was notoriously fickle. After a week of fair weather, a bed of calla lilies planted with optimism could be wiped out with a single breath of frost. There were no sure things in the garden, just as there were no sure things in love. Success was a matter of faith, and the knowledge that what you got out of it mattered less than what you put in.

"All right," Jack said. "I'll try."

Within a week, he was well into the transformation. He was given tools, a moderate budget, the freedom to order plants over the phone. He didn't stretch the climate zone the way he usually did, but chose only cold-hardy banana trees, tough bamboos, winter hibiscus. He convinced the hospital's director to give him nautical rope (under close supervision, should the depressives get a hold of it), which he fabricated into swinging bridges between the trees. The other patients got wind of an alternative to bingo, and specialists arrived. Michael, the recovering addict, preached the hardiness and versatility of hemp; Caitlyn, feather light after a season of bulimia, took to the oak branches like an elf and helped build the tree houses; the autistic twins weeded meticulously, never left a bed until the last taproot was gone.

The day Mel Herrara reduced the dosage of lithium, Jack stared at the pink in his variegated palms and cried. The garden wasn't particularly unusual or avant-garde, but for some reason he loved it without measure.

When he wiped his eyes and emerged from the trees, he found

Blanche Armstrong wearing gardening gloves, blue jeans, and a man's plaid shirt. The group came to Fairhaven every Thursday, whether or not Jack got out of bed to join them. Louis Fields had reworked his schedule at the day care; the four of them helped with the gardening or appropriated the visiting room, tuning the television to *Santa Barbara* and playing cards.

"The magic hasn't left you, Jack," she said.

His uncertainty, ironically, was the clearest sign yet that he was getting well. When he'd been manic, he'd changed his mind a thousand times but never doubted his vision. Now he questioned the need and artistry of every design element; he struggled to make the smallest decision. Yet once the choice was made, he delighted in the play of light through the native ferns, the heady smell of the indigenous coastal redwoods after a rain. He waited until Elizabeth's letters stopped coming, then read them through twice. He packed them in a box with elder leaves and snowdrops, put it away in his closet. Put it to rest.

"Jack," Blanche said. "Someone's here to see you."

He followed Blanche's gaze, caught a glimpse of blue and red silk atop the two-story hospital wing, the vivid zigzag of an S. He let out his breath at the mischievous glint in his sister's eyes. He hoped he never forgot how lucky he was to have one person who always showed up.

From somewhere in the garden, a patient applauded. Caitlyn leaned out from the boughs of the sycamore and yelled, "Hey, Superman!"

Jack turned suddenly to Blanche. "Gary wants you back."

Blanche pulled her gaze from the rooftop. She looked at Gary, whose tics accommodated him suspiciously, rolling into the gaps between planting, waiting until after each scrape of the trowel.

"Really? You heard him think that?"

He no longer heard much but the obvious, but in most cases that was enough. "Go on, Blanche," he said. "Can't you tell when you're adored?"

She stood there a moment longer, hesitant, too old for her own good, then she blushed like a school girl. She stepped into the garden, hesitated behind Gary just as a tic shook him from head to toe. She put her hand on his shoulder. Both of them sighed at the same time.

Jack headed toward the peony bed near the patio while the schizophrenics stared at the roof and yelled, "Fly! Fly!" He wasn't entirely used to color yet, which was only part of the reason the red stopped him cold. Annie emerged from the patio, her hair nearly the shade of the sun itself. He raised his hand to shield his eyes; love and regret were almost unbearable, as close as a man came to being blinded.

"Jack," she said, stepping forward slowly. Her hair was down, even more colorful than he remembered—auburn and chocolate and a strand or two of white. He hadn't even given her credit for being beautiful.

"Look at this place," she said, smiling. Her gaze took in the jungle, the swings, the tree-climbing patients, dressed in jeans and sombreros. "You were always so worried about what you could accomplish on medication. And look at this. It's perfect."

Of course it wasn't, with its lopsided beds, the lawn too narrow for the scale of the new plantings, a jungle without any truly tropical vine. The grounds were in need of a new sprinkler system, low-voltage lighting, a hundred more interesting flowers, and he was giddy at the opportunity to show it all off to her, every last endearing flaw.

It was hard to say who was shaking more, so he just held her, smoothed her hair until strands came off in his fingers, like slivers of sunlight. He wanted to show her everything, but some gardens needed to be eased into. This garden, he decided, could wait.

Readers Guide

SUMMER OF
Glorious Madness

by

CHRISTY YORKE

Questions for Discussion

1) Why does Will and Beth's marriage disintegrate? Do you think they could have done more to try and work it out? Or do you think separating was the only option left to them when they finally faced facts?

2) Both Will and Beth benefit from their separation, despite their failed affairs. Discuss what each of them brings back to the marriage as a result.

3) Chloe seems like a pretty typical teenager. Do you think her infatuation with Skitch is the result of low self-esteem—something that might have been avoided with better parenting? Or do you think all teenagers are susceptible to unworthy romances?

4) Will and Beth are good parents but they are also emotionally absent in different ways. Discuss how this affects Chloe. How does the eventual revitalization of their relationship benefit their daughter, too?

5) Beth has little luck treating her Thursday patients until Jack Bolton joins the group. What changes for Kayla, Louis, Gary and Blanche? How does Beth change and grow as a psychiatrist?

6) Beth's mother was bipolar and died tragically. Discuss the many ways this impacts Beth's life. How does this play into her attraction to Jack Bolton? Do you think Beth finds some resolution to her childhood issues because of this romance?

7) Each character in the novel faces their own fears: Beth must delve into the horrors and surprising joys of bipolar disorder, Jack fears losing his artistry with plants, Beth's Thursday patients worry that they might never get well, or that they will recover and lose what little uniqueness they have. How have these fears held them back? What does Will fear? Chloe? Stuart? Do some fears, like Beth's terror of flying, serve a purpose by keeping her safe from at least one potential danger? Are these fears worth holding on to?

8) Jack is driven by a need to create perfection. To what extent does this prevent him from finding it? And how does this contribute to the world's view of him as crazy? Do you believe perfection is possible, and can be found in compromise?

9) Allowing herself to become emotionally and physically involved with Jack Bolton is a definite breech of ethics. Do you think Beth made the right choice? Why?

10) Discuss the pros and cons of Jack's bipolarity. How does this illness serve as an enormous gift? How does it destroy his life? Can the ecstasy and creativity of short-lived mania be worth the price of depression? Do you believe artistry and mental illnesses such as mood disorders are biologically linked? Can artists lead quiet, normal lives and still create masterpieces? How many famous poets, writers, and artists can you think of who led uneventful lives? Extravagant and eccentric lives? Tragic ones?

11) Chloe's pregnancy is a blow to both her parents. Do you think they handled her situation well? And do you think they would have handled it the same way before their separation?

12) What did you learn about mental illness from this book? Would you agree, as the author seems to suggest, that the line between sane and crazy is sometimes rather arbitrary? Where would you draw that line?